Westminster Public Library
3705 W 112th Ave
Westminster, CO 80031
www.westminsterlibrary.org

INTERFERENCE

OTHER TITLES BY BRAD PARKS

Stand-Alone Novels

Say Nothing

Closer Than You Know

The Last Act

The Carter Ross Series

Faces of the Gone

Eyes of the Innocent

The Girl Next Door

The Good Cop

The Player

The Fraud

INTERFERENCE

BRAD
PARKS

THOMAS & MERCER

Text copyright © 2020 by MAC Enterprises Inc.
All rights reserved.

Published by Thomas & Mercer, Seattle

www.apub.com

Amazon, the Amazon logo, and Thomas & Mercer are trademarks of Amazon.com, Inc., or its affiliates.

ISBN-13: 9781542023399 (hardcover)
ISBN-10: 1542023394 (hardcover)

ISBN-13: 9781542020374 (paperback)
ISBN-10: 1542020379 (paperback)

Cover design by Anna Laytham

Printed in the United States of America

First Edition

For Melissa. Again and again.

Because when you marry a dazzling woman—and she also turns out to be the best mother imaginable—you really ought to dedicate more books to her.

PREFACE

When Albert Einstein first theorized what is now known as quantum entanglement, it was only to highlight the absurdity of it.

Entanglement is this seeming impossibility, predicted by the equations of quantum mechanics, that every now and then, two particles can be born with an intrinsic connection to one another. Once that happens, they are never again truly apart. You can separate them across galaxies, and the relationship remains: poke one, and the other feels it.

Immediately. With no delay. No matter how far they may have traveled.

To Einstein, this meant quantum mechanics was fundamentally broken, offensive both to the laws of nature and common sense. He derided entanglement as "spooky action at a distance." Surely, there could be no hidden interaction that travels faster than light, which he believed to be the universe's ultimate speed limit.

And yet, in recent years, quantum entanglement has been verified in laboratories many times, in experiments of increasing elegance and certainty, using both particles and entire systems of particles. Scientists have demonstrated that once you determine certain properties of one member of an entangled pair, you instantaneously and irrevocably change the other. And this mysterious coordination remains intact at every distance yet measured.

In other words, Einstein was wrong. Quantum entanglement really does exist, even if no one understands how it's possible. It raises all kinds of disquieting questions about the true nature of our universe and about the secrets it may be hiding, not the least of which is:

If this could happen with particles, or even systems of particles . . . . . . what about human beings?

CHAPTER 1

Had I known about the phone call I would receive at 11:09 a.m., I would have wrapped myself around Matt so tight he never could have left the bed that morning.

Or begged him to take the day off.

Or contrived some clever, wifely way to guarantee he was in a different area code from his laboratory.

But that's the thing about those 11:09 a.m. phone calls that capsize your existence: life's biggest waves clobber you when you're not looking.

So, blithely unaware, I let him slip away before the sun rose, as he so often did. In addition to being a physicist, Professor Matt Bronik was an unreformed nerd, if that's not too much of a redundancy. At age thirty-nine, he was still so excited by his research he bounded out of bed every morning like a schoolboy—a strapping, six-foot-tall, balding, bearded schoolboy—eager to get off to his lab at Dartmouth College because he *just couldn't wait* to find out what happened next.

His area of expertise was quantum mechanics, which I had a hard time describing without making it sound like magic. All those tiny particles, many of them too small to have ever been seen, leaping around willy-nilly, acting in ways that disregarded human logic.

Matt spoke about his work in generalities, knowing the specifics were far too obscure for me—and nearly everyone else. He liked to joke that only twelve people in the world actually understood what he did. "And," he was always quick to add in his self-deprecating way, "only five of them actually care."

This, naturally, didn't make him any less enthusiastic about it.

Being as I didn't suffer from quite the same level of internal motivation, I lingered in bed for as long as possible, at which point I needed to be shaken out of it.

Quite literally. I have hearing loss. It started in my early thirties, and now, in my midforties, it was profound enough that no alarm clock could break through the bubble of quiet that surrounded me when I slept without my earpieces in. What I had instead was a contraption that began vibrating my bed. The pulses grew stronger until I finally succumbed to its demands.

On the rare mornings when he actually did linger in bed, Matt still whispered in my ear, giving me the pleasure of feeling his breath and the low vibration of his voice. I could no longer hear his gentle North Carolina twang or make out the actual words, but I always told him it was better that way.

What woman wouldn't like a husband who always says the perfect thing?

Still, I had to admit: Matt did pretty well for himself even when I wasn't imagining the script. I was five years older than him and was really starting to feel, well, forty-four. My once-lustrous brown hair had become dull and gray streaked. My hourglass figure was sliding south such that it now more resembled a spoon. And I hated what was happening to my neck.

Matt earnestly insisted I was only becoming more beautiful as I aged, which just meant that in addition to his other talents, he was also a gifted liar.

Alas, there was no whispering this morning. Matt's side of the bed was cold by the time my half began shaking at six thirty. I resisted it as long as I dared, then put in my hearing aids and began focusing on Morgan, our irrepressible nine-year-old.

Matt and I had always planned on having more children until we actually had one. Then we decided that was enough. Being a family of three seemed to fit us. Matt was always reminding me the triangle is the strongest shape in nature.

Once I got myself ready and Morgan off to the bus, I reported to my job at Baker Library, Dartmouth College's stately main branch. I work in cataloguing and acquisitions, the perfect position for someone with hearing loss, because it doesn't require a lot of conversation.

It was the first Monday of February—another cold gray day in Hanover, New Hampshire, a place where winter only feels like it lasts forever. A little after ten, I got a text from Matt. He was just getting out of a meeting with Sean Plottner, a rich alum who was considering making a substantial gift to Dartmouth. The meeting had gone a little too well, apparently, because Plottner had taken up nearly an hour of Matt's day.

Otherwise, I was just sitting at my desk, typing an email, when my phone began flashing, which I saw before the faint ringing sound managed to penetrate my hearing aid.

And because my phone had a digital clock on it, I could tell you with precision:

It was 11:09 a.m.

The call was coming from the main number at the Dartmouth College Department of Physics and Astronomy, which was how Matt's work number appeared on my caller ID.

Matt didn't bother calling most of the time. He knew that even though my phone was equipped with captioning, I preferred text or email. He only called when he wanted to say something lovely and endearing.

Or naughty. Which was why I answered with, "Hey, sexy."

And then I both listened and watched as the screen spit out, "Hello, Brigid, it's Beppe Valentino."

I blushed. Beppe was Matt's department chair, a theoretical physicist whose Italian accent sometimes challenged my phone's voice recognition software.

"Oh, Beppe, I thought you were—"

"I know. Look, I'm sorry, but something's wrong with Matt. He's having some kind of seizure."

CHAPTER 2

Sean Plottner had never been sure when the boredom set in.

Definitely not during the first billion. He was all in during the first billion.

The second billion had kept his attention as well. He loved the chase, the deal, having his investing talents more widely acknowledged.

Even the third billion had been mildly stimulating, what with how he made it during a recession, when everyone else was recovering from mortgage-backed stupidity.

But at a certain point—perhaps by the fourth billion, definitely by the fifth—the boredom had descended and solidified around him, like something gelatinous he could never fully slough off.

Now forty-six years old, Plottner had bought everything he could think to buy, visited everywhere he felt like going, done the requisite rich guy things: fast cars, fast people, golfing in Antarctica, flying in zero gravity, shuffling through various extravagant hobbies, all while continuing to amass a fortune that grew faster than he could spend it.

The boredom remained.

Take these visits to his alma mater. Plottner was always a little uncertain who the dog was in the dog-and-pony show the Dartmouth development people put on whenever he came to campus.

He was pretty sure the staff member—or the student, or the gymnasium, or whatever it was he had come to visit—was *supposed* to be the dog.

But half the time, he was the dog. Like they were actually showing him off.

Check out this loaded alum we've got, Professor! See how he follows us like he's on a leash?

Hey, kids, this is what a multibillionaire looks like! Wanna hear him bark when we ask for money?

Most of the time he just went along with it, nodding and smiling—because that was appropriate behavior, because his family's name was on a dorm, and because it beat just sitting around one of his six houses.

None of it was actually interesting.

Until, suddenly, on the first Monday morning in February, it was.

He felt like it had been a long time since he had heard something new, seen something truly exciting, or met someone who shifted his eyes away from the mundanity of his billions and prodded his thoughts toward something more profound.

And it happened in the most unlikely place:

A physics professor's lab.

Matt Bronik was the guy's name. Plottner didn't know physics, but he did know people. And Bronik had that rogue brilliance, that spark, that ineffable quality that Plottner had made his billions by being able to sniff out.

The professor had grown up in, of all places, Clinton, North Carolina, a podunk town that revolved around hogs—both the rearing and rendering of them. Bronik had told the story of how his elementary school was downwind from the hog-processing plant. On hot days, the stench was so overpowering they had to let school out early.

Local farmers said it smelled like money. Bronik insisted it smelled like dead pigs.

The Bronik family owned a diner, and Matt had spent his childhood helping out in the kitchen. Except where everyone else was slinging hash or making sweet tea, young Bronik was seeing Fibonacci sequences every time he cut an onion.

Plottner got the rest of the tale from the development people: Bronik won his first national mathematics competition when he was eleven. Then he won a bunch more. That, in turn, led to a full scholarship to Massachusetts Institute of Technology; and a PhD in physics from Princeton; and a postdoctoral fellowship at Delft University of Technology in the Netherlands; and, ultimately, his current appointment, a tenured professorship at Dartmouth College.

It was the kind of quirky backstory that, in Plottner's experience, evinced true genius. Not the run-of-the-mill kind. The once-in-a-generation kind.

This was what he had been waiting for—and who he had been waiting for—without even realizing it.

It went to something he had been thinking about a lot lately: legacy. It was one thing to be rich. It was quite another thing to be someone the world would keep talking about long after you were dead.

Like Carnegie. Or Rockefeller. Someone whose vision and future-focused pioneering drove the country forward and defined an age.

Philanthropy was part of that, of course. How many libraries had Carnegie given? How many buildings carried Rockefeller's name? Etch yourself into the stone, and they can never forget you.

But generosity alone wasn't enough. Anyone could stroke a check.

Plottner wanted to be part of something that was bigger than money or fame, something that would make him a part of a larger narrative.

The story of humanity itself.

Matt Bronik just might be able to do that for him.

And so even now, with the dog-and-pony show over, Plottner couldn't stop thinking about what he had seen and heard in that lab. For the first time in ages, he was feeling that old restlessness, the way he used to get when he wasn't sure whether a deal was going to come together.

It was unsettling.

And invigorating.

"Theresa," he called out.

Theresa D'Orsi, his omnipresent personal assistant, who had been with him earlier that day for Professor Bronik's presentation, appeared.

"Theresa, what do you say we get into the physics business?"

"Sir, before you dive in headfirst with Professor Bronik, why don't we reach out to someone who knows physics—someone not connected to Dartmouth—who can tell us a little more about this?"

"That's a fine idea," Plottner said.

He said it like this was an unusual occurrence. It wasn't.

Theresa disappeared. Plottner felt himself bubbling over like newly opened champagne.

The boredom was definitely gone.

CHAPTER 3

I knew it was bad when they wouldn't let me in to see him.

Everything I learned came from a series of updates, delivered to me in the intensive care unit waiting area at Dartmouth-Hitchcock Medical Center by a succession of harried health care providers.

With all of them, I gestured to my hearing aids, so they knew about my condition, then stared hard at their mouths so I wouldn't miss a word.

Even still, each update begged more questions than the last.

It started with the emergency room doctor, the first to see Matt when he was admitted. According to her, Matt's eyes had been alternating between open and closed, and he was "agitated"—enough that the EMTs had strapped him down, to keep him from hurting himself.

He was rambling (all nonsense) but wasn't responding to commands. She couldn't determine whether he was in some minimally conscious state or a coma, nor could she say when he'd come out of it.

My next update came from a cardiologist, who said the most immediate issues were Matt's heart rate and blood pressure, both of which were dangerously low.

I asked whether he had suffered a heart attack. The cardiologist said Matt's initial enzyme levels suggested no, but it was something they were still considering. Both the cardiologist and the neurologist wanted to give him a CT scan, but they couldn't do that while he was moving around so much—and they didn't dare give him something to settle him down while his blood pressure was so low.

The update after that came from the neurologist. His name was Dr. Reiner, and he seemed just as baffled as everyone else. Matt had finally responded to the fluids and norepinephrine he had been given, but he still wasn't snapping out of whatever spell he was under.

"What are you thinking happened?" I asked. "Did he have a stroke?"

"We don't think so," Dr. Reiner said.

"You don't *think* so?"

"Strokes tend to be hemispheric. They impact one side of the body or one part of the body. We're not seeing any evidence of that right now. Our biggest concern at the moment is that his oxygen levels were very low when he first got here. It's possible he's still suffering the effects of that."

"Low oxygen levels . . . that means, what, brain damage?"

"It's too early to say."

"What do you mean?" I said.

The panic had been building up from deep inside me, volcano-like, for a while by that point. And I was now battling with everything I had to keep it down where it belonged.

"Until he wakes up and we can assess his functioning—or until we can safely sedate him and give him an MRI—we're pretty much in the dark."

"An MRI? And what . . . what would be the purpose of that?"

"We could determine if there had been any structural damage to his brain or if there might be something else going on."

"Something else like what?"

He bowed his head a little bit and mumbled something indistinct.

"I'm sorry, what did you say?" I demanded.

The panic was now getting dangerously close to spurting out. It took all my resolve to keep the lid on it.

Dr. Reiner looked up like it pained him to have to repeat himself. "It might be a tumor."

"A tumor," I echoed.

"If it's not a stroke, and it's not a heart attack, a tumor is a strong possibility, yes."

My body began shaking. I felt myself swaying from side to side.

"Mrs. Bronik, I don't want to scare you, but right now we're just glad your husband is alive," Reiner said. "Until we have a chance to run more tests, anything else I might say would be speculation. We're just going to have to wait and see."

Once I realized he had nothing else useful to tell me, and I could stop concentrating so damn hard on just having to hear him, the eruption came. I was suddenly on my knees, doubled over, sobbing.

The fall knocked out one of my hearing aids, but I could still hear the pathetic series of primal moans emanating from my diaphragm and forcing their way out of my throat.

Matt was the smartest person I had ever met. And second place wasn't close. I could barely process the notion that there might be something wrong with his extraordinary, beautiful brain.

My thoughts immediately turned to Morgan. How would he turn out with a deaf mother and a brain-damaged, tumor-ridden father—or, dear lord, no father at all? What would that do to him? Didn't he need at least one fully functioning parent?

All spouses develop roles. In our marriage, Matt was the vibrant one, a basketball nut who could play two hours of pickup hoops and still have the energy to roughhouse with Morgan. I was the broken one, the medical ne'er-do-well who went to the audiologist with hope and came home with heartbreak.

But even though I had never said this out loud, I had always felt like there was a larger purpose to my suffering. I was the repository for our family's entire share of crappy luck. I had taken the whole load of it so Matt and Morgan could go forth into the world happy, strong, and healthy.

That was why this shouldn't have been happening.

All our crappy luck was supposed to have been used up already.

Dr. Reiner was gone by the time I pulled myself together. I only managed to do so out of some sense that I needed to stay clearheaded for Matt.

And Morgan. He would be getting off the bus from school soon. I texted my sister, Aimee, who lived in nearby Quechee, Vermont. Three years older than me, she was divorced, self-employed, and childless—in other words, the perfect aunt. She texted back that she would drop everything to help, like she always did.

Around three o'clock, I was finally permitted to enter Matt's room. He had a tube running into him just below his collarbone. A variety of medical devices—monitors and whatnot—surrounded him, and even my lousy ears could make out the steady beep that represented his heart rate. There was a ventilator, but the mask was hanging on the hook, not strapped to Matt's face.

He was breathing on his own, his chest rising and sinking rhythmically.

His eyes were closed.

In some ways, he looked like he normally did. Matt kept what little hair he had shaved to a stubble, a concession to his male-pattern baldness. His graying beard was neatly tended, as usual.

It was around the eyes where his appearance was shocking. They were sunken, like he had abruptly aged from thirty-nine to sixty-nine.

A nurse who was holding a computer tablet looked up at me and said something. I was so fixated on Matt I wasn't really looking at her until the end. I thought the last word she said was *moment*.

I'll just be a moment.

Would you like a moment?

Something like that.

"Thank you," I said, hoping it was the right response.

She spent a few more seconds consulting her tablet, then nodded at me, making room for me to approach the bedside.

Matt was wearing this mesh vest that wrapped around his body twice and was strapped to the bed rails in several spots—to restrain him, I supposed. One of his arms was by his side. The other was folded on top of him. It looked so sinewy strong it seemed hard to believe the person attached couldn't make it move if he wanted to.

His legs were covered by a thin white hospital blanket. His ankles were bound by these two fuzzy cuffs that had also been attached to the bed rails.

There was no chair by the bed, so I just stood at his side.

"Matty, it's me, baby," I said.

The only answer was the metronomic beeping.

I grabbed his hand, the one that was down at his side. I had been expecting maybe it would feel stiff or cold, but it was pliant, alive, and very warm—warmer than mine.

"I love you, Matty. We're going to get through this. You're going to be fine. Just fine. And I'm going to be with you every step of the way, okay?"

The nurse had walked away, perhaps not wanting to be a part of this private exchange.

"We're going to figure out what's going on. And it's going to be . . ."

I stopped, not knowing how to finish the sentence. I didn't know what the hell it was going to be.

"The main thing is I love you. And Morgan loves you. And . . ."

I was faltering, but I forced myself to keep going.

"A triangle is the strongest shape in nature. You always say that. You, me, and Morgan. We're the triangle, and we're—"

Suddenly Matt was trying to sit up. His teeth were clamped against his lower lip. Spit sputtered out of his mouth. As soon as he encountered the vest and the straps that were restraining him, he began moaning in frustration and straining against them, turning a terrifying shade of crimson.

He was having another seizure.

"Matty, Matt honey, you've got to relax," I said. "It's me. We're in the hospital. You're—"

A guttural noise—something that sounded like "Iwann-iwann-iwann-iwann"—came pouring out of him. His efforts to overcome the straps only intensified. The veins on both sides of his neck popped like tiny snakes. I seriously thought he was going to rupture something. Matt had this penchant for doing sit-ups, push-ups, and burpees when he felt like getting his blood moving, and they had created a powerful body that did not tolerate being tied down.

An alarm bell started clanging. The nurse had returned.

"What's happening?" I asked, dimly aware the question had come out as a shriek.

I couldn't hear her reply, but I said, "Can't you *do* something?"

A doctor had come rushing in, half shoving me aside. I put my hand on Matt's shoulder, just to keep some part of me in contact with him.

"Matty, you have to calm down," I implored. "You're going to hurt yourself. I'm here. I'm here. I'm going to take care of you. It's okay, it's—"

I stopped.

Hearing is something of a specialty of mine, even if I'm not very good at it. And therefore, something in me knew: Matt couldn't hear me right now.

He was trapped in a world even more silent than mine.

Here, but not here.

Any talking I did at this point was strictly for my own benefit, which struck me as especially pointless.

Instead, I closed my eyes.

I am a member of that vast, indistinct, perpetually confused congregation of the spiritually nonreligious. Which is to say I believe in something; I just can't tell you what.

On some core level, I know there is something bigger than me out there, something I feel when I stand on top of a mountain, or gaze up at the stars, or look into my child's eyes, something that has long moved humanity to search for metaphysical answers.

At the same time, I know what my husband has told me about the unfathomable vastness of the cosmos and about the extraordinarily high mathematical likelihood that other intelligent life must exist.

Given those truths, it seemed self-centered to believe that the Bigger Something would be too terribly concerned about the trifling affairs of one member of one tiny species, scrambling around one rocky planet, rotating around one unremarkable star somewhere out toward the edge of one insignificant galaxy.

Therefore, I am ordinarily skeptical about the efficacy of prayer.

Maybe it's because so many of mine have gone unanswered.

But at the moment I had nowhere else to turn.

As Matt bucked and thrashed, I screwed my eyes shut.

And I prayed.

I prayed harder than I ever had in my whole life.

CHAPTER 4

I didn't leave Matt's bedside, nor release my grip on him, for the entire next hour.

That was why I had such a good view of the tiny changes taking place in him.

His eyes, in the rare moments they opened, were no longer quite as unfocused as they had been. They would actually look at me, even if the stare was still blank.

His hand, which had been resting on his chest, moved in a way that, to me, seemed intentional.

His facial expressions changed too. Like a computer inside of him had rebooted.

Then his eyes opened. And he looked right at me.

"I must have died," he croaked weakly. "Because you sure look like an angel."

I immediately burst into tears.

Whatever had happened, he was Matt again.

I hadn't lost him.

"Oh, Matty," was the first thing I managed to choke out.

It didn't get much more articulate for a while after that.

Eventually, both for my benefit and for the doctors'—who were as mystified by his sudden recovery as anyone—Matt recounted what he could remember.

He'd woken up early, like usual, and had his normal breakfast: two granola bars and an apple, which he ate during his drive to Dartmouth. Once there, he went immediately to his lab and got to work.

Reiner asked what that entailed. Matt said, "Playing with lasers"—which was the flippant description he used in social settings when he didn't really want to get into it. Reiner just let it go, so Matt continued with his narrative.

He worked until nine, when he had his meeting with Sean Plottner, which took place in the lab.

Plottner left by ten, and Matt didn't have to teach until eleven, so he went back to work. He was deep in it when he said a strange feeling came over him. One moment he was normal. And then suddenly he was hit by something overwhelming—yet weightless and invisible—that knocked him out.

From there, his memory fragmented into wispy strands and bits of fabric that he couldn't begin to piece together into any kind of whole tapestry.

He remembered straining against the strap that held him down. And the anxious face of an EMT peering down at him. And that someone was, at some point, pinching his chest with what felt like a giant set of tweezers—probably when he had the tube inserted.

But, like a dream whose details he was struggling to recall, he couldn't put any of what had happened in logical order.

The rest we pieced together by talking with the worried physics department colleagues who started calling to check in.

When Matt didn't show up for his eleven o'clock class, one of the students alerted Beppe Valentino of Matt's absence. Beppe and David Dafashy, another physics professor, started looking for him while Sheena Aiyagari, Matt's postdoc, went to his classroom in case he showed up there.

It was David who found Matt, still in his lab, unresponsive, stooped over in a zombielike state. They called an ambulance.

And now? He was exhausted from his labors against the restraints, and his skull was being hammered by what he described as "a tequila headache times fifty."

But, otherwise, it was like nothing had happened to him. His vitals were normal. His body seemed to be functioning fine again.

He ate some dinner—the doctors wanted him to regain some strength and also make sure he could metabolize food without a problem—then they started running tests.

A lot of tests. Ones they had done before. Ones they hadn't.

There was a full lab workup, including a tox screen, followed by an alphabet soup of machine scans: CT, EEG, MRI, MRA.

When a nurse confirmed they intended to keep Matt overnight, I ran back home to tuck in Morgan and thank Aimee for coming to our rescue, then returned to the hospital. They had moved Matt out of the ICU and into the neurology wing.

We passed the night sleeping fitfully, with the usual interruptions from the medical industrial complex that can make a hospital the worst place ever to actually get better.

One by one, as test results came back the next morning and into the afternoon, the doctors began ruling out possibilities.

It wasn't a heart attack. His heart was structurally perfect, and thumping along fine.

It wasn't a tumor. The MRI came back clean.

It wasn't botulism. Or any other common critter.

It wasn't poisoning, at least none that showed up on the tox screen.

Brain damage was also no longer being discussed.

A stroke was still a possibility, but a distant one. The only culprit that hadn't been completely ruled out was a transient ischemic attack—a TIA, as it's known. TIAs can apparently be difficult to diagnose, because the small blood clots that cause them are long gone by the time doctors go to look for them.

Except Matt was awfully young for a TIA and didn't have any of the risk factors that led to one. Plus, TIAs usually lasted minutes, not hours.

Around three o'clock the next afternoon, Dr. Reiner came into the room, having just consulted with the cardiologist.

"I don't know if this is good news or bad news, but there's nothing wrong with you," he announced. "Or at least nothing we can find. If I hadn't seen you nearly dead yesterday, I would say you're the healthiest thirty-nine-year-old in New Hampshire."

"So, basically, the lights went out yesterday and now they're back on," Matt said.

"Pretty much," Reiner said.

"Must not have paid my electricity bill."

"More like a storm came and knocked out your service, which was then restored," Reiner said.

They were tossing about these metaphors in such a jocular way, like all the dire potential diagnoses had been a big joke, like the uncertainty and ambiguity left behind were not at all troubling.

I was trying not to let it infuriate me.

"Doesn't it all strike you as," I started, groped around for a way to conclude my sentence, then concluded with a meek, "a little strange?"

"Disorders of consciousness are a strange thing," Reiner said. "If you're having trouble walking, we look at your legs. If you're having trouble breathing, we look at your lungs. But where do we look when you're having trouble with your consciousness? Where is consciousness located? Can we stick a needle in it? What causes someone to go unconscious? What makes them wake back up? We're not really sure.

"As just one example, we don't actually understand why anesthesia works. We know certain drugs bind to certain receptors, sure, but that doesn't explain the totality of what happens when someone zonks out for surgery. Nor does it explain why some people can later recount things that were said in the operating theater while they were supposedly under. The mechanism behind general anesthesia simply isn't understood all that well. I'm afraid what happened to your husband yesterday falls into the same category. Something caused his brain to check out for a while. And then it recovered. Call it a medical mystery or a medical miracle. Either term works for me."

Matt smiled. "Doctor, we have a saying where I come from: You can put wings on a pig, but that don't make it an eagle."

Reiner grinned back. "I'm not sure I—"

"Mysteries are for novelists and miracles are for preachers," Matt said. "I'm a scientist. I believe the causes for things are natural, not supernatural. *Something* happened to me, even if it didn't show up in all those tests you gave me. You must have a hypothesis that doesn't involve divine intervention. One scientist to another, just give me your best guess as to what's going on here."

"Okay," Reiner said, taking in a deep breath and then letting it go. "My best guess—and this is really only a guess—is that we could be looking at some kind of conversion disorder."

"What's that?" I asked.

"It's neurosis where corporal symptoms appear without any apparent somatic or physical basis, so we say the mental condition is 'converting' itself into physical form. It's possible this could result in this kind of fugue state, where you're able to shuffle around but not interact meaningfully with the outside world. We've seen instances where a conversion disorder can cause blindness, paralysis, all kinds of things."

"In other words, you think I'm crazy," Matt said, still smiling.

"Crazy or just incredibly stressed by something," Reiner said. "Think of it like when someone gets some truly terrible news—the death of a loved one, something traumatic. They hear the news and they faint. That's a conversion disorder. The brain doesn't know what to do with a mental shock, and so it shuts things down for a little while, just to give itself a chance to work things out. Have you been under a lot of stress?"

Matt and I exchanged a quick, meaningful glance. He hadn't published a paper in a year and a half, nor did he have anything in the pipeline. And, yes, that was stressful. Matt felt like he had reached a go-big-or-go-home juncture in his research, where he couldn't just pump out another article about the gradual progress he was making. Until he got a major result, no one really wanted to hear from him.

He kept saying he was close. But in some ways there was no more fraught place than finding yourself on the brink of a greatness that continued to elude you.

"No more or less so than usual," Matt said.

"A certain amount of stress is unavoidable," I said.

"Well, yes. But he still has to take care of himself," Reiner said to me, then turned to Matt. "Make sure you're eating well and getting good sleep. If you start to feel overwhelmed by something, give yourself permission to take a break and perform some self-care—go on a walk or do whatever you do that rejuvenates you."

"Take two spoonfuls of slacking off and call me in the morning," Matt said.

"That's right. Just take it easy."

Then Reiner added the words that my superstitious side wished he hadn't:

"And hope whatever this was doesn't come back."

CHAPTER 5

The most painful seven days of Emmett Webster's life—168 hours he wished he could bury somewhere near the center of the earth—were finally coming to an end.

He couldn't believe it had only been a week. It felt like so much longer.

Wanda had died on Sunday morning. The three days that followed were a numbing blur of grief and logistics. The viewing had been Thursday evening, the memorial service Friday morning. By Friday afternoon, the love of Emmett Webster's life had been committed to the ground forever.

Wanda Elaine Webster. Cherished wife, mother, and grandmother. Friend to all. May she rest in peace.

Emmett's friends and colleagues in the New Hampshire State Police had come out in force for the whole thing. Cops were great when it came to funerals. There was something about the occasion—the air of crisis, the fellow officer in need, the rigid formality of the event—that appealed to a cop's nature and training.

They were around death a lot. They knew what to do.

Maybe that explained how Emmett was able to get through that initial phase of mourning with such stoicism. He simply went into cop mode.

For the eulogy, he had told the story of their first date. They went bowling. They were so pumped just to be with each other she rolled a 167 and he rolled a 212. Neither one of them had bowled that well before—or since.

They were married six months later. Three kids followed in five years. The next quarter century went by in a cheerful churn of seasons.

She had been the feisty one, the one who wore every feeling she had directly on her face. He was the plodding, steady type, the kind of cop who solved cases with stoic persistence. Clashing styles, to be sure. But they were always better together than apart. Fact was, you needed sunshine *and* clouds to make a rainbow.

At the viewing, he must have had the same conversation, or slightly different variations thereof, no less than a hundred times. He'd tell the person how Wanda had recently been diagnosed with what had been called "mild" sleep apnea. They were still figuring out what to do about it—whether she needed the mask or whatnot. She had decided to sleep on the couch in the den because she worried her snoring would wake up Emmett.

That's where he found her the next morning. In the den. Sudden cardiac death, triggered by sleep apnea.

At least she didn't suffer, the person would reply.

Yes, it was a blessing.

But really? Seriously?

There was plenty of suffering.

His.

And she was dead, the woman who was at the geographic middle of fifty-four-year-old Emmett's happiness for more than half his life. How was that any kind of blessing?

He spent Saturday with the kids and grandkids, who overfilled the family house in Concord. They looked at pictures. They watched videos. They told stories.

Oh, everyone had their moments—they couldn't believe Mom was gone, they missed Grandma—but with all five grandchildren under the age of six, it was basically just chaos. No time to really think about anything. Emmett had switched from cop mode to grandpa mode, forcing cheer as he played with dolls and trucks.

Then they left. All three kids. All three spouses. All five grandkids. They had to go back to their regularly scheduled lives.

And now it was again Sunday morning—one week, exactly, since Wanda had died—and Emmett was alone.

Powerfully alone.

He wandered from room to room, still expecting to find Wanda in one of them. Everyplace he went was drenched with memories of her.

Upstairs—their bedroom, the bathroom—still smelled like her.

The kitchen? Forget it. Even in death, her vivacious presence filled the space.

In the dining room, there were three easels, each containing a poster board filled with pictures. Wanda, the most gorgeous bride ever, walking back down the aisle, newly married. Wanda with Emmett in dress uniform, on the long-ago day when he had been promoted to detective. Wanda with the kids in various stages of development, with their trophies, dance outfits, and diplomas. Wanda with grandchildren, smiling brightly.

He had to get out of there. Fast.

That's how he found himself in the den.

Which was probably the last place he should have been.

He asked himself, not for the first time, whether it would have mattered if he'd done something different. If he had forced her to get the stupid mask. Or if he had insisted she wear those breathing strips they had gotten from the drugstore. If he had just kept her in bed with him, because her snoring wasn't *that* bad. Something.

Suddenly he couldn't handle the den anymore either. He was on his feet and moving. Down the stairs, to the basement, where Wanda almost never went.

It would be safer for him there.

He clicked on a pull-chain light. There was his workbench, built into the left side of the far wall.

And, to the right, his gun safe, where he stored his hunting rifles and service weapon, a Smith & Wesson M&P 45.

He looked at his tools for a moment, all neatly arranged. Then, in a kind of trance, he walked to the gun safe, spun the dial, and opened the door.

His hand went for the Smith & Wesson, reflexively checking the magazine.

Full. And he knew there was one in the chamber.

He slid the magazine back in, hearing it snap into place. He lifted the gun, feeling the weight of it. The grip fit his palm perfectly.

This could be so easy.

No more suffering.

And it would either be Wanda, waiting for him on the other side, or it would be nothing. Both possibilities were better than what he was feeling now.

His index finger, which had started in its automatic resting spot outside the trigger guard, had somehow worked its way inside.

One week. One miserable week. The previous Saturday night, before they went to bed, everything in their lives was settled, everything made sense. She had retired after thirty-two years in the Concord City Clerk's Office. He was a month away from finishing thirty distinguished years of service to the New Hampshire State Police, the last eighteen of them as a detective with the Major Crime Unit.

They had bought an RV, a Leisure Travel Vans twenty-four-footer. They had been planning their retirement for years, calculating and recalculating their pensions, saving and working—overtime for him, every chance he got; an extra job for her at the outlets during the holidays—so they could go wherever they wanted, do whatever they wanted.

Visit the kids. See the country. Spend their golden years together.

Emmett and Wanda.

What a pair.

Now that the unit was broken, now that there was no together anymore, what was he still doing here? What was the point?

He fitted the barrel of the gun into the soft underside of his chin.

Just to see how it would feel.

And it felt, well, inevitable. The pain had been unbearable, and he didn't see how it would do anything but get worse as the days, weeks, and months without Wanda passed.

If he didn't do it now, he was just going to do it later. Why not get it over with? It wouldn't hurt. At least not for very long.

Really, what was he afraid of?

He began applying gentle pressure to the trigger. Not enough to send the bullet on its way. But it was definitely heading in that direction. Just a little more squeeze and then—

His phone rang.

He pulled it out of his pocket.

Gracie. His youngest. The pregnant one.

He put the gun down so he could answer.

"Hello?"

"Hey, Dad, what are you doing?"

"Nothing."

"Good. Go to your computer. I just sent you an email. I want you to pull it up right now."

Emmett had a flip phone, as all of his children knew. If you sent Dad an email, he still had to check it on his laptop.

"I'm down in the basement. I'm not—"

"Just go to your computer."

Emmett did as he was told, leaving the gun behind, walking into the kitchen, flipping open the lid on his laptop, clicking on Gracie's email, which consisted only of a picture.

An ultrasound photo.

"What . . . what's this?"

"That," Gracie said, "is your granddaughter. Isn't she adorable? Look at that little face. The technician was supposed to send us the picture after our last checkup, and it finally just arrived. I think it's Mom, working her magic. She knew we need a little pick-me-up."

Or maybe she knew they weren't the only ones.

Emmett tilted his head, and, yes, you could see the baby's face.

"How about that," he said.

"And we decided on the plane ride back we're going to name the baby Wanda. Is that okay?"

"Oh, Gracie," Emmett said, his throat squeezing.

"Love you, Dad."

And Emmett managed to choke out, "Love you too."

CHAPTER 6

I felt like I was tiptoeing all through the next two weeks, just waiting for the phone call saying that Matt had lapsed into another fit.

That had become my euphemistic name for what happened to him: a fit, like the whole thing—being plunged into a catatonic state for reasons that eluded medical explanation—had been nothing more than a childish tantrum.

Without telling Matt, I packed a bag that I kept in my car, just in case. And I established with Aimee that all I had to do was text her a 911, and she'd know to come running again.

In the meantime, I lived in a kind of suspended animation. Normally, I tried to get out for a hike at least once a week—as long as the weather wasn't *too* terrible. Ever since I started losing my hearing, hiking had become my preferred method of self-care. Often, the family joined me. Mount Cardigan State Forest and Gile State Forest were our go-to spots, with Mount Moosilauke thrown in if we had time to make the drive.

But there was no way I was going to risk Matt going into a seizure while we were on top of a mountain somewhere. And I didn't want to go alone either. It felt irresponsible to wander out of cell phone range.

As it was, every time my phone rang—in the office, while I was out doing errands—my first thought was that I'd have to dash back to Dartmouth-Hitchcock for more tests, hand-wringing, and dread.

And I didn't know which was more terrifying:

That we didn't know what had triggered the fit.

Or that we didn't know what made him come out of it.

If there was a next time, would it last longer than six hours? Like six months? Or six years? Or . . .

I didn't voice any of these fears to Matt, because I knew he wouldn't have any answers either. It became the great unspoken, looming over everything.

Without my having to nag him, Matt voluntarily dialed back his work schedule. A bit. He decided the problem was simply stress, and that natural medicine—pumping up his exercise regime—was his best option. He made more time to participate in the noontime pickup hoops game at Alumni Gym that locked Dartmouth professors, students, and administrators in mortal basketball combat. He was coming home with bruises and scratches to show for his enthusiasm.

Otherwise, the greatest risk to his health was that I might mother-hen him to death about his eating. I did my best to rid the house of corn syrup and insisted we add kale smoothies to our dinnertime regime, as if the whole problem with Matt's diet was that it wasn't trendy enough.

Matt actually liked them.

Morgan? Less so.

"*Daddy* was the one who got sick," he moaned. "Why should *I* be punished?"

Otherwise, I slowly allowed myself to believe that impending doom might not be shadowing me at every turn, and we stumbled around finding our new normal.

It was early Monday evening, two weeks postfit. With Morgan at swim practice and Matt still at work, I was in the kitchen starting dinner, singing, something I only did when I was sure I was alone, when it didn't matter if I was horribly (and unknowingly) off key.

Music had actually been what got Matt and me together. Like a lot of math types, Matt was a naturally gifted musician for whom playing piano seemed somehow intuitive. I was a singer from the cradle on, taking voice lessons as a child, doing all the musicals in high school, then becoming a member of a popular a cappella group in college.

When he was in grad school at Princeton and I was a young reference librarian in nearby West Windsor, New Jersey, he was a last-second emergency fill-in accompanist for a community choir I had joined.

I had noticed him before our holiday concert because, let me be honest, he was hot. His lifelong basketball obsession had given him a chiseled physique, plus he had these puppy dog brown eyes that I could just tell served as a window to a lovely soul.

After the show, in which I had a solo, he shyly approached me and told me I had the most gorgeous soprano voice he had ever heard. Then he said he was missing his family in North Carolina and asked, in this adorable country twang of his, if I might sing his favorite carol, "I'll Be Home for Christmas," while he accompanied me.

"What key?" I asked.

"Just pick one," he said.

I sang; he played, transposing on the fly, perfectly and beautifully. Matt didn't merely strike the keys; he caressed them, coaxing a sound out of the piano that made me wonder what else his hands could do.

It was probably a good thing a small crowd gathered around to listen, because otherwise I would have jumped him right there.

Romance ensued. I assumed music would continue to be a large part of our relationship, and of my life in general. Until, around the time I turned thirty, I started having trouble with harmonies. Then it was melodies. Before long, I was struggling to even match pitches. It was mortifying.

Finally, I went to an audiologist, who gave me the devastating diagnosis: bilateral otosclerosis, a progressive hardening of the stapes, the tiny bone in the middle ear that transfers sound from the eardrum to the inner ear.

What's more, my stapes bone was pressing on the nerves of my inner ear, causing more damage. It was an extra layer of hell that made my hearing loss more severe and eliminated numerous treatment options, including surgery. And it was only going to get worse.

We had just gotten married but were still childless, so I tearfully told Matt if he wanted to leave me—because he didn't want to raise a baby with a woman who might not be able to hear it cry, or spend his old age with a woman who might not be able to hear him at all—I completely understood.

"Brigid," he replied gently, "how many times do I have to tell you I'm only with you for your body?"

One joke at a time, we somehow made it this far. And now here I was, pounding flat some chicken breasts, climbing to a fortissimo in "Ave Maria," when I turned and jumped about six feet.

Matt was sitting at the kitchen peninsula.

"Jesus, Matt," I said, my hand to my thumping heart.

"Oh, please don't stop," he said.

I huffed at him, my way of saying I wasn't engaging in this again, the *why don't you sing to me anymore, you sound beautiful / no I don't* argument.

"What are you doing here?" I asked, glancing toward the clock. It was quarter after five. On Mondays, Matt normally stayed at the office until it was time to pick up Morgan from swimming at six.

"I wanted to talk to you while Morgan wasn't here."

"Okay, hang on," I said, putting down the mallet I had been using and washing my hands.

Then, as I dried them on a dish towel, I stood directly across from him. "What's up?"

"You remember that alum, Sean Plottner?"

"The rich one."

"Is there any other kind?"

"What about him?"

"He offered me a job this morning," Matt said.

"Really? To do what?"

"Research. And only research. No teaching. No grubbing for grants. No faculty meetings. I would work for his company, Plottner Investments, in New York."

"New York," I said, trying not to immediately freak out over the prospect of tearing Morgan away from the school he loved and the only home he'd ever known.

"That part might be negotiable. But I'm still not taking the job. Or at least I don't think I am."

"Okay," I said, a little mystified. "Then why do you look like you're Hamlet and it's deep in act two?"

"Because of what the offer was."

I raised my eyebrows.

"He started at five hundred thousand."

"A year?" I said, dropping the dish towel.

Matt nodded. It was four times his current salary.

"To do research."

"Yes."

"What kind of research?"

"Exactly what I'm doing now. He would set me up in a lab with the same equipment. But I'd be doing it for him."

"You said he 'started at' five hundred. Did it go down when he realized how ridiculous that number was?"

"No, it went up," Matt said. "When I didn't immediately accept the offer, he doubled it."

"Doubled it?" I said, because I was sure I must have heard him wrong.

"A million dollars a year," my math-savant husband confirmed, in case I was incapable of doing the calculation.

"Oh, Matty," is all I could think to say.

"I still don't think we should take it."

"Why? Because of New York?"

"No, because . . . I don't get the best vibe from Plottner. He's basically just another Wall Street guy."

Matt had repeatedly expressed his dismay that the financial sector was gobbling up some of the world's most brilliant mathematicians and that rather than using their gifts to tackle the world's thorniest numerical dilemmas or improve the human condition, these geniuses were now engaged in the zero-sum game that was making bets on the stock market.

"Beyond that," Matt continued, "I don't even know if he really understands what he's getting into. I mean, yeah, I *think* I'm close to a breakthrough. But I've been thinking that for a while now, haven't I? And until I actually bring it home, I'm just another struggling scientist going around dishing out pithy aphorisms about how many airplanes the Wright brothers crashed. What if a year from now Plottner gets bored or impatient and decides he's wasting his money? Dartmouth isn't going to take me back. And these kind of positions . . ."

He didn't need to complete the thought. A tenured Ivy League professorship was the most sought-after prize in American academia, not to mention the most recession-proof job of all time.

"Well, you know enough people," I said. "You'd land on your feet somewhere."

"Yeah, but where? Say I hang on for a year or two with Plottner before he pulls the plug. It will have been that much longer since I published anything. I'd be lucky to get an interview with Southern North Dakota College for the Directionally Challenged."

"I'm sure that's not true."

"It's more than that, though," Matt said. "If I work for Plottner Investments, I am no longer part of the community of scholars, creating knowledge for the sake of knowledge, freely sharing my ideas. He would own whatever I did. I wouldn't get to publish a paper unless he okayed it. Let's say I *do* finally have a breakthrough and he makes me sit on it?"

"Why would he do that?"

"Because he wants to patent it and sell it to the highest bidder," Matt said. "He's an investor. He's not offering a million dollars a year—plus benefits, plus lab setup costs, plus whatever—simply because he wants to see Plottner Investments get a one-line mention in *Physical Review Letters*. My work would remain under lock and key until he said it wasn't."

"And then there's my health."

I felt a small catch in my breathing. The great unspoken was being spoken.

"What about it?"

"Dr. Reiner said I need less stress. Not more. What if taking this job makes it come back? Moving to New York is stressful. Starting a new job is stressful. Working for a guy like Plottner is stressful."

"Okay. You're right. Turn it down."

"I know. But *a million dollars a year*?"

"Money isn't everything," I said.

"But it's to do something I love."

"That's true."

"And no more grant proposals."

"That too."

"And . . ."

His voice trailed off.

"What?" I asked.

"I don't know. I just feel like it would be . . . selfish of me not to take this," he said. "There's Morgan's college to think about. And I could retire my parents."

Matt's parents still spent seventy hours a week at the diner. Matt worried they were working themselves into the grave. They had been trying to sell the business for a few years but hadn't been able to find a buyer.

We stopped and stared at each other. I looked into those puppy dog eyes of his and tried to divine what was really happening deep inside.

What I saw was a man legitimately torn.

A million dollars was a lot of money for anyone, but especially for a kid who grew up in a diner in Clinton, North Carolina.

"When does Plottner need an answer?" I asked.

"He didn't say. We left it that I'd talk to you, and then we'd talk again soon."

"Which way are you leaning?"

"The risk-averse part of me leans toward no," he said. "But then, as soon as I try to live that decision, I feel crazier than a bag of monkeys. Who turns down a million-dollar-a-year job?"

"Right," I said.

"Let's sleep on it and see how we feel in the morning," he suggested.

"Okay," I said. "We'll sleep on it."

We slept.

Or, in my case, pretended to sleep until sometime well after midnight.

Growing up in the Philadelphia suburbs, I never would have described my family as rich. But we had always been comfortable. I had the privilege of never worrying about where my next meal came from, of being able to plan for the future while taking the present more or less for granted.

Ditto with my adult life. Even when Matt was a broke grad student and I was riding the reference desk in West Windsor, the second-most junior librarian in the system and paid accordingly, we had everything we truly needed. I could sing for free. And ramen noodles weren't so bad.

These days, we weren't just comfortable. We were *very* comfortable. Truly, working for Dartmouth College was the quintessential golden handcuffs.

Still, we had our worries. Hanover real estate wasn't cheap, and our mortgage payment gobbled up a big chunk of our paychecks. We probably weren't saving enough for Morgan's college, the cost of which only grew more astronomical with each passing year. And retirement? Don't even start.

All those qualms would be eliminated if Matt was making a million dollars a year.

A lot of things got easier with a salary like that.

Plus, there was always hopeful talk about the cutting-edge treatments for hearing loss that might soon be coming and could significantly improve my condition.

They were all expensive. And none were covered by insurance.

What would it be like to hear again? To sing again?

To not have to wonder if I'd be able to know what my sweet boy's voice sounded like when he became a man?

I immediately chastised myself for even thinking about that. Matt had enough pressure on his research already. There is this incredible urgency that physicists feel as they age. Albert Einstein was twenty-six when he had his annus mirabilis, his miracle year. Werner Heisenberg was twenty-five when he published his uncertainty principle. Niels Bohr wrote his famous trilogy of papers when he was twenty-eight. Erwin Schrödinger was considered an old man when he was doing his best work at thirty-nine.

There were far fewer examples of people whose best work came in their forties and beyond, the wall Matt was now staring at. It had long been my role in his life to remind him there was more to life than winning the Nobel Prize. He often thanked me for bringing balance to his worldview and "saving" him from the unhappy life of a narrow-minded, workaholic physicist. Is that what I should do again here?

At least now, at Dartmouth, he still had his teaching, which he enjoyed. Did we really want to put him in a place where his research would be everything?

At some point, I finally drifted off. Matt made his usual five o'clock exit. Or at least I assumed he did: when the bed started buzzing at six thirty, his side was already empty.

I got Morgan off to school, then groggily made my way to Baker Library.

Around ten, my phone started flashing.

It was the Dartmouth College Department of Physics and Astronomy.

Matt. Probably asking whether I wanted to start looking for apartments in Manhattan.

"Hey, what's up?" I said.

"Brigid, it's Beppe," he said gravely. "It's happening again."

CHAPTER 7

I texted Aimee a 911, then raced to Dartmouth-Hitchcock.

At the information desk, a gray-faced woman asked, "Can I help you?"

"Yes, I'm Brigid Bronik. I'm looking for my husband, Matthew Bronik. He was just brought here in an ambulance. I'm not sure if he's in the ER or if he's been moved somewhere else already."

"Can I see some ID?"

I hastily produced my driver's license. The woman glanced at it just long enough to verify my name, then started typing.

"He's in the ICU. It's—"

"I know where it is. Thank you."

I hurried off through the hallways. When I reached the ICU, a nurse asked me to stay in the waiting area, just like last time. Matt had the same alarmingly low blood pressure and heart rate.

Around eleven, the cardiologist came out and told me Matt was responding well to fluids and norepinephrine and we were "out of the woods" after some nervous moments, at least as far as his respiration and oxygen levels were concerned.

At noon, Dr. Reiner escorted me into Matt's room, where he looked mostly the same as he did last time. The hospital gown. The tube stuck in near his collarbone. The gadgets surrounding him.

Except this time he had a nasty gash on his forehead. Reiner said the EMTs found him that way and surmised he hit his head when he lost consciousness.

Reiner wanted to at least try a CT scan, hoping Matt would be still and they could get pictures of his brain while the fit was still ongoing. After that, he was transferred to neurology.

I recognized one of the nurses there, a woman named Yvonne who gave me a grim smile of recognition.

Back again?

I just nodded. No one wants to be a repeat customer in the neurology wing.

Time passed slowly. Whenever Matt got riled up and began fighting against those awful straps, it got even slower. He was hurting himself, but there was nothing anyone could do about it.

At one point, Reiner came by to say he had read the CT scan. It didn't provide any firm answers as to what was happening.

"Does that mean he'll come out of it again?" I asked.

"Maybe? I'm afraid if I told you anything else, it might be a lie."

I continued my vigil, talking to him when I could think of anything to say, remaining watchful for any changes in him.

He kept alternating between closed eyes and half-lidded vacant ones. Periods of frightening agitation—moaning, sputtering, struggling against his restraints—were followed by calm.

When he started getting upset, I'd massage his bare scalp, something he liked—or at least he did when he was conscious. It was difficult to tell whether it was having any effect.

Now and then, I'd put an ice bag on his forehead. The wound there was so angry and swollen, I figured it might help.

Mostly, I waited. And watched.

The first real sign of life came around 5:30 p.m., and it came from Matt's tongue.

It was searching out his teeth, like he was checking to see if they were all there.

Other signs soon followed. A flexed hand. A shifted leg.

Then, with his eyes still closed, he said, "Do you think this place gives frequent-flier miles? We've got to be halfway to a ticket for Bora Bora by now."

He had been out for roughly eight hours. I felt like, one forehead gash aside, it had taken as much of a toll on me as it had on him.

We ran through the same battery of tests, plus a few extra "just in case" ones.

Once he recovered from his headache—he described it as "thunderous" this time—Matt was an agreeable, good-natured pincushion, joking and quipping his way through the whole thing.

I made a quick trip home, where Aimee had everything under control. Morgan loved his time with his aunt, who followed the rules just enough to give him the structure he craved but playfully bent them just enough to be fun.

Then I returned to the hospital and spent a long, uncertain night by Matt's side.

The next day, morning soon blurred into afternoon.

I wasn't aware of the exact time when Dr. Reiner appeared and gave us a rundown of everything he had learned from the tests.

Or, rather, everything he hadn't.

He concluded by saying, "I have to be honest: at this point, we're looking for zebras."

"Zebras?" I said, sure I had misheard him.

"Have you ever heard the expression 'When you hear hoofbeats, think horses, not zebras'? Well, in this case, we've looked for all the horses. So we're left with zebras."

"Great," Matt said. "I've always wanted to go on a safari."

"I keep going back to the similarities between this attack and the last one," Reiner said. "It was the same time of day, which makes me wonder if it's some kind of narcolepsy. I'm going to order a sleep study to see if it tells us anything. I'm afraid that's going to mean another night at the hospital."

"Seems like I'm going to keep getting those one way or another if we don't figure this out. Might as well plan it."

"The other thing that's the same is where it happened."

"The lab," Matt said.

"Is there *anything* in there that might have caused this? You said you play with lasers. Could you have zapped yourself unconscious?"

Matt shook his head. "We're not exactly talking about Luke Skywalker's lightsaber here. It's very low powered, very delicate. I use it to gently nudge around things that could fit on the head of a pin with room to spare."

"Still—"

"You'd have better luck knocking down the Empire State Building with a flyswatter. I could run the thing over your body all day long and you'd never feel it."

"Okay, what about some kind of contaminant?"

Matt, who was sitting in bed, crossed his arms and frowned. It was not a look I normally attributed to him.

"What?" I said.

"I'm not sure I would call it a contaminant. And I can't imagine how it would . . ."

"Matty, what are you talking about?"

He took in a deep breath, then let it go.

"It's nothing," he said. "Forget it."

"No, not forget it," I said. "This is not a 'forget it' kind of time. You've got something really scary happening to you, and we have to figure out what."

"It'll help me to know more, not less," Dr. Reiner said.

Matt looked back and forth between the two of us before finally settling on Reiner.

"This is . . . something I can't advertise," Matt said. "Some of my funding comes from the Department of Defense. They haven't explicitly told me *not* to tell people about what I've been doing, but they've cautioned me against loose talk. Particularly with foreigners or people I don't know well. I'm not saying it's *you* they'd be concerned about, but I wouldn't want you discussing this with colleagues."

"Doctor-patient privilege applies to whatever you say right now. I'm ethically bound to keep this to myself."

"Okay," he said. "I don't mean to make this sound all cloak and dagger. But I *have* been working with viruses."

I felt something squeezing in my chest. Viruses? Since when?

"I see," Reiner said.

"I suppose that could be viewed as a contaminant of sorts."

You suppose? I wanted to interject. *And you're just now mentioning this?*

If we hadn't been in a hospital, talking to a doctor, I never could have kept my poise.

"What kind of virus?" Reiner asked.

"The tobacco mosaic virus," Matt said. "It's a real scourge where I come from. But it's a good, solid, well-studied virus. It's very stable. It can survive at a wide range of temperatures or in a vacuum. And it's pretty commonly available for research purposes."

"What, exactly, have you been doing with it?"

"How much do you know about quantum physics?"

"I pretty much peter out at Schrödinger's cat."

"Okay, so let's start at the top," Matt said, slipping into professor mode. "The quantum world is a very strange place. Particles can make sudden leaps from one place to another and leave no footprints behind as to how they did it. Or they can pass through solid walls, which we refer to as quantum tunneling. It's all very unsettling and very difficult to imagine, even for people like me who deal with it all the time. The way we reassure people is by telling them it's okay for all this weirdness to exist, because it's all happening on an incredibly small scale. Here in the world we can see, what we call 'classical' physics rules the day. Newton's apple still falls from the tree and that sort of thing. Or at least that's what we thought. But it turns out it's more complicated than that."

"It usually is," Reiner said.

"In the last few years, we've been able to get larger and larger objects to act in these bizarre quantum ways. To 'interfere' them, as we say. We started with particles, which are incredibly small—ten to the negative fifteen meters. Then we moved up to atoms, which are ten to the negative ten meters. Then we were dealing with molecules like carbon-sixty, which we call a buckyball. It's ten to the negative nine meters, which is still very, very small, but absolutely huge compared to where we started. Then we got to clumps of atoms, getting up to ten to the negative eight meters. And now?

"A group of researchers at Delft University of Technology interfered a silicon wire that is ten to the negative six meters. That's billions and billions of atoms, plunged into a quantum state. We've reached the point where no one knows exactly how large we can go. Where does quantum physics end and the classical world begin? The limits appear to be technical rather than theoretical."

"Matt did his postdoc at Delft," I added quietly.

"Now, so far, we've only been talking about inanimate objects. But the smallest life-form, a virus, is ten to the negative seven meters. And some bacteria aren't much larger. We've already surpassed that sizewise. Could we actually interfere a living thing? Or is life, in fact, the dividing line between the quantum world and the classical one? Is there something about a living thing—about consciousness, perhaps—that simply won't comply with those weird quantum rules? Or can life go quantum too?

"It's one of the biggest questions in physics, in all of science for that matter, and there's a guaranteed Nobel Prize in it for whoever gets the answer. Because if life can go quantum, it literally changes existence as we know it. What if we can have viruses or bacteria or even microanimals like tardigrades making quantum leaps or traveling through solid walls? We literally may never look at the world the same way again. So that's been the goal of my research. To see if I can get a virus to demonstrate quantum interference."

Interference. It was actually the perfect word to describe what this virus had done to our lives.

"How come you didn't tell me about this?" I asked quietly.

He looked at me apologetically. "I don't know. I feel like I got my PhD and then tenure by playing it safe, just doing the kind of predictable, incremental science you need to move your career ahead. Once I got tenure, I was ready to take a moon shot. But at the same time it's so audacious, I felt almost silly talking about it. To some people, saying you're trying to interfere a virus is like saying you want to bike to Mars."

"No, I mean why didn't you tell me after the first fit?" I asked. "Seriously, medical science is powerless to explain what's happening to you, and you didn't think that maybe spending half your day with a quantum virus had anything to do with it?"

"But the tobacco mosaic virus doesn't infect humans," he said. "At least it shouldn't."

"What do you mean?"

"Well, this is the part, I admit, I'm a little unsure about. I keep mutating it by accident."

He said this simply, like he was referring to spilling a cup of water in a bathtub. I was gripping his bed rail so hard I was sure I was breaking blood vessels.

"A *mutated* quantum virus," I said, and even I could hear that I was now yelling. "Even better. I guess now I understand why you never told me the details about your research, because I would have asked if you had lost your damn mind. It seriously *never* occurred to you this was why you were freaking out?"

Matt just sat on his bed, shrinking quietly.

"*Oh* my God," I said. "You basically have *no* idea what this thing is or might be capable of, do you?"

"I wouldn't say no idea," he muttered.

"Well, then, what? What have you created? We don't even know whether it's the mutation that's doing this or if it's because you're taking these mutated creations and trying to send them into quantum orbit. How do you know you haven't done something that made a plant virus capable of infecting humans? Or that you haven't enabled this one particular virus to make some kind of quantum leap into your brain? You're basically playing God here. Well, congratulations, Prometheus, you've stolen fire and now it's burning you."

I pointed to Reiner. "He ought to order a psychiatric evaluation not because of conversion disorder, but because you really *are* crazy."

"This virus definitely sounds like something we need to look into," Dr. Reiner said, as if this profound understatement might make Professor Bronik's hysterical wife calm down.

I let go of the bed and grabbed Matt's hands.

"Matty, please, *please* tell me you're going to stop messing with this thing."

"But it's my work," Matt said quietly. "I've spent years building toward this. This is . . . it's everything. It's my whole career."

"Yeah? And I'm your wife. And somewhere out there is your son. We're your family. And we need you. We need you more than a Nobel Prize. I'm worried that if you keep doing this, next time it won't be six hours. Or eight hours. It'll be forever. Or no one will get to you in time with a shot of norepinephrine and we'll find you dead on the laboratory floor. You have to ask yourself: What's more important, your work or your life?"

He didn't answer, just kept gazing down at his bedsheets.

"I'm serious, Matt," I said. "And I need an answer. Right here, right now. What's it going to be?"

He looked up.

"You guys, of course," he said.

"You promise?"

"Yes."

"Thank you," I said, releasing his hands, though his performance was less than entirely convincing.

Then he added: "At least until we figure out what's going on."

And that's when I began to suspect this was a promise he never intended to keep.

CHAPTER 8

There were those who called Sean Plottner a narcissist.

But, seriously, if you had enough money to buy a plane—not lease it, not enter into one of those chintzy time-sharing arrangements, actually buy it—you'd name it after yourself too.

Especially a plane like this. The Gulfstream G550 had a range of 6,750 miles, which meant it could go from New York to Tokyo without refueling. Its engines could push a top speed of Mach .885, with a cruising altitude up to 51,000 feet, and it could practically land on a piece of chewing gum, which enabled it to avoid the more crowded airports.

And so, yes, he had christened this magnificent vessel the *Plottner One.* And whether you called him a narcissist or an egomaniac or simply vainglorious, the truth was he had been called worse. When he was in college, he was the guy everyone hated—the slacker who skipped class all semester but still got straight As. He withstood three accusations of academic dishonesty from incredulous professors, none of whom could believe the burnout had aced the final exam without cheating.

Then there was the Securities and Exchange Commission, which had equal trouble believing Plottner's investing success was solely the product of hard work and insight.

Plottner had received four separate target letters, informing him the SEC was looking into allegedly suspicious trading activity. None of the investigations had gone anywhere. He had yet to be indicted or even charged.

And, in fact, there had been a few flops, some near misses. Maybe just enough that those investigators could convince themselves Plottner was legit.

But there hadn't been many.

He was on his way to another potentially big score now. Having spent a few days spearfishing (ostensibly) and paying to get laid (primarily) in the Florida Keys, he was on his way to Houston to meet with a group of researchers.

And, sure, he could have just Skyped in. A lot of rich guys did. But Plottner had learned long ago that if something was important, there was no substitute for being there in person. You discovered so much about whoever you were dealing with, most of it nuanced and unspoken.

As the plane ascended and angled west, he was seated in the main cabin along with two other passengers, two people who went more or less everywhere with Plottner.

One was Plottner Investments' director of security, Laestrygones "Lee" Michaelides, a thirtysomething former officer from the First Infantry Division of the Hellenic Army—Greece's famed special forces unit—with an inscrutable face and a phlegmatic demeanor.

He didn't talk much. Or at all. People who had been around him a fair amount and still had never heard him speak wondered if he suffered from selective mutism. Then again, given his measurables—six feet six, 260 pounds, 6 percent body fat—a stern glance was usually sufficient to get his point across.

The other was Plottner's personal assistant, Theresa D'Orsi, who was battle tested in her own way, having handled Plottner's most inane requests for twenty years. Now in her midfifties, she wore small round glasses and modeled both efficiency and discretion. At least part of this was legally mandated: her employment contract included a nuclear-powered nondisclosure agreement.

Plottner One had just cleared ten thousand feet when the plane's satellite phone rang.

Theresa answered it and was soon approaching Plottner, cupping the phone.

"It's Matt Bronik from Dartmouth," she said.

Plottner nodded, accepted the phone. "Matt," he said. "So nice to hear from you. Have you been thinking about my offer?"

"I have. A lot," Bronik said. "It's very, very generous. I'm sure I would have enjoyed working for you, and believe me, this was an exceedingly difficult decision. But I think, in my heart, I'm just not made for the business world. I'm an academic. And this isn't the right time for me or my family to be leaving Dartmouth."

"I see," Plottner said.

And then, because he was never one to give up easily, he said, "Is there some way I might be able to make it the right time?"

"I appreciate that, but I really don't think so. To be honest, I've been having a little bit of a health issue that's forced me to step back from my research. So I'm not sure how much good I would be to you anyway."

A health issue? Was that actually true, or was it just an excuse? Plottner was tempted to ask for details, but he wasn't going to pry.

He could make the college-development people pry for him.

"I understand," Plottner said.

He was tempted to double the offer, right there. Two million bucks a year. That could surely clear up a lot of health issues. Everyone had a price, right?

But, no. That wasn't how he wanted to do this.

"Well, obviously, I'm disappointed. I think your research is very exciting, and I wanted to have the Plottner name be a part of it in some way."

"I appreciate that. I really do."

"And as far as I'm concerned, the offer remains open," Plottner said. "Perhaps you'll change your mind."

"That's very generous of you. Thank you."

"All right then. I hope we part as friends?"

"Absolutely."

"Very good, very good," Plottner said.

And then, like an idea was already forming in his head, he added: "Perhaps we'll talk again someday."

Plottner hung up. For perhaps ten seconds, he sat with the phone clutched to his chest. For Plottner, this passed as crippling indecision.

Then he called out, "Theresa."

She appeared at his side without a word.

"Tell Houston we have to cancel. We're going to New Hampshire."

Because there was no substitute for being there in person.

A few minutes later, as long as it took to file a new flight plan, *Plottner One* began gently banking north.

Maybe other people would have given up more easily.

They weren't the sort of people who had planes named after them.

CHAPTER 9

As the end of February gave way to the beginning of March, I allowed myself a few degrees of cautious optimism about Matt, even as I continued to worry about a relapse.

There were certain viruses that, once they got inside you, never truly left. They could lie dormant and then strike at any time, couldn't they?

We had established protocols that if he didn't show up in certain places at certain times, people knew to start looking for him, because it meant he was slumped over somewhere. His Where's My Phone app was activated, and he wasn't allowed to go out of range. He had also started wearing a medical alert bracelet.

But I really hoped that as long as he stayed away from that virus, he'd be okay.

Which was why I remained vigilant for any sign he was weakening in his resolve. I felt like a jealous wife, except instead of searching for lipstick smears on Matt's collar, I was finding excuses to touch his hands when he came home. The latex gloves he wore at the lab were dusted with cornstarch, and they sometimes left residue behind.

I had also secretly enlisted a spy: Sheena Aiyagari, Matt's postdoc. She and I had always been closer than Matt's other postdocs, if only because she was more socially skilled than the rest—even if that was, admittedly, a low bar when it came to physics PhDs. At department gatherings, which were mostly a bunch of men talking about Higgs bosons, she had always gone out of her way to ask about Morgan or the latest at the library.

Otherwise, she was fairly typical of the breed of physics postdocs: smart, serious, and focused. She was of South Asian ancestry and had grown up in India, though she finished high school at an American boarding school. She had gone to Cornell as an undergrad, then Berkeley for her PhD. And now she was a postdoc, working as a teaching assistant for undergrad classes and doing research under Matt's tutelage, sharing lab space with him.

Which meant she was around him a lot. And she had promised me that if she saw him working with his laser—or if she was aware of any other sign he was dipping back into his research—she would notify me immediately.

Otherwise, we were slipping along without incident.

Then came the first Tuesday of the month.

And another one of those phone calls from the Dartmouth College Department of Physics and Astronomy.

"Brigid," Beppe began. "I'm so sorry, but—"

"Where is he now?"

"The ambulance just left."

It was a few minutes before two.

"Did you find him in the lab again?" I asked.

I could already feel the anger building in me. If Matt had gone behind my back with the virus, I was going to be truly and righteously pissed.

"I'm not sure," Beppe said. "All I saw was the EMTs carrying him down the stairs. There was a group of us gathered at the landing and I asked, 'Has anyone called Brigid?' No one had, so—"

"I appreciate it. Thank you, Beppe."

"I'm sorry," he said again. "Let me know if there's anything I can do."

I assured him I would, then started grimly going through a routine I now felt like I could do by rote. I texted Aimee. I told my boss what had happened. I drove to Dartmouth-Hitchcock.

When I reached the information desk, it was staffed by the same gray-faced woman as last time.

"I'm Brigid Bronik, here to see my husband, Matthew Bronik," I said, digging out my ID and handing it to her before she could ask.

She accepted it and started typing.

And frowning.

"I'm sorry," she said. "We don't have a record of a Matthew Bronik being admitted today."

I stood there, stumped. "Well, is he . . . I mean, if he came here in an ambulance, he'd be taken to the ER, right?"

"All I can tell you is we don't have a record of a Matthew Bronik being admitted today," she repeated robotically.

"But how—"

"Maybe he hasn't been admitted yet. You can have a seat if you like," the woman said. "Next, please."

"But he has to be—"

"I'm sorry, ma'am," the woman said firmly, "I don't have any information. Have a seat, please. Next."

Her eyes had moved to the person in line, a man who had already advanced to the desk.

I walked away, muttering an insincere "Thank you," managing to muzzle the more choice words I may have preferred.

But, really, I didn't need some icy health care bureaucrat to tell me where my husband was. It was either the ER or the ICU.

Start with the ER. I followed a series of signs until I arrived. The woman staffing the desk there was younger, friendlier.

"Can I help you?" she asked.

"Yes, I'm looking for my husband, Matthew Bronik. He was just brought here in an ambulance."

I held out my license.

She accepted it. But then the same scene repeated itself: typing, followed by frowning.

And no Matthew Bronik.

"Are you sure they brought him *here*?" the woman asked.

"Well, no, but . . . where else would they take him?"

"It's possible they went to Alice Peck Day. We've been very busy this afternoon. Every now and then the EMTs decide a patient will be seen faster over there."

I tamped down the brief spurt of panic that accompanied this news. Alice Peck Day was a small community hospital in nearby Lebanon that had been swallowed up years earlier by the ever-expanding Dartmouth-Hitchcock medical colossus. They didn't have nearly the facilities that Dartmouth-Hitchcock did.

But they would still have the ability to check his medical alert bracelet and then could administer the drugs and fluids he needed to get his blood pressure up, right?

"Aren't they affiliated with you?" I asked. "Wouldn't he still show up in your system if he was there?"

"Sometimes they're a little slower to get people entered," the woman said apologetically. "Hang on."

She picked up her phone, dialed. A short exchange ensued, during which it was firmly established that, no, Alice Peck Day didn't have Matthew Bronik either; and no one matching Matt's description had been brought in.

I thanked the woman for her time, then immediately began the trek toward the ICU.

Maybe the EMTs had taken him straight there. On account of the bracelet. He just hadn't been entered into the computer yet because in the ICU they had more pressing things to worry about than paperwork.

But when I arrived, a woman in scrubs told me they had no patients named Matthew Bronik.

Without bothering to do my incredulous double-checking, I just thanked her and went straight to what was always our end destination: Neurology.

I hadn't bothered to remove my winter jacket, which was filled with down and quite toasty, so I was sweating by that point. I didn't have a tie to pull back my hair, which was probably going in eight different directions. I'm sure I looked a little deranged. I'm also sure I didn't care.

The first person I saw in Neurology was Yvonne, the nurse I had befriended on my previous visits. I could tell she recognized me.

When I stopped in the hallway, she stopped too.

"Hi," I said. "I know this sounds ridiculous, but Dartmouth-Hitchcock seems to have lost my husband. Is he here by any chance?"

She said something in reply, but her head was turned, so I couldn't hear it. I repositioned myself so I could see her mouth.

"I'm sorry, what did you say?" I asked, feeling stupid.

"I haven't seen Dr. Bronik," she said loudly and slowly.

"Would you mind checking the computer for me?"

Maybe someone, somewhere, had finally thought to log him in.

Yvonne went behind a desk.

And no.

Still no Matthew Bronik.

"Maybe check with Dr. Reiner?" Yvonne suggested.

I thanked her for the idea, then found a quiet spot in the corner of the Neurology waiting area. I hated having to make important phone calls on my cell phone. It had the same kind of captioning as my landlines, but I couldn't read and listen at the same time. I had to stare at the screen, wait until I was sure the person was done talking, then respond. It made it like I was on satellite delay.

Nevertheless, the office manager was patient with me. And once I explained what was going on, she agreed it was troubling and volunteered to get Reiner on the line.

Finally, some help. Surely, if anyone could cut through medical bureaucracy, it would be an insistent doctor.

I walked Reiner through my journey from the information desk, to the ER, to the ICU, to Neurology. When I was done, there was nothing on my screen for a short while. Then the words started coming.

"Well, I'm sure he'll turn up. I'm going to have my office manager keep Matt's record open. If there's a new entry, we'll know immediately and we'll call you, okay?"

I momentarily returned the phone to my lips to say, "Thank you."

He started talking again. I was getting tired of the screen and the delay, so I just mashed the phone's earpiece against my hearing aid and hoped for the best.

"In the meantime, why don't you check with Hanover Emergency Medical Services?" he suggested. "I'm sure they'll have a record of where they took him."

"That's a good thought. Thank you, Doctor."

"Let us know when you find him, okay? I want to be able to see him immediately."

"Thank you, Doctor," I said again, then hung up.

I looked up the number for Hanover EMS. When a man answered, I explained my situation.

His answer was definitive:

"We haven't made any pickups at Dartmouth today."

He was a natural shouter. I didn't need my screen.

"Are you sure?" I asked.

"I'm the dispatcher, ma'am. I know where all our units are, all the time, and I haven't sent any squads to Dartmouth. I'm sorry."

"Is it . . . is it possible a different ambulance service picked him up?"

"Your husband works at Dartmouth?"

"Yes."

"Not UMass Dartmouth. Dartmouth College in Hanover, New Hampshire?"

"Yes," I said, exasperated.

"Well, then I don't know what to tell you. We're the only game in town. We cover Hanover, Norwich, Lyme, the whole area. If your husband was picked up by an ambulance, it would have been us. But we haven't made any trips to Dartmouth today."

"Do you have any idea where he might be?" I asked, aware I sounded frantic.

"I'm sorry. All I can tell you is, he's not with us."

I ended the call, now damp everywhere from sweat. I finally shed my down jacket, stood up, and took a few deep breaths.

Then inspiration struck: Matt had the Where's My Phone app. My phone was programmed to track his.

I pulled out my phone, swiped, and prodded. But elation was soon followed by disappointment.

The blue blob was centered on Wilder Hall. It had been left behind.

Just in case, I called his number. It rang twice; then my screen read: "Hey, Brigid. It's Sheena."

"Hi," I said into the mouthpiece, keeping my eyes on the screen. She was soft spoken.

"If you're looking for Matt's phone, he left it on his desk in the lab." I grunted to signify my disgust.

"But I don't think he was working on the virus," she added.

"What makes you say that?"

"Because I came up here not long after he made his departure and the laser was cold. If he had been using it, it would have been warm. It takes a while for the thing to cool down."

"Oh," I said.

"I've been keeping an eye on him like I told you I would. I just didn't want you to think he had gone behind your back or anything."

"Then why did he get sick?"

"Who knows? Maybe there are still some traces of the virus around that he accidentally came into contact with?"

"But you've never gotten sick," I pointed out. "And you're in there all the time."

"Maybe I just didn't touch the same things or my immune system fought it off," she said. "How's he doing anyway?"

"I, uhh, I don't know. They . . . can't find him."

Just saying the words made me feel crazy.

"Isn't he at the hospital?" Sheena asked.

"No, I'm here now. They have no record of him. His doctor doesn't know where he is. The ambulance people say they haven't done any pickups at Dartmouth today."

"But how is that possible?"

"I'm trying to figure that out. Sheena, did you actually *see* Matt get taken out by the EMTs?"

"Well, yeah. It was kind of a big thing, you know?"

"What, exactly, did you see?"

"I . . . I was in my office and I heard . . . kind of a commotion. Then someone said, 'Oh no, Professor Bronik must be doing that thing again.' Everyone was sort of gathered on the stairs. He was strapped to the stretcher and just completely out of it. Exactly like last time."

"And you saw him on the stretcher?"

"A bunch of us did."

"Did you see him get loaded into the ambulance?"

"No, I just went back to my office, but . . . Brigid, what's going on?"

"I don't know," I said. "I just don't know."

Sheena offered me the same reassurances as everyone else. I quickly chased her off the phone.

Then I turned toward the window in the waiting room and looked out on a world that was still spinning at its usual thousand miles an hour, oblivious to the terror I was feeling.

Beppe Valentino and Sheena Aiyagari were brilliant scientists, not people prone to delusions. They had both seen the same thing: Matt taken out of his lab on a stretcher.

From there . . . well, from there, the trail ended. No one, it seemed, knew anything.

It was giving me the same feeling I sometimes got when Matt talked about his work. And every time I said "I'm not sure I get it," Matt just smiled and replied, "Don't worry. Neither does anyone else."

The most famous and venerated proof of quantum mechanics is the double-slit experiment. By demonstrating that light acts as both a particle and a wave, it neatly shows what's known as quantum superposition—the head-scratching fact that a single particle can seem to exist in multiple places at the same time.

Which is utterly baffling.

Except it was still less baffling than what was suddenly going on with my husband.

He didn't seem to exist anywhere at all.

CHAPTER 10

Without even realizing it, Emmett Webster was staring at the picture. Again.

It was the one of the Leisure Travel Vans twenty-four-footer, which he and Wanda should have been in right now. They probably would have been poking their way through the Carolinas, looking for the ultimate roadside barbecue, luxuriating in early spring weather that wasn't even a rumor yet in New Hampshire.

Instead, here he was, sitting in a cubicle at New Hampshire State Police headquarters, the result of a series of decisions that no one besides him seemed to like very much.

The first was that he wasn't going RVing. He couldn't really afford it anymore—their calculations had involved two pensions, not one. Plus, traveling the country with Wanda felt like an adventure. Doing it by himself felt like being a long-haul trucker.

This was much to the distress of his children, who thought Dad was giving up on his dreams.

The second was that he wasn't retiring. Maybe a little of that was also financial. It was mostly that he had already seen what having too much time on his hands looked like.

This was much to the distress of his bosses, who had been hoping to get him out of the way.

There was a new colonel in charge of the New Hampshire State Police, some young guy who had come in from Massachusetts to allegedly clean house, even though Emmett thought the house was just fine the way it was.

The colonel had already promised Emmett's job in Major Crime to someone else, another guy from Massachusetts, which had resulted in Emmett being reassigned to Missing Persons.

It had been a week and a day since he had started there. He had, at first, been quietly hopeful. There was something about Missing Persons that felt like it could be a calling. After all, he missed Wanda every damn second.

Except, like so many other units, Missing Persons had a new captain: Angus Carpenter, another Masshole brought here by the colonel.

So far Carpenter had made it clear he hadn't wanted this transfer to happen, that he had fought it and lost, and that therefore he considered Detective Webster's presence as welcome as hemorrhoids.

The captain hadn't bothered to find out that Emmett had the highest homicide clearance rate in Major Crime three out of the last four years, or that he performed better than most of the new recruits on the PT tests, or that his marksman scores were as good as anyone's on the whole force.

Worse, the guy hadn't given Emmett a case yet. How was Emmett supposed to prove he wasn't some deadweight dinosaur if he didn't actually get some work to do?

So there he was, staring at that picture, when in walked Captain Carpenter, the buzz-cut bastard, and began his idea of an exchange of pleasantries.

"Detective," Carpenter said.

"Captain," Emmett replied.

"We have a report of a person missing from Hanover."

Emmett took a clean notepad out of his desk drawer. The younger cops put everything on computer. Emmett was an analog guy, and would remain so as long as someone, somewhere, was still making pens.

"The name is Matthew Bronik," Carpenter continued. "He's a physics professor up at Dartmouth. His wife called Hanover PD, saying her husband was taken away in an ambulance after having some kind of seizure, but now no one can find him. Hanover PD checked with Hanover EMS and with Dartmouth-Hitchcock, then called us. I'm sure it's some kind of paperwork screwup."

"Got it, Captain," Emmett said. "I'll run it down."

Carpenter left without another word. Emmett was already a little deflated. This professor was probably at the hospital as a John Doe. Or Dartmouth-Hitchcock spelled his name wrong. Or it was something else benign and obvious.

Something that couldn't possibly turn into a real case.

Which was why Carpenter gave it to Emmett.

Still, he started making calls. He leaned heavily on Dartmouth-Hitchcock, getting a high-level administrator who knew all the tricks with the patient database. They went through every possible spelling of Bronik, and Matthew or Matthews as a last name instead of a first name, and all the other permutations they could think of.

Nothing hit. And there were no John Does in any of their facilities.

His next call was to Hanover EMS, where he got a dispatcher who said, "I heard from the wife already. We haven't seen the guy."

Emmett made him double-check anyway. And, in fact, every single one of their rigs was accounted for.

Then Emmett called every other hospital on both sides of the Connecticut River, large and small, within an hour drive of Hanover.

And the urgent care centers.

And the other area EMSs.

Nothing. Nothing. Nothing.

Cops develop instincts, especially after thirty years. And Emmett was getting the feeling something strange was going on. There were certain kinds of people who had an unfortunate tendency to slip through society's cracks. People who were addicted to substances. People who didn't have homes. People who suffered from mental illness. People who lacked documentation. They vanished largely because the system wasn't set up for them, and maybe—when Emmett was being cynical—because the system didn't care about them as much.

None of that applied to a Dartmouth professor.

Dartmouth professors didn't just disappear.

An hour later, Captain Carpenter was again standing at the entrance to Emmett's cubicle.

"Found him?" Carpenter asked.

"Not yet, sir."

Carpenter's face registered annoyance.

Before he could say anything, Emmett added, "But I will. Don't worry, Captain. I got this."

CHAPTER 11

Would it be six hours this time?

Or eight?

Or longer?

Beppe's call had come in at 1:57. It was now closing in on eight o'clock.

I was sitting in our living room, distractedly swiping at my phone. I had that irrational worry that if I didn't keep the screen lit, I might miss an incoming call.

From the corner, a grandfather clock—a family heirloom that ended up with me when no one else wanted it—seemed to be ticking slower than usual.

It reminded me of one of Matt's favorite Einstein quotes, his famous tongue-in-cheek description of relativity: Time moves a lot faster when you're sitting with a pretty girl than when you're sitting on a hot stove.

This was pure hot-stove time.

Really, where was Matt?

It wasn't like he had been stricken and then wandered off, doing his zombie walk. Nor was he lying in a ditch somewhere, undiscovered.

He had been taken away by trained medical professionals. They were taking care of him, weren't they?

I was at once furious—*someone* had to know *something*—and out of my mind with worry.

That he wouldn't come out of it this time.

That some doctor or nurse had screwed something up badly, and now some health care executive was trying to figure out how they were going to explain it to Mrs. Bronik in a way that she wouldn't sue them.

Except I should have heard from one of those people by now. I had made it clear to everyone I could think of that, whatever was going on with Matt, I wanted to know.

After the hospital, I had visited the Hanover Police Department, where an officer promised to "look into it."

Then I made another round of phone calls, checking all the places I had already checked, making sure everyone was on high alert.

After that, I went home. Aimee was there to greet me, having met Morgan when he got off the bus, then parked him in front of apple slices and math homework.

She was just as stymied as I was about Matt's disappearance, which only unnerved me further.

Aimee was competence personified, the kind of person who had a solution for everything. We had been typical sisters growing up: mortal enemies 2 percent of the time, best of friends the other 98—pretty much, whenever we weren't bitterly fighting about something.

We drifted apart for a while after college as we went our own separate directions. Then our relationship went through a metamorphosis in our late twenties and early thirties.

Within the span of a few years, our parents died way too young and unexpectedly—a car crash for Mom and an aneurysm for Dad. Then Aimee went through a hellacious divorce, and I started losing my hearing. At every traumatic turn, we leaned on each other until it became our only way of getting by.

After Morgan was born, she was coming up from her home in Connecticut so often to help out I finally convinced her to move here. She made her living as a forensic accountant. Most of her work was online or over the phone. There was no reason she couldn't relocate.

Having her so close bonded us further. Sometimes we're so simpatico I swear we're thinking with the same brain. It can get a little silly at times. Like, for example, there was my down jacket. The first time I wore it, Aimee scrutinized it, then burst into laughter. She had ordered the exact same jacket, in the exact same color (black), from the exact same catalogue (L.L.Bean), two days before I had. We called them our twin jackets.

Our running, if macabre, joke is that I'd walk through fire for her, and she'd take a bullet for me.

She was not only my best friend; she was Morgan's de facto second mother—except more fun than the first one.

She was also the person I automatically turned to in times of crisis. So when not even Aimee could guess what had happened? I was adrift.

I had tried to distract myself with chores, but I couldn't even concentrate enough to fold laundry.

Dinner, likewise, had been pointless. I made mac and cheese for Morgan and ordered takeout for Aimee and, ostensibly, for myself. Except I was too nervous to eat anything.

As I got closer to the six-hour mark and still had not heard from anyone, I was mostly just counting on Matt. He was going to come to—somewhere—and immediately ask to call his wife.

Or maybe it would be eight hours. But it would happen. Eventually.

Over the last half hour, my vigil had become especially quiet. I didn't dare reach out to anyone else because, one, I had contacted everyone I could think of already; and, two, I didn't want to miss Matt's call.

So I just sat there in silent misery, swiping and fidgeting.

At 8:05, Morgan padded softly into the room, with Aimee just behind. She had been keeping him distracted, but the magic of Uno and Monopoly had slowly worn off.

Our normal bedtime routine started at eight. Morgan should have been under the thrall of Matt's narration of Harry Potter by now. They were in their third rereading of the series and had once again reached book five.

"Have they found Daddy yet?" he asked, his brown eyes—identical to Matt's—searching mine.

"Not yet, honey," I replied.

Aimee added, "I keep telling him Daddy is somewhere. We just don't know where."

"I wish Daddy was the kind of doctor that made people better and not the kind of doctor that does physics," Morgan said. "Then he'd be able to cure himself."

"Me too, honey."

Without another word, Morgan climbed onto the sofa and nestled himself against me, his small body squirming until it finally settled. His warmth radiated against me.

Aimee joined me on the other side, and the three of us spent a few moments like that. It was difficult to say who was comforting whom. Aimee adored Matt too.

"Do you want to get Harry Potter and I'll read it to you?" I asked Morgan, reaching for normalcy.

"No. I don't want Daddy to miss any of it. We're just about to get to one of the parts with Grawp. He *loves* doing Grawp."

I squeezed Morgan a little tighter with one hand. With the other, I swiped at my phone, which was on my lap.

Still nothing.

Morgan shifted, his sharp elbows digging into my side.

The grandfather clock ticked some more.

Then the silence was split by four insistent raps on the front door.

I vaulted off the couch, hurried over, looked through the peephole. There was a fiftyish white man standing on the front porch. He was graying at the temples. He wore a blue parka and khaki-colored slacks. He was already attempting to wipe the winter grit off his thick boots and onto the bristle doormat, like he anticipated he would shortly be inside.

He was holding up a gold shield.

A police officer.

Come to tell me . . . well, something.

"Hold on a moment," I called out.

I shot a glance at Aimee. Morgan didn't need to be a party to whatever scene was about to unfold. She read my mind instantly.

"Morgan, honey," she said immediately, "let's go brush our teeth and get our pj's on."

There was a sharpness to her tone—combined with the strain on my face—that sent him scurrying upstairs, his socked feet flying. As soon as he was out of sight, I opened the door.

"Mrs. Bronik?"

"Yes."

"I'm Detective Emmett Webster with the New Hampshire State Police. I'm in charge of the investigation. Can I come in, please?"

"Yes, absolutely," I said, stepping back into the narrow hallway that served as our foyer.

He entered, bringing an envelope of cold air in with him, then worked his boots into the small rug that was supposed to catch what the doormat did not.

"I just have a few preliminary questions to ask," he said, pulling out a notepad. "I know this is a difficult time. We're trying to move quickly at this stage."

Stage? What stage?

"When was the last time you saw your husband?"

"Early this morning."

"What time was that?"

"Around five a.m. He's an early riser. I saw him getting dressed and I think I mumbled something at him. He came over and kissed me, and that was it. I rolled over and went back to sleep."

"Did you hear from him after that?"

"No. Just the phone call from his department chair at one fifty-seven saying he had been taken away in an ambulance. From there I went to the hospital and, well, I assume Hanover Police told you the rest, right? About his fits and all that?"

"They did, thank you. Was there anything unusual about today? Did he indicate he expected any kind of disruption in his normal pattern?"

"No."

"Can you think of anyone who would want to harm your husband? Anyone who had threatened him recently or might wish him ill will?"

I paused, confused. Matt had been plenty of a threat to himself lately, but that didn't seem to be what this detective wanted to know.

"No, everyone loves Matt and . . . I'm sorry, why are you asking? Do you know where Matt is or not? Has he come out of his fit yet?"

Webster tilted his head. Now he was the one who looked confused.

"Has anyone else from law enforcement talked to you?" Webster asked.

"No. Why?"

"No one from Hanover Police called you?"

"No."

"And the K-9 unit didn't come here?"

"The K-9 unit?" I asked, as confused as I was alarmed. "What are you talking about?"

The detective sighed, put away his pad, bowed his head a little.

"I'm very sorry, Mrs. Bronik. My understanding was that you knew this already. Lyme Police found an ambulance abandoned off a dirt road not far from the Dartmouth Skiway about an hour ago. We believe it was the ambulance that carried your husband, but it was completely empty inside."

CHAPTER 12

The whole time he was talking to her, Emmett Webster couldn't figure out:

Why is this lady so calm?

Why isn't she more hysterical?

Does she actually get what's going on? She seems to be tracking me, but she has those hearing aids . . .

For a moment or two, he was getting that dreary itch, asking himself if he was actually talking to his prime suspect, wondering if this was another seamy life insurance scam or a woman looking for the cheapest possible divorce.

Emmett hated those cases. Didn't they realize what a gift marriage was? And how easily that gift could be taken away?

Sure, there could be rough times. But you were supposed to put the work in. There was a reason why no wedding officiant ever said, "Do you promise to love each other only as long as it's easy?"

Then, once he realized no one had told her what was going on, calm wasn't the problem anymore. The poor woman went through a heaving, sobbing, no-doubt-about-it meltdown. And it only got worse when her kid came downstairs and asked why Mommy was crying.

Emmett was patient with the whole thing, of course. Pushing too hard at this point wouldn't accomplish anything. And, truly, his heart went out to her.

But there was also part of him that was thinking, *Okay, lady, we don't have time for you to be* this *hysterical.*

The only thing that really saved it was when the woman's sister stepped in. Aimee was her name. She projected a sturdy, capable air.

Emmett took the sister into the next room, so the kid wouldn't hear, and gave her a quick rundown of what he knew: that the ambulance didn't belong to Hanover EMS, that it had generic markings and was owned by a company that rented out ambulances, that the abductors may well have been imposters who dressed as EMTs.

To Emmett's gratitude, she immediately took charge. An older sister, obviously. She whisked the kid off to bed with promises the police would find his father, then came back downstairs and herded Emmett and Brigid back into the living room.

Emmett remained standing. Aimee guided her sister onto the sofa, where she held her hands and started speaking in a low, urgent voice.

"I know this is a nightmare," Aimee said. "But you *have* to pull it together. Right now, Matt needs us. The first forty-eight hours are the most critical time, isn't that right, Detective?"

"That's correct," Emmett said.

Actually, it wasn't. No one needed Emmett to start spouting statistics. But three hours was actually the more important window. In 75 percent of cases where an abduction ended in a homicide, the killing was later determined to have happened within the first three hours.

Fact was, if the people who had taken Matthew Bronik planned to kill him, he was already dead.

"So we're going to be strong, okay?" Aimee continued. "We're going to be strong for Matt. We're going to do belly breaths, just like Mom used to make us do. Okay? And then we're going to focus."

Emmett watched as the woman counted down from ten, taking a big breath each time, encouraging her sister to do the same. And, remarkably, when they got down to one, Brigid was no longer crying.

"Okay, good," Aimee said, then stood and faced Emmett. "So what's going on with the investigation right now? How can we help? Who's out there looking for him?"

"We have a K-9 unit searching the area around the ambulance," Emmett said. "Best-case scenario is he's still somewhere nearby. A cabin or something. If he is, those dogs will find him. They're amazing."

"And if he's not nearby?"

"It becomes more difficult," Emmett admitted. "Our public relations unit is right now putting out Professor Bronik's picture. That'll go on websites, on Twitter feeds, and to the TV stations and newspapers. The more eyes we have looking for him out there, the better."

"Can't you issue an Amber Alert?"

"I'm afraid that's only for children."

"Okay, what about roadblocks or—"

"That wouldn't help us much at this point," Emmett said. "Professor Bronik was last seen at roughly two p.m. We didn't find the ambulance until seven thirty. That was our first indication this was something other than a paperwork mix-up at a hospital somewhere. Assuming it took his abductors a half hour to ditch the ambulance and transfer to a new vehicle, they still had a five-hour head start. They could have driven anywhere from New Jersey to Canada during that time."

Aimee jammed her fists against her hips.

"So that's it?" she asked. "You just hope someone out there sees him by accident and—"

"No, that's not it," Emmett assured her. "That's not it by a long shot. I assure you this is going to be a very proactive investigation. To begin with, my captain has notified the NCIC, the National Crime Information Center. Every jurisdiction in the country will have access to information about Professor Bronik.

"The next thing—and I've done this too—is requesting camera footage from Dartmouth Safety and Security. They tell me they don't have any cameras inside Wilder Hall, but there are some outside that area. They're poring through the tapes for us right now."

"That's good," Aimee said.

"We'll see," Emmett said. "If the people who took Professor Bronik did enough planning to rent an ambulance and dress as EMTs, they probably knew there were going to be cameras. They may have obscured their appearance in some way. Still, it's worth a shot. The Crime Scene Unit is working the ambulance right now to see if it gives us anything. They'll probably spend the night on that. In the morning, I've got them headed to Dartmouth. They'll dust Professor Bronik's lab for prints; then they'll obtain prints from anyone who had a legitimate reason to be in that lab. If there are prints that don't belong, that could be a lead. Maybe one of these EMTs got careless and left us a present."

"What about hair and fiber?" Aimee asked.

This isn't an episode of CSI, Emmett thought but kept his expression neutral.

"Those kind of analyses take weeks, if not months," he said. "We'll have fingerprints back in a few hours. That's more the kind of time span that will be useful to us right now."

"Okay, what about, I don't know, highway cameras, or facial recognition software, or—"

Again, too much CSI.

"We're going to use anything we can, I promise," Emmett said. "But all that technology, it only starts to become useful when you can find a direction for it. And right now we need that direction. We need to use the computers we were born with."

He tapped his skull, then turned to the wife, Brigid. The tissue she had been using to dab her face was now crumpled in her hand.

"I'm sure your husband is a great guy, and I know it's hard to think about someone you love in any kind of negative light," Emmett said. "But the fact is, someone has put a lot of effort into this. There has to be someone who stands to gain from his disappearance. Think hard.

Has he crossed anyone lately? Was there someone angry with him for some reason?"

She had been staring hard at Emmett's face as he spoke. When he finished, she took a few moments to think it over.

"Well," she said finally. "Matt *did* just turn down a job offer, but—"

"From whom?"

Brigid immediately started shaking her head. "That's not . . . that couldn't be it. Forget I said it."

"Mrs. Bronik, you may think it's nothing. But everything at this point is something."

"If you don't tell him, I will," Aimee said.

"I don't want to cast aspersions," Brigid began. "It's not—"

"Just tell him!" Aimee demanded.

"Fine," Brigid said, then turned to Emmett. "There's this rich guy, Sean Plottner. He runs an investment company. He tried to hire Matt—"

"For a million dollars a year," Aimee interjected.

"When was this?" Emmett asked.

"A few weeks ago."

"And how did Plottner react? Was he angry?"

"No. Matt said he was perfectly nice about it. I think Plottner was hoping Matt was going to change his mind. And I don't think . . . I mean, Plottner is a multibillionaire. Would he really be involved in something like this?"

Emmett had been a detective long enough to know that people involved themselves in all sorts of things they shouldn't.

On a fresh page of his notebook, he printed the name SEAN PLOTTNER in block letters.

Ask him some questions. Catch him in a lie or two. Tie him to the ambulance rental financially . . .

"It's something to look into. Nothing more," Emmett said. "Are there any other—"

His phone rang. Emmett recognized the number for Haver Markham, the young, whip-smart head of the Crime Scene Unit.

"Excuse me," he said to Brigid. Then: "Webster here."

"It's Haver," she said. "I'm out with the ambulance. You with the wife right now?"

"Yeah."

"Can you ask if she knows her husband's blood type?"

Emmett repeated the question for Brigid, whose color was rapidly draining from her face.

"B negative," she said.

Emmett told Markham the answer.

"Then I got some bad news," she said. "Whoever was in this ambulance tried to wipe it down, and they did good enough to fool the naked eye but not good enough to fool a blue light. We found blood on the side of one of the floor plates. When we pried up the plate, we found more that had seeped underneath. It was B negative. That's pretty rare. Less than two percent of the population."

Mindful of not wanting to say too much around Brigid and Aimee, Emmett asked, "How much was there?"

Markham easily picked up on his guarded tone. "If you're asking whether the guy is still alive, I couldn't tell you. It depends how much was above it that got wiped up. We found enough under the plate that I didn't have any trouble collecting samples, but beyond that? Couldn't tell you."

"So it's a definite maybe?" Emmett asked.

"Yes, that's fair. A definite maybe."

CHAPTER 13

Before this, the longest night of my life was when Morgan was born.

I had felt the first hint of a contraction—a real contraction, not the false-alarm Braxton-Hicks type—around seven o'clock. My birth plan, a carefully constructed document that had gone through six drafts and much anguished consideration, had dictated I labor for several hours at home, peacefully, with music playing and scented candles burning, while easing in and out of a warm bath.

We had come up with this in the Netherlands, where Matt was finishing up his postdoc at Delft. Our childbirth class was for English-speaking expats from the UK and America, but it was taught by a Dutch woman who assumed we would be completing pregnancy in the Netherlands, where giving birth at home with a midwife—and without an epidural—was a common practice.

Even though we moved to New Hampshire when I was twenty-four weeks, we stuck with our Netherlands plan. So when I went into labor at thirty-seven weeks, a little on the early side, we didn't panic at those first contractions. Matt just drew a bath.

Then my water broke. And my very American obstetrician ordered me to report to the hospital for a round of antibiotics.

Still, we were going to stay the course. In addition to the bath and the candles—which were no longer options—the childbirth class instructor said poetry, read aloud by the woman's birthing partner, could be very soothing, a kind of meditation that relaxed the mother's brain and helped her maintain a more Zen-like state.

Matt brought Elizabeth Bishop, Robert Hayden, Rainer Maria Rilke, and Maya Angelou with us to the hospital.

And as my contractions started coming closer, Matt continued reading.

Until about three o'clock in the morning. He was working his way through *Sonnets to Orpheus* when I suddenly clamped his arm in a death grip and, in between breaths, hissed, *"Would you shut . . . the hell up . . . and get me . . . some goddamn drugs!"*

It became part of the story we always told about my delivery, not to mention one of Matt's running jokes: *Whatever you do with Brigid, don't read her Rilke.*

But now? In the dark of this night? Long after Aimee had chased away the television news crews that wanted interviews and ordered me to get some sleep? When the lights were off and I was in bed, except I was so far from slumber I might as well have been lying on coals? When the pillow next to mine was undented by a human head?

The only thing I wished for in the world was to have my Matty next to me, reading me poetry.

Detective Webster had departed not long after he had received the call from the Crime Scene Unit. He wanted to be up at what he referred to as "the scene"—with the unasked, unanswerable question being: The scene of what?

An abduction?

Or a murder?

Detective Webster asked me to stay at home, in case the abductors tried to contact us with a ransom demand.

Or something like that.

Really, I got the sense they were just trying to keep us out of the way.

The Crime Scene Unit had come by to collect samples of Matt's fingerprints off items he had touched, but that was the last I had heard from law enforcement.

I could guess what the cops were thinking. Blood would lead to a body, which would lead to a long night, after which they would all go home.

If they ever thought about that spot in Lyme again, they would just think about that cold, strange night when they found what was left of that poor Dartmouth professor.

These were the kind of thoughts spinning in my mind on brutal repeat, and I wished I could make it stop.

But it wouldn't.

There are the things the brain anticipates, even if just in the dark crevices where the creepy things live, the things no one wants to talk about.

But, yes, you prepare yourself to lose a spouse in some horrific way. Whether it's a car crash, a sudden heart attack, or a terrible act of violence, you think: *That could happen, and here's how I would react, and here's how I would attempt to move on.*

You might even ponder the unforeseen act of emotional brutality. The affair with the colleague. Some unforgiveable relationship sabotage. A midlife freak-out that involves a commune or a cult. Even if any of those things would be wildly out of character for Matt, they still felt like they were in the realm of possibility.

This did not. This scenario did not exist in even the creepiest of creepy crevices. The notion that my husband could be . . . just . . . taken.

And maybe we would hear from the abductors. Or maybe there would never be a word. Or any answers as to what happened.

Maybe this was the beginning of a long, awful narrative poem that would continue for the rest of my life. And when I drew my last breath, I'd still be wondering:

What *did* happen to Matt?

No, I had to stop thinking like this. Just because there was blood, that could have just been an accident. The wound on his forehead could have reopened. Those things bleed profusely, even when they're not serious.

I thought back to the morning, when he kissed me goodbye. Even though it was dark, I could tell he was wearing one of my favorite shirts—a fitted long-sleeve North Carolina T-shirt that hugged his body just so.

That shirt. I remembered when Matt got it. His beloved UNC was deep in an NCAA tournament run, and he had felt this childlike need to show his colors.

It was so ridiculous, his college-basketball fetish. But it was also part of the reason I loved him. His thing with basketball was real. And authentic.

And relatable. There was so much else about Matt that defied my relatively common understanding. Because he was *so* smart, and he understood concepts that were far beyond the comprehension of most humans. He talked about things like the shape of the universe (why did that matter again?), or how black holes warped space-time (come again?), or how neutrinos carried stories from billions of years ago (huh?), and he just lost me altogether.

But then he wore his Tar Heels shirt, and moped when his team lost, and made enthusiastic love to me when it won, and suddenly I felt like I understood him.

And loved him.

Loved him more than anything.

Because he wasn't perfect, but he was *mine*.

And this was the thing that was now coming to me at whatever o'clock in the morning, when sleep was impossible, when every thought was grim, when there was a bloody ambulance floating on the backs of my eyelids every time I closed my eyes:

I would fight for what I loved.

For him.

Tooth and nail. Fangs, claws, whatever.

I would do it for Morgan, who worshipped his father—and, more to the point, deserved to be raised with one, rather than without one.

I would do it for myself, because giving up on Matt was giving in to a misery that was unimaginable.

And I would do it for our triangular family, which was the greater unit by far.

Granted, deciding this didn't make it any easier to find sleep. My thoughts were jumping wildly about. Part of what makes quantum mechanics so difficult to comprehend—and so different from the simpler models of physics that came before it—is that it's a world where no one can tell you exactly how something is going to play out.

There's no certainty. Just probability.

Einstein hated this. *"Gott würfelt nicht,"* he fumed.

Commonly translated as: God doesn't play dice with the universe.

And yet there I was in the dark of night.

Thinking about dice.

Hoping God rolled them in my favor.

CHAPTER 14

Emmett Webster's night had included maybe four hours of sleep, most of it poor.

State police guidelines said that if a detective was more than an hour from home on a case, he could elect to spend the night in a hotel. Emmett always kept toiletries and a few changes of clothes in his car for just such an occasion.

Not in the guidelines was that Angus Carpenter had already explained to Emmett: that if a three-digit number showed up on his expense report, there'd be consequences.

Which was fine in some parts of the state. Not in tony Hanover. That's how Emmett ended up at the cheapest place in the area, an off-brand motel called the Tuck Inn that advertised a "free waffle breakfast" but, judging from the number of overdose calls the local rescue squad had to handle at that location, seemed to attract a crowd that was there for something else.

In the morning, waking up in a strange place turned out to have an unexpected perk: he didn't immediately start looking for Wanda.

That made up for the fact that free waffles turned out to be the frozen variety, heated in a toaster and served with sugar-free imitation maple-flavored syrup, a condiment that tasted only marginally better than the plastic bottle it came in.

As he sawed through the waffle with a plastic knife distinctly unsuited to the task, he opened his laptop and got to work. Whether the critical window in this investigation was three hours, forty-eight, or something in between, the fact was the clock was ticking.

The Crime Scene Unit's report on the scene in Lyme had not given him much to go on. The blood from the ambulance had been sent to the lab for analysis, but that would take weeks.

The ambulance itself was owned by a company in Manchester. He would attempt to run down who had done the renting as soon as business opened.

In the meantime, he decided his first move would be on what was, at this point, his lone suspect: Sean Plottner.

Emmett had dealt with rich guys before and, therefore, knew the perils. Rich guys had rich lawyers who would invent civil rights that had not previously existed; or they would make the administration of Miranda rights last all afternoon, primarily because they were getting paid eight hundred dollars for every hour they could make pass.

The trick—the only trick, really—was to get the drop on the guy and get him to talk *before* the lawyers moved in.

So, first, Emmett had to find him.

Which turned out to be predictably difficult. Plottner wasn't in the DMV database. He probably owned homes all over, but his official residence was somewhere like Florida, which had no state income tax.

Emmett tried state police records next and found some arrests from back in the nineties. Drug possession and DUI.

In both cases, the address listed was a student box number.

He looked for property records next. But if Plottner owned anything in the state, it wasn't in his own name. Rich people had LLCs for that sort of thing.

Next, Emmett tried googling "Sean Plottner New Hampshire," and that was where he got a hit. Someone had bought a property—the top of a whole mountain, basically—for $21.9 million. It was one of the largest private real estate transactions in state history, and a reporter had done a little digging and discovered the purchaser was investment billionaire Sean Plottner.

From there, it got easier. There weren't exactly a surfeit of $21.9 million real estate transactions to check. Emmett found the one in question, matched the block and lot number to an address on a rural route outside Orford, and got underway.

Upon arrival, he was confronted with a formidable iron gate, sturdily anchored by huge stone pillars on either side. He slowed to a stop, rolled down his window, and pressed the button on a call box, aware his every action was being caught on one camera he could see—and probably several he couldn't.

"May I help you?" a woman's voice asked.

"Emmett Webster, New Hampshire State Police, I'm here to see Sean Plottner."

"May I ask what this is regarding?"

"I wanted to ask him some questions for a case I'm working on."

Emmett waited for a response. None came at first.

Then: "Is this about Matt Bronik?"

So much for getting the drop on the guy.

"Yes," Emmett said.

He was bracing to be told that Mr. Plottner was not available, that an appointment to speak with him could be scheduled at a later time, that questions could be submitted in writing—some kind of rich-guy stall tactic like that.

But, to his surprise, the gates began opening.

The woman said, "Drive ahead to the main house, please."

Climbing up the side of the mountain through a series of switchbacks, Emmett felt like he had left New Hampshire and entered Switzerland.

There were occasional breaks in the trees where he'd see a horse barn, or tennis courts, or a rolling field. And then he'd continue his slow ascent through the forest.

He had traveled at least a mile before he even got a glimpse of the house, sitting all the way at the top of the mountain. It was enormous and fronted by a massive stone retaining wall.

Like a fortress.

Emmett continued through the switchbacks until the terrain leveled out. He parked in a roundabout and climbed the front steps, which consisted of seven huge pieces of granite, stacked on top of each other, gracefully carved into semicircles.

On either side, two stone-inlay columns rose to a section of gabled roof two stories up.

At the top of the porch—and, really, it was more portico than porch—was a granite tile landing that led to two fourteen-feet-tall double doors made of a handsome dark wood that may have been mahogany. They had been set into a marble archway with exquisite stained glass at the top.

Emmett had knocked on a lot of doors in his career, none as grand as this one. He lifted a heavy iron knocker and brought it down three times.

The echoes that came back suggested a house that was every bit as large inside as out.

Emmett was expecting a butler—maybe several—but the door was answered by Plottner himself. He was wearing corduroys, a button-down shirt, and a V-neck cashmere sweater, all casually elegant and, undoubtedly, more expensive than what Wanda had bought on sale for Emmett at the outlets.

"Hi, Sean Plottner," he said easily, extending a hand.

"Emmett Webster."

They shook.

"Come in, please," Plottner said.

He then led Emmett through a grand entryway, underneath a curving double staircase, and down three steps into a sitting area that could have entertained twenty comfortably.

The focal point of it was a series of broad picture windows with a view that was nothing short of stunning.

"The real estate agent said you can see five states and Canada," Plottner said as Emmett gaped. "But I think he was just trying to get a commission. Anyhow, take a seat, please."

Emmett lowered himself into a leather easy chair. Plottner flopped on a couch nearby, leaning against the arm and crossing his legs.

"I heard about what happened to Dr. Bronik," he said. "It sounds awful. Do you have any leads yet?"

Emmett deflected the question by asking one of his own. "How do you know Professor Bronik?"

"I was introduced to him during one of my visits to Dartmouth. I'm an alum, as you probably know. My family has a long history of philanthropy with the college. The development office is always trying to get me excited about what's going on there so I'll feel like separating myself from more of my money."

"When did you first meet him?"

Plottner cast his eyes toward the ceiling, decided the answer wasn't up there, then called out, "Theresa!"

Emmett felt his phone buzz in his pocket but ignored it.

A tidy woman with round glasses appeared, seemingly out of nowhere.

"Yes?"

"What day did we visit Professor Bronik's lab?"

She immediately consulted a tablet she was carrying.

"February third. It was a Monday. The appointment was at nine a.m."

"There you go," Plottner said.

"And you offered to pay him a million dollars a year based on that one meeting?" Emmett asked.

"That's right."

"Why? You're not exactly running a physics lab."

"No, that's true. But I just get a feeling about people sometimes—which people are capable of generating revolutionary breakthroughs, which people are worth putting my money behind. They tend to be people who look at problems differently, or have unconventional perspectives. In Matt Bronik's case, what got me interested was his background. He's a certifiable genius who grew up in Pig Snout, North Carolina. He thinks of himself as an outsider. He *thinks* like an outsider. And yet he still has all the knowledge, training, and expertise of an insider. That's practically a formula for innovation. I'll back that guy every time.

"I'm wrong about my feelings sometimes, but I've been right an awful lot too. And I've learned when I have that feeling, I need to back those people as fully as I possibly can. A million dollars a year—or call it two million, by the time I got him a lab and an assistant and whatnot—was a relatively small bet, from my perspective, with a potentially enormous payoff."

Emmett's phone buzzed again. He again ignored it.

"Except he turned you down," he said.

"That's right."

"Why?"

"He said he was having some health issues, though I couldn't tell you what they were. Beyond that, I got the sense he didn't like that I would own his work product. He wanted to be able to publish his work, to share it freely with the world."

"And you wanted to be able to profit off it," Emmett said.

"That's right. I don't apologize for that. That's what I do."

"How did you feel when he turned you down?"

"Disappointed, of course. But . . ."

He finished the thought by shrugging.

"That's it?"

"That's it."

He smiled and recrossed his legs, automatically smoothing his pants legs as he did so.

Almost like keeping things smooth was a reflex.

Emmett felt like he hadn't asked any hard questions yet. It was time to start, if only to see how Plottner would react.

"What were you up to yesterday?" Emmett asked.

"You mean, was I busy kidnapping Matt Bronik?" Plottner asked back. The smile hadn't left his face.

"It's just a question, Mr. Plottner."

"I was at Dartmouth, actually. But I didn't see Professor Bronik. I had some morning meetings with the president and the provost. I'm sure they'd be willing to confirm that. The meetings were over around noon. I had lunch at Latham House in Lyme—I have a weakness for their beer pretzel—then I came back here. Theresa can confirm that. So can Andrew, my chef, who made dinner for us; and Lee, my security director. I can make any of them available to chat with you alone, if you like. I have nothing to hide."

Emmett would check with the Dartmouth administrators later. The employees were less useful. He was sure that even if Plottner had something to do with this, he wouldn't have done the wet work himself.

Still, it was interesting that the man would admit to having been near Dartmouth College when the abduction occurred.

"That's not necessary," Emmett said. "Like I said, it's just a question."

"Do you have any leads other than me?" Plottner asked.

His tone was not passive aggressive, even if the words were.

"That's not something I can really discuss," Emmett said.

"So that's a no," Plottner said, hefting a sigh. "Well, I do hope you manage to find one. In the meantime, here's my number if you need anything else."

He pulled a sleek silver business-card holder out of his pocket and handed Emmett a stiff piece of card stock with his name and phone number embossed on it.

"Theresa, make sure you put Detective Webster through if he calls."

"Of course, sir," she said.

"Good. She can be pretty vicious otherwise," Plottner said, adding a wink. "Is there anything else I can do for you?"

Emmett's phone buzzed yet again. He couldn't remember the last time he had felt so manhandled during an interrogation he was supposed to be running.

At the same time, he also knew he had nothing on Plottner, other than a reflexive distrust of smug billionaires.

And that wasn't exactly something you could take to a judge to get a search warrant.

"No," Emmett said. "Thank you for your time."

CHAPTER 15

No sympathy. None whatsoever.

If I stopped to pity myself, or to think about Matt, or about Morgan losing his father, I might never have the wherewithal to start moving again.

Action was my only refuge.

Aimee had spent the night in our guest room rather than drive back to Queeche, but I declined her offer of assistance with the morning routine and bravely forged ahead, making breakfast for Morgan, then getting him ready for school.

It wasn't so strange, doing this part alone. Matt was never around during this time of the day anyway.

The one moment I faltered was when I made the mistake of fetching the *Valley News* from the front porch and opening it up to see the headline "Physics professor missing in possible abduction."

Underneath were Matt's portrait and a dark, grainy picture of the abandoned ambulance, cocked sideways and half-buried in the brush.

My hand shot to the side of the doorframe and gripped tight. Few people realize how much we use our hearing to locate ourselves in space. It's part of the reason old people fall so much—it's actually their ears failing them as much as their legs. An unexpected part of my disability was how bad my balance had become, and this was almost enough to knock me off my feet.

I knew Aimee had shooed away those television reporters the previous night, but . . . to see this now, splattered across the front page; to be forced to objectively acknowledge the horror of what was happening; to realize my family had become a lurid headline for the consumption of drowsy voyeurs over their breakfasts.

If I was going to get jarred off the rails, this was when it would happen.

Instead, I refolded the paper, shoved it back in its plastic sleeve, and tossed it in the snow under the shrubs.

For Morgan's sake, I told myself.

Then I was going again. After I dressed, I walked Morgan to the bus stop, watched him climb aboard. I returned to the house, told Aimee I had some errands to run, and was soon underway toward Dartmouth and Wilder Hall.

Detective Webster had his investigation, and I'm sure he would do it well. I had my own questions, things I wanted to see for myself.

I couldn't even say exactly what I was looking for. I just had this feeling I would know when I found it.

Besides, anything was better than standing still.

I parked in my usual spot near Baker Library, then made that familiar walk to Wilder. Except as I made the final turn, I saw two decidedly unfamiliar trucks stopped outside the building in a no-parking zone—two trucks that, in combination, had surely never graced Dartmouth's campus during its quarter millennium of operations.

The first was shiny and black. It had STATE POLICE and MAJOR CRIME UNIT stamped prominently on its side.

The second was more mysterious. It was a boxy thing with heavy tires, maybe twenty feet long, and painted in drab olive. Like it belonged to the military.

Its diesel engine was running. Leaning against the front bumper, smoking a cigarette, was a man with buzz-cut hair and army fatigues. I counted three stripes on his sleeve. A sergeant.

He paid no particular mind to the middle-aged lady coming his way. I walked, tentatively now, a little closer.

On the side of the second cab was a seal that consisted of the medical symbol—two snakes intertwined around a torch—and the words *Protect Project Sustain*.

Stenciled underneath was the acronym USAMRMC.

One Google search later, I was on the website for the US Army Medical Research and Materiel Command.

Obviously, the army had been alerted Matt was missing.

I continued toward Wilder. Behind the two trucks were a pair of American-made sedans, both black.

Inside the first car, resting on top of the dashboard, was a folder with a sticker on it. Another acronym. NICBR, with the *I* represented as a DNA-style double helix.

Once I entered Wilder, I pulled out my phone again. I was soon on the website for the National Interagency Confederation for Biological Research.

It was bare bones, calling the confederation "a consortium of eight agencies with a common vision of Federal research partners working in synergy to achieve a healthier and more secure nation."

Wikipedia was slightly more forthcoming. It described the National Interagency Confederation for Biological Research as "a biotechnology and biodefense partnership."

Biodefense.

Because Matt's virus could be used as a weapon?

I resumed my journey, climbing the wooden staircase that dominated the middle of Wilder, trying not to think about how Matt had been brought down these steps, strapped to a stretcher, a mere eighteen hours earlier.

When I reached the second floor, I was confronted with yellow crime scene tape stretched across the entrance to the Physics and

Astronomy Department. Taped to the middle, like a fly caught in a spider's web, was a printed sign:

DO NOT ENTER
AREA SEALED
UNTIL FURTHER NOTICE
BY ORDER OF
THE DEPARTMENT OF DEFENSE

I paused, a little stupefied. The Department of Defense was really sealing off the entire department?

A quick jog up to the third floor confirmed that yes, it was trying; but someone else didn't like it very much.

The yellow tape hung in tatters. The **DO NOT ENTER** sign lay on the floor, partially crumpled.

I walked toward Matt's lab without seeing anyone. The third floor of Wilder Hall was a disjointed rabbit warren of hallways and offices, having been added to, subtracted from, and reconfigured far too many times to retain any logic. It had been built in an era long before central air. The retrofitting of that particular advance had involved adding ducts that hung from the ceiling and were roomy enough for a large child to crawl through, which only added to the blocky, haphazard feel of the place.

The offices were all dark and closed. There was shouting coming from somewhere farther down, but I had no chance of discerning the substance of it.

Still, I thought I heard the word *colonel*. And *general*. And—

"Ma'am, ma'am, ma'am."

The words came out like the barks of a small insistent dog. The man who uttered them was approaching fast. He was anywhere from midthirties to midforties, with vampirically pale skin, a Young Republican haircut, and an Old Republican dark suit. A curly cord of some sort protruded from his ear and snaked down the back of his shirt.

"You can't be here," he said. "This area is sealed."

The shouting down the hall was continuing, but I did my best to tune it out so I could focus on the man in front of me.

"I'm . . . I'm Brigid Bronik. Matt's wife."

This halted the man's progress. Shocked him, even. Made him momentarily forget his purpose.

Then he quickly rediscovered it.

"And I'm—"

He said his name too indistinctly. People do that all the time. They assume that because *they* know their name, I must know it too.

"I'm sorry, I didn't hear you. Could you say that again?"

I turned one of my ears slightly toward him, so he wouldn't miss my hearing aid. It was something I hated having to do—directing people's attention to my impairment—but this was too important to get hung up on my usual vanity.

"Gary Evans," he said more slowly and distinctly. "I'm with US Army Counterintelligence."

I could feel my mouth hanging open.

"I'm sorry for . . . for what happened to your husband," he continued. "But you still can't be here. We've sealed off the entire second and third floors until further notice. I'm afraid you have to leave."

Whether consciously or not, he had spread his suit jacket just slightly, giving me a glimpse of the sidearm he had tucked in his shoulder holster.

"Please, ma'am. This way," he said, and was now herding me away from the shouting, back down the hallway from where I had come.

"Do you know anything about where Matt is?" I asked, allowing myself to be guided away.

"I'm sorry, ma'am, I can't answer any questions right now. You have to leave."

I slowed down so I could turn and look at his mouth as he spoke. He clearly didn't like this. He hadn't actually touched me yet, but I had the sense his next step would be to grab my arm if he felt he needed to.

We had reached the staircase, and he kept right on herding. It was only at the landing to the second floor that he stopped.

"Can you find your way out?" he asked.

"Yes," I said meekly.

"Okay. Thank you."

Then he added, "I'm sorry about your husband."

"Thank you," I said, then continued back out of the building, past the sedans and trucks.

The sergeant, having finished his cigarette, was now back in the cab, the engine still running. I continued my retreat all the way back to Baker Library.

Once in my office, I closed the door and sat at my desk, still trying to make sense of what had just happened.

National security? Biodefense? What kind of tiny Frankenstein have you created, Matt?

Using my desk phone, I called Beppe Valentino, hoping he might have more answers than I did at the moment.

"Brigid. How are you doing?" I heard/read.

"Awful. Why has the Department of Defense sealed off the physics department?"

"That's complicated," Beppe said. "I'm at the house right now. Why don't you come over? We probably need to talk."

CHAPTER 16

It was Sean Plottner's favorite feature—the house's real selling point, though it hadn't been included in the multiple listing service report because, as the agent discreetly explained, revealing it publicly "wouldn't be prudent."

That's because it wasn't on top of the mountain but, rather, inside it: a 2,400-square-foot apartment, accessible from the main house via a secret door and an elevator, some thirty feet farther down.

The space was comfortable, well appointed. It had its own natural source of water—a spring that came from deep underground—and a generator that could fully power operations even if cut off from the solar panels on the surface. A third of the space was dedicated to food storage and stocked with MREs and other nonperishables.

Bombproof? Check.

Radiationproof? Check.

Soundproof? But of course.

The agent had been careful not to describe it as a "bunker," because that word upset some people. Instead, he deemed it "an ideal feature for the security-conscious owner."

It was certainly an ideal spot for some of the property's more sensitive security apparatuses—the monitoring of all the hidden cameras, motion-sensing devices, and microphones that littered the estate. Guests could be spied on from virtually any nook or cranny of the house, not to mention much of the 850 acres around them.

This was where Plottner had retreated not long after the detective had made his departure. He went straight to a room with three large screens and an even larger man stationed in front of them. Ramrod straight in the command chair, Lee Michaelides was almost as tall sitting as Plottner was standing.

"Is he gone?" Plottner asked.

Lee, never one to use words when gestures would do, merely nodded.

"Did he stop on the way? Try to snoop around at all?"

Lee shook his head.

"Were you listening to our conversation in the living room?"

Another nod.

"Why do you think he suspects me? Just because of the job offer? Or is there something else?"

Lee didn't bother replying to a question he couldn't answer.

"Why do people always suspect me of things?" Plottner said.

The question was half-rhetorical, half-whining. So, again, Lee stayed quiet.

"Show me him leaving, please," Plottner said.

Lee quickly cued up the footage: First Plottner getting into his car, a dark-gray unmarked police sedan. Then the sedan pulling away. Then the car at various spots as it snaked down the mountain.

And, no. No stops.

"Okay, thanks," Plottner said.

He puckered his face for a moment, then said, "I think this detective needs some fresh leads. Let's make sure he has more than he can handle."

Without wasted movement, he walked over to a nearby desk, placed his laptop on it, opened the lid, then clicked on the Facebook icon.

Plottner loved Facebook, and not just because he had bought a pile of its stock at its IPO—another brilliant investment that would net him several hundred million dollars whenever he chose to cash out.

No, he loved it because the Plottner Investments Facebook account had hundreds of thousands of followers—from professional money managers to day traders and amateur investors—all of whom wanted to know what Sean Plottner was going to do next.

Plottner enjoyed being able to speak to them directly, without the obfuscation of traditional media.

He clicked "Live." After a brief countdown, he was soon looking at his own image on the screen.

"Good morning. I have an important announcement to make, and I'd ask that you all share it as widely as possible."

He paused very briefly, watching the visitor count quickly grow from a few hundred to a few thousand before resuming.

"A friend of mine, Dr. Matthew Bronik, has been abducted from his lab at Dartmouth College. I will offer a million dollars to anyone who provides the New Hampshire State Police information that helps ensure his safe return."

CHAPTER 17

By the time he cleared the cell phone dead zone that covered the outskirts of Orford, Emmett Webster had six missed calls.

All from Haver Markham, the head of the Crime Scene Unit.

Emmett highlighted her number, hit send, and almost immediately heard: "Where are you?"

"I was interviewing a suspect."

"How far are you from Hanover?"

"About twenty minutes, give or take."

"Okay. We need you here. I'm at Dartmouth, in Wilder Hall. You might want to hurry."

"Why?"

"Because there's this guy named Gary Evans who has become a real pain in my ass. I don't know if I want to arrest him or shoot him. Maybe both."

"Be right there," Emmett said, and put the pedal down.

Eighteen minutes later, he knew he had found the right spot when he saw the Crime Scene Unit's shiny black truck.

Just off its bumper, pacing, was Haver Markham.

To Emmett, Markham wasn't just a different generation. She was a different breed entirely: five feet three, strawberry blonde, and, not to put too fine a point on it, female. And unlike Emmett, who had learned crime scene analysis haphazardly, on the job, Markham had gone to school for it specifically. And Emmett had no problem admitting she was far better at it than he ever would or could be. Specialization had its benefits.

Except right now, the specialist was fuming.

"I was waiting on you before we escalated this thing," Markham began as Emmett approached. "This is your investigation, so it's not my call. But for the record, I say we escalate."

"What's going on exactly?" Emmett asked.

"These G.I. Joe jackasses upstairs won't let us into Bronik's lab, that's what," she spat, gesturing toward a drab-olive truck parked nearby.

"Why not?"

"Why don't you ask them?" she said hotly. "They're up on the third floor doing a circle jerk. Maybe they'll let you in on it. They didn't seem to want to invite me."

"Ah," Emmett said.

He entered Wilder and climbed the stairs. Markham was smart and skilled. But she was also young and easily addled. There were times when a veteran's touch was needed.

At both the second and third floors, he encountered crime scene tape and signs telling him the area had been sealed by the Department of Defense. The sign on the upper floor was spiderwebbed with lines, having apparently been balled up and then flattened back out.

"Hello?" Emmett called out. "Anyone here?"

Nothing happened for about thirty seconds, so Emmett repeated himself, a little louder. That prompted a man with short hair and a dark suit to appear. Before Emmett could say anything more, the man preempted him by barking, "You can't be here, sir."

Emmett held up his shield and spoke softly. "I'm Emmett Webster, New Hampshire State Police Missing Persons. I'm the lead investigator into the abduction of Matthew Bronik. Who are you?"

The man stopped on the other side of the police tape.

"Gary Evans, United States Army Counterintelligence."

"Thank you . . . Mr. Evans? Major Evans? I'm sorry, I—"

"Agent Evans."

"My apologies. Can I ask why you aren't giving my Crime Scene Unit access to Dr. Bronik's lab?"

"You can ask, but it's not something I can answer. I've already told your colleague this area is off limits until further notice. It's a matter of national security, which supersedes any and every reason the New Hampshire State Police might have for getting into it."

Emmett accepted this placidly. While there could be exceptions, the very simple jurisdictional hierarchy was that state beat local, and federal beat state.

There was no fighting the feds, as Haver Markham had learned. There was also no escalating against the feds, as Markham was also perhaps beginning to appreciate.

But maybe there was a chance to finesse them.

"Look, we're all on the same team here," Emmett said. "I'm trying to figure out what happened, and I'm sure you are too. Let's work together. My people are pros. They'll be very careful. If you need to be in there with them to oversee what they're doing or set limits on—"

"Not going to happen."

"I understand you have a job to do, but so—"

"Not going to happen."

"There has to be some kind of—"

"I can't let you into that lab under any circumstances."

"This guy has a wife, a kid," Emmett pleaded. "We're—"

"Sir, I have work to do, and you're preventing me from doing it. I'm asking you nicely to leave. If you refuse that order, I will take action and have you detained."

Emmett was starting to understand why Markham yearned to resort to gunplay.

"Very well," he said, then retreated back down the stairs.

So much for the veteran's touch.

He delivered the news to Markham that they were stymied for the moment. She just grumbled about how the feds had probably ruined the crime scene anyway, then got her crew back in the truck.

Meanwhile, Emmett's phone told him he had missed another call.

A few button pushes later, he heard, "Detective Webster, this is Steve Dahan"—the Dartmouth College Safety and Security director Emmett had spoken with the previous evening. "I've found some footage that I think you're going to want to see."

CHAPTER 18

I drove to Beppe's house, even though it was within walking distance of campus.

Anything to keep moving forward quickly.

Two cars were parked in the short driveway of the Valentino residence. One was the practical salt-stained all-wheel-drive Subaru Outback that so many Dartmouth professors drove you'd think the college handed them out at convocation.

The other, hiding under a canvas cover, was a Maserati GranTurismo convertible that always struck me as an odd choice for a mild-mannered theoretical physicist.

Then there was the third car, the one that stayed in the garage all winter. It was driven by Beppe's wife, whom I only barely knew. She departed Hanover in roughly mid-October, when the first snowflakes began to fly, and was not seen again until mid-April. She spent the time in Italy, in a villa in Calabria, down at the tip of the boot.

I was never sure how that worked—a marriage where you spent half the year apart. It seemed very European.

Being as this was not Mrs. Valentino's season, I thought her husband would be home alone. So when I rang the doorbell of his four-bedroom Cape, I expected an appearance from Beppe, who was short, lithe, and fair skinned—northern Italian, not southern—with thinning brown hair swept back from a widow's peak.

Instead, I was met by a handsome man of medium height and heavier build, with thick, dark curly hair and a complexion that was swarthy even at the end of winter.

David Dafashy. He had gotten tenure a year before Matt and had informally mentored him through the process. David and his wife, Mariangela, had a daughter who was maybe five or six.

As one of the few younger families in the department, we had spent time together socially. Though only sporadically. It seemed like we had dinner together every six to eight months, swore we would do it more often, then let another six or eight months pass before we did it again.

Dafashy always had a bit of an exotic air about him. I had heard him speak of his father, an Egyptian immigrant who hailed from the small Nile River city of Dafash, which accounted for both the family name and David's olive skin. The Dafashys seemed to be very British Empire Egyptian, so while David was born and raised in Virginia, his accent skewed slightly English. He came off as refined, cultured, and perhaps a tad pedantic—all of which fit in very well with the Dartmouth faculty.

He opened the door wearing an appropriately grim expression.

"Hi, Brigid," he said in a hushed, funereal voice. "Come on in. Beppe was just making some more coffee."

I followed him into an eat-in kitchen, where I was immediately enveloped in a hug by Beppe Valentino.

"Brigid," he purred.

I'm pretty sure he had never hugged me before.

Then again, my husband had never been abducted before.

"How are you holding up?" he asked when he released me. "I can't imagine what this is like for you."

"About how you would expect," I said.

"Have a seat," he said, gesturing toward a high-top table that was set in a small nook surrounded by windows. Two coffee mugs sat atop it already. Beppe was soon placing a third in front of me.

"David and I were just discussing the Wilder situation," Beppe said.

"Yeah. What happened? Were you just working and they came in and ordered you out?"

"No. It was already sealed when we got there. They must have come in the middle of the night. David and I arrived at the same time, around seven thirty. They wouldn't even let us go into our offices to grab a few things."

"Can they do that? Kick you out of your own space?"

"I just put in a call to the college's lawyers to see if we have any options, but the short answer is yes," Beppe said. "As soon as the government decides something is a matter of national security, it has a great deal of authority to do whatever it wants, however it pleases."

"And this is . . . I mean, I know what Matt was doing was dangerous to him personally. But is it really a matter of national security?"

Beppe and David exchanged uneasy glances.

"She deserves to know," David said.

Beppe turned to me. "This is all . . . confidential, I guess you might say. Ever since the Manhattan Project, the military and the physics department have been what you might call forced bedfellows. The things we're doing, even things that seem strictly theoretical at times, can have applications that go far beyond the lab table, sometimes far more quickly than anyone realizes."

"Especially Matt's area," David said. "Quantum physics has become the new space race. It's us against the Chinese, and in certain areas they're winning, which absolutely terrifies Uncle Sam."

"You know what Matt was attempting to do, yes?" Beppe asked.

"Interfere a virus."

"Right. But what about how he was going about it?"

"I know it had to do with a laser . . . and he said something about accidentally mutating the virus, but . . ."

Beppe breathed in deeply and turned to David. "You want to take this? I feel like this is more your area."

David, who had been taking a sip of coffee, put down his mug.

"Of course," he said. "How much has Matt told you?"

"Assume I know nothing," I said.

"Okay, then. The conventional way we get things to demonstrate quantum interference is to make what's called a Bose-Einstein condensate. It chills the particles down to near absolute zero, at which point they line up and dance with each other like good quantum particles should. A number of very prominent teams have tried to do the same thing with viruses and bacteria, hoping they could find one that could withstand the extreme cold of a Bose-Einstein condensate. The problem is, life doesn't like things cold and orderly. It prefers them warm and messy. Even the hardiest viruses were getting killed.

"Matt felt like those teams were going about things all wrong. He wanted to work with the virus on its own terms, to see if he could manipulate something about the virus itself that would allow him to coax it into a quantum state at room temperature."

"Which may have been simply impossible," I said.

"Not necessarily," Beppe cautioned. "We are just starting to discover that there are all kinds of natural quantum processes happening within organisms. As just one example, consider photosynthesis. It's far more efficient than classical theory suggests it should be. How? We suspect it's quantum tunneling. The electrons are essentially taking shortcuts. Now, like I said, that's *within* an organism. We're still not talking about the whole organism. But it at least gives us hope that quantum biology does not necessarily need to happen in the deep freeze."

"But what made Matt's approach different also might be what makes it dangerous," David said. "The other teams were essentially looking for a tiny little unicorn—that rare, rare virus that might be able to survive the rigors of a Bose-Einstein condensate. Matt, on the other hand, was working with a very common virus. If his technique worked on that virus, it could potentially work with *any* virus."

"Like, what, the flu? Ebola?" I asked.

"Take your pick," David said. "Frankly, it's far more troubling that Matt's illness may have been caused by a virus not known to infect humans. No one thought the tobacco mosaic virus was any kind of threat. That's why Matt's lab was only biosafety level two and was allowed to exist quite happily on the third floor of Wilder Hall. But if he's managed to make the tobacco mosaic virus pathogenic? What if merely putting a virus into a quantum state makes it capable of eluding our immune systems? The implications for the battlefield—or for life in general, really—are deeply, deeply disturbing.

"You have to understand, the vast majority of viruses crawling around this earth aren't dangerous to us. They've evolved to attack other organisms. But that also means they're completely foreign to us. Our bodies would be utterly defenseless. And even if you could quickly come up with a vaccine against one, another one could come along. If this got into the wrong hands . . ."

He didn't need to describe the nightmare for me.

I was already having it.

"And so you think the fact that he was getting sick means . . . well, it means he must have succeeded, right?" I asked.

"I couldn't tell you," David said. "Matt always kept his cards close to the vest. He didn't want to be the scientist who constantly ran around shouting 'eureka' when he wasn't a thousand percent sure of what he had."

Beppe cut back in: "There's one person who would know."

"Who's that?" I asked.

"Sheena Aiyagari," he said, pulling out his phone. "Let me call her."

CHAPTER 19

It was likely no accident that the Dartmouth College Office of Safety and Security was located just past frat row.

If nothing else, Emmett thought, it saved them a lot of gas on Friday and Saturday nights.

Shortly after showing his badge, Emmett was escorted into the office of Steve Dahan, where the most prominent decoration was a large picture of a much younger Steve Dahan, wearing desert camouflage and the campaign hat of the United States Marine Corps.

Dahan still had a marine-inspired flattop, though he had gained some thickness around the middle since his oorah days. Emmett could guess it was because the man spent most of his day doing exactly what he was right now: sitting behind a desk.

"Thanks for coming so quickly," Dahan said, rising to greet Emmett.

"You're the one doing me a favor," Emmett replied. "So thank you."

"I was on a student-life committee with Matt Bronik a few years back," Dahan said. "He was a great guy. Down to earth. Not full of himself like some of these professors. Still very smart, obviously. But also very thoughtful. Those two things don't always go together, as you know."

Emmett nodded. He was no grammarian, but he nevertheless noted Dahan's use of the past tense to describe Bronik.

Dahan tilted his twenty-seven-inch flat-screen computer monitor so Emmett could see it. Dahan talked as he clicked.

"Anyway, let's get cracking. We have a hundred and fifty cameras spread across campus, all of them networked. I have an application that lets me look at any camera, anytime, from anywhere. I love it. I can't tell you how many times it's saved me from coming in on a day off."

Emmett was sure it had. He also remembered a time, not too long ago, when a day off was actually a day off.

"Now, a hundred and fifty cameras sounds like a lot. But the main campus is two hundred and seventy acres, so it's actually not as much coverage as you might think. Some of our cameras are designed to be very obvious. We place them to be a deterrent to anyone who might be thinking about doing something they shouldn't. Some are not so obvious. We're sensitive about not placing any in or near the dorms. We don't want students to think we're spying on them."

"Security and privacy do tend to compete with each other," Emmett noted.

Now appearing on the screen was a side view of the front of Wilder Hall, shot from several stories up.

"Exactly," Dahan said. "I think I told you we didn't have anything in Wilder, either internal or external. That's such an old building it's very difficult to retrofit anything modern onto it in a way that's unobtrusive. The Admissions Department blows a lid if we do anything that makes this place look like anything other than a stately two-hundred-fifty-year-old college worth every penny of the seventy-five grand we want parents to pay for it. The closest thing we have is from the top of Fairchild, which is next door. Luckily, this is one of our better high-resolution cameras."

"Great," Emmett said.

"Okay, here we go. I've put all this on a thumb drive for you, but I wanted to preview it for you in case you had any questions. As you can see, this was yesterday afternoon, a little before two o'clock," Dahan said, jabbing his finger on the time stamp at the bottom of the screen, which read 13:49—what civilians referred to as 1:49.

Emmett watched as an ambulance, lights flashing, cruised up to the front of Wilder Hall. Its markings were generic—it just said AMBULANCE, without any reference to Hanover—but who would think to question that?

Moments after it stopped, three men jumped out: one from the driver's door, one from the passenger door, and one from the back.

They were wearing dark-blue EMT uniforms, but something was definitely off about them. Emmett had seen more than enough EMTs in his time. They typically owned a small number of uniforms—three, four, five, whatever—and cycled through them regularly, wearing each one so frequently it soon melded to the body it was intended for. The patches warped, the pocket flaps curled, the colors faded.

These uniforms were all crisp. The patches were like boards. The pockets were straight. The colors sharp.

Like they had never been worn before.

And there was something else: their heads were covered in blue scrub caps, their eyes with clear-plastic safety glasses, their mouths with white masks.

Like they were about to enter a surgical theater.

Or were the medical equivalent of bank robbers.

"Can you pause it?" Emmett asked.

"I could," Dahan said. "But I've been over this a bunch of times now, and you'll get your best look at them when they come back out."

"Okay," Emmett said.

"Nothing happens for the next little while," Dahan said, clicking the fast-forward button.

The image sprang to life. Students streamed in and out, walking four times faster, then eight times faster, as Dahan clicked and reclicked. When the clock reached 13:56, he slowed it back to regular speed.

"Okay, they're about to come back out," he said.

Sure enough, the three men reemerged. This time the stretcher had a human form strapped to it.

A human form with a nearly bald head, a beard, and a light-blue long-sleeve T-shirt.

"That's Bronik, all right," Emmett said.

"Yeah," Dahan said. "And you're going to get your best view of the perpetrators right about . . . here."

He clicked pause, then zoomed in.

"I've given you the best stills of all three of these guys on your thumb drive," Dahan said. "But this is basically what you'll see."

Emmett peered hard at the screen. Between the scrub caps and the masks, very little of the men's faces were exposed. Just a narrow strip around the eyes. And even that was covered in the safety glasses.

But there were two noticeable features about the men's eyes. Their lids did not have a crease in them. And their shape was distinctly almond.

Matt Bronik's abductors had East Asian ancestry. And there was something about the way they moved—a foreign feel to their gait—that made Emmett think they weren't American.

"You making of this what I'm making of this?" Dahan asked.

"Sure am," Emmett said. "Looks to me like Professor Bronik was kidnapped by three Chinese nationals."

CHAPTER 20

Sheena didn't answer her phone.

I just sat there, feigning patience, as Beppe left a message to please call, then sent a text saying the same thing.

Ten minutes passed. Twenty.

Nothing from Sheena.

Beppe served more coffee. David was telling stories about Matt. They were heartwarming—all about how Matt was beloved by everyone from the students to the janitors—but I wished he would stop.

It felt like he was rehearsing anecdotes for Matt's funeral.

As the minutes continued to pass, I quickly grew impatient.

"Why isn't she answering?" I finally asked. "Don't people her age treat their phones like another appendage?"

"She probably did what David and I did: went to Wilder, found it closed, then returned home," Beppe said. "Then she put her phone down. She doesn't know we're trying to reach her."

"Where does she live?"

"I certainly don't know," David said, throwing his hands up with perhaps a bit too much flair.

"Hang on, I can get her address from the department roster," Beppe volunteered and was soon thumbing his phone. "She's in Sachem Village."

"That's the graduate-student housing off Route 10, isn't it?" I asked.

"That's right."

"Great, let's go," I said, already standing.

David was still seated. "What, and just knock on her door?"

"Exactly."

"Well, I can't do that."

"Why not?"

He stirred uneasily, shooting an urgent glance at Beppe that seemed to be laden with meaning.

"I'm just not comfortable intruding on her personal space like that," David said. "It feels . . . inappropriate, especially for men who are in a supervisory role over her."

Then I finally got it. Mariangela had been a doctoral candidate when David first met and began wooing her. He was an assistant professor ten years her senior at the time, so it set off some tongue clucking around the department. Then she got pregnant. There was talk it would cost David a chance at tenure.

He survived the scandal. Barely. This was ultimately pre-#MeToo and before college policies regarding professors and their underlings were quite as zero tolerance. The relationship was clearly consensual. There wasn't exactly anyone lodging a complaint.

Once they got married and had the baby, everyone more or less moved on, and the cloud that hovered over Dafashy's career cleared. Or so I thought.

"Under the circumstances, I'm sure she'd be fine with it," I pressed.

We were both now looking toward Beppe, who as a college department chair had long experience brokering peace agreements between squabbling grown-ups.

Beppe didn't take long to deliberate.

"Why don't you just go, Brigid?" he said. "She might be more comfortable talking with only you anyway. With three people it could feel like an interrogation."

"Okay, fine," I said, eager to get moving. "Call me if you hear from her in the meantime?"

"Of course," Beppe said.

He smiled warmly. I still felt like I was missing something—some knowledge that Beppe and David clearly shared. But I had bigger problems than whatever they were colluding about.

I thanked Beppe for the coffee, bid them both farewell, and made for the door.

On the drive toward Sachem Village, I was interrupted by a text with some hopeful news from Aimee: Sean Plottner had offered a million-dollar reward for information leading to Matt's safe return.

It was currently rocketing around the internet, moving at the speed that only a trending topic could, and it would surely help motivate any would-be eyewitnesses out there.

Which was very generous. It was also one more piece of information I couldn't adequately parse. Matt had turned down the job offer. Why was he still worth some small portion of the Plottner fortune?

Or maybe that was the thing: it was so small it wasn't that big a deal to Plottner. To him, a million dollars was just a friendly gesture, a nice donation to his favorite charity.

There was no time to think about it further. With the aid of Google Maps and the address provided by Beppe, I had arrived in front of a gray-sided multifamily home. It had a two-story section in the middle, with one-story wings on each side. There were three front doors altogether.

Sheena's was the one on the right. I walked up a short concrete path and was confronted with a door guarded by one of those numeric keypad locks. Just to the right was a doorbell. I rang it.

And waited.

There was no movement inside. It appeared to be a two-room unit, with a living room that flowed into a kitchen in front and a bedroom down a hallway behind. If Sheena was in the back, she might not hear.

I rang again.

Still no answer.

I looked around to see if I could tell whether there was a car nearby that might have belonged to Sheena—something with, say, a Cornell window decal or physics-related bumper sticker.

There was nothing obvious.

Of course, it was also possible Sheena didn't have a car. Campus was less than two miles away—a long walk, but a relatively short bike ride.

I knocked this time. When that provoked no more response than the bell, I walked back down the path.

Except when I reached my car, I didn't feel like giving up just yet. I turned, looked at that multifamily home, and was soon walking toward the middle door.

Sheena's neighbor.

Who might know where Sheena was.

This time when I rang the bell, the door was opened by a harried-looking young woman with long light-brown hair she appeared not to have brushed yet—likely because of the wide-eyed baby on her hip and the runny-nosed toddler crowding her legs.

"Hi, can I help you?"

"I'm sorry to bother you. I'm trying to track down Sheena Aiyagari. Have you seen her?"

"May I ask who you are?"

"Yes, my name is Brigid Bronik and—"

The woman's hand flew to her mouth, and her eyes grew wide. "Oh my gosh. I'm so sorry. I heard this morning on the news and . . . have they found him? Or . . ."

"Thank you. And no. He's still missing. That's why I'm looking for Sheena. She works with Matt. But she's not answering her phone, so I thought I'd stop by."

"I actually haven't seen her since yesterday," the woman said. "I've been really worried."

I felt a chill, like a hard wind had just blown, except the air around me was still.

The toddler was attempting to go outside to play, forcing the woman to use her legs to block the child's escape. She looked down and said something I couldn't hear but could easily imagine.

Honey, not now, Mommy's talking to a grown-up.

Then she looked up again and asked, "Could you actually come inside for a moment?"

"Of course."

The woman planted the toddler in front of *Dora the Explorer*, then returned to the foyer, the baby still clinging to her contentedly.

"My name is Lauryn, by the way. Lauryn Ward."

"Nice to meet you. Are you and Sheena friends, or . . ."

"Yeah, I would say so. Do you know her well?"

"Sort of," I said. "More through my husband than anything."

"Oh, she's a total sweetheart. We don't get to spend a ton of time together, because she's so busy. But she's been a total godsend. Maybe she just feels sorry for me, I don't know, but sometimes she'll just stop by with a cup of coffee and chat a little bit. Or she'll stay with the kids for a few minutes so I can run out to the store without having to get them all bundled up."

"That's very kind of her."

"It's a lifesaver. Are you a mom?"

I nodded.

"So, yeah, you know. Anyhow, Sheena is . . . I mean, I don't want to sound like I'm a nosy neighbor or something, keeping tabs on her. But I guess I sort of keep a lookout for her. It can get a little lonely here. My husband is doing his residency at the hospital right now, so his schedule is crazy. Our neighbor on the other side is a single guy who acts like family is something contagious he doesn't want to catch. Sheena is one of the only grown-ups I get to see outside of a doctor's office or a mommy group. And she's usually home by nine o'clock at the latest, every night, without fail."

"But not last night?"

"No. I get my daughter down around eight-thirty or eight forty-five, then I tidy up the kitchen before I go to bed. That's normally when I see Sheena's headlights swinging in, if she isn't home already. But I didn't see them last night. And then this morning when I woke up and I didn't see her car, I seriously thought about calling the police. I didn't even realize she worked with your husband . . . do you think it's connected somehow?"

My heart was thumping too hard for me to respond. I couldn't bring myself to say it out loud. But it was becoming increasingly clear:

Sheena had been abducted too.

CHAPTER 21

Emmett watched Matt Bronik's abduction video three times, then stared at the still photos for a while.

If, by some chance, he came across these men again, he wanted to be able to identify them as quickly and as surely as possible.

The trick he had developed for doing this with suspects was to focus on one unusual feature, something he was unlikely to find in anyone else, and memorize it—almost like he was taking a picture of it with the camera in his brain.

In this case, one of the men had very distinctive eyebrows, shaped like sickles. Another man had a forehead with a sharper-than-normal slope to it. Like he was a Neanderthal. The third man was the easiest. On the front of his throat, peeking just above his collar, there was a tattoo. It appeared to be a dragon.

These were the men who had Professor Bronik. They were already ten steps ahead of Emmett and were, if anything, currently extending that lead.

Emmett had to close the gap somehow, and he had to do it with his own government handcuffing him. How was he supposed to find these men if he couldn't even get access to the place where they had committed their crime?

And if it was some foreign entity, what was he, a New Hampshire State Police detective, supposed to do about it? He didn't even have a current passport.

It used to be when Emmett started feeling hopeless about a case, he would talk to Wanda. And Wanda, with all her positive energy, would know exactly what to say.

Wasn't that one of the secrets to a lasting marriage? When one person was down or doubting themselves, the other person lifted them up, made them believe.

Made them better than they would be alone.

Now all he could think about was what Wanda would have said, then try to give himself the same pep talk.

She would have told him to keep his head down, keep working the case, keep chasing down every lead. She would have reminded him what he was so ultimately good at: that plodding persistence of his. If he kept turning over shovelfuls of new information, he'd eventually dig down to the truth.

So. One scoop at a time. He still had to reach out to the company that owned the ambulance. It was a place that specialized in renting out emergency vehicles and other large equipment to rescue squads and municipalities whose original vehicles needed repair or were out of service for some reason.

He made the call, identified himself, and was soon on the phone with a manager. After he read off the vehicle identification number from the Crime Scene Unit's report, she pulled up the record and informed him that the truck had been rented by a Yiren Jiang of 12 Badger Street in Nashua, New Hampshire. He had used a New Hampshire driver's license—probably a fake—as identification. The deposit had been paid in cash. The rental had started the previous Wednesday, and he had picked it up on Monday.

Unfortunately, her office didn't have any cameras. But she did have originals of the paperwork, which Jiang may have touched.

Emmett said he'd send a trooper over to collect it as evidence, then ended the call.

Emmett next dialed Captain Angus Carpenter. He wanted the captain to send troopers to the ambulance-rental place and to 12 Badger Street.

"Carpenter."

"Hi, Captain. It's Emmett Webster."

"I know, Detective. We have caller ID, remember?"

Such warmth between them.

Emmett plowed forward: "I tracked down that ambulance. It was rented from a business in Manchester by a man with a Chinese name who—"

"Slow down, Detective, slow down. Could you just send this to me in an email instead?"

Email. Why was it nothing seemed to exist these days unless it appeared in a damn email?

But Emmett said, "Yes, sir."

"Thanks. I was actually about to call you. I just talked with the colonel about the Dartmouth situation."

Emmett's sense of foreboding was immediate. He couldn't think of a single time when this particular colonel had been anything but bad news.

"Yes, sir?"

"We're off the case."

Emmett took a deep breath before responding.

"And why is that, sir?"

"The colonel wants this turned over to Major Crime. He feels this isn't a missing persons case anymore. It's a homicide, and we need to start treating it that way."

"Sir, with all due respect, we don't know that yet. And I think it sends a bad message to the family, like we've given up hope."

"The family will be fine. Major Crime has more resources than we do. And this case is going to need it. Some rich guy just posted on Facebook that he was offering a million-dollar reward for anyone who had information about the good professor, and the crackpots are already coming out of the woodwork."

"What rich guy?" Emmett asked.

"Sean Plottner. He's some investing guru."

He might be a lot more than that, Emmett thought but did not say. He wasn't ready to start spitballing theories of this case when Carpenter was just going to allow it to be taken away.

"Anyhow, email me whatever leads you have and I'll make sure they're followed up," the captain continued. "Otherwise, you're done."

"We found blood in an ambulance. That's not the same as finding a body," Emmett said.

"Sorry. Colonel's mind is made up. I don't like it either. But when the colonel gives an order, I follow it. This is now a homicide. Unless you can prove him wrong?"

"I believe Professor Bronik is still alive, yes."

"And why is that?"

"Because Bronik isn't a heavily guarded head of state or some elusive figure," Emmett said. "He's a college professor. If someone wanted to kill him, they could have just knocked on his door and shot him. But whoever did this went through a lot of trouble to abduct him instead. And they wouldn't have done that if all they intended to do was put a bullet behind his ear."

Carpenter absorbed this silently for a moment.

"That's a fine theory," he said after a pause. "But it's nothing more than a theory."

"So is the colonel's belief that this is a homicide. The difference is, I've been working this case, so my theory is actually based on something."

Carpenter sighed noisily. "Look, you want to finish up your shift chasing down what you have? Fine. You're already out there. But unless you come up with some kind of evidence that Bronik is still alive, your time on this case is done. I want you to pass your notes along to Major Crime, and then I want you back in here at noon tomorrow, behind a desk, with your ass in a chair. Is that clear?"

"Yes, sir."

"And you'll send me that email?"

"Yes, sir."

"Good."

That was how the call ended.

Because he was Emmett, he showed little reaction.

That's not what Wanda would have done. She would have hung up, then given Carpenter a one-finger salute.

CHAPTER 22

For the second time in less than twenty-four hours, I found myself reporting someone missing.

I made this call to Detective Webster, because I suspected all the Hanover Police would have done is pass it on to the state police anyway. He took it in without much commentary.

He then said he had pictures of the people who took Matt, and asked if we could meet somewhere so I could look at them. I suggested my house.

On my way back home, I called Beppe, told him my fears about Sheena, and about the mugshots I was about to see. He asked if he could see them, too, and of course I said yes. The more eyeballs, the better.

That was how, thirty minutes later, everyone converged at my house.

Aimee immediately took charge of the hosting. Already that morning, she had found some overripe bananas and worked magic on them, baking them into a bread whose delectable fragrance still lingered in the kitchen.

As Beppe and Detective Webster arrived, Aimee hung up their coats and directed them toward the dining room, where we had a large farm table that had been made out of reclaimed lumber—Matt's favorite piece of furniture in the house, bought with the proceeds of an undergraduate teaching award he had won a few years back.

She then insisted we have a hot beverage with our fresh banana bread, and generally lorded over us the way only Aimee could.

When you're a man, they call this taking initiative. When you're a woman, they call it being bossy.

Whatever. I was just thankful—and not for the first time—for my incredible sister, whose simple acts of hospitality put air into a room that otherwise might have lacked it.

Detective Webster seemed to appreciate her, too, nodding as Aimee set down a plate in front of him, then taking a large bite.

"This is delicious," he gushed. "I haven't had anything this good since my wife died."

I felt an awkward smile stretch across my face. Webster seemed too young to have lost a spouse.

The next thought crashed into me: *Is that what people are going to say about me someday?*

Webster cleared his throat and set his laptop on the farm table, getting us down to business by loading a video and pressing play.

I was soon assaulted with the shocking sight of my husband being abducted, which I watched with my hand clutched to my throat. Mostly, it was just surreal, seeing these men carry my inert husband out of Wilder Hall—and out of my life—with no more apparent difficulty than two guys carrying an empty dresser.

After the video was done, Webster clicked on close-ups of the three suspects and told us how he had started thinking of them. They were, in order: a man with sickle-shaped eyebrows, a man with a Neanderthal-sloped forehead, and a man with a dragon tattoo on his throat.

"Do any of these men look familiar to either of you?" he asked. "Have you seen them around? Do you know who they are?"

I stared hard at the screen, looking at the men who had turned my existence upside down, feeling an ample measure of revulsion but not the least shred of recognition.

"No," I said. "Should I?"

"Probably not. But I have to ask."

Beppe took his turn studying the pictures next, and similarly came up blank.

From behind us, where she had been watching silently, Aimee said something. I didn't catch the beginning, but I turned in time to see her say, "Something that's been bothering me."

"What's that?" Webster asked, turning toward her.

"Beppe, you saw Matt being carried down the stairs. And it looked like he was having one of his fits, right?" Aimee said.

"That's right," Beppe said.

"And on that video, he certainly appears to be out of it. So how did those fake EMTs know to arrive when Matt was spazzing out? The last two times he's had a fit, there's been no warning. Even he didn't know he was about to have one. So how did *those* guys know?"

She finished the question with an emphatic point at the screen. The room fell silent.

"Great question," Webster said after a pause. "It's possible his abductors knew about Dr. Bronik's medical problem and used it to their advantage. They drugged him, knowing that when they carried him out, everyone would just assume he was having another attack."

"So it's an inside job, then," Aimee said. "Only people in the physics department knew about Matt's fits."

"Not necessarily," Beppe said. "There are students who have seen him carried out too. And they're not all physics majors."

"Still, an inside-Dartmouth job," Aimee said.

No one had anything to say about this for a moment or two.

"Maybe they just got lucky and drugged a guy who was already having a health problem?" Webster suggested.

No one responded. The word *lucky* didn't seem to belong anywhere near this.

Webster moved on to his next item of business. He had received a scan of the driver's license that had been used to rent the ambulance.

The man with the sickle-shaped eyebrows was using the name Yiren Jiang.

The license, however, was a fake. Yiren Jiang didn't exist in the DMV database. And police had confirmed the address he used in Nashua didn't exist.

Webster asked whether Matt's research had anything to do with China, which prompted a lecture from Beppe about the quantum space race. He concluded by talking about a hundred-million-dollar satellite called Micius, which was allowing the Chinese to smash records when it came to demonstrating quantum entanglement.

Matt had often talked about entanglement, which to me was perhaps the most mind-boggling bit of quantum sorcery out there. Once a pair of particles have been entangled, they can be separated by any distance—a thousand miles, a thousand solar systems, it doesn't matter—and yet they still somehow remain coordinated with each other. Smack a particle in one place, and its partner immediately says "Ouch."

"So if the Chinese are already doing so well with this satellite and whatnot, why would they need to kidnap Dr. Bronik?" Webster asked.

"Anything I said would be speculation," Beppe said. "But I will say that lately it seems like they're stuck."

"Stuck how?"

"Normally, when you've got a technological edge like the Chinese do right now, you keep putting out papers and filing patents, just to remind everyone you're still top dog," Beppe said. "Instead, they've gone very quiet. Now, it's possible that means they're about to come out with something really big—or they've already gotten there, and they've decided not to tell us. But it's also possible they've hit some kind of dead end. I was Skyping with a colleague from Australia about this the other day. The line he used was 'The silence from the Chinese has been rather deafening, don't you think?' And I agreed. Maybe they've stalled, and they think something Matt knows will get them unstalled?"

I jumped in with, "And let's not forget they also took Sheena. Maybe it was actually *her* work and they felt like they also needed her adviser."

"Just slow down a moment," Webster said, holding up his hands like a traffic cop. "Are we sure Ms. Aiyagari is missing and not just away from her phone? I realize she didn't come home last night, but I don't want us to hit the panic button just yet. She's a young single woman. Maybe she just spent the night at her boyfriend's place?"

Beppe was shaking his head. "There's no boyfriend. Sheena has a fiancé who lives in India."

"What about a friend's couch? I don't want to sound the alarm over someone simply because she's not answering her phone."

"I understand," Beppe said. "But Sheena is a very reliable young woman, not the type of person who just disappears. I've been reaching out to everyone in the department. She shares an office with two other postdocs. Late yesterday afternoon, she told them she was going to the library for a while. That's the last communication anyone has had with her as far as I know."

"I talked with her, too, but it was before then," I said. "She answered Matt's phone when I called it. But at that point, I still thought the whole thing was some kind of mix-up with the hospital. Sheena didn't know anything, of course."

The unknowns were starting to form overlapping layers.

Was this, in fact, a double tragedy? I wondered how they had abducted Sheena. Had they drugged her too? Just grabbed her off the street? Had Sheena and Matt shared that ambulance at some point? Were they now being held in the same place?

So many questions.

Including one that was now coming back to the forefront of my mind.

"Beppe, can I ask you something about Sheena?" I asked. "When we were at your house earlier, and I suggested we go knock on her door,

David shot you this look that I could only describe as alarmed. What was that about?"

"That's a long story," he said, sighing heavily.

The physics department chair ran his hand through what remained of his thinning hair. I waited for him to continue.

"I don't even know if I should be telling you this, or if it's relevant," Beppe said. "I'd ask you to treat this with . . . a certain degree of discretion."

"Of course," I said.

"About a month ago," Beppe said heavily, "Sheena accused David Dafashy of sexual harassment."

CHAPTER 23

Sean Plottner was back aboveground, sitting in his office, staring out the window but not seeing the view.

Theresa appeared behind him.

"Sir," she said.

He turned. She was holding the phone.

"It's Sam Ellis," she announced. "He says you'll want to talk to him."

Sam Ellis was Plottner Investments' social media guru, a millennial with a smart mouth and fast fingers who annoyed Plottner with talk about "touch points" and the need to be "buzzy" on his "socials." Ellis's life was a seemingly endless series of selfies. He knew nothing of personal privacy, spoke of algorithms in reverential tones, and placed in Instagram influencers the kind of faith once reserved for biblical prophets.

Plottner accepted the phone and said, "Yes?"

"Hey, it's Sam," he said. "Love the video. Have you looked at your numbers? The views are going up so fast it's like watching a national debt counter."

"Great," Plottner said flatly.

The moment Facebook views had dollar figures attached to them, he would start taking them seriously. Otherwise, he didn't understand the fascination. If people needed attention so badly, why didn't they just get a dog?

"The comments are the usual mix of morons and trolls," Ellis said. "Most of it is useless. I've been sifting through it anyway. I sent a few people on to the New Hampshire State Police, but there's one guy who refuses to deal with the cops. He swears he knows where Bronik is, and he says he'll only talk to you directly."

"Oh?" Plottner said, his interest piqued.

"The guy's name is supposedly Tom O'Day. It's pretty obviously a fake account. It was just opened. There's no sign of any friends or public posts. I did a reverse image search, and the profile photo was ripped off from the Facebook account for another Tom O'Day, a retired federal lobbyist from Fredericksburg, Virginia. I contacted *that* Tom O'Day just to make sure, and we chatted. Nice guy. Likes mystery novels. He reminds me of my grandpa. Anyhow, I then messaged the fake Tom O'Day and told him I knew he was a fraud, and he admitted Tom O'Day was not his real name."

"Nice work," Plottner said.

"Thanks. He said his info was legit even if his account wasn't."

"Okay, so let's assume for a moment he's not completely full of it. What does he claim to know?"

"I'm not sure. I tried five different ways to get more out of him, told him your time was valuable, told him I couldn't get access to you unless I knew what it was about, and so on. None of it worked. He's adamant it's you or nothing."

"Okay, then it's me he gets," Plottner said.

"Are you sure? It's probably another troll. Or it's some joker who thinks he can scam you out of an easy million dollars."

"I'll take that chance," Plottner said. "In the meantime, I want you to document your entire interaction with this Tom O'Day. Take screenshots. Note dates and times. Then type it up and send it to the lawyers. Got it?"

"You're the boss."

"Thank you again," Plottner said. "Good work."

He hung up, then turned to his laptop and opened Facebook. He clicked on the message chain between the Plottner Investments Facebook account and the fake Tom O'Day.

Plottner reviewed what had been written so far, then started typing.

"This is Sean Plottner," he wrote. "I understand you wanted to work directly with me. I'm here. What can you tell me about Professor Bronik?"

Plottner hit send. Almost immediately, he saw little periods jumping around, telling him someone on the other end was typing.

"How I know you are true Sean Plottner?"

"Because I'm telling you I am. Why would I lie?"

"Prove it. Go live and now record new message. Show me this is true you. Show me you is serious."

Plottner's brow wrinkled. He didn't like being told what to do by anyone, especially someone with atrocious grammar.

But on the off chance Tom O'Day really knew something . . .

He clicked the "Live" button and waited for the countdown before he began speaking.

"This is Sean Plottner. There have been some questions about whether I'm serious about this reward. Let this be confirmation that yes, I'm very serious."

He clicked it off, then returned to the message screen just as a handful of the idiots who had been watching him live started up a new round of inane comments.

"Satisfied?" Plottner wrote.

The dots danced, then spit out: "Yes. Thank you."

"So let's get down to it. Where is Matt Bronik?"

"You are too fast."

Plottner rolled his eyes.

Tom O'Day was typing, and soon Plottner received his next missive. Which was: "I am yet not telling you."

"And why not?" Plottner immediately replied.

"I am need more than 1 million. You have more than 1 million. You give it to me."

"Why? A million dollars for what you know is more than fair. And it's a lot more than what anyone else will offer you."

The periods moved.

"I have expensive," Tom O'Day wrote.

Did he mean he was expensive? Or he had expenses? English clearly wasn't this guy's native tongue. He only seemed to be fluent in wanting more money—perhaps the most international language of all.

"How much this is worth to you?" Tom O'Day wanted to know.

Plottner almost smiled. He loved a good negotiation. And, therefore, he knew never to be the first to name a number.

"That depends," Plottner wrote. "What kind of condition is Professor Bronik in?"

Plottner waited for the dots.

They were still.

"Has Professor Bronik been hurt in any way?" he typed.

The screen remained static.

"Do you know exactly where he is or are you just guessing?"

Still nothing.

Then, finally, the dots started waving at him.

"I am go," Tom O'Day wrote. "I am contacting you at a later time. I am need more than 1 million. Goodbye."

Plottner narrowed his eyes. He didn't like this negotiating ploy, but he also couldn't help but respect it.

It's exactly what he would have done.

CHAPTER 24

I felt the words *sexual harassment* like a shock wave.

My thoughts went to Mariangela; to their daughter, a little girl who was deep into Disney princesses; to the fears so many faculty spouses felt about the youthful temptations that surrounded their partners.

Detective Webster, meanwhile, had actually leaned forward, eager to explore this new piece of information.

"What, exactly, did she allege?" Webster asked.

"That he constantly made advances and wouldn't take the hint she wasn't interested," Beppe said. "David never actually touched her. But according to her, he made it very, very clear he wanted to. She said it started pretty much the moment she arrived here. He would wait until no one else was around and then give her compliments. But they were always very calculated."

"What do you mean?"

"He wouldn't just come out and say 'I like your lips.' He would say 'That lipstick is a really good shade for you.' Or he would say 'That blouse really complements your figure.' You get the idea."

I was already shaking my head.

"So that if Sheena ever said anything to anyone, David could claim he was just making idle talk about women's fashion," I said. "I had no idea he was that kind of slimebucket."

"Sheena said she found it inappropriate but harmless. Except it escalated," Beppe said. "He started making inquiries about her fiancé, asking why he was still in India, why they weren't married yet. He'd make comments like, 'If I was your fiancé, I would want to be with you every night.' Again, he was very clever about it, always careful to make sure he put things in the hypothetical. But Sheena said there was no mistaking the sexualized undertone."

"Did he ever put any of this in writing?" Webster asked. "Emails? Texts?"

"Nothing. It was always in person. She said he would sometimes lurk around her office but only come in if she was alone."

"Obviously, after Mariangela, he knew he had to be careful," I said.

When Webster asked what I meant by that, I told him about Dafashy's romantic history.

Beppe continued with Sheena's story: "She says she was mostly just resigned to putting up with it. But then there was this conference on quantum sensing in Montreal he was trying to get her to attend—with him, of course. He said it could come out of his budget. He talked some about all the people he could introduce her to and how it could do wonders for her career. But then he would also slip in what restaurants they would go to and what drinks they would order there and whatnot. She said she felt like he was building it up in his mind as some kind of romantic getaway. She told him she didn't like his constant innuendo, that she wasn't interested in him as anything other than a colleague, and to please stop coming into her office."

"Which I'm guessing he didn't," I said.

"No. According to her, he just ramped up with how Montreal could really help her career and how she needed to think about what would happen when her postdoc was over. That's when she finally came to me."

"How long ago was this?" Webster asked.

"Probably about six weeks ago?" Beppe guessed. "I'd have to look at my calendar to know for sure."

"Okay, and what did you do at that point?"

"At her request, I spoke to David. She thought that would be the jolt he needed to make him realize she was serious. I was expecting he would say she was misconstruing basic friendliness and he would immediately back off. Instead?"

Beppe moved his head side to side. "He denied everything. Absolutely everything. He said it was absurd to suggest he would notice or comment on a woman's lipstick. He admitted he was registered to go to the conference in Montreal. But he said he never mentioned it to Sheena. He insisted that everything she alleged was fabricated."

The room fell silent for a few seconds.

"Wow," I said at last. "That's ballsy. Detestable, but ballsy."

Aimee, who had taken a seat at the table next to me, said, "He must have known that with his history no one would give him the benefit of the doubt. He had to hope she couldn't prove anything."

"Or she's making it up," Webster said. "I'm not saying she is, or that it's even likely, but it is possible. Until there's evidence one way or the other, we can't make assumptions."

"Why would she invent something like that?" Aimee asked.

"Because she's mentally ill? Because she has a grudge against Dafashy for some reason we're unaware of and she knows he's made himself an easy target in this particular area? Please don't misunderstand me: I'm not trying to be the man sticking up for another man. If the allegations are true, it's reprehensible behavior. But that's still an *if*. Until we have corroborating evidence, we don't know for sure."

"See?" I said. "That's how slimebuckets like David Dafashy sow doubt."

Webster pointed his next question at Beppe: "If it came down to his word versus hers, who would you trust?"

"I honestly don't know," Beppe said. "I've known David a long time. When Sheena first came to me, there was part of me that thought, 'Well, that's David being David.' He's always fancied himself a ladies' man. At the same time, he's never lied to me. At least not that I'm aware of. But I don't think Sheena is lying either. As a scientist, I'm fascinated by the number of times that humanity has posed an either-or question only to learn the answer is really 'both'—for example, nature versus nurture. Maybe there's a way they're both telling the truth? But I also don't see how that's possible. The whole situation is very difficult."

"So what did you do after you talked to David?" Webster asked.

"I went back to Sheena and told her that he denied everything. At that point, she said she felt like she didn't have a choice, that she had to make a formal accusation of harassment. I then referred the matter to the dean of faculty's office."

"That's who handles the investigation?"

"Correct," Beppe said.

"At risk of stating the obvious, I assume David had a lot riding on this," Webster said. "He could have lost his job over this, yes?"

"Oh, absolutely," Beppe said. "The dean of faculty would make a recommendation to a committee that would then have final say. But the college policy is now zero tolerance. He would have his tenure revoked immediately."

"Do you have any idea how the investigation was going?"

"A little. I didn't get all the details. But as David and Sheena's supervisor, I was kept in the loop to a certain extent," Beppe said. "There was supposed to be a hearing this Friday."

"Friday," Webster repeated. "And I assume each of them was going to have a chance to speak?"

"That's right. They were also going to be allowed to submit questions in writing for the other."

"And was anyone else going to testify?"

"Well, yes—"

And then, midbreath, he stopped himself.

"Oh my goodness," he said.

He was blinking rapidly now, almost like something had hit him in the head. I had never seen him looking so bewildered.

"I'm sorry, this is all happening so fast," he said. "I just, I didn't even think about the implications."

"Of what?" I asked.

"Didn't Matt tell you?" Beppe asked, then answered his own question: "No, of course he didn't. He would have kept something like this to himself."

"Tell me what?" I asked.

"Sheena was going to have one supporting witness, and it was Matt," Beppe said. "I never felt like it was appropriate for me to ask him about it, but I presume he must have overheard David's overtures at some point, and that's why Sheena wanted him to testify."

I felt myself going as wide eyed as everyone else in the room. The complainant and the lone material witness in a sexual harassment case were now both missing. It pointed a big bright flashing arrow at the person who benefited most from their disappearance.

And, apparently, no one needed to tell Detective Webster to follow it.

"Do you know where David Dafashy is right now?" he asked.

"He was at my house this morning," Beppe said. "Then he said he was going home for a little while."

"All right," Webster said. "I'll go talk to him."

CHAPTER 25

According to the Department of Motor Vehicles, David Dafashy lived in Hanover, just off Route 120.

This technically wasn't Emmett's case anymore. But that didn't mean he had turned off being a detective.

Besides, he didn't have to be back at his desk until noon tomorrow.

While sexual harassment wasn't Emmett's area of expertise, criminal behavior was. You always knew you were dealing with an amateur when they tried to talk their way out of things, relying on their charm or your stupidity to allow them to get away with their misdeeds.

Only two kinds of people denied absolutely everything: Hardened criminals, who had already learned that everything they said to law enforcement would be used against them.

Or the truly innocent.

Which sometimes made it very difficult to distinguish one from the other.

Could Dafashy have hired three Chinese men to kidnap Matt Bronik and Sheena Aiyagari? Was Dafashy hoping the looming presence of China—the rival to American supremacy in so many areas, including quantum physics—would be distracting enough that suspicion would never fall on him?

It was an elaborate scheme, though Dafashy surely had the intelligence to plan it out.

He also had the motive. If Dafashy were drummed out of Dartmouth on a sexual harassment charge, he wouldn't only lose his job. He'd lose his career. The days when universities looked the other way on such malfeasance were over. College presidents now lived in fear of the social media mob turning on them.

In academia, sexual misconduct was the new leprosy. Dafashy would become untouchable.

Emmett was soon parking in front of a modern-looking house set in a cluster of similar structures, each no more than a few feet away.

When Emmett knocked on Dafashy's door, it was answered by a woman with long dark hair, serious brown eyes hidden behind tortoiseshell glasses, and the kind of facial symmetry normally found on models and high-end restaurant hostesses. She appeared to be in her early thirties.

"Hi, I'm looking for David Dafashy," Emmett said.

"I'm sorry, he's not here," she replied coolly.

"Are you Mrs. Dafashy?"

"I'm David's wife, yes."

"Mariangela?"

"That's right. Mariangela Sechi. Can I help you?"

Emmett introduced himself.

"Missing Persons," she said. "Is this about Matt Bronik?"

"Yes, ma'am."

"Why don't you come in?"

"Thank you," he said, entering an open-floor-plan downstairs area.

On one side of the room there was a sitting area—on the other, a home office. The desk was covered in piles of paper of varying heights. A laptop rested on one of the piles.

Behind the desk, hanging on the wall, were diplomas from a variety of institutions. In the corner, there was a low table covered in pink, purple, and green LEGOs.

"I read about Matt this morning online, and I've been in total shock ever since," Mariangela said. "I wanted to reach out to Brigid just to offer support. But then I didn't want to bother her and . . . how's she doing?"

"She's hanging in there," Emmett said. "Her sister, Aimee, is with her, so that helps."

"Oh, thank goodness. I can't even imagine. Have a seat, please."

She pointed him toward an armchair and took a spot on the couch, shoving aside a blanket and two stuffed animals, a pair of floppy-eared rabbits. There was a quiet command to her movements. She had a poised, intelligent air.

"You know the Broniks fairly well, then?" Emmett started, just to get her warmed up.

"We're not best friends or anything, but yeah. There aren't a lot of people with school-age kids in the physics department, so we kind of gravitate toward each other. My daughter is a few years younger than their son."

"I think Brigid mentioned your families socialized."

"Now and then. Once the term gets underway, everyone is usually pretty busy."

"You look like you're pretty busy yourself," Emmett said, nodding toward the paper-strewn desk. "Do you work at the college too?"

"No, I do freelance copyediting for scientific journals," she said, almost like it embarrassed her.

She cleared her throat. "But I'm sure you didn't come here to listen to me talk about my boring job. Is there some way I can help?"

"I wanted to ask a few questions about Matt Bronik and Sheena Aiyagari," he said.

Mariangela's poise did not survive the mention of the young woman's name.

"What does *she* have to do with this?" Mariangela asked, lacing the pronoun with acid.

"Sheena is missing too. No one has seen her since late yesterday afternoon, not long after Professor Bronik was taken."

Mariangela took a beat to absorb this information. Her face, so hard at the first mention of Sheena, had melted into confusion.

"Sheena too?" she asked. "And you think it's connected?"

"It's a theory we have to pursue," Emmett said, aware he sounded too much like a cop. "I assume your husband told you about the accusation Sheena made against him?"

"Yes. He denied it, naturally. But David denies a lot of things."

"You don't believe him?"

Mariangela grabbed one of the plush rabbits she had earlier cast aside and settled it in her lap.

"Sometimes I think I don't believe anything about David anymore."

"What do you mean?"

She blew out a big breath and looked up at the ceiling. "This is really hard to talk about. I'm sure you heard about the circumstances under which David and I met?"

"I did."

"Yeah, so . . . I was a PhD candidate. And when I got pregnant, I wanted to have an abortion. I knew once I had a baby there'd be no way I'd finish the program. David was the one who talked me into keeping the baby. And part of the reason I allowed him to convince me was . . . this sounds stupid now, but I had never wanted anything the way he seemed to want us. He was so adamant that we would be together, and we would be this beautiful family, and I let myself believe the fairy tale. I had always wanted to be a mother anyway—not at that point, but eventually. And there are certainly worse things than being the wife of a Dartmouth professor. So I decided to speed up 'eventually.' We got married, I had the baby, and I started to get ready for happily ever after."

She let loose a derisive chortle. "And then came Leonie."

"Who's Leonie?"

"Leonie Descheun. She was a postdoc. From France. She actually sort of looks like me—a little geeky, dark hair, except hers is curly. Anyway, the baby was fourteen, eighteen months, maybe? I was pretty deep in that and David was obviously distracted by something, but whatever. Then we were at the department holiday party and it was just so obvious—the way he was following her around, the way he looked at her. I don't know if he actually slept with her or not. But he so clearly wanted to that I was . . . shattered, really. Obviously I wasn't as special as I thought."

"Sometimes affairs of the heart are worse than real affairs," Emmett interjected.

"Oh, I know. The only thing that saved our marriage is, thank God, she went back to France. As soon as she was out of the picture, David kind of returned to normal. And I thought, 'Okay, that sucked. But we survived.'

"Then came Sheena, and . . . I don't know. It was like, is this what my life is going to be? Is there always going to be another Leonie, another Sheena, another skirt he's going to chase until either his libido cools down or he gets himself fired? Can I really deal with that?"

"So you believe Sheena," Emmett said.

"Absolutely."

"Why?"

"Because from what I was told, he was hot to take her to the Quantum Sensing Gordon Research Conference."

"In Montreal?"

"Yeah," she said.

She breathed out sharply again before announcing: "That's where David and I slept together for the first time. He was even trying to take her to the same restaurant, Les Jardins. It was this very fancy place—white tablecloths, people to scrape away bread crumbs for you, every bottle of wine seventy-five dollars or more. Definitely not the kind of place you take a colleague. It's like, 'Jesus, David. Couldn't you come up with new moves?'"

"I'm sorry," he said quietly.

"Don't be. It's not your fault I'm stupid."

Emmett looked down at the carpet. He didn't really understand men like David Dafashy. Sure, Emmett could look at another woman and see that she was attractive. But he never had a desire to take it further. Once he got with Wanda, he had all he ever needed.

Mariangela ended his brief reverie by saying, "I still don't understand what any of this has to do with Matt."

"Apparently, he was going to testify at Sheena's hearing."

"Oh," she said, looking away. And then, as the realization of what this could mean reached her, she turned toward Emmett sharply. "So you think David—"

She couldn't finish the sentence.

"I'm looking into a lot of theories at this point," Emmett said, still cop-like. "But, yes, I have to ask: Do you think it's possible David had Matt and Sheena abducted so he wouldn't have to face this sexual harassment charge?"

Mariangela had worked her hand inside her glasses and was rubbing her eyes as she shook her head.

"I don't know. I really don't know," she said in a moan.

"Do you know where David was yesterday afternoon?"

"I assume at his office. But I couldn't tell you."

"What about last night? What time did he get home?"

She resettled her glasses back on her nose. "This isn't his home anymore. He hasn't been living here for a little while now. After I heard about Sheena, I told him I couldn't stand to look at him. He denied it and pleaded with me to reconsider but . . . I guess you could say we're separated, on our way to divorce. He's renting a room in Hanover. The last time I saw him was Sunday. He took our daughter ice-skating and returned her around three thirty or so.

"But as for yesterday afternoon? Or last night? Or this morning? Sorry. I can't help you. As far as I know, he could have been anywhere."

CHAPTER 26

My vow to keep moving was being tested now that I had nowhere to go.

Detective Webster was off chasing after David Dafashy, which left . . . what, exactly?

"Are you sure there's no way to get into Wilder?" I asked Beppe, who was mostly just staring into the remains of his coffee. "I know it's probably a waste of time, but I keep thinking, I don't know, that I'll see something."

Or maybe it was just wanting to feel closer to Matt.

"That seems to be in the hands of the Department of Defense," Beppe said.

"Do we have any way of forcing them to let us in?"

"I heard back from one of the college lawyers right before I came over," Beppe said. "She told me that when the government claims eminent domain, like they have here, the onus is on us to make a case as to why the top two floors of Wilder Hall should be unsealed. The matter would be heard in front of a federal judge. We'd be the plaintiff. And merely saying, 'This is really inconvenient to a bunch of students and professors' isn't good enough. We have to prove there is a public interest that would be served by opening the space back up, and it has to be more compelling than the government's need to keep it closed."

I doubted my baseless hunch that I'd find something useful in Matt's office would qualify.

"Oh," I said.

Aimee, who had been making more tea and trying to force more banana bread on us, had returned to the table.

"I'm just surprised that Matt never mentioned this whole thing about Sheena and David," she said. "He really never said anything about it?"

"Not once," I said.

"Obviously, I was never very good at the marriage thing," said Aimee, whose wedding and decision to divorce had been nearly simultaneous events. "But isn't that something you'd tell your wife? That you had been asked to appear at a sexual harassment hearing?"

"You know Matt. He detests the rumormongering part of academia. Didn't Dad ever whip that quote on you about great minds?"

"Great minds discuss ideas; average minds discuss events; small minds discuss people," Aimee said. "I still don't see how he didn't tell his wife."

"There's a lot in this world we don't see," Beppe said cryptically. "The vast majority of it, actually."

"What do you mean?" Aimee asked.

"If you took the entire electromagnetic spectrum—from short gamma ray bursts all the way to the longest radio waves—and stretched it out between New York and Los Angeles, the part that is actually visible to the human eye would be about an inch long. The other twenty-five hundred miles is invisible to us."

I didn't reply. I felt like I was on that cross-country trip right now, and I had already missed the inch I was supposed to see.

"Huh, how about that," Aimee said. "I wonder what—"

A phone rang. Beppe's. It had been sitting on the table in front of him.

He looked down at it idly, then did a double take.

"It's Sheena," he said sharply.

He practically fumbled his phone before getting it up to his face. "Hello, it's Beppe."

I was staring at his mouth, which was slack as he listened to Sheena talk.

Then he said, "We've been worried about you. Where are you? Are you okay?"

More listening.

"Slow down, slow down," he said. "Why are you scared? I don't—"

He stopped, let Sheena speak, then said, "I'm with Brigid Bronik. We're sitting in her dining room. Do you know anything about Matt? You know he's missing, right?"

He was staring straight ahead, looking mostly perplexed by whatever he was hearing.

"Well, we can't meet at Wilder. That's been . . . yes, exactly," Beppe said. "Would you like to come here, or—"

He held perfectly still. The questions were practically exploding inside me, but I kept silent.

Beppe's side of the conversation continued: "Okay, yes, I understand . . . fifteen minutes . . . I'm sure Brigid will want to come, yes . . . Just relax, everything will be fine . . . Okay, we'll see you soon."

Beppe lowered his phone.

"She wants to meet us in fifteen minutes on the seventh floor of the stacks at Baker Library. She said that's the only place she feels safe."

"What's going on?" I demanded. "Does she know anything about Matt?"

"I think she knows something but she's not really making sense," Beppe said. "Mostly, she just sounds terrified."

CHAPTER 27

In the various profiles that had been done about him—first in business publications; later, after his fortune had grown to sufficient levels, in glossy lifestyle magazines—writers almost always used one word to describe Sean Plottner's drive:

Obsessive.

And, yes, Plottner had to admit, he obsessed better than most.

His current obsession was seeing just how long Tom O'Day and his fake Facebook account could withstand the scrutiny of Plottner and his rather sizable stake in the company.

He started with his frontline contact at Facebook, a woman from the investor-relations department whose title might as well have been "adult babysitter." Her basic function was to make sure large shareholders like Plottner stayed happy and didn't do anything radical that would make life miserable for the CEO or the board.

And, at first, she was failing spectacularly. Because when Plottner told her he wanted to know everything about a user allegedly named Tom O'Day, she had, ridiculously, thrown *policy* in Plottner's face.

Specifically, Facebook's data policy, which it now took very seriously—after getting in trouble for not having taken it as seriously as it should have—which placed tight restrictions on what user information Facebook could disclose to third parties.

Plottner responded by asking if he should instead make his request of Mark Zuckerberg, which made the investor-relations woman sound nervous, but didn't immediately alter her response.

Policy was policy. They had to follow policy.

Then Plottner asked if he should go live and announce that he had shorted his Facebook shares over deep concerns about the competence of the management team.

At that point, the investor-relations woman said she'd get back to him.

Over the next twenty minutes, Plottner paced and practiced a series of threats and ultimatums that were heard only by his director of security, Lee Michaelides.

Who, as was his custom, said nothing in reply.

Then the investor-relations woman called back. She had been in touch with Facebook's legal department, which—lo and behold—had determined that since this so-called Tom O'Day had clearly violated the terms of the user agreement, he was no longer protected by the data policy, which meant they were free to share his information.

And, therefore, Plottner should expect a call from one of Facebook's network engineers.

Plottner paced some more. Now and then, he yelled to Theresa or grumbled more at Lee.

A half hour passed. He couldn't stand to wait for anything.

Finally, Theresa was standing at his office door, clutching the phone.

Plottner grabbed it before she could finish saying "It's the engineer from—"

"Talk to me," Plottner said into the phone.

"Hello, sir. My name is—"

"Yeah, yeah. I get it. Just tell me what you know."

"Well, sir, Tom O'Day opened his account this morning, using a Gmail address and a password that appears to have been randomly generated. His first log-in came earlier this morning from an IP address in Slovenia."

"Slovenia," Plottner repeated.

"The next log-in came about an hour later from India."

"India?"

"After that it was Ukraine."

"So he's using a VPN."

A virtual private network, the method of internet entry preferred by hackers, child pornographers, and others who wanted to obscure their electronic tracks. It was the equivalent of being at the receiving end of a long tunnel: you could see where someone came out, but not where they entered.

"That's right, sir."

"Can you overcome that in some way?"

"Short answer? No. The best I can do is keep monitoring this account in case he stops using the VPN. If the same IP address pops up twice, we'll know that's really him. Unless you'd rather we just erase the account?"

"Absolutely not. Keep it open. I want to continue being able to talk to this guy."

"Yes, sir."

"Was that Ukraine log-in his last one?"

"Yes, sir."

"When was that?"

"About an hour and fifteen minutes ago."

Which was when O'Day had chatted with Plottner.

"Okay. Can you keep an eye on his account for me? Maybe . . . write a program that sends me an email whenever he logs in?"

"Sure, I can do that. It might take me about an hour or so. See, the way the network protocols are set up—"

"I don't care," Plottner said. "Just get it done."

"Okay. Anything else, sir?"

"Yes. Can you document the previous log-ins and send them to me? I want a record of all of this."

A man who had been the subject of four SEC target letters had learned to be careful.

He wanted his actions to be well accounted for in case there were any accusations.

CHAPTER 28

I had never covered the ground between my house and the Dartmouth College campus faster.

Beppe was somewhere behind me, in his own car, either keeping up or not.

Where had Sheena been all this time? Why hadn't she been answering her phone? And what *did* she know about Matt?

The questions kept racing in my frantic mind as I parked in my usual spot near Baker Library, then marched inside, speed hiking like I was coming down from the top of a mountain and there were storm clouds closing in fast.

Without stopping, I charged to the entrance of the stacks, a nine-story structure that was home to a good portion of Dartmouth's more than two million volumes.

There was an elevator, but it was notoriously slow. I went for the stairs, whose steps were made of polished gray slate, worn down in the middle by nearly a hundred years of footsteps.

At the top of the seventh floor, I reached a door.

It was locked—which I should have known. But I wasn't thinking clearly. Behind the door were study carrels used by grad students and undergraduates who were working on a thesis or an independent study. The area was off limits to the general public.

That's why Sheena felt safe there.

My keys were down in my office, many floors below. I didn't want to have to go down and fetch them, so I knocked.

I couldn't really tell if there was anything happening on the other side—any sound, any movement. I knocked again.

From the landing below me, Beppe rounded into view.

"I haven't been up here in years," he said.

"I knocked. She hasn't answered."

"Hang on. Let me call her."

Beppe jabbed at his phone, then brought it up.

"We're here," he said, listened for a moment, then replied, "Yes, it's just us."

Then: "Yes, I'm sure."

He hung up and announced, "She says she's coming."

Ten seconds later, the edge of the door separated from the jamb by perhaps an inch, and a tiny sliver of Sheena's face appeared, peering warily from out of the crack.

She had a gruesome bruise under her right eye, a large smudge several shades darker than her light-brown skin. Her black hair was pulled back in a rough ponytail, exposing a two-inch-long cut near her hairline.

"Come on," she said, opening the door a little more widely, but only by a foot or two. "Quickly."

Beppe and I filed past. Sheena gave one hard look down the stairwell, then immediately closed the door. She tested the handle to make sure it was still locked and, satisfied, was immediately on the move again.

She said something that might have been "Follow me." She had already turned down the hallway behind her.

I tailed her around the corner. Sheena was a small woman, no more than five feet tall, but she moved her short legs with purpose. Slung over her left shoulder was a brown leather bag that she was clutching fiercely with her left hand.

She stopped at a door midway down the next hallway and stuck a key into the lock. She opened it and gestured for Beppe and me to enter.

The room was spare, barely larger than the desk it contained. In front of the desk was a wooden chair. To the left of the desk was a window that offered a sweeping view of the north side of the Dartmouth campus.

Sheena closed the door behind us and, again, checked the handle.

"Okay," she said and took a deep breath, like it was her first in quite some time. "Let me make some room for you."

She cleared some books off the ledge, which was wide enough for one person; then she made room on the desk, which could accommodate another.

I took the desk. Beppe took the ledge. Sheena turned the chair around so she could sit facing us, then set her bag down in between her feet.

"Sorry, I know it's a little cramped in here," she said again. "But they won't be able to find me here."

"Who?" Beppe asked.

"The men."

"What men?"

She held her hands up in a pleading fashion. "Let me start at the beginning. I think that's the only way this is going to make even a little bit of sense. Is that okay?"

"Of course," Beppe said.

"It was around four o'clock yesterday afternoon. I had been here for, I don't know, maybe an hour or so. I was sitting in here, reading. And then it just . . . hit me."

"What hit you?" I asked.

"I don't know. I think . . . the only explanation I've been able to come up with is . . . you call them fits, right? What Matt has been having?"

I brought a hand to my mouth.

"It came out of nowhere, just like Matt's. One second I was normal and the next thing I knew everything just felt . . . strange. And then, boom, nothing. I blacked out. I literally have no idea where the next six hours went. I have these weird memories of it that are . . . almost like a dream. There's nothing really concrete. I'd wake up for a split second, but I couldn't really control my body. And then I'd go back under. The next thing I could really tell you with any certainty is that it was dark out, and I was lying right here."

She made a sweeping gesture, indicating the floor in front of her. "I had a huge headache. I was covered in dried blood. And I had this," she said, pointing to her blackened eye. "I must have fallen or something. Anyway, I went into the bathroom and washed the blood off my face and looked at my eye, and then I came back here and I kind of just . . . rested for a while."

"You didn't call for help?" Beppe asked.

"Oh my God, no. By then I had taken stock of everything and I had figured out that I must have had what Matt was having and I just . . . I didn't want anyone to know. At least not until I had a chance to think about things more."

She turned to me. "I'm sorry, but you should hear how people talk about Matt. They think he's either crazy, or dying, or contagious, or I don't know. And I can't . . . I'm not tenured. I don't even have a job lined up for next year. Physics is such a small world, and all I could think was that if word got out there was something wrong with me . . ."

"No one in physics is going to discriminate against you because of a health problem," Beppe assured her.

"Really?" Sheena spat. "Just like no one in physics is going to discriminate against me because I'm a woman?"

Beppe looked down at his hands.

"Anyhow, I obviously knew Matt had suffered a fit and that Brigid was having trouble finding him. It never occurred to me he had been kidnapped. I just assumed he would turn up. So I thought I'd go home and sleep it off, and then in the morning I'd talk to him. I knew I could trust him to be discreet. So I just got in my car and went home. It was probably eleven or so?"

I thought about the neighbor who had been expecting Sheena to be home by nine o'clock.

She took a deep breath and pushed it back out. "I got to my place and I was walking up to my front door when all of a sudden this guy came around the corner of the house and started coming toward me. And then I realized another guy was coming up from behind me. They were both Asian—Chinese, if I had to guess."

I gasped. Chinese men. Just like the video. It made sense there were only two of them this time. One would have stayed behind to keep watch on Matt.

"I don't even really know what happened next," Sheena said. "I just have this image of them, kind of leering at me. And they were coming at me really slowly, like they were expecting me to try to run, but they weren't worried because they knew they had me surrounded and they knew they could outrun me. And that's what gave me the time I needed."

"To do what?" I asked.

"Pepper spray," she said, reaching into the bag at her feet and drawing out a small metallic cylinder. "I gave it to them good, right in the face like you're supposed to do, and then I ran for it. I got back to my car and I tore out of there and I haven't been back to my place since. I just went to a hotel and threw the chain across the door."

"Why didn't you call the police?" Beppe asked.

"Because they *were* police. It was dark, and I didn't get a good enough look to see what kind, but they were definitely wearing police uniforms."

"Those were EMT uniforms," Beppe said softly. "Fake ones, but . . . the men who abducted Matt were wearing EMT uniforms."

"Oh," she said. "Well, I guess I was pretty freaked out, so I just went to the hotel and locked myself in. And just to, I don't know, calm myself down, I turned on the TV. That's when I heard about Matt. The way the TV was talking about him, it was like he was already dead. But I knew he wasn't."

"What do you mean?" I asked, and I could feel my heart throbbing in my damaged ears.

"This is going to sound crazy," she said. "It feels crazy to even say it out loud. But . . . ever since I came out of the fit, I've felt this weird connection to Matt. It's like . . . I know he's out there. I can sense him. Sometimes I know I'm moving closer to him, and then other times I know I'm moving away. It's wild. But I swear, Matt is alive."

I was getting light headed, suddenly incapable of getting enough air into my lungs. My mind only had room for one thought, and it kept playing on repeat.

Matt is alive.

Beppe seemed to be shocked by this news as well, but he recovered faster.

"How could that be?" he asked.

"I don't know. I've been thinking a lot about it obviously, and my theory is . . ."

Sheena's voice trailed off for a moment; then she looked at me. "Did Matt ever mention anything to you about entanglement?"

"Spooky action at a distance," I said. "Once entangled, two particles are never again truly apart."

"Right, but specifically that the viruses he was working on were showing signs of being entangled with each other?"

"Matt didn't tell me much," I said.

"Are you suggesting . . . ," Beppe said but couldn't finish the thought.

"On Sunday afternoon, I was cleaning up some stuff in the lab and I cut myself on some glass," Sheena said. "It sliced right through my gloves. I was working near where Matt normally worked, and I think I must have been infected by the same virus that infected him, the tobacco mosaic virus. There was an incubation period—roughly two days—and then I had the fit. And now? Ever since I've come out of it, I've had this feeling about him. It's almost like twin sense or . . . I don't know."

She bowed her head for a moment before bringing it back up. "But I think our brains have become entangled."

CHAPTER 29

During thirty-two years with the New Hampshire State Police, Emmett Webster thought he had seen and heard it all—every crazy story, every odd twist, every color of behavior in the human rainbow.

This was a new one. Even for him.

"So let me get this straight," he said, having hurried to Baker Tower at the urging of Beppe Valentino. "This woman and Professor Bronik, they've both been infected by this quantum virus, and now she has quantum ESP?"

"I wouldn't call it ESP," Beppe said. "She can't tell what he's thinking. It's more, she can feel his presence."

They were sitting on the sixth floor of the stacks, huddled in two chairs by the window, talking in low voices.

One floor above them, still ensconced in her study carrel, was Sheena Aiyagari, the young woman who wasn't missing after all.

She was, apparently, just leery about talking to Emmett. Which was why Beppe was trying to smooth the way, explaining what had happened to her over the previous twenty-four hours.

"All right, so this quantum whatever-you-want-to-call-it. Entanglement. ESP. Whatever. How is this," Emmett started, then stopped himself because he wasn't sure of how to word the question. "I guess what I'm trying to ask you is: You're a scientist; you're supposed to be skeptical about everything. What do you make of this?"

Beppe put his elbow on the desk in front of him and rested his chin in his hand for a moment.

"Detective, do you know what the *x* in *x-ray* stands for?"

"No."

"Neither does anyone else. When x-rays were first discovered, all the scientists knew was that very short wavelength light could seemingly pass through solid objects. The experimenters had no idea why or how, so they called the rays of light they were sending out *x*—like it was a variable they would go back and define later. There are all kinds of things in the history of science that seemed fantastical or even impossible when we first tripped on them, things that completely defied explanation. Quantum theory is another one of those things. I'll be traveling to Copenhagen later this year to celebrate the centennial of Niels Bohr's institute there. Do you know who he is?"

"Sort of," Emmett said. "And by 'sort of' I mean 'not really.'"

"He's the father of quantum theory. He pioneered what's known as the Copenhagen interpretation. That means we're a hundred years into our efforts to understand quantum theory. And, in some ways, it's been a disaster. We still can't grasp some very fundamental aspects of the quantum universe. We're pretty good with the *what* of it. We're very bad with the *how*. It's like we're waiting for another Einstein to come along and help us make sense of it all. And until he or she arrives, we're still wandering in the dark.

"But, in other ways, the last hundred years have been a raging success. The best century in human history. Quantum theory is the most accurate, most well-verified scientific hypothesis the world has ever known. Everywhere we look, we keep finding quantum mechanics is really wonderful at explaining some of our greatest mysteries.

As just one example, how do migratory birds navigate such huge distances with such precision? Well, a few years back, some researchers from the UK discovered they do it with the help of entangled electron pairs in their eyes. How do salmon know how to return, after five years of swimming in the open ocean, to the exact same spot they were born in order to spawn? We suspect it's the same kind of mechanism."

Beppe spread his hands. "Now, a quantum virus is, quite literally, a new animal. We have no idea what it's capable of or how it might change the world. We do know that viruses are capable of transferring their genetic material into human beings. After that, all bets are off. So if you're asking me whether it's possible that two people infected with a quantum virus might have developed some kind of connection that allows them to sense where the other is? I have to be honest: if the birds and the fish can do it, I'm not ready to rule it out for human beings. With quantum theory, I've learned to accept the *what* and try not to get too caught up on the *how*."

Emmett sighed—for him, a demonstrable display of emotion.

What to believe? He had read stories about police solving crimes with the help of psychics who claimed to be able to locate crime scenes or find bodies, and had actually done so with an accuracy that had no logical basis.

Then again, he had also read stories about psychics who had played the police for idiots.

Fact was, people believed what they wanted to believe, and they did so as fervently as they wished to—whether it was that a man could change water into wine, that something called the United States of America was worth dying for, or that the lyrics of a song were truly life altering.

Was this more right or less crazy than any of those ideas?

"Okay, walk me through this again," Emmett said.

"You're still having a hard time believing me."

"I am," he admitted.

"Then I'm glad I talked to you first. Sheena was very nervous about involving law enforcement at all."

"Well, sorry to tell you, but—like it or not—law enforcement is involved."

"I know, I know. I'm just saying, she's pretty overwhelmed right now. She's had this strange thing happen to her, and then two men tried to abduct her. At first, she thought they were cops. She's still trying to figure out who she can trust, or whether she can trust anyone at all. It might be helpful if you act like you believe her—or at least suspend your disbelief a little bit. I realize this is a lot to take in for you too. But, really, what do you have to lose?"

What little credibility I have with my new boss.

Maybe even my job if he decides I've lost my mind.

"I'm just not sure I understand it, that's all," Emmett said.

"I'm not sure I do either. Basically, it's that when she moves, she can sense whether she's getting closer to him, or whether she's moving further away. It's less like quantum ESP and more like a quantum compass."

As soon as Beppe said the word, Emmett felt an idea creeping up the back of his spine.

"A compass, huh?" he said.

"That's right."

"Do you think we could use *her* like a compass?" Emmett asked. "Maybe she could point us toward Professor Bronik."

"We could try," Beppe said.

It was probably a stupid idea. If anyone at the barracks heard about it, they'd laugh at him, call him an old fool.

But what the heck. The case wasn't even his anymore. Captain Carpenter had written him off. Major Crime hadn't even bothered to call him. No one was expecting anything from the old nag who didn't even realize he had been put out to pasture.

Maybe he didn't have anything to lose after all.

The first small flakes of an Alberta clipper were falling, almost immediately sticking to the nearby walking paths.

Emmett was now standing with Sheena in the middle of the Dartmouth Green, the nearest large open space he could find.

"So you can feel Professor Bronik's presence right now," Emmett said, deciding he would try to believe whatever came next.

"If I concentrate on the feeling, yes. It's . . . not as strong as it was last night. But it's still there."

"Then I want you to walk in the direction that makes you feel him more."

Sheena closed her eyes. She took two halting steps north, then stopped. She turned in the opposite direction, which from the look on her face seemed to be better, but still not quite right.

Emmett cast a glance over his shoulder. Brigid and Beppe were watching from nearby, the snow dusting their hair with white.

Sheena veered more easterly, now aimed more toward the end of Dartmouth Row. She left the walking path, opening her eyes briefly as she scaled a foot-and-a-half-high snowbank, then closing them again. Her hiking boots crunched as they broke through the crusty top layer of snow and eventually settled on the softer stuff underneath.

She was walking with determination now, more sure of herself, and had settled into a relatively straight path. Emmett followed her at a short distance, trying to keep his boots quiet so he wouldn't distract her.

"Yeah," she said, stopping after she had traveled about twenty feet or so. "He's definitely this way."

"The direction you're facing now?" he asked.

"That's right."

Like a lot of cops, Emmett had started out on patrol. Knowing where he was—and what direction he was heading—had become almost second nature, one he kept with him even when he became a detective. So he knew that Sheena was walking basically east, with a little south thrown in. Call it 110 degrees.

It was nearly the opposite direction from where the ambulance had been found in Lyme. But that made sense. The kidnappers didn't want to abandon it near where they planned to hole up.

"And do you think he's close, or . . ."

"Not especially," Sheena said.

"How not close?"

Sheena frowned. "I'd just be guessing."

"Your guess is going to be better than mine."

"He's miles away but not *too* many miles. Ten? Fifty? I don't know. Boston is that way, right?"

"More like Portsmouth," said Emmett, then pointed in a more southerly direction. "Boston is that way."

"Well, he's definitely not *that* far. I don't think. I don't know."

"But he's that direction."

"Yes."

"You're sure?"

"No, I'm not sure," she said, exasperated. "All I know is that I blacked out and that when I woke up, my face was a mess and I had this weird feeling on . . . on an almost cellular level. I've never experienced anything like this before. I'm not 'sure' about anything. I'm just doing the best I can."

Emmett showed little reaction. At least outwardly. Inwardly, he was still thinking, *This is nuts, right?*

But in for a penny . . .

"You're doing great, just relax," he said and then got to the part of the crazy idea that would really have the guys back at the barracks rolling. "Do you think if we got in my car, you could keep pointing me in the right direction?"

Sheena blinked at him through the snowflakes that were pelting her face.

"You mean, like, guide you? Tell you where to go?"

"Exactly."

She looked out blankly into the distance, toward whatever it was that only she could see and feel.

"I don't know," she said. "I guess I could try."

CHAPTER 30

I rode in the back seat, driver's side. Beppe sat next to me.

Sheena was up front.

Detective Webster was both driving and talking, but since I was directly behind him, I had basically no chance of hearing him. I caught stray words here and there. He seemed to be either giving directions or asking for them.

In response to whatever he said, Sheena simply replied, "Okay."

We traveled in silence. I kept looking at Sheena, who mostly had her eyes closed in concentration, only opening them every now and then to take a peek at where we were going.

I felt a strange sense of jealousy. Why hadn't *I* been infected? I slept with Matt every night. Couldn't he have passed me the virus so now I'd feel a connection to him?

As we neared Interstate 89, Webster started talking again.

Sheena said, "Take the highway."

Soon enough, we merged on Interstate 89 South, joining a steady stream of cars and trucks that had no idea what odd science experiment was happening in the unmarked dark-gray police sedan next to them.

The speed limit was sixty-five. The snow, which wasn't sticking to the roadway, had no impact on the driving of New Hampshire folks who were, by that point in the winter, inured to it.

We continued for a few miles. Beppe hadn't spoken. Like me, he didn't want to distract Sheena. Webster kept his hands fastened at ten and two on the steering wheel.

As we neared the first exit, he started talking again. A full paragraph came out of his mouth, of which I heard only a few syllables.

When he was done, Sheena said, "Yeah, this one."

Webster slowed and we exited the highway, then wound around a cloverleaf that spat us out to the right. A sign said we were traveling toward Enfield, a town twenty minutes from Hanover that I had passed through many times on my way to Mount Cardigan.

We climbed a steep hill; then the road bent left.

The moment it straightened out in the new direction, Sheena said, "This isn't right. We're going the wrong way."

Webster said something that must have mollified Sheena, because she just closed her eyes again.

We plunged downhill again, passing through a patchwork of forest and farmhouses. Webster began talking again. I got the sense he was familiar with these roads and was narrating what would come next, asking Sheena which way she wanted to go.

Except this time, Sheena didn't reply.

There was a right-turn lane. Sheena still hadn't answered.

Webster spoke again.

"I'm sorry, I . . . I don't know," Sheena said. "Could you pull off for a second?"

Webster gently applied the brakes and nudged the car onto the shoulder. Two of his wheels remained on the pavement. The other two were up on the brown-black glacier that had been shoved to the side of the road by plows from storms past. That dirty snow was starting to get a fresh coat of white.

He wasn't talking, so I looked anxiously toward the passenger seat.

"I feel like I want to go that way," Sheena said, pointing in a direction that was neither straight, nor right, but in the middle.

Webster said something that seemed to annoy Sheena. "Okay. Go straight, I guess," she said. "But remember this spot. We may have to come back and go the other way."

We started rolling again, passing through Enfield, which consisted of a disjointed string of houses and commercial establishments. There were numerous auto repair shops, all of them strewn with old cars out front. A Family Dollar. A thrift store. The markers of semidepressed rural America.

Eventually, the buildings petered out, and we passed back into the countryside, frozen and forested.

More silence.

Then this from Sheena:

"I want to go right, except . . . I'm getting this weird . . ."

Webster said something.

"Nothing," Sheena said. "It's just . . . it's almost like . . . I don't know, there are two of him all of a sudden. One is stationary and the other is getting further away."

Further away? That wasn't right. Unless the kidnappers were on the move?

I clenched my fists. Beppe saw it and shot me a sympathetic look.

We kept going, passing a large meadow on our right. Sheena's eyes were open, and she was looking out at the open area like she wished to go that direction.

She said something to Webster—with her head turned away from me—and Webster replied.

Another mile or so down, just past a large yellow building with some U-Haul trucks parked outside, Sheena said, "Take a right here."

We were now leaving Route 4 and the way to Mount Cardigan, taking a road I had never been on before. It was called Potato Road, just a narrow country lane cutting through the woods.

We crossed a small wooden bridge, then reached a four-way inter-section with another, even smaller road.

"Straight," Sheena directed.

Soon the pavement was replaced by packed dirt. The snow had painted it with a thin layer of white, such that our tires were leaving vivid brown marks as we rolled through.

At the intersection of the next small dirt road, Sheena again said, "Straight."

Then she added, "I feel like . . . I could be wrong, but like we're definitely getting closer."

I sucked in my lower lip, electrified by this development. Not knowing what else to do with the sudden spurt of nervous energy, I reached out and grabbed Beppe's hand, squeezing it hard. He shot me a strained smile.

The road narrowed further. The trees formed an arch over it, blocking enough of the snow that the dirt was barely covered in spots. Now and then we passed a house or trailer. Otherwise, it was just forest.

Webster slowed as we approached another intersection. Sheena pointed diagonally to her left and said, "I wish I could go that way."

I looked where she pointed. There was no road in that direction.

We continued straight instead. Webster had slowed to twenty-five miles an hour. A dirt road went angling off to the right. Sheena didn't even look at it.

Shortly after, there was another small dirt road that jutted off to the left.

"Take this one," she said.

Webster did as he was told, except a few hundred feet later, we dead-ended at a cabin that appeared to be empty for the winter. Beyond it lay a small lake.

"Sorry," Sheena said as Webster began turning around.

He soon returned us to the small road we had just been on. The snow was coming down harder now, falling on the frozen lake, which was visible through a stand of leafless trees. The road skirted the water for a short while until we reached a T.

Sheena was confident this time. "Definitely left. But I'm still getting this weird split feeling."

What does that even mean? I wondered.

The road meandered along the south side of the lake; then the water was gone, and it was nothing but woods again. If you were going to abduct someone and then find a really isolated place to hide, you could scarcely improve on where we were now, this seemingly forgotten stretch of wilderness.

Webster had slowed further, probably afraid of sliding off the road into one of the many thick trees that lined it.

Then, to the left, there came a small lane, barely wide enough for a car. It was more rutted and cratered than anything we had seen so far. I wasn't sure if Webster's sedan could handle it.

Sheena's eyes were open wide. "Try that way. I feel like this might be it."

I caught a glimpse of the sign that marked the path, then had to stifle a small gasp.

It was called Riddle Hill Road.

CHAPTER 31

Emmett felt every rock and pothole as his car lurched along the rough road surface, which sloped steadily upward.

Next to him, Sheena had scooched forward in her seat and was scanning the road eagerly, like she was expecting to see something familiar any moment.

At the top of the hill, the road bent to the right. To the left was a driveway.

It had ruts where tires had pressed down the snow. Unlike the summer places on nearby Grafton Pond, someone had been here recently.

"This is it," Sheena said in a whisper, eyeing the driveway. "That way."

Determined to see this through—to wherever it was leading—Emmett didn't question her. He just turned the wheel.

At the bottom of the driveway was a patch of mud and brown slush. One of his tires spun briefly, but the rest of them maintained enough traction to keep churning onward. There was a reason the New Hampshire State Police only bought four-wheel drive vehicles.

After a few hundred feet he could just glimpse a clearing with a house in the middle. It had green aluminum siding, badly faded, and looked nearly as old as the massive pine trees that grew behind it. The roof appeared to be as much moss as shingle and would probably collapse under the weight of a heavy snow someday soon.

There was a chimney on the left side of the structure. It had a faint ribbon of smoke coming from it.

Someone had a fire going.

He braked. From this spot, about a hundred yards away from the house and downhill from it, still surrounded by trees, with the snow swirling, he was relatively sure no one inside would have noticed him yet.

The engine idled softly. His wipers were still going, sweeping snow off the windshield before it could accumulate.

Sheena wasn't saying anything. From the back seat, Brigid and Beppe squirmed, shifting position so they could get a better view out.

At what, was the question.

A place that was harboring dangerous kidnappers?

Or just some random shack that was giving Sheena the willies?

He reached for the two-way radio that was fastened to his dashboard. He lifted the handheld transmitter off its perch and pressed a button on the side.

"Dispatch, this is forty-seven," he said.

"Go ahead, forty-seven," a female voice responded.

"I'm on Riddle Hill Road near Grafton Pond. Are you seeing me?"

Forget quantum GPS. The dispatcher had real GPS. Every car showed up as a number on a map that the dispatcher kept up on her screen.

"I've got you, forty-seven."

"Do you have any units nearby?"

He waited, then heard, "I have three thirty-one patrolling four-A in Springfield."

That was five, maybe seven minutes away. Not bad, considering how remote they were. Emmett had been thinking he'd be lucky to have anyone within fifteen minutes.

"Can you send it up my way? I've got—"

And here he paused. This was the point of no return. This was no longer just his own private wild-goose chase. He was now summoning another officer to his aid. He'd have explaining to do if this turned out to be nothing.

But he had come too far to stop now.

"I've got a residence that may or may not contain Matt Bronik, the professor who was abducted," he continued. "I'd like some backup before I go in."

"Got you, forty-seven. Hang on."

His eyes were still fixed on the house, looking for more signs of life or movement.

After a short pause, the dispatch came back on: "Three thirty-one is on his way as fast as he can get there."

"Tell him to come quiet."

"You got it."

"Forty-seven out."

Emmett rested the transmitter back on its hook but kept the radio on in case the dispatcher gave him an update.

"You really think he's in there?" he asked.

"I don't . . . I don't know anymore. I feel something in there. But I also feel something that way," Sheena said, pointing off to the right. "And it's getting further away."

Emmett barely stopped himself from shaking his head. Seriously, what the hell was he doing?

"All right, can everyone stay here?" he said.

No one responded, so he turned toward the back seat and said, "I need a yes on that. I don't know what's going on out there and I can't be worrying about my back *and* yours. So you'll stay here, please?"

Once he heard three yeses, he got out of the car, a chilly blast of air hitting him in the face as he stood. Very gently, so as not to make any noise that might alert anyone inside to his presence, he closed the door.

Then he took a few steps forward and crouched next to his bumper so he could study the driveway. Whoever had come up and down had stayed in virtually the same line, wearing down the same section each time. But, very faintly, he could make out fresh tire tracks. They were wider than a passenger car's—left by a van or light truck, perhaps—and appeared to have been made after this particular snow had started but had since been covered over by new snow.

Like someone had just left. Maybe ten minutes earlier? Twenty? It was hard to tell.

He stood and studied the house. There were no lights on, but it was also just after noon, about as bright as it could get on a snowy March day in New Hampshire. Anyone inside wouldn't necessarily need lights. He wished he had some binoculars or even his hunting rifle, which had a scope on it, so he could get a better look.

The smoke from the chimney continued to drift upward until it was carried away by the sporadic wind gusts cutting through the trees.

Emmett trained his ears on the house—could he hear anything?—but the falling snow had a way of dampening ambient noise. The first thing he heard, from the road below, was the sound of an engine approaching.

It was revving hard and hot. Probably a younger officer, driving just the way Emmett would have when he was that age and had been called off catching speeders so he could assist a detective on a potentially big case.

Perhaps thirty seconds later, a Dodge Charger, painted in forest green and copper, with the chevron of the New Hampshire State Police on the side, pulled up the driveway. Emmett walked toward it, holding his finger to his lips. The last thing he wanted was this kid—and Emmett was sure it was a kid—slamming his car door, alerting whoever was inside the house that they had company.

The officer who got out was, as expected, maybe twenty-four, with short blond hair and a face that could barely dull a razor. His nameplate said JENKINS.

Emmett introduced himself, then explained the situation, skipping the part about how they had arrived at that house, in particular. Jenkins nodded along and seemed eager for whatever came next.

"All right, then, let's go," Emmett said. "Keep it quiet and steady. Don't do anything crazy. But keep your guard up. This could be anything or nothing."

Emmett strode forward, his feet kicking up small plumes of snow. After a hundred feet, he was out of the trees and in plain sight of anyone inside the house who happened to be looking his way. The final two hundred feet was all open.

Jenkins was just behind him, his hand already on his weapon. He had thumbed loose the leather strap that kept it in place but had not yet drawn it. Emmett's gun was in a holster on his hip.

A hundred feet left. Emmett had yet to see any sign of movement in the house. The snow was thick enough that their footprints didn't go all the way through to the ground underneath and cold enough that it squealed slightly as their boots twisted on it.

Fifty feet now. Still nothing from inside. There were three main windows on the front of the house—two to the left of the front door and one to the right. Neither had curtains or blinds, but because the house was set atop a small hill, Emmett could only see ceiling when he looked inside.

He took three more steps.

Then, in the distance, a dog barked.

Or maybe it didn't.

Emmett halted.

So did Jenkins.

"You hear that?" Emmett asked.

"Hear what?"

"I think someone called 'Help.'"

"Uh, okay," Jenkins said.

Emmett took out his radio and spoke softly. "Dispatch, this is forty-seven. I've got three thirty-one here with me."

"Go ahead."

"We just heard a call for help inside the house. We're going in."

"Okay, forty-seven. I've got four-eighteen en route, but he's still twenty minutes out."

"I'm worried we don't have that kind of time. We're heading in."

"Roger that. Be careful."

Emmett stowed his radio and turned to Jenkins. "I'll take the front door, you take the back. Move, move."

Jenkins took off, racing around back. Emmett ran toward the front door, reaching under his jacket for his pistol, which he soon gripped firmly in his right hand. There were three wooden steps leading up to a small landing in front of the door. Emmett took them in two strides.

He pounded on the front door with the butt of his gun.

"State police, open up," he said.

He counted to three. "State police. I heard someone calling for help. I'm coming in."

After trying the handle—locked—Emmett studied the door for a split second. His boots were heavy and steel toed, but his door-kicking-in days were long over.

There were small slits of frosted glass on either side of the front door. Using his gun as a cudgel, Emmett jabbed the one on the right. The glass came away from its rotting frame in one piece, falling to the floor below and shattering. He reached inside and thumbed the lock.

"State police," he said again as he shoved open the door.

There were rooms to the left and right and stairs in the middle, just slightly off center from the door. The floors were pine and deeply scuffed. The walls were a grungy white. The ceiling in the small foyer had a gaping, brown-ringed hole in it, probably from where a pipe had burst. No one had bothered to replace the drywall.

Leading with his gun held low, Emmett took two steps inside.

What he didn't immediately see was furniture. The room to the right, which may have been a sitting room or an office, was completely empty save for the dust and bug carcasses that littered the floor. The floor of the room to the left, which was larger and also included the fireplace, appeared to have been more recently disturbed. There was dust and debris by the walls and in the corners, but the middle of the room had been worn clean by foot traffic.

The fire was still going. It had been stoked recently. The two top logs still had unburned portions on the top.

Someone had been here. Or still was.

But who?

Not the owner. Clearly, judging from the dearth of furniture, no one lived here.

So kidnappers?

Or just squatters?

Emmett closed the door behind him. The fire, he quickly realized, was the only source of heat in the house, which was otherwise cold and dead feeling, like the electricity had been cut off.

He stopped and listened. For breathing. For the shifting of weight on the floorboards above him. For anything that indicated he was not alone.

Anyone in the house would have heard him by now. Which meant either no one was there.

Or they were lying in wait.

Emmett walked as quietly as his wet boots allowed, leading with his pistol, checking first the room to the right, including the closet. There was nothing.

He turned to the living room next and passed through it quickly. There was no place to hide in there.

Behind the living room was an eat-in kitchen. Here there were more signs of recent habitation—potato chip bags left out on the counter, crumbs on the table.

Still, there were no appliances out, no pots or pans or trivets or cutting boards or anything else suggesting permanent residence.

Jenkins was standing on the deck that butted up against the back of the house. Emmett let him in through the door and, in whispers, told him what he had observed so far.

Jenkins just nodded.

Using hand gestures to signal his intentions, Emmett worked his way down the short hallway behind the kitchen. It led to a closet that had apparently served as a pantry, a laundry room, and a half bath, all of them as vacant as the other rooms had been.

Emmett walked into the bath and lifted the lid on the toilet. It was bone dry inside. Whoever had eaten those chips had not been using it.

There was, clearly, no one downstairs. But that still left the second level. Emmett pointed in that direction. Jenkins nodded again.

They walked around to the staircase. Emmett brought his gun up when he reached the first step. If you were going to ambush someone, this would be as good a place as any.

He climbed the stairs quickly, his eyes up the whole time. Jenkins, in a crouch, trailed behind.

It was colder on the second level, almost as cold as it was outside. The heat from the fire had only made it so far. At the top of the stairs was a bathroom. Two bedrooms were on either side. The doors were half-open.

Emmett checked the bathroom—nothing—then went to the bedroom on the right. He peeked cautiously in, then shoved the door quickly, in case anyone was hiding on the other side.

It slammed against the wall. The sound echoed through the house. Emmett swept through the room and its lone closet.

One room to go. He repeated his procedure, slow then quick, moving tentatively then decisively.

But there was no one here.

No one at all.

He reholstered his weapon and rejoined Jenkins in the small upstairs foyer.

"What do you think?" the officer asked.

The tracks in the driveway. The potato chip wrappers. The fire.

"Well, someone was here," Emmett said. "But I think we just missed them."

CHAPTER 32

If there was one aspect of being an obsessive billionaire that Sean Plottner wished he could live without, it was what might be called his competitive spirit.

Once he started something, he had to finish it. By winning.

Sometimes it felt like the winning mattered more than the actual objective.

And so—even though there were a million ways Sean Plottner could have spent his billions to entertain himself, distract himself, or pamper himself—he wasn't interested in any of them.

All he really cared about at the moment was nailing down Tom O'Day and beating him at this high-stakes game they were suddenly playing.

What kind of money was he looking for here? If it was two million, okay. Four? Well . . . fine. But there was a limit, right?

Especially when Plottner couldn't even be sure he'd ever get a return on his investment.

More immediately, when *would* Tom O'Day go on Facebook again?

Plottner finally got an answer to that last question at 1:15 p.m., via an email from an account that showed up in his in-box as "Friendly Facebook Bot." It told him that Tom O'Day had just logged in from an IP address in Vancouver.

Finally.

"Theresa!" he called out in his excitement. "Theresa, he's back! It's Tom O'Day!"

"Great," Theresa called, halfheartedly, from somewhere downstairs. "Do you need me for something?"

"Just note the time, please."

Plottner opened up Facebook in his browser. He clicked on Messenger, bringing up his previous exchange with O'Day, but didn't type anything.

He just waited.

And waited some more.

Negotiations were all about perceived leverage. And you had to shift as much of it as you could into your own corner. If you waited for the other guy to make the first move, you planted that little seed that he must want it more.

Except . . . what was O'Day doing? Why wasn't he reaching out? It's not like he had any other Facebook friends. There was only one reason O'Day had an account: to wring money from Plottner.

So why wasn't Plottner seeing anything appear in that Messenger window now?

Negotiations were about discipline too. Being tougher. Holding your ground. Staking your—

Finally, he couldn't help himself. To hell with winning the negotiation.

"I've been thinking," he typed, "and I may be willing to offer more than a million dollars for Professor Bronik."

The dots began dancing.

"How much more?"

"First things first. Can you prove you actually have him?"

The response was quicker: "How do I prove?"

"I want a photograph of him," Plottner typed. Then he imagined Tom O'Day mining the internet for photos of Bronik. How to make sure this was authentic and not photoshopped?

He needed a photo that was fast and unique. Something impossible to fake. What was the most unlikely thing for a physics professor to do?

Suddenly, he thought of that famous Albert Einstein snapshot—the one where the mischievous physicist stuck out his tongue—and started typing.

"I want a photograph of Bronik sticking out his tongue. And I want it in the next five minutes or the deal is off."

Set deadlines. Even if they're artificial. Yet another important tactic.

"Okay," Tom O'Day wrote back. "I be back."

"I'm setting the timer on my phone. It starts now."

Plottner did as he promised, then turned his eyes back to the screen. A minute passed. Then two.

He realized he had his fists balled. He relaxed them. This reminded him of the early days, when he had made a big play on a stock and stared at the ticker to see which direction it was moving.

Three minutes. Three and a half.

What if Tom O'Day called his bluff? Would Plottner really walk away? That hardly felt like winning. That was like stopping the game, taking his ball, and going home.

Four minutes. Four minutes, fifteen seconds.

Dammit.

Plottner swore at the screen, exhorting it to do something.

Four forty-three. Four forty-eight. Four fifty-two.

Four fifty-nine.

And . . .

Nothing.

CHAPTER 33

I stayed in Emmett's idling car as another state trooper showed up, a middle-aged guy with a husky build who disembarked from his patrol vehicle and barely glanced at Beppe, Sheena, and me as he passed.

Then the Crime Scene Unit truck, the one I had seen parked outside Wilder earlier, pulled up behind the patrol vehicle. The first person who emerged was a young woman with strawberry-blonde hair sticking out from under a knit cap. She was followed by two other men. All of them carried briefcases.

Next, there was an unmarked car, from which a pear-shaped younger man with a red beard emerged.

All of these people disappeared into the little green house. None came back out to tell us what was going on.

In the front seat, Sheena's eyes were closed, as if the effort of having guided us this far exhausted her too much to keep them open any longer.

Or, maybe more simply, because she had slept so poorly the previous night.

I kept peering ahead anxiously. The more time passed, the more I realized I wasn't going to get the happy ending I hoped for—the one where they rescued Matt, who was scared but basically unscathed, and brought him out to be smothered in kisses by his loving wife.

If that was the case, it would have happened already.

"What's taking so long?" I whispered to Beppe.

He shook his head. He'd just be guessing.

We sat there, in that information vacuum, for a seemingly interminable amount of time. What had they found? Couldn't someone come back to the car and put me out of my agony?

But the flow of law enforcement officers only seemed to go in one direction.

Then, prompted by nothing I could discern, Sheena stirred, lifting her head.

Without a word, she unclipped her seat belt, opened her door, and got out.

I briefly looked toward Beppe, who seemed as confused by this as I was. I quickly scrambled out and ran to catch up with Sheena.

"Where are you going?" I asked.

"To the house," Sheena said, like this should have been obvious.

"But we told Detective Webster we'd stay in the car."

"I know. I just . . . I keep getting these two feelings. One says he's in the house. One says he's getting further away. I can't tell which is right. It's driving me crazy."

Sheena was marching with resolve, her black ponytail a magnet for the swirling white snow. I scurried after her. From the corner of my eye, I saw Beppe had also left the car.

She climbed the stairs without breaking stride and entered the little green house like she owned it. It was all I could do to keep up.

But I still caught the bizarre looks Sheena got as she barged into the living room. Detective Webster and the pear-shaped man with the red beard, who looked like they had been in the middle of an argument, stared at her like she was stepping off a spaceship.

Webster recovered from his shock first.

"I asked you to stay in the car," he said.

"And I didn't," Sheena replied.

Right. Like what else did he need to know?

She was studying the empty living room with the eyes of a scientist ready to release her findings.

"He was definitely here," she said simply.

I felt my soul lurch.

"Oh, Christ," the pear-shaped man said, the disbelief as plain as his eye roll.

"How do you know?" Webster asked.

"How do you know you're standing here?" Sheena asked. "How do you know this isn't just an elaborate computer simulation? How does anyone know anything? I'm not in the mood for an epistemological debate at the moment, Detective. I just know. I feel it right now."

"Oh, Christ," the pear-shaped man said again.

Sheena kept going, wandering to the eat-in kitchen. The woman with the strawberry-blonde hair was sitting at the table, her attention fixed on a laptop screen. She was wearing blue nitrile gloves. A small scanner was affixed to her computer via a USB cable.

"He was in here too," Sheena announced.

She pointed at the table. "He sat right there."

I stared at the table like it was either charmed or hexed. I couldn't decide.

Then she gestured toward the back porch. "They let him go out that door a few times. Maybe to pee or something, I don't know. But not for long. He never went to this half of the kitchen or down that hall."

Webster and the pear-shaped man had followed her in.

The pear-shaped man started with, "Now, how can you—"

"She's not wrong," the woman with the strawberry-blonde hair said. "Okay, I don't know about the peeing-off-the-back-porch part. But those potato chip bags we found? There are few things better for matching fingerprints. It's a shiny surface. And anyone eating chips gets a ton of grease on their hands to supplement the oil they have already. I just lifted a print off one of the bags that was a fourteen-point match for Bronik. There's no question he was here. Or at least his fingers were."

This brought a hot silence to the room.

Then:

"Wow," Webster said.

"Oh, Christ," the pear-shaped man said for a third time, but it was very different.

Like he believed.

"I should be a little more explicit: it's not really *him* I feel," Sheena said. "I was thinking about this while we were waiting in the car. It's not him; it's the virus itself. Like any virus, it can live outside a host for a certain duration. And there are traces of it all over this house. I feel it stronger in the other room. That's where he must have slept, by the fire. He was there all night, doing a lot of breathing. Does he snore?"

The question was directed at me.

"Uh, no. I mean, when he's sick, yes. But otherwise—"

"Well, whatever he was doing, he expelled a fair amount of the virus by the fireplace. This room, less so. My guess is he just came in here to eat. It's not nearly as strong in here. And that's why I don't think he went into the rest of the kitchen or down that hallway at all. I get no feeling from there whatsoever."

"So he *was* here," Webster said.

"Of course he was here," Sheena said. "I keep telling you that."

"And, again, she's not wrong," the strawberry-blonde woman said.

More silence. The pear-shaped man tugged at his beard. None of the officers were absorbing this new information fast enough. And they certainly weren't moving on to the next logical questions.

So I did it for them.

"Okay, we know he was here," I said. "But where is he now? And why did he leave right at the moment we were closing in?"

Beppe chimed in. "I've been wondering that myself. We're in an abandoned cabin in a remote area. Unless the owners came back—and it doesn't look like they're planning to—your chances of being tripped on out here are practically nil, at least until blackfly season ends and summer people start arriving. They could have stayed holed up here for a while. And yet judging by the freshness of the tracks in the driveway, they took off just before we got here. How is that possible? Was it just luck?"

Everyone was looking at Sheena, who had established herself as the only person offering answers.

"Yeah, about that," she said; then she turned to me. "You might not like it."

"What do you mean?" I asked.

"There's only one person who could have possibly known we were coming," Sheena said. "And it's Matt."

Even in that chilly kitchen, the heat quickly rose to my head. Now I was the one who couldn't process information fast enough.

Sheena continued, "It only stands to reason that if I can feel Matt—or at least the virus he's carrying—don't you think *he* can feel the virus in *me*?"

I had been so focused on our journey toward him, I hadn't thought about that possibility. I started to stammer, "So . . . wait . . ."

"He knew we were getting closer and he decided it was time to leave. That's why I started getting that split feeling as we were coming here. I was still feeling the virus he left behind in this house. But the virus inside him had started to move."

"Why would he do that?" I asked, feeling stupid and desperate.

"I'm sorry, Brigid," Sheena said quietly. "I'm not saying this makes sense. And I couldn't even guess why this might be. But you have to start being open to the possibility that Matt doesn't want to be found."

CHAPTER 34

The timer on the phone would have reached fifty-three minutes—but only if Plottner hadn't shut it off in sheer frustration after twelve.

He spent some of that time ranting at Theresa, who took in her boss's tirade calmly. Tolerating his mania was just part of the job.

That mental sixth gear of his, the one that had made him so unfathomably wealthy, was clearly engaged. The only difference here was that whereas normally people leaped at the possibility of having some of the Plottner fortune tossed their way—and therefore accommodated his sudden and crushing interest in them—O'Day seemed indifferent.

Really, where had he gone? Hadn't he agreed to the five-minute deadline? Was he merely off faking a photograph, or was this it, and Plottner would never hear from the guy again?

Plottner continued pacing and grumbling until, finally, Friendly Facebook Bot informed him Tom O'Day was back, this time checking in from Tempe, Arizona.

Plottner didn't bother waiting.

"Where have you been?" he typed, his fingers pummeling the keyboard. "I told you five minutes."

Tom O'Day's response: "Complicated."

What did that even mean? How complicated was it to take a photo?

"Do you have the photo or not?"

O'Day: "I have it."

The dots began moving.

But nothing new appeared.

Plottner felt like he could have stared through the other side of the screen. How long did it take to upload a photo? What internet speed was this guy using? Dial up?

Then the image appeared.

It was small. Plottner enlarged it so he could get a better look.

And, yes.

No question.

It was Matt Bronik.

The professor was staring straight at the camera with contempt. He had Band-Aids on his forehead, wore a dirty white V-neck T-shirt, and was sitting against a plain wall painted in a neutral color.

And he was sticking out his tongue.

Just like Plottner asked.

Still, Plottner had wanted the picture delivered forty-eight minutes earlier. Had fifty-three minutes been sufficient time for Tom O'Day—who obviously knew his way around a computer—to work some kind of magic with an airbrush?

He couldn't take this to the state police and claim he had made contact with the kidnappers until he was absolutely sure he wasn't being played. Plottner squinted at the blown-up picture, looking for telltale signs of manipulation, little places where lines weren't quite straight or the shadows suddenly changed hue.

He didn't see anything that aroused suspicion. It might have been the real thing.

Or it might have been an outstanding counterfeit.

And Plottner had an idea how he could find out.

"You took too long with this," Plottner typed. "This could be fake."

O'Day: "It not fake."

Plottner: "Convince me. Let's see another photo. I want him sticking his thumb up this time."

O'Day: "No. No more photo. It too difficult."

Difficult? What did that even mean? What could be so difficult about taking a picture of a guy you were holding captive?

Plottner typed, "If you can't even get me a photo, how am I supposed to have any confidence you can get me Bronik?"

He leaned back, waiting for the dots.

They never appeared.

Seconds became minutes. Minutes started adding up. Once again, neither Plottner's frustration nor his money seemed to matter.

Tom O'Day was gone again.

CHAPTER 35

They were all just standing there, hands shoved in their pockets, none of them sure what to do with this wild idea that their abduction victim wasn't really a victim.

Then Emmett's phone rang.

He excused himself from the kitchen and walked into the living room to take the call.

"Webster here."

"Pretending to hear someone call for help?" the terse, Masshole-ish voice of Captain Angus Carpenter said.

"Excuse me, sir?"

"Don't play dumb, Detective. The patrol officer reported it to the patrol supervisor, who reported it to the patrol captain, who reported it to the colonel, who just chewed my ass."

Emmett never lied. Lying was wrong.

Except when it fit into a certain moral space. Wanda, borrowing from some fancy philosopher, used to put it like this: If a madman who wanted to murder your wife came to the door and asked if she was there, wouldn't you say no?

We're all liars sometimes.

"I wasn't pretending, Captain," Emmett said.

"Look, I don't go for this cowboy crap," Carpenter said. "Maybe that's how the New Hampshire State Police used to operate, but it's not anymore. You either have probable cause or you don't. Do I make myself clear?"

"Yes, sir."

"So that's issue number one. Issue number two is: Why are you wasting perfectly good officers' time with this . . . this crackpot who says she can sense where our vic is? I will *not* have you making a mockery of this unit, of this organization with this—"

"Sir, you—"

"—ridiculous fantasy. We are in the real world here. And we are real police who follow real leads based on real evidence. I can't believe I'm even having to—"

"Sir, with all due—"

"I'm not done talking," Carpenter snapped. "You'll know I'm done talking when no more sound is coming out of my mouth. Now shut up and listen, Detective. Because I'm going to give two choices. Either you take whatever vacation time you have accrued—and I mean all of it—and disappear somewhere in that RV you stare at until I'm done being pissed at you, or I haul your ass in front of the disciplinary committee for inventing probable cause and, if I can find it anywhere in the regulations, for following the delusions of a crackpot. Which is it going to be?"

Emmett didn't hesitate. "Neither, sir. Not until this case is over."

"You're done with this case. Hasn't O'Reilly gotten there yet?"

Emmett looked toward the kitchen, where Connor O'Reilly, the red-bearded Major Crime detective, had probably blasphemed a few more times.

"He's here, sir, but we're not handing off this case."

"The hell we're not."

And then, in his very dry, matter-of-fact Yankee way—without sounding like he was gloating—Emmett told him about the still-burning fire, the fresh tire tracks, and the fingerprint match Haver Markham had discovered.

"You told me that if we found evidence Bronik was still alive, we could keep the case," Emmett said. "Well, Captain, there's your evidence."

The other end of the line was suddenly very quiet.

"Hello, sir?" Emmett said. "You still there?"

"I'm here, I just . . . you really got a print?"

"Would you like me to put you on the line with Haver Markham?"

"No, no. I . . ."

His voice trailed off again. But when it came back, it did so in a different tone. Less Masshole. More actual human being. "This woman, she was really able to lead you . . . like some kind of human bloodhound?"

"Sir, I honestly don't know what's going on. I can only tell you what I've seen. And, yes, she was able to guide us through the wilderness, down roads I presume she's never seen before, straight to the abandoned house where Matt Bronik was, perhaps as little as an hour ago."

"Okay, then," Carpenter said. "I'll call the colonel and let him know what's going on. In the meantime, if this woman really is a bloodhound, let's get her back on the trail. She almost found our vic once. Do you think she can track him down again?"

Ten minutes later, Emmett was back in his car with Sheena next to him.

Brigid and Beppe were in the back seat.

Jenkins and O'Reilly were trailing in their own vehicles.

Emmett led them and the crime scene truck up the driveway to the top of the clearing so they could turn around. Then he got himself aimed back down the hill so this caravan—minus the crime scene truck, which was staying behind to look for more evidence—could follow him.

The snow had stopped, the clipper having passed through. The sky behind it was clearing. Bright sun was already starting to poke through the clouds, which were being carried away by a stiffening breeze.

Sheena was shifting her weight. She couldn't seem to get comfortable.

"You ready to do this?" Emmett asked.

"I guess," she said.

Then she added, "I still don't know if he wants to be found."

"It could have just been a coincidence, them leaving like that. Maybe the kidnappers' plan all along was to stay on the move, and we just happened to barely miss them. We won't know until we try again."

"Okay," she said, like she wasn't convinced. "I'll do my best. It's just . . ."

"What?"

"The feeling is all mixed up right now. There's here. Then there's wherever he is right now. And it's getting weaker all the time. It's like I'm losing signal strength."

"You still feel it some, though?"

"Some, yes. I just can't explain how strange everything feels right now. Even time itself is getting weird. It shouldn't be today anymore, but somehow it still is. It's like I'm being sucked into a black hole or something."

"What does that mean?"

"Nothing."

From the back seat, Beppe volunteered: "There's a classic thought experiment proposed by Einstein in which he imagined what it would be like to get dragged into a black hole. His prediction was that as you got closer, the immense gravitational pull of the black hole would accelerate you closer and closer to the speed of light, such that time would actually start to move much slower for you—and, therefore, relatively speaking, much faster everywhere else. Galaxies would start spinning around you like pinwheels, which would mean thousands of Earth years were passing by. But to you, it would still seem like a fraction of a second."

"Uh-huh," Emmett said.

Which was about how much sense this made to him.

"Well, let's just give this another try," he said. "At this point we have nothing to lose."

"Okay," Sheena said.

He looked in his rearview mirror and saw the other cars, lined up behind him. He released the brake and got rolling down the driveway, gripping the wheel tightly as his car jounced over the ruts and potholes.

At the bottom of the driveway, Sheena said, "Left."

She was leaning forward in her seat again. Her jaw had a determined set to it.

He turned with purpose. It felt different this time. This wasn't a wild-goose chase anymore.

It was a hunt.

There was a chance the kidnappers—and that's how Emmett was still thinking of them, no matter what Sheena said—were hurtling along a highway at sixty-five miles an hour, making it difficult to catch up.

But Emmett didn't think so. If these Chinese men were bounding from one abandoned house to the next, they would stay close.

There were a lot of places like that around here.

Riddle Hill Road meandered to the right, though it remained a small track, wide enough for one car and no more. After a half mile or so, they came to a T.

Emmett stopped and turned toward Sheena, who had her eyes closed again. Her face was squeezed with concentration.

"That way," she said, pointing left.

This new road was wider. It took a sharp bend to the right, then straightened. They continued straight through an intersection. Sheena didn't even glance at it.

Emmett had a rough sense that they were tracking toward a small town called Grafton Center. And not that it was the center of much, but if the Chinese men were really looking for another abandoned cabin, it wasn't the way to go.

Except before they could get there, Sheena pointed to the right.

"Go that way," she said, sending them down something called Williams Hill Road.

They weren't on it for long.

"Take this road," she said.

It was another right. Livingston Hill Road.

"You got it," Emmett said.

They were pointed back toward the boonies now. Behind them, Jenkins and O'Reilly—probably already wondering when and where this was going to end—were having no problem keeping up.

On the right, they passed marshland, frozen solid, with big dead trees sticking out of the white earth. On the left were more houses, all of them visible from the road, making them unsuitable for the Chinese men.

Emmett slowed for another T, having reached Kinsman Highway, a dirt road that was no kind of highway at all.

"Right, please," Sheena said.

The back seat remained quiet, though Emmett could practically feel the tension rolling off Brigid. This had to be excruciating for her, not knowing whether she was being led to her husband or just to another empty house.

They had taken such a strange series of lefts and rights Emmett's sense of direction was momentarily confused. He felt like he couldn't get his bearings.

He peeked over toward Sheena, who was staring straight ahead with intensity. In relatively short order, Kinsman Highway had two turnoffs to the right, neither of which she even seemed to notice.

The road went straight for a while. But as it continued, Emmett was getting reoriented, and it was giving him a bad feeling. They were definitely in the kind of country that would have a quiet hideaway, but . . .

Sure enough, they had arrived at a familiar place. They were just coming at it from a different direction. He stopped the car.

"What's wrong?" Brigid asked, her first words of the journey.

"That's Riddle Hill Road," Emmett said. "We've just gone in a big circle."

In the passenger seat, Sheena sagged.

"I'm sorry," she said. "I tried."

CHAPTER 36

After we finished that big heartbreaking loop to nowhere, we drove back to Hanover.

I didn't speak for most of the ride. Neither did anyone else.

Sometimes, there's just nothing to say.

As we neared town, Sheena announced she needed a change of clothes and a shower. She was just afraid to go home and do it. Those Chinese men were still out there.

She suggested that Webster could just take her back to her hotel room, but no one liked the idea of her being alone.

Eventually, we arrived at a plan. Webster drove us first to Sheena's house. With Beppe and Webster keeping watch outside, Sheena and I approached her front door.

She keyed in her code, which I couldn't help but see: 4-3-2-1.

It reminded me of something Matt would do. He could solve a multivariate equation in the time it took me just to read one, yet when it came to ordinary things—like a door's pass code—he couldn't be bothered. Half his passwords were *password*.

Once Sheena had packed a bag, we hitched a ride with Webster back to my house.

From there, we split up. Detective Webster was taking Beppe back home, then going to find David Dafashy now that Beppe had put him onto the correct address.

Emmett's final instruction to me was to call 911 if I saw anyone or anything that looked remotely suspicious approaching the house.

Truly, I didn't need the encouragement.

It was a half hour later by the time Sheena emerged from the shower, dressed in clean jeans and a sweater. She had toweled off her hair and left it down to air-dry.

The cut at her hairline looked a little better. The bruise under her eye was worse.

Morgan had returned from school by then. He took one look at Sheena, and I could practically read the thought bubble forming over his head—*Is that what my daddy looks like right now?*—before he excused himself to play in his room.

Aimee, back in hostess mode, had made a sandwich for Sheena, who objected, saying she wasn't hungry. Except she was already two bites in by the time I joined her at the table.

"How are you feeling?" I asked.

"Forget about me," Sheena said, between bites. "How are you?"

"I'm not thinking about that right now."

Sheena nodded and chewed. Aimee had sat down with us.

"I'm still trying to get my head around so much of this," I said. "Do you mind if I ask you some questions?"

"Not at all," Sheena said.

"When you said maybe Matt didn't want to be found—"

"That was just speculation. I don't know what I'm talking about. I'm sure—"

"No, wait," I said. "I was thinking while you were in the shower. Let's say, for sake of argument, that Matt really doesn't want to be found. He's running away from something—or someone—and he had good reason to think this someone or something is a significant threat. What if he staged his own abduction?"

"Brigid, honey," Aimee said. "Maybe you shouldn't—"

"Hear me out. You were actually the one who opened this door for me when you asked the question about how those EMTs knew to arrive right when he was having a fit. Detective Webster thought they drugged him. But what if Matt was faking it or . . . or if he had finally gotten so he could predict when he was going to have a fit? That would explain the timing. You said it was an inside job, and you were right. It was really the ultimate inside job."

"I don't know, Brig," Aimee said. "I just can't see Matt doing something like that to you and Morgan. Don't you think he would have at least told you what was really happening so you wouldn't panic?"

"No, because he needed me—and all of us—to act like it was real. Whoever he's running from needs to be convinced, and part of that convincing is his family acting the part. And maybe he *will* find a way to contact us and let us know he's all right—just not yet."

I liked that part of the theory best. Sure, I would be temporarily furious with Matt for putting us through this emotional turmoil.

But it was still so much better than any of the alternatives.

"So let's go back to February," I continued. "He starts having these fits. Maybe he didn't know at first it was connected to his work, but after the second one, he sure did. That the virus was capable of infecting him meant he had finally succeeded in having the breakthrough he had been working toward for years."

Sheena was shaking her head. "I don't think he had, though," she insisted. "I'm in the lab with him all the time, and I never saw anything or heard anything that made me think he had interfered the virus."

"And yet aren't you living proof that he did?" I asked.

She had no reply to that.

"Okay, so he knew something big was happening. And he worried that once the news got out, it would catch the attention of . . . someone. Someone he feared. I don't know who, obviously. It was someone scary enough he decided he needed to disappear. And to make it look really convincing—like he didn't have a choice in the matter, so the people who he was afraid of wouldn't come after him—he faked his own abduction. Maybe he just needed to disappear for a while so he could finish working on this, then publish the paper? I don't know. The thing he didn't expect was that you would have been infected by this virus, too, and that you would then develop this connection. That's been the unexpected wrinkle in his otherwise perfect plan.

"But it doesn't change the fundamental question, which is who is he afraid of? And why is he running from them?"

Having thrown out the question, I leaned back. My face was flushed.

Sheena had lapsed into a thousand-yard stare, almost like she had left the room.

Aimee was drawing circles on the table with her finger. Without looking up, she said, "Not the Chinese."

"Why not?" I asked.

"Because if it was the Chinese, he would have gone to the Department of Defense and said, 'Hey, guys, can you help me? I think I'm in trouble here.'"

"Maybe he did, and the DOD just isn't telling us. Maybe that's why the DOD is right now camped out in Wilder, because they need to make it look real too. In reality, they helped Matt disappear, and he's told them to protect the lab from whoever he's afraid of."

"But then why would Matt make it look like the Chinese were the ones who abducted him?" Aimee asked. "The Chinese would know they hadn't sent their own people to do it. The gig would be up too fast. It has to be someone here in America, someone who would be fooled by the China ruse."

"Then it's the government itself he's running from," I said. "Maybe he was afraid the military wanted to use this new quantum virus for some frightening new weapon or something else he didn't want to happen, and that's why the DOD is all over his lab. The military is right now trying to find whatever secrets Matt was keeping from it."

Aimee had stopped drawing circles.

"I don't know," she said. "I've never been a huge fan of government conspiracies. Have you ever worked with the government? Individually, there can be some good people. But collectively, they can barely get out of their own way. I don't see where they're smart enough to carry off some grand conspiracy."

"Then it's David Dafashy trying to derail this sexual harassment allegation and save his miserable career?" I asked. "Detective Webster seems to think it's possible. Maybe it really was just bad timing that the kidnappers happened to leave right as we got there."

We lapsed into silence.

Then Sheena seemed to rejoin us.

"I think I have an idea about how we might find Matt," she said. "Ever since I became aware of the feeling—the compass, or whatever you want to call it—I've been feeling it slowly weakening. It's almost like it's a radioactive element with a short half life, constantly decaying. But if I can get back into the lab and work with the virus the way Matt did, maybe I'll be able to reinfect myself. It'll refresh the feeling, and then I can find him again."

"That would be great," I said, "except the lab's closed."

"What if I can change that? Beppe was saying Dartmouth could go before a federal judge and make the claim the lab needed to be open, but only if there was a compelling public interest. What if finding Matt is that public interest? What's more compelling than rescuing a father and husband who has been abducted?"

I didn't know if it would work.

But I was absolutely willing to try.

At that point, I would have tried anything.

"Okay," I said. "Let's call Beppe."

CHAPTER 37

Emmett could feel his brow lifting with incredulity as he surveyed the hovel that was David Dafashy's apartment.

It had been slapped onto the back side of an ancient house in Hanover, almost like a lean-to, having probably been added long ago when someone's mother-in-law needed a place to die. Its windows looked like they leaked out whatever warmth managed to accumulate inside.

The whole house would likely be torn down whenever the current owners sold. But, for now, the back portion was being rented out to whoever was desperate enough to need it.

Emmett knocked on the battered front door, which was soon answered by a man with curly dark hair who was wearing a heavy, rough-hewn mackinaw. Probably on account of the windows.

"Can I help you?"

"David Dafashy?"

"Yes?"

Emmett introduced himself.

"What can I do for you, Detective?"

His accent was ever-so-slightly English. Emmett thought it sounded affected.

"I wanted to talk to you about Matt Bronik."

"Absolutely," Dafashy said, then stood aside. "Come in, please."

Emmett looked around for a place to scrape his boots. There was none. Only wall-to-wall carpet worn in the middle by about fifty years of foot traffic.

"Sorry about the condition of the place. I'm just renting it while my wife and I take a little break. It came furnished, so I took it," Dafashy said. "Have a seat, please."

He pointed to a blue easy chair that was in the corner of the living room, opposite a plaid couch. In the middle was a coffee table with inlaid plastic tiles.

Emmett hadn't seen the rest of the place, but even as temporary lodging, it was a pretty hard fall for a tenured Dartmouth professor.

Dafashy seemed pleased that Emmett had dropped in, like this was a social call. There was nothing wary in his demeanor. He probably believed he could talk his way out of this.

Which was fine. Let him try.

Emmett pulled out his notepad.

"How can I help?" Dafashy said.

"Well, let's start with yesterday afternoon," Emmett said.

"Oh, right. Well, yes, I was there."

"In Wilder?"

"Yes. I didn't see him on the staircase like some of the others did. But I might be able to give you a list of names of the people who did see him, if that helps. I'm not sure if anyone really got a good look at the kidnappers. From what I understand, they were wearing masks. Everyone thought it was some kind of medical thing. It didn't occur to us there was anything underhanded going on. Matt had been having these attacks, as I'm sure you're aware, and we thought this was just another one. To think those men who had him on that stretcher weren't what they seemed, it's deeply unsettling."

"How long did you stay in Wilder?"

"Oh, I don't know. Until five thirty or six? None of us had any idea there was anything amiss."

"And where did you go next?"

"Here. Well, I stopped to get takeout, but then I came back here. I didn't know what happened to Matt until I saw it on the news. That was, what, ten o'clock? Ten fifteen? Then I went online to read about it, because I thought maybe the TV newspeople were, I don't know, mistaken or something. I couldn't believe it."

"So you were here all evening?"

"Yes."

"Can anyone verify that?"

Dafashy opened his mouth to answer, but then his face changed, like it had suddenly occurred to him that Emmett wasn't just making conversation.

"Oh, wait, you think I . . . these are merely routine questions, right? You're asking everyone this?"

"Don't worry about everyone else," Emmett said evenly. "Just answer for yourself. Can anyone verify your whereabouts?"

"No, I . . . my landlords are in Florida. They're retired. They don't come back until April."

"What about anyone else? Did anyone stop by?"

"No," Dafashy said. "I was just here all evening. By myself. I ate the Thai food. Then I reviewed an article for an editorial board I sit on. And then I just watched television. I . . ."

Even as Dafashy's voice trailed away to nothing, Emmett remained mute. Suspects who kept talking often said far more than they ever intended. And Emmett was going to avail this man of that opportunity.

Dafashy laughed nervously. "You can't possibly think I . . . I would do something like this to Matt. We're . . . it might be a stretch to say we're best friends, but we were hired within a year of each other. I mentored him through tenure. We're very close. Ask anyone. Why would I want to harm him?"

Emmett glanced down at his notepad before looking back up again. Time to turn up the heat a little.

"Professor Dafashy, I know about the accusation Sheena Aiyagari made against you."

"*That's* what this is about?" Dafashy said.

The accent had dimmed. There was now a snarl in his voice. "That little . . . did she tell you to come here? Did she tell you I had something to do with this? She's lying. She's flat-out lying. And in any event, how could her . . . her preposterous claims have anything to do with Matt?"

"He was going to testify against you at the hearing on Friday, wasn't he?"

"He was going to testify, yes. But I wouldn't say he was going to testify *against* me. When I saw his name on the witness list, I confronted him immediately. He said he had no idea why Sheena asked him to appear. I asked him if he thought I had harassed Sheena and he said no. As far as I was concerned, Matt was a *good* witness for me. He was going to clear my name."

Which, conveniently for Dafashy, was impossible to disprove as long as Bronik was missing. But to Emmett it seemed unlikely Sheena would put Matt Bronik's name on her witness list unless he had seen or heard something that would help her cause. Emmett would have to ask her about that.

"So you deny ever coming on to Sheena," Emmett said.

"Absolutely. Categorically. The whole accusation is fallacious."

"Fallacious?" Emmett repeated.

Dartmouth professors and their fancy words.

"Yes. Listen, I'm not sure how I'm going to articulate this at the hearing, because I'm afraid I'll get excoriated by the PC police. But I don't go for dark-skinned women, okay? I'm not attracted to them, physically. So for Sheena to go inventing this fantasy that somehow I've been trying to get her into bed? Yes, it's fallacious. A logical fallacy."

Emmett wasn't sure how to reply. It was certainly a novel defense: *I couldn't have committed sexual harassment because I'm actually a racist.*

Dafashy continued: "You're looking at me like I'm abhorrent, and maybe I am. You don't know what it's like to grow up Arab in the suburbs of Virginia. Thank God I don't have a particularly Arab-sounding name. My brother and I were the only nonwhite kids in the neighborhood. It wasn't so noticeable in the winter, but in the summertime, at the pool? We'd get so dark kids actually teased us that we were black. They called my brother Cleotis Jamal. They called me Theotis Tyrone. They tortured us. I spent my whole life trying to be white. I would check *white* or *Caucasian* in boxes on standardized tests or college applications. Part of that was dating white girls and I guess it became . . . well, a preference. So I can assure you I didn't make any advances on Sheena Aiyagari."

"What about Leonie Descheun?" Emmett asked. "She's white. Did you make any advances on her?"

Emmett saw a flash of rage pool inside Dafashy for a moment before he succeeded in swallowing it.

"You've talked to my wife, obviously," Dafashy said stiffly.

"Yes. Is she lying to me too?"

"No. I wouldn't say she's lying. I would say she has an overly active imagination. And you can tell Mariangela I said so."

"So you didn't sexually harass Leonie."

"No. Absolutely not. I was professionally cordial with her, the same way I was professionally cordial with Sheena. I never laid a hand on either of them."

"Sexual harassment isn't necessarily about touching someone," Emmett said.

"You know what I mean. I'm not stupid. I know where the line is. I didn't cross it with either of them. What happened with Mariangela is going to follow me for the rest of my career and obviously it's put a target on my back for this sort of thing. But if anything, that's made me *more* careful. Not less so. And if you don't believe me, if you want to believe my wife or Sheena, well, I guess there's nothing I can do about that. But it has nothing to do with Matt. There's no connection."

"Except the same people who took Professor Bronik away on the stretcher also attempted to take Sheena," Emmett said. "So the Bronik abduction and the failed Aiyagari abduction are very much connected. The only difference is she got away."

Dafashy narrowed his eyes at this. Emmett couldn't fully read the expression, but there was something going on behind those eyes.

"She saw these men?" Dafashy asked. "The people who kidnapped Matt?"

"She did."

"And let me guess, they were Chinese, am I right?" Dafashy asked.

Emmett wasn't going to answer the question. He wasn't comfortable sharing details of his investigation with a suspect.

But Dafashy didn't wait for confirmation. He didn't seem to need it.

"I knew it," Dafashy said, growing very excited. "Don't you see? It all points to what I was telling Brigid this morning. When it comes to quantum mechanics, we're in a space race against the Chinese. They're hell bent on winning. And they'll do anything. *Anything.* Sheena is Matt's postdoc. She shares a lab with him. She would know more about his research than anyone. Doesn't it stand to reason that the Chinese would want both Matt and his assistant? You have to see that's what's really going on here. The Chinese are behind everything."

Or, Emmett thought, *that's what you want people to think.*

"That's certainly a theory to pursue," Emmett said guardedly.

"A theory to pursue! Is that all? She saw the men who did this and yet you're bothering with me? You should be getting her with a sketch artist. You should be focused on the Chinese."

"We don't know they're Chinese," Emmett said. "They might be US citizens who just happen to have Chinese ancestry."

"So you need to have incontrovertible proof they're Chinese before you start exploring the most obvious explanation? That's patently inane."

Emmett wasn't sure how he had allowed himself to be maneuvered into discussing investigation strategy with a suspect, but it was a corner he needed to get out of.

"I'm not saying that," he offered lamely.

"No, what you're saying is it's easier to pin this on me. Horny Professor Dafashy, who had one momentary lapse in judgment years ago when he got his TA pregnant. Yes, he must be the one who did it."

"I'm just asking questions here, Professor."

"Well, if you have any more of them, you can ask my lawyer."

"You have a lawyer?"

"Not yet. But I'll be getting one," he said. "You can have your witch hunt, but I'm not going to play the role of the lady with the pointed hat."

Dafashy stood. So did Emmett. The suspect had invoked his right to counsel. There was no law that dictated Emmett needed to stop asking questions because of it, and with someone less sophisticated, Emmett might have tried to do just that.

But that wasn't going to work here. Dafashy was too smart.

So Emmett simply handed the man a business card, then left, all the while replaying what had been a rather remarkable performance.

It was, by turns, friendly and combative. Dafashy had attempted to be persuasive, and when that failed, he turned belligerent. He had hopped on the China angle with fervor, and when that suggestion wasn't met with unbridled enthusiasm, he took a turn toward paranoia, then lawyered up.

In other words, he had acted like the hundreds of guilty suspects Emmett had interviewed before him.

Was there truth in anything he had said? Emmett had always felt that people who dismissed harassment claims as being he-said-she-said—and therefore impossible to untangle—were just being lazy. At the very least, you could learn more about the truthfulness of the he and she involved.

Emmett believed in the legal concept of *falsus in uno, falsus in omnibus*—the Latin phrase that translated as "false in one thing, false in everything." And there was at least one part of Dafashy's story that would be relatively easy to check.

Emmett took out his phone and dialed Beppe Valentino.

After a brief exchange, Emmett got down to the reason for his call: "Do you have contact information for Leonie Descheun?"

It was three thirty East Coast time, nine thirty Paris time. Which made it late to call the cell phone number that Beppe had been able to dig up.

But not too late.

Emmett needed three tries to get the number right—a New Hampshire State Police detective didn't exactly make a lot of international calls, so he forgot the 011 prefix—but finally he heard the flat double beep of the European ringtone.

After three rings, a woman answered.

"Hello?"

She sounded French, so it came out more like "'ello"—with a silent *h*.

"Leonie, this is Emmett Webster, I'm a detective for the New Hampshire State Police. Beppe Valentino from Dartmouth gave me your number. Do you have a few minutes to talk?"

"Yes, of course, how can I help you?"

"I'm just doing a background check and wanted to ask you a few questions about David Dafashy."

Leonie's reaction was not one Emmett expected.

She said, "Okay," then added a giggle.

"What's so funny?" Emmett asked.

"Nothing. I'm sorry. Go ahead."

Emmett didn't know what to make of that. So he started with, "You know Dr. Dafashy?"

"Yes, of course. He was a professor at Dartmouth, where I was doing a postdoctoral study."

"Was he your adviser?"

"No, emm, not directly. That was more Beppe. I am a theorist, like Beppe. But David was interested in my area of study."

"So you interacted with him a fair amount?"

"Some, yes."

"How would you describe those interactions?"

"Oh, he was very friendly. He is a very nice man. He was interested in being a mentor to me, wanting to help my career."

"How so?"

"He knows a lot of people at different places. Physics is very small, but within physics, the name David Dafashy is a little famous, you know?"

Emmett had been doing this long enough to know when someone was holding back. And he was getting that feeling now.

"Did you ever get the sense his interest in you was more than just professional?" he asked.

And there it was again. That giggle.

"You're laughing," he said. "Does the question make you uncomfortable?"

"No, no. This is . . . I don't want to sound like I am bragging. But, yes, I think maybe he likes me? He was very sweet. He was always telling me I am beautiful and asking why do I not have a boyfriend."

"And how did you respond to that?"

"When a man tells me I'm beautiful? I say, 'Thank you.' What should I say?"

"But were you threatened by his behavior at all? Did you ever think about reporting him?"

"Oh, nooo. This is nothing. In France, we are used to men like this. This is why when #MeToo happens in America, Brigitte Bardot, she comes out and says, 'I found it charming when men said I had a nice backside.' It is different with men and women here. At François Mitterrand's funeral, his wife and his mistress were treated with equal respect. I am not saying this is right. Cheating is wrong. I am just saying it happens a lot."

"Do you think Professor Dafashy wanted you to be his mistress?"

Another giggle.

"This is hard to answer," she said. "It is not like he comes out and says, 'Leonie, I want to have an affair with you.'"

"So what did he say?"

"Well, there is this conference he goes to. It is in Montreal, which is a very romantic city, you know? And he says, 'Leonie, you should come with me to Montreal. Leonie, you should have dinner with me. Leonie, we will drink wine together.' And even though he is not saying it, I am knowing what he means, what he wants."

"And how did you respond?"

"Ohh, I know he has a wife and a little girl. I am not a, a what-you-call-it, a home-wrecker. But I want to be kind to him. So I say, 'I'm sorry, I am busy, I cannot go to this conference with you.'"

"By any chance did he mention the name of the restaurant he wanted to take you to?"

"Oh, yes. It is called Les Jardins. He thinks maybe because I am French, I will like this, yes?"

Les Jardins. Just like it had been with Mariangela and Sheena. And yet somehow Emmett was supposed to believe he had no feelings for Leonie? Or that he hadn't harassed Sheena?

Falsus in uno, falsus in omnibus.

"Yes," Emmett said. "I'm sure that's exactly what he thought."

"Is everything okay? Has something happened to him?"

"No, he's just fine. Thank you for answering my questions."

"I am not sure what I have even told you," she said. "This is not so helpful, I think?"

"No, no, it's very helpful," Emmett assured her before ending the call. "You told me everything I needed to know."

CHAPTER 38

Tom O'Day had vanished again.

It had been hours now, and Sean Plottner had heard nothing from him.

Friendly Facebook Bot had alerted him to one log-in, from Germany. But O'Day had not seen fit to write a message.

Plottner had Facebook open and was checking it every few minutes. Where was goddamn Tom O'Day? What was taking him so long? Didn't he want a payday?

Plottner was starting to think he might never get an answer. Then, during one of his many Facebook checks, he saw he had a new message.

Not from Tom O'Day.

From someone called Michael Dillman.

And the contents made Plottner freeze.

"You're not working with Tom O'Day anymore," it read. "You're working with me now."

Whoever this was, his English was certainly improved. Plottner leaned close to the screen and inspected the thumbnail-size profile photo. It was a picture of an aging white man whose face was consumed by a bushy mustache.

Another stolen picture? Another fake account? Logging in from a VPN, just like O'Day?

"Theresa!" Plottner yelled. "Get that Facebook engineer on the phone. Get him now. Better yet, get him five minutes ago."

Plottner was still staring at the screen, letting all these thoughts rumble through his mind, when the dots started moving.

Michael Dillman was typing.

The message came in: "If you want to see Matt Bronik again, you'll answer me now."

"Who are you?" Plottner hastily typed.

"That's incidental. What matters is we each have something the other wants. You want Matt Bronik. I want money. We can make a deal."

Yes. A deal.

Plottner loved making deals.

Was this actually Tom O'Day, switching accounts, trying to gain leverage in negotiations by pretending to be someone else? No. How would that help him? Having two entities who both claimed to have abducted Bronik would actually weaken each negotiator's position—if not obliterate it altogether, if it muddled the question of possession.

This Michael Dillman was a new actor.

"What happened to Tom O'Day?" Plottner typed.

He didn't really care, of course. He just wanted to see what Dillman was willing to reveal.

"He is no longer your concern," Dillman replied.

"How do I know you have Matt?"

Much more quickly than last time—no more dial up, apparently—a photo appeared. It was Matt Bronik, with the same Band-Aids, the same plain wall, the same dingy lighting.

But the T-shirt was different.

It had a brown-red stain across the chest, dots that arced from left to right in a crescent-moon shape, growing slightly smaller toward the tail.

Like a blood spatter.

The other striking thing about the photo was that he was sticking up his thumb.

Michael Dillman had clearly been in contact with Tom O'Day somehow. Because that was the photo Plottner had last asked for. Otherwise, how would Dillman know?

Except Plottner was already shaking his head as he messaged: "This is no good. I asked for this picture hours ago. My eight-year-old niece could have faked a photo in that amount of time."

"Okay. How can I convince you?"

"I want a video. Not tomorrow. Not in five hours. I want it in five minutes. And whatever your monetary demand is, I want Matt to say it on the video."

The reply was immediate: "Okay."

Plottner was pleased with his cleverness. Not only would he get the proof of life he needed, but he had subtly claimed a leg up in the negotiation by making Michael Dillman name his number first.

Theresa appeared. "I've got the Facebook engineer," she said.

With his eyes on the screen the whole time, Plottner confirmed with the engineer that Michael Dillman had entered Facebook via a VPN. So there was no tracking him.

Plottner hung up. It had been three minutes already.

Then a video arrived.

Bronik's face was squared in the middle of the frame, but he was not looking at the camera. His eyes were cast down, at something he appeared to be holding.

Plottner hastily hit the triangular-shaped play button and unmuted the sound. He was soon hearing Bronik's unmistakable North Carolina twang, reading from a piece of paper.

And there was no question in Plottner's mind:

This was the real thing.

This was the convincing evidence he had been waiting for.

This was something he could take to the state police with total confidence.

CHAPTER 39

For someone accustomed to the deliberative pace of a university—where there's always tomorrow, and the next day, and the month after that—I could scarcely believe the speed at which the legal system was moving.

It turned out that when Beppe called them, the college's lawyers, working in conjunction with a law firm in Concord, had been moments away from filing a claim challenging the Department of Defense's use of eminent domain—which included a request for an emergency injunction that would, in effect, reopen the top two floors of Wilder Hall.

As soon as the lawyers heard about Sheena, they enthusiastically included her claims in their brief, then made me a plaintiff.

When you're throwing legal spaghetti against the wall in the hopes that something sticks, it always helps to have more noodles.

They filed *Dartmouth College and Brigid Bronik v. Department of Defense, et al.* with the US District Court of New Hampshire in Concord. And then they waited for a response.

But not for long.

The case was assigned to the Honorable Benjamin Stuart Parsons, which may or may not have been a stroke of luck. According to the outside counsel, Parsons had been on the bench for twenty-five years, long enough that he had stopped caring what anyone, including the Department of Defense, thought of him. He was notoriously impatient and raged against the torpidity of the federal judiciary, hearing more cases in most years than any two of his colleagues, believing in the adage that justice delayed was justice denied.

He was also fiercely independent and wildly unpredictable, considered just as likely to tell the Department of Defense to pack up its bags and go home as he was to tell the elite private college to stop its whining and let the army do its job.

Literally, anything could happen.

But whatever was the case, it would happen quickly. Judge Parsons called us to his chambers for a conference, scheduling it for five o'clock, regular business hours be damned.

We, the plaintiffs, had said this was an emergency; to Parsons, everything was an emergency.

It was not, according to the lawyers, a formal hearing. That would come later. But there would be a court stenographer present. We would be on the record, under oath. We would be given a chance to present as much of our case as the judge would let us.

And would it help to have the wife of the missing professor there? And the postdoc who might be able to find him if she could get back into the lab?

Yes, it absolutely would.

Which meant we had to hurry. I barely had time to put on a dress appropriate for a meeting with a judge. Sheena was resigned to the clothes she had on, because the trip back to her apartment would have made us late.

We just hopped in my CRV and took off. I explained to Sheena I didn't talk and drive at the same time—it required me taking my eyes off the road for too long—so we rode in silence.

As soon we hit the highway, Sheena fell asleep again.

I could feel my body slowing down as well. The lack of sleep from the night before was finally bearing down on me. To stave off exhaustion, I sipped a diet soda, letting the much-needed caffeine percolate into my bloodstream.

All the while, my mind continued racing. How quickly would renewed contact with the virus strengthen her feeling for Matt? Would she need to have another fit before it triggered?

Or would it not work at all? Was it possible that, without Matt also renewing his infection, the connection between them would slowly dissipate, like ripples in a pond, until it was so flat as to be indistinguishable?

Then there was the other vexing issue that refused to leave my thoughts: Even if Sheena's spooky feelings did return, would Matt allow himself to be found? Would we simply chase him from one hiding spot to the next, barely missing him every time?

And if that was the case, what did I do then? Just wait for him to come in from the cold?

The whole thing was like one of the tandem trucks in the lane next to me, rumbling down the side of the White Mountains. And there I was next to them, in my little Honda CRV, merely hoping not to get run over.

It was seven minutes to five when we arrived at the Warren B. Rudman US Courthouse, an imposing building whose facade was done in 100 percent cheerless gray New Hampshire granite.

We passed under an arched glass entryway, then through a metal detector, after which we were directed to the fifth-floor office suite of Judge Parsons.

A law clerk escorted Sheena and me into a room with narrow rectangular windows and a long conference table. There were ten chairs, only one of which was occupied. As the clerk departed, a woman in a blue skirt suit, with long blonde hair and empathetic blue eyes, stood up.

"Mrs. Bronik, Ms. Aiyagari?" she said in a melodious voice. Even with the digital flatness of my hearing aids, I could tell she was a singer.

"That's us," I said.

"I'm Jen Sopko. I'm with the law firm of Farley, Gibson & Wrobel here in Concord. I'll be arguing this case on Dartmouth's behalf—and on your behalf, since you're now a plaintiff too. It's nice to meet you."

We exchanged handshakes.

"Is anyone from Dartmouth coming?" Sheena asked.

"This isn't really their area of expertise," Sopko said, then lowered her voice. "And Judge Parsons is known for being sort of prickly when he feels like one side is trying to flex its muscle by bringing in a mob of attorneys. We decided the fewer of us, the better."

It wasn't three seconds after she made that observation that the door opened again. Six people in suits—men and women, tall and short, white and black and brown—filed in.

So much for not having a mob.

They began introducing themselves. The lead counsel was Greg Tufaro, who had short kinky hair and the handsome face of a man who belonged on television. He represented the Department of Defense. After that, I lost track of names and agencies. They just kept piling on top of each other.

When they were through, the law clerk said, "Are we expecting anyone else?"

Each side looked at the other. When no one answered, she said, "Okay. I'll let the judge know everyone is here."

For five uncomfortable minutes, we tried to avoid staring at each other. Outside, the sun was sinking low. The occasional wind gust buffeted the building.

I thought about Morgan, who would probably be hungry for dinner soon. Aunt Aimee had it covered, but I still got that stab of maternal guilt. When Matt talked about particles being in two places at once, I understood it as a mother. I always existed in two places simultaneously as well: wherever circumstance had placed me, and wherever Morgan was.

The only interruption during those next few quiet minutes was when the court reporter walked in and took her seat in the corner, where her steno machine had already been set up.

When the door opened again, the frame was filled by a man a shade above six feet tall, with wiry gray hair that had stubbornly refused to recede. He wore a blue-and-yellow-striped bow tie.

The lawyers stood up. Sheena and I followed their lead.

"Good afternoon, everyone," the judge said in an accent that would have been at home in a Kennedy family reunion. "Have a seat, please."

He took the spot at the head of the table and then introduced his law clerks, both of whom acknowledged the lawyers from the corner where they were standing.

"I appreciate all of you coming on such short notice, and I'm going to value your time as much as I want you to value mine. It is right now," he said, then glanced at his watch, "five-oh-three. Mrs. Parsons likes me to be home by six, because she won't start her manhattan until I get there. And, believe me, you don't want to get between Mrs. Parsons and her first manhattan."

As lawyers on both sides grinned, he glanced at the court reporter. "That's not on the record, is it, Francine?"

From the corner, the court reporter said something that made everyone laugh nervously. Naturally, I didn't catch it. But I pretended like I had and laughed too.

"Okay, good," Parsons said. "But from now on everything else is on the record, so let's get started. It's my intention to issue a preliminary verbal ruling this afternoon and then follow up in writing later. Ms. Sopko, I've read your filing. I want to hear, in three minutes or less, why I should grant you an injunction."

"I'm not sure I can do it in three minutes, Your Honor," Sopko began. "I—"

"You're already wasting your time, Counselor. And mine."

"Okay, Your Honor. Our argument has two sides. One is that the DOD has overreached by shutting down two entire floors of a very important college building. It's displacing dozens of professors and hundreds of students, so every hour they continue to do that is actually hundreds of hours of disruption. And it's doing this for essentially no reason. Just because Professor Bronik walked down a hallway on a regular basis doesn't make it vital to national security. If the DOD wants to keep Professor Bronik's office sealed, we understand and can abide by that.

"Our second argument is, admittedly, more unusual."

"I'll say," the judge interjected.

I couldn't help but note his skepticism. I worried he had already made up his mind and was now just going through the appearance of due process.

"Are you familiar with quantum physics, Your Honor?" Sopko asked.

"My parents wanted me to be a doctor," he said. "I became a lawyer because I couldn't handle the science classes."

"Don't worry, neither could I," Sopko said, smiling warmly at him. "But that's okay. Because you don't actually need to know quantum physics to understand our argument here. You just need to understand evidence. Ms. Aiyagari was able to lead the New Hampshire State Police to the abandoned house where Professor Bronik was being held. A crime scene unit found a fingerprint that was a fourteen-point match, so there's no doubt he was there. I have just received a sworn statement from Detective Emmett Webster affirming all of this."

She slid a two-page document toward Parsons. Then she pushed another copy toward Tufaro on the other side of the table.

Parsons extracted a pair of plastic reading glasses from his shirt pocket and hung them crookedly on the end of his nose. He skimmed the first page, then glanced at the second page.

"You're right," Parsons said. "You're going to need more than three minutes."

"What I would like to stress on behalf of my plaintiff, Mrs. Bronik, is that speed is of the essence. Every minute matters here. Until Professor Bronik is returned safely, his life will be in considerable danger. And while Dartmouth College sees him as an important part of its faculty, he is far more important to his family as a husband and father to a nine-year-old boy."

Parsons looked at me. My throat had swelled at the mention of my son. I could feel my face flushing.

"His name is Morgan," I choked out.

"Thank you," Parsons said softly, then turned to Sheena. "Ms. Aiyagari, can I ask you some questions?"

"Yes, Your Honor."

"Raise your right hand, please."

Sheena complied.

"Do you swear or affirm that everything you're about to say is the truth? If so, say yes."

"Yes."

"And you understand that even though we are not in a courtroom, everything you say in front of me right now is subject to the penalties of perjury?"

"Yes, sir."

"Very good. Ms. Aiyagari, if you could, help me understand this . . . thing that happened to you."

Sheena talked him through the events of the previous evening and the day at hand. Parsons peered at her intently from over his reading glasses.

I couldn't tell what he thought about any of it. But he was at least listening. When Sheena was through, he removed the reading glasses and stuffed them back in his pocket.

"Ms. Aiyagari, you seem very lucid, so forgive me for this question. But I have to get it on the record. Are you under the influence of any drugs? I know you don't have a lawyer present, so I'll remind you that you may invoke your Fifth Amendment right against self-incrimination if you wish."

"No, sir," she said. "I've never done drugs."

"Are you taking any medications that might have a strange reaction with each other? Any medication at all, for that matter?"

"No, sir. I took some Tylenol last night and this morning because my face hurt. That's it."

"And would you be willing to submit to a drug test for this court? It would be voluntary, so we'd have a probation officer meet you at your home or workplace, whatever you prefer. It wouldn't take more than five or ten minutes."

"Yes, sir."

"Okay. Now, this house where you led the detective. Had you ever been there before?"

"No, Your Honor."

"You had never seen it in your life."

"No, sir."

Parsons was bobbing his head faintly as he continued to study Sheena.

"And you think if you're able to go back into your lab and work with this virus, you'll really be able to tell us better where Professor Bronik is?"

"I honestly don't know what will happen, Your Honor," Sheena said. "But I think it's the only thing that might work, and I'd like to have the opportunity to try."

Parsons glanced at his watch. "Okay, there are probably a lot of other issues that I'm sure we'll explore when we have a full hearing, but in the interest of time, I'm going to turn this over to the defendant. Mr. Tufaro? Try to keep it short."

Tufaro straightened in his chair.

"Thank you, Your Honor. The key fact from our point of view is that Professor Bronik's work was considered extremely sensitive and important to the Department of Defense and our close partner, the National Interagency Confederation for Biological Research. I hope you understand that I can't go into details in a document that could become part of the public record. But it pertains to biological warfare, or biological agents that could possibly be unleashed on the public. And because of the unique nature of what Professor Bronik was doing, the DOD would have no immediate ability to combat it. There are no vaccines, no antidotes. Without delving into scare-mongering, this is as serious as anything you could imagine in your worst nightmares.

"Beyond that, the government's use of eminent domain in matters of national security is well-settled law. The takings clause has been understood for hundreds of years to mean the government can seize private property. And there are numerous examples, particularly during the Cold War, of the DOD using eminent domain during times when Congress had made no formal declaration of war. We haven't had much time to review this—we barely had time to get here. But we've been scouring Westlaw to find examples of where the government's claims of national security were successfully challenged, and so far we haven't found a single one."

He paused to let that sink in. When he resumed, his tone was softer. "Mrs. Bronik and her son obviously have our sympathy. But we have an entire nation of citizens whose needs we need to think of as well. And, if anything, Ms. Aiyagari's testimony only underscores our need to carefully protect this research, because we really *don't* understand its full power and what it might be used for. We're still assessing that threat level. Frankly, the unknown makes it even more frightening. The moment Professor Bronik was abducted, it triggered a lot of alarm bells that made the DOD feel it had to act, and act decisively to contain the risk before something catastrophic resulted.

"In closing, the government's responsibility is very clear here, as is its authority. And that's why we'd ask you to immediately deny this request for an injunction."

Parsons had been listening carefully. When Tufaro finished, Parsons folded his hands in front of himself in a contemplative, almost prayerful gesture.

"How much longer do you think the DOD will want to continue controlling access to this area?" he asked.

"That's difficult to say. I'm told that we'll probably want to keep Wilder Hall on lockdown for at least another week."

A week. Or more.

I felt like the previous day had lasted a year. How was I going to survive a week? And would that already be too late for Matt?

"Is it possible to speed that up?" Parsons asked.

"Not really," Tufaro said. "This isn't the kind of work you want to rush. Without boring you with the details of what our hazmat teams do, it's a very laborious process, and it has to be done with due caution. You can't just spray some Clorox and walk away. The team is due in tomorrow morning and will get to work right away. We have to make sure the threat is fully contained and eliminated."

"Eliminated! You're going to kill the virus?" Sheena interrupted, her voice climbing with each syllable.

Parsons turned toward her. "Ms. Aiyagari, I'll ask the questions here."

"We're not going to kill it," Tufaro said. "We'll take it to Fort Detrick in Maryland. It's biosafety level four—the highest level. It will be stored there until such time as Professor Bronik returns or . . ."

He didn't finish the thought, nor did he need to. Everyone knew what the alternative was.

Sheena, meanwhile, was clearly intent on ignoring the judge's admonishment. "But if you take the virus away, there's no point. I'll never get this feeling back. I won't be able to find Matt. You'd be killing him. Is that what you want?"

"Ms. Aiyagari, please," Parsons said, more sharply this time.

Sheena's mouth finally closed. But she had no trouble meeting his gaze.

Parsons crossed his arms and leaned back in his chair. I could guess that he had been leading up to a very judicial kind of compromise, telling the Department of Defense to speed things up a little, then saying, "Look, Dartmouth, this is the best we can do."

But there would be no splitting the baby this time.

No easy answers.

He wasn't looking at anyone now, his eyes searching the dimming light outside the window for answers. I could practically see the machinations of his decision-making process. His breath seemed to have gotten short. His arms rose and fell across his chest each time he inhaled, then exhaled.

Then, suddenly, he was looking directly at me.

"Mrs. Bronik, my heart goes out to you and your son," he said. "Truly, it does. And please understand how difficult this is. In making a decision like this, I have to weigh the potential harm and the potential good of each possibility. In this case, the threat the government is talking about is theoretical—something bad *might* happen if this virus falls into the wrong hands. At the same time, the threat against your husband is also theoretical—something bad *might* happen to him if Ms. Aiyagari can't find him.

"So I'm weighing two theoretical threats against each other. Except, on one side, the threat pertains to potentially thousands or millions of people, while on the other side, it pertains to just one man. That's some harsh math, I realize. But—"

There was a knock on the door. It didn't distract me from my misery over what was about to happen, but it did seem to derail the judge.

Annoyed, he started to say, "Now what the—"

"I'm sorry, Judge," said a woman as she stuck her head in. "They said it was an emergency and that it pertained to the Dartmouth case."

She opened the door wider to allow two men to enter. One was a massive stone-faced man with a build so powerful he barely fit into his suit.

The other—who seemed quite comfortable walking into a roomful of strangers and taking charge—had a large head, a long face, and stooped shoulders.

I recognized him instantly, but only because I had googled him so many times.

"Hello, Your Honor," he said. "My name is Sean Plottner."

CHAPTER 40

For Sean Plottner, the path to a Concord courtroom had started with the Matt Bronik video.

Plottner had sent it to his contact at the state police, a captain by the name of Angus Carpenter, the man Plottner had first been put in touch with when he offered the reward. Perhaps a bit starstruck by Plottner's money—it happened a lot—the captain had reviewed the video and found it highly credible.

Just as Plottner had hoped he would.

Then Carpenter began oversharing about what was happening on the state police's end. He told Plottner a remarkable story about a young Dartmouth postdoc guiding a detective to an abandoned house where Bronik had been held.

She had gotten there perhaps twenty minutes late. But, still, the police found Bronik's fingerprints at the residence.

Carpenter presented the narrative as if it was the manifestation of something supernatural. Didn't it beat all? Wasn't it incredible?

Plottner was not quite as awed. He had listened to Bronik talk about his work for an hour. The quantum world was a place where the incredible was business as usual.

Carpenter had finished by telling Plottner about the emergency injunction request now pending in federal court. That's what led to a team of Plottner's lawyers hastily drafting an amicus brief in the matter of *Dartmouth College and Brigid Bronik v. Department of Defense, et al.*, which mostly consisted of a transcript of the Bronik video.

And, sure, he could have filed it with the court and left it at that. Except Plottner knew all about judges and their bubble of self-importance. He had learned, the hard way, to show obsequiousness in the face of federal judicial might.

All it took was one pissed-off judge to seriously mess up your day.

Besides, there was no substitute for being there in person.

The helicopter made quick work of the trip from Plottner's house to a helipad near the federal courthouse in Concord. And before long, Plottner was entering the chambers of the Honorable Benjamin Stuart Parsons with the formidable shape of Lee Michaelides in tow.

Plottner was met by a staff member, upon whom he began impressing the notion that no, this really *couldn't* wait.

Lee had nothing to add. But his presence may have been persuasive, because moments later they were escorted into the judge's conference room.

"Hello, Your Honor," he said. "My name is Sean Plottner. I own Plottner Investments. This is Laestrygones Michaelides, my director of security. He goes by Lee."

"Laestrygones," Parsons said in disbelief, slightly dumbstruck as he looked at Lee. "Aren't the Laestrygones the tribe of man-eating giants from the *Odyssey*?"

"Yes," Plottner said. "That's why I keep him well fed."

Lee stood behind his boss with no expression on his granite face. If he even understood they were talking about him, he never let on.

"Forgive our interruption," Plottner continued. "I've filed an amicus curiae in this matter. It mostly pertains to a video of Dr. Bronik that I'd like to show you. I think it will be of great interest to everyone in this room."

"And who are you again?" Parsons demanded.

"Sean Plottner," he said again, like that alone should have been enough to settle matters. "The video won't take more than thirty seconds of your time. If I may, Your Honor?"

Plottner was holding up his laptop, looking for the judge's permission to set it down. If the man didn't say anything soon, Plottner was going to proceed as if he had been granted permission—as was his usual response to most things in life.

But with one final look at Lee, then a glance at his watch, Parsons said, "Fine. Be quick."

Plottner set down the computer and opened the lid. The video was cued up, so an image of a bandaged Matt Bronik had already appeared on the screen.

The lawyers either craned their necks to see the monitor or were now scrambling for a view.

Once he felt people were properly in place, Plottner turned the sound up all the way, then pressed play.

Bronik's voice soon filled the room.

"This is Matt Bronik," he read from a piece of paper. "I am being held against my will. My captor wants five million dollars in cash to ensure my safe return and he wants it by noon tomorrow, or I will be killed."

There was a catch in his throat as he said the word. Then he continued: "Further instructions will be forthcoming. I ask you to take this request very seriously, as I have no doubt—"

And then he lifted his eyes from the paper and, clearly off script, blurted: "I love you, Brigid, I love you, Mor—"

But before he could say anything else, the screen went dark.

Plottner, who had already seen the video a dozen times, had been watching the reactions of the people in the room.

A car bomb could scarcely have left them more shell shocked.

The first sound was a barely stifled sob from a middle-aged woman in a dress on the far side of the conference table. It wasn't difficult for Plottner to guess this was Bronik's wife.

A young dark-skinned woman—this must have been Sheena Aiyagari, the postdoc with the paranormal abilities—placed her hand on the wife's back in an attempt to comfort her.

The lawyers who had needed to get up to see the video were now returning to their seats.

"How did you acquire this?" the judge asked.

Briefly, Plottner told the judge about the reward, then described the interactions that led to the video—first with Tom O'Day, then with Michael Dillman.

"It's all documented in the amicus curiae," Plottner finished. "I also had my social media person sign an affidavit, which I've attached."

"And are the state police trying to trace where this video came from?" Parsons asked.

"I'm afraid they won't be able to," Plottner said. "I've been in touch with a network engineer at Facebook. Both Tom O'Day and Michael Dillman have been accessing internet via a virtual private network. Facebook is essentially blindfolded as to where they're coming from."

"Well," Parsons said, "this certainly changes things."

Plottner didn't know what, exactly, the judge was referring to. But the man had already turned to Aiyagari. "If I were to let you into the lab, is it possible this feeling would return before noon tomorrow?"

"I believe so," she said. "That's my theory of how this would work. But until I have a chance to try, I won't know for sure."

Parsons frowned for a moment, then looked at the lawyer to his left.

"Mr. Tufaro, I certainly understand the government's concerns about the sensitivity of Professor Bronik's work. But as you can see, the threat to Dr. Bronik is no longer theoretical. It's very real."

The judge gave one final pause. But, having seemingly wrestled his doubts to the ground, he said, "I'm granting the plaintiff's injunction."

Tufaro's expression soured.

"Can the DOD remain on premises to provide security?" he asked.

"I don't know how that would work," the judge said. "What this injunction essentially says is that this lab belongs to the plaintiff again. It's their lab, so it's their call. I would hope the plaintiff has given some thought to how it will keep the lab secure?"

He said the last part with a hopeful lift of the eyebrows.

"Dartmouth has already told me they have a plan in place for that," Sopko said. "The head of their safety and security office is a former marine."

"Okay, Ms. Aiyagari," Parsons said. "The clock is ticking. Get to work."

CHAPTER 41

Emmett didn't really have time to stop and eat.

But he was starving.

The banana bread made by Brigid's sister—delicious as it was—had ceased fortifying him several hours earlier, and he hadn't had the chance to do anything about it through the late afternoon.

Almost immediately after hanging up with Leonie Descheun, Emmett had heard from Angus Carpenter, who sent Emmett the video of Matt Bronik and transcripts of Facebook exchanges between Sean Plottner and people who went by the names Tom O'Day and Michael Dillman.

The captain then asked for a sworn statement from Emmett, something that was needed to help get the lab back open.

Writing was never Emmett's strength, and ordinarily it might have taken him even longer to sputter through the narrative of what he had experienced earlier in the day. But, mindful that Matt Bronik was running out of time, he choked it out as quickly as he could.

And now, because he felt like he was going to fall over if he didn't eat something soon, he was at a burrito joint on Main Street in Hanover.

It was around five. He was three bites in when his phone rang.

"Webster here."

"It's Carpenter," he heard.

"Did you get the statement?"

"I did. Thanks. But that's not why I'm calling. You're needed out near Canaan."

"What's out near Canaan?"

"I don't know yet. I just got the message that O'Reilly asked for you. He said you need to hurry."

"Okay," Emmett said. "Where am I going?"

Carpenter gave him the address. Emmett was out the door moments later, walking toward his car as he took bites from his burrito.

More than a little of it fell on the sidewalk. The New Hampshire State Police Diet Plan.

It took the better part of a half hour to reach the destination Carpenter had given him on Fernwood Farm Road, which was near Canaan Street Lake.

The dirt road was, by rural New Hampshire standards, well populated—one house every tenth of a mile or so. Most of what was in between had once been farmland but had now grown back over.

Emmett was nearing his destination when he had to slow down. A state trooper was blocking the road, which told Emmett he had found the right place.

The trooper directed him to pull his car off to the side. Emmett went the rest of the way on foot. The sun was lowering. The wind had picked up. The temperature had dropped at least ten degrees.

Emmett walked until he saw the Crime Scene Unit truck, occupying the middle of the small road. With all the flashing police lights, and the general confusion lent by too many people in uniform with no actual purpose, Emmett couldn't tell what was going on.

"Emmett," he heard.

He turned to see Connor O'Reilly, whose bulk was wrapped in a jacket that went midway down his thighs. His red beard always reminded Emmett of a leprechaun's.

"Detective," Emmett said.

"Hey, just to get this out of the way: Sorry about earlier. You were right, I was wrong. My bad."

They had been arguing about what had happened in that abandoned house on Riddle Hill Road before Haver Markham came along and settled the argument. Emmett was already over it. After a certain age—was it forty? fifty? or was it after your wife died?—taking everything personally required too much energy.

"No problem," Emmett said.

"Thanks. And thanks for coming out. Anyhow, here's what I got: A lady is out walking her dog when Rover starts going nuts and runs into the forest. She goes into the woods to see what Rover is all fired up about—we've already identified which footprints are hers, by the way—and she sees what I'm about to show you. She freaks out, calls 911, and here we are. The scene isn't too contaminated. Markham got out here about thirty minutes ago, and she's been staring daggers at anyone who gets too close. You want to follow me? We're going around it and approaching it from the side."

Emmett said, "Sure."

O'Reilly plunged into the brush, crunching along in shin-deep snow. There was a dense stand of dead, dried thicket by the side of the road. But once they cleared it, getting into the forest proper, the walking was easier.

The ground sloped upward. They covered about thirty yards until O'Reilly slowed and walked, more hesitantly now, to his right. Emmett matched his pace. He could hear and see the younger man's breath.

Finally, in the gloaming, Emmett could make out two human shapes in the snow.

O'Reilly reached into his jacket and brought out a MagLite. He clicked the flashlight on and aimed it at one dead man, then another.

Emmett recognized them immediately.

The man with the dragon tattoo on his throat.

And the man with the sickle-shaped eyebrows.

"Not a lot of Chinese people out this way," O'Reilly said. "I was wondering if maybe these were two of your suspects from the Bronik thing."

"Yeah," Emmett said. "That's them."

Emmett worked through this new revelation methodically.

There had been three men involved in the abduction.

Two of them were now dead.

It was possible that was the plan all along. You need three men to pretend to be a team of EMTs. Then you need three men to carry out the next phase—two to grab Sheena Aiyagari, the other to stay with Bronik.

But then at some point three becomes superfluous. A liability even—too many moving parts. Especially if you've decided Sheena is either no longer a priority, or no longer possible to abduct now that she's alerted to the threat.

You only need one man to hold someone hostage, assuming the hostage is tied up, making the other two expendable.

Were these the two who had failed with Sheena? Was her dose of pepper spray only the beginning of their punishment? Had someone decided to dispose of them when they weren't needed anymore?

Possibly.

But then why dump the bodies here? Fernwood Farm Road was more populated than the Riddle Hill Road area. This was New Hampshire, for goodness' sake. If you couldn't find a place more than thirty yards from a road where people walked their dogs, you weren't trying very hard. It would be almost inevitable bodies would be discovered.

It made it seem like this hadn't been someone's original plan. This was a plan gone wrong. This was improvisation, perhaps born of desperation.

"Shine your light on that one, if you don't mind," Emmett said amiably, like he was studying fauna on a nature walk.

O'Reilly pointed the beam at the first man. He still had on the blue EMT pants but had ditched the top part of the uniform—the part that would have made him look like an EMT, which law enforcement might have been looking for. He was wearing a tight black sweater with a black T-shirt underneath.

Just above the collar of the T-shirt, roughly where the dragon's snout was, his throat had been slit. The line across was straight. The cut was deep enough and wide enough it appeared to have severed both carotid arteries.

The murder weapon would be a serious knife—a butcher knife, a hunting knife, even a machete—not some piddly switchblade someone had kept in their pocket.

"It didn't happen here," Emmett said. "There would be more blood. A lot more."

"Markham says the guys were dragged up here from the road," O'Reilly said. "There's a pretty obvious path. No blood, so they must have been dead for a while. The drag marks obscured some of the boot prints, but not all of them. She's working on them over that way."

O'Reilly pointed downhill, where Haver Markham and another crime scene tech were bent over one particular spot in the snow.

"Show me the other guy," Emmett said.

O'Reilly shifted his beam to the man with the sickle-shaped eyebrows. Just above those eyebrows were two round holes, leaving little doubt as to how he met his end.

The entry wounds were small and neat. Nine millimeter, Emmett guessed. The murder weapon was probably a pistol with a short barrel, something that could have been carried concealed.

It wasn't difficult to guess the order of operations: The one with the slit throat had been the first victim, when the perpetrator needed to be quiet. The gunshot victim came when noise no longer mattered.

"I'm sure it's making Markham nervous, having us this close," O'Reilly said. "You seen enough yet?"

"Yeah, for now," Emmett said.

They began crunching back down the hill. Emmett was still working through things. This was now a ransom case, but it hadn't started out as one. If it was, they would have heard a demand from the kidnappers sooner—not roughly twenty-six hours after the initial abduction.

Plus, Matt Bronik was not especially wealthy. His research may have been worth a lot of money, but he was not. If it was treasure these Chinese men were after, wouldn't they have snatched someone whose family actually had it?

No, this only became about money once Sean Plottner entered the picture and offered a million dollars for Bronik's return. That was what had triggered the initial contact from Tom O'Day.

Except now Tom O'Day was more than likely one of the men lying in the snow by Fernwood Farm Road. That was why the Facebook account had changed from Tom O'Day to Michael Dillman.

Because Tom O'Day was dead.

Which meant Michael Dillman was likely the third man, the one with the Neanderthal forehead—or someone else altogether, someone Emmett didn't know about yet.

Then again.

Maybe it was someone he *did* know.

Emmett was back on the road now, though he was barely even seeing it. He was picturing a small section of that Facebook transcript Carpenter had sent.

Plottner: Who are you?

Dillman: That's incidental.

Incidental.

Dartmouth professors and their fancy words.

Was Michael Dillman actually David Dafashy?

Emmett was now trying on a new theory. Dafashy hired three Chinese men to abduct Bronik and Aiyagari. Dafashy had paid his mercenaries well . . .

But not *that* well. Not a million dollars.

Once word of Plottner's offer got out, one of the Chinese men, alias Tom O'Day, realized he could greatly improve his payday. So he reached out to Plottner, eager to cash in.

Somehow, Dafashy discovered that one of his mercenaries—or maybe two of them?—had betrayed him. With things about to spiral badly out of control, Dafashy acted. He killed Tom O'Day and his accomplice.

Then Dafashy, as "Michael Dillman," messaged Plottner and made a demand for five million dollars. Not because he had any intention of returning Bronik or collecting any reward. But because it was more distraction, more confusion, more plausible deniability for Dafashy, who could point to the escalating ransom demands as evidence this had nothing to do with him.

The whole thing was misdirection, leading a detective—or a dean of faculty investigation, or a jury—away from the sexual harassment angle.

But Bronik would never be allowed to return and testify. That much was certain.

So while parts of this were improvisation, none of it was desperation. This was the calculated brilliance of a man who realized he had stumbled into a second red herring, that of the ransom demand. The quantum space race—the notion that the Chinese were stealing Bronik and his research—was still the first.

That's why the bodies had been so easy to find. It was exactly what Dafashy wanted.

Emmett was now flashing back to his last interaction with Dafashy.

We don't know they're Chinese, he had said. *They might be US citizens who just happen to have Chinese ancestry.*

Dafashy had fired back: *So you need to have incontrovertible proof they're Chinese before you start exploring the most obvious explanation?*

Emmett started working his way back up the hill, toward Haver, watching for stray footprints, being careful not to disturb any of the drag marks.

"Haver," he called out, when he was close. "Do you have a moment?"

She turned, said something to her crime scene tech, then approached Emmett.

"What's up?" she asked. She had obviously been outside for a while. Her cheeks were flushed red from the cold.

"O'Reilly said you got close to the victims."

"Yeah, what about them?" she said. Not rudely. Just impatiently. She had work to do.

"You check their pockets by any chance?"

"I did. But if you're hoping the killer was thoughtful enough to leave their wallets and IDs on them, you're going to be a little disappointed."

"Did you find anything at all?"

"One of them had what looked like some kind of coupon on him. The other had a scrap of thermal paper with printing on it—possibly a receipt. I bagged them. They're in the truck now. But good luck getting anything from them."

"Why?"

"It's all in Chinese."

Of course it was.

This was Dafashy at work.

Giving incontrovertible proof.

CHAPTER 42

Even as I stood up, even as my legs started moving, even as I managed to propel myself out of the conference room without falling over, I had the feeling I wasn't entirely in control of my body.

I was under the influence of . . . what, exactly? An excess of cortisol. A dearth of oxygen. The chemical cocktail the body created when it was confronted by absolute terror.

It had seized me the moment that video clicked on.

And it wasn't letting go now that it was over.

Fearful I might pass out—and not wanting to make a scene—I asked for directions to the ladies' room. One of the clerks led me to a private bathroom used by the judge and his staff.

There, I sat on the lid of the toilet, trying to collect myself.

I knew Matt must have been afraid, of course. But to actually *see* him looking that scared, to hear his voice sounding so strained, to read his body language as it screamed out in panic.

We all have our illusions in this world, and we cling to them. We think we're standing on a broad, sturdy cruise ship of an existence when really we're floating in a life raft. We construct webs of safety for our families and ignore the hungry spider in the corner. We convince ourselves that the terrible things we read about will always happen to someone else.

Matt had always been at the center of those illusions for me. He was the light shining under the bed, showing me there were no monsters.

That light had now been snuffed out. The monsters were in the room.

Unless . . . was this more of Matt's plan? His not wanting to be found? It seemed impossible he was that good an actor. The emotions of that video—the terror, the trauma—they seemed far too real to have been faked.

But there was still the unresolved issue of how he vacated that cabin just as Sheena was bearing down on him.

Or had that truly been happenstance?

Not wanting anyone outside to feel like they needed to come in after me, I stood up and splashed some water on my face. Then I walked shakily back into the judge's waiting room.

The lawyers had their phones out and were talking dates and times. I couldn't focus on anything that concrete. My head was down. The floor was still swaying slightly, even though no one else seemed to be having the same trouble.

Maybe Sheena could regain her sense of Matt in time, but if not . . .

Five million dollars. Where would I get five million dollars? And by noon the next day? We had a little equity in the house, our 401(k) s, a 529 plan for Morgan, and a small rainy-day fund. None of them were as robust as they probably should have been, and they didn't come close to five million.

Suddenly, there was someone standing directly in front of me. The person had said something, but I had been too wrapped up in my own distress to register what it was.

I lifted my head. It was Sean Plottner. The man who had only ever been a Google search to me.

"Mrs. Bronik," he said for perhaps the second or third time.

"Hi," was all I could manage.

"That video," he said. "That was really something. Are you okay?"

"I'm fine," I said, though I could tell he didn't believe me any more than I did. So I added, "It just threw me for a little bit of a loop."

"Completely understandable," he said. "But right now every minute matters. I've got a helicopter waiting a short drive away. I've offered Ms. Aiyagari a ride back to Hanover, and she says she'll go if you will. It will cut your transit time down considerably and get her to the lab that much faster."

"But I . . . I can't," I said. "My car is here."

"I'll have someone drive it back for you," he said. "Just give me your key."

He pulled his phone out of his suit jacket and ordered his secretary to take care of the details. It was a short conversation. Then he turned to me and said, "Key, please."

It occurred to me that Plottner was the kind of man who got what he wanted, one way or another. If I argued, I would just be slowing us down.

And I didn't want anything to delay Sheena's return to the lab. I reached into my purse and grabbed my keys, separating the Honda key from the ring. Then I handed it to Plottner.

"Okay, glad we've got that handled," he said. "Let's go."

I started walking. That massive block of a bodyguard—Lee was his name?—followed a little too closely, like he was going to grab me by the scruff of the neck if I tried to make a run for it.

We were soon back outside. A stretch black limousine was waiting. Lee sped around us with surprising agility, given his size, and was holding the back door open.

The moment we were seated, Lee tapped twice on a smoked-glass partition that separated the back cabin from the driver. The car immediately rolled away from the curb.

"The helipad is five minutes from here; then we'll be scooting along quite nicely," Plottner said.

He leaned back. The car was new and permeated by the scent of expensive leather. Plottner seemed like the kind of man whose whole life smelled that way.

"Now, as to the issue at hand," he said. "Do you have five million dollars to meet this ransom demand?"

"No," I said.

"Well, I do. But if I were to allot these funds, I would expect a return on my investment."

"What do you mean?"

"It's pretty simple, really. I'd want Matt to come work for me. On the terms I already proposed: a million dollars a year, working as an employee of Plottner Investments in New York. He would report to me directly—or to my director of operations, whichever he preferred. We can put it in writing. In fact, I'd insist."

I shifted in my seat. The leather squealed.

"The other possibility is that Ms. Aiyagari is able to find your husband by noon tomorrow," he said. "We can all root for that, I suppose. But if she can't, I certainly hope you would consider having your husband work for me to be an acceptable alternative to what the kidnappers have proposed."

"I guess we'll have to see," I said.

This was all too dizzying to even think of another answer.

"Yes, though I do hope it works out with us. I'd love to be in the physics business. I've always found it quite fascinating, even if I don't totally understand it. Like Schrödinger's cat. I assume you're familiar with it?"

"Of course," I said.

In Schrödinger's imagination, there was a cat closed in a box along with a vial with cyanide and an atom of radioactive material. If the atom decayed, a radiation detector would trigger a hammer to break the vial, releasing the poison and killing the cat.

But the trick is, no one can predict when an individual atom will decay. There's a chance it has. There's a chance it hasn't. Until you opened the box and observed the cat, you could say the cat was both alive *and* dead.

Crazy, sure. But that's quantum superposition. Until you nail it down, anything that's possible remains possible.

"I've always had a bit of a problem with it," Plottner said. "The physicists want me to believe that during the experiment, the cat is both alive *and* dead. But I don't buy that. Just because a camera is out of focus doesn't mean the world is blurry."

"What do you mean?"

"That cat isn't truly alive *and* dead. The whole time, it's either one or the other. Maybe the scientist outside the box doesn't know. But inside the box, the cat knows."

He paused over this point, as if to magnify its significance.

Then he repeated, "The cat knows."

CHAPTER 43

From the relative warmth of the back of the Crime Scene Unit truck, Emmett inspected what Haver had bagged off the dead men.

He didn't learn much. Other than that he hadn't magically developed the ability to read Mandarin.

Still, the mere presence of those characters told him enough. Each man had one small item—just one—left behind on his person. A coupon. A receipt. They were meaningless scraps of paper, the kind of things you might not notice if you were ransacking a man's pockets before you dumped his body. And yet they would neatly link each man to China.

It felt like the kind of highly calculated thing a brilliant professor would think to do.

Emmett was just leaving the truck when his phone rang.

"Webster here."

"You out in Canaan yet?" Captain Carpenter asked.

"Yes, sir."

"How's it going?"

"Just got a look at the victims. They're the guys who abducted Bronik. Two of the three of them, anyway."

"Okay. I was just talking with the colonel, and we've worked out a division of labor moving forward. Major Crime is going to continue working the homicide scene. We're going to keep our focus on Bronik."

"Yes, sir," Emmett said.

"We just got word that the judge granted Dartmouth's injunction. Looks like your bloodhound will be back on the trail soon."

"Yes, sir."

"Once you're done out there, why don't you head back to Hanover. If she starts getting that feeling again, I want us to be able to run it down."

"Yes, sir."

"All right," Carpenter said.

Then, before hanging up, he added, "Good stuff."

It almost sounded like a compliment.

Emmett wouldn't let it go to his head.

He had pocketed his phone and was off to look for O'Reilly when he heard the low rumble of a diesel truck, coming from the south. He peered toward the source of the noise until he saw a boxy truck, painted in drab olive, the same military vehicle he had seen parked outside Wilder Hall that morning. It was being followed by two dark government sedans.

The vehicles halted.

O'Reilly, who had suddenly appeared at Emmett's side, muttered, "Oh, Christ."

A man in a dark suit with a short haircut emerged from the first sedan. He had a cord snaking away from his ear. Emmett recognized Gary Evans of United States Army Counterintelligence.

Evans started walking toward Emmett, trying to muster a self-assured stride even as his wing-tipped feet slipped in the snow every third step or so.

"Whose crime scene was this?" Evans demanded.

Was this. That darn past tense again.

"It's mine," O'Reilly said, in present tense.

"Well, it's not anymore," Evans said. "The army will take it from here. We appreciate your cooperation."

O'Reilly might have been summoning a response, but the attention of all three men was pulled toward the woods, where there was a crashing noise coming their way: snapping branches, leaves rustling under snow, pricker bushes scratching against fabric.

Then Haver Markham burst out of the thicket, wild eyed, looking like a five-foot-three, strawberry-blonde Sasquatch.

"What's this"—she inserted a colorfully profane description of the army counterintelligence representative—"doing here?"

"There's no need for name-calling," Evans said snippily. "I was merely informing these gentlemen that we are relieving you of jurisdiction."

"The hell you are," Markham spat.

"I'm going to ask you to please cease and desist all activities and turn over any evidence you may have gathered to us," Evans continued. "If you would please also—"

"Under whose authority?"

"Do we really need to go through this again? Because in addition to the national security concerns from this morning, we now throw in the specter of international espionage."

"I heard you boys just lost in court," Haver said. "So now you're going to come take a crime scene from us out of spite? Real nice. Has your dick always been this small or did you have it surgically reduced?"

The corners of Emmett's mouth lifted just slightly for a moment before he got control of them. He admired her spirit.

But state beat local.

And federal beat state.

This cause was lost. There was a bigger picture to think about. They'd never get the army's cooperation on anything if they tried to fight it every step of the way.

"Sorry, Agent Evans, she doesn't mean anything by that," Emmett said. "We'll clear out. Good luck here. Hope you find your spies."

Haver was drawing breath to object, but Emmett silenced her with a fierce glance.

"Thank you, Detective," Evans said stiffly.

"Just do us a favor," Emmett said, holding out a business card for the man. "Keep us in the loop, okay? We still have a civilian with a wife and child missing here. There's been a ransom demand. Every bit of information counts, and every second matters."

Evans took the business card.

"Of course," he said.

Maybe the veteran's touch would actually work this time. Really, it was the only play he had.

Emmett herded O'Reilly and Markham away before they said anything they'd later regret.

"Why are you just giving up like that?" O'Reilly asked.

"We're probably better off to have this with the feds right now. They have resources and contacts we don't have. We were at a dead end out here anyway. We're looking at two Chinese nationals dumped by the side of the road. And it's great to get a cast of a boot print, but we have to be realistic that we really don't have a legitimate chance to find the foot that was inside that boot."

"How did Agent Asshole even know we were here?" Markham grumbled.

"Probably NCIC," Emmett said, using the acronym for the National Crime Information Center. "Captain Carpenter has been updating it continuously in case Bronik's captors take him out of state."

Markham replied to this by offering another observation about the size of Gary Evans's manhood.

"Let's just keep our eyes focused on the road ahead, not the road behind," Emmett said. "The lab at Dartmouth is back open now. Why don't you take your guys back there and have a crack at it?"

CHAPTER 44

From the back bench seat of the helicopter, I watched the sun lower itself until it was resting perfectly on top of the Green Mountains of Vermont, like the red rubber ball in a song my father used to play.

It perched there for just a few minutes before making its exit, leaving the aircraft to fly toward the dusty pink-and-peach hues left behind.

Matt was down there—somewhere—huddled in a blood-spattered T-shirt, alone with his terror.

Could he hear the chopper passing overhead? Did he know what a hopeful sound it might be? Did he know how hard everyone—the police, the lawyers, and most of all Sheena—was working to rescue him?

Did he know there was such a beautiful sunset?

Would he live to see another one?

That last thought came completely unbidden, and I immediately tried to erase it.

I looked across the aisle, where Sean Plottner and his bodyguard were sitting. They were both wearing ear protection, as were Sheena and I. Lee stared at the fuselage, unblinking and expressionless, almost Plasticine, like an android that had gone into sleep mode but could snap into action instantly if commanded.

Plottner was buried in his phone. As I looked at him, I found myself thinking of something I read long ago in a German-literature class. It was the story of Doctor Faust, who famously sold his soul to the devil in exchange for knowledge.

In this case, it wasn't knowledge being sold. It was knowledge being bought.

I couldn't help but wonder if I was dealing with the devil all the same.

By offering to pay the five-million-dollar ransom in exchange for Matt's employment, was Plottner actually just seizing an opportunity he had created in the first place?

I played out the scenario: Matt turned down the job, so Plottner had Matt kidnapped, faked a ransom demand—which he received on his own Facebook account—and then swooped in with this generous-seeming offer to "save" him in exchange for Matt doing what Plottner wanted all along.

Would a billionaire do something so risky, something that could land him in prison if he got caught?

Or was that *precisely* what a billionaire did, because he had been raised in such extreme privilege and had spent a lifetime bending rules to his desires and skating away from the consequences?

That would clearly preclude Matt faking his own disappearance. And the question of how the kidnappers had known to evacuate just as Sheena was bearing down on the cabin had an easy answer too: Plottner had hired people to follow her. They had watched her leave Hanover and probably been able to follow us at least as far as Potato Road before falling back to avoid being spotted.

But by then they could have notified others that Sheena was getting close.

It fit. But was it true? I felt like my mind was spinning at least as fast as the rotors overhead.

I shook my head, trying to focus on what was real. Sheena was going back to the lab. And if she failed, there was Sean Plottner's generous offer.

It *was* generous, right? Yes, of course. It's just that it came with strings attached.

Heavy ones.

More like chains.

But that's all it was. Just an offer.

Matt would forgive me if I had to say yes to this, wouldn't he? It's not like I had a choice. What was I going to do, tell Plottner no thanks and invite the kidnappers to go ahead and kill my husband because he was too pure to consider working for private industry?

No, if Sheena couldn't find Matt, this was clearly the second-best option. I looked over at her, buckled in the next seat over, smiling thinly at her.

Sheena nodded back. There was no smile on her battered face. Only determination.

She was obviously under stress, both from the abduction attempt and from what had followed. It's not like she had asked to serve as a medium to her kidnapped postdoctoral adviser.

But she was holding up as well as could be expected.

Before too long, the helicopter began its descent and was soon hovering over our landing pad.

As soon as the bird set down, Plottner tugged off his ear protection. Sheena and I did the same. The pilot came around and opened the door.

At the edge of the helipad were two Lincoln Town Cars. Plottner led Sheena and me toward the first one. A driver was already holding the back door open. Plottner stopped short of it, gesturing for us to get in.

I read his lips as, over the roar of the helicopter motors, he said, "I'm sure we'll talk more soon."

"Yes, of course," I said solemnly.

Sheena said something I didn't catch.

"You bet," Plottner said. "Good luck."

He rapped the top of the car twice before heading toward his own Lincoln. Our driver confirmed we were going to Wilder Hall, then got rolling.

I quickly called Aimee, updating her, then asking how Morgan was doing, reading her answers on my screen. Aimee promised she was keeping her nephew distracted.

Then I talked briefly with Morgan, forcing cheer into my voice so he would think Mommy was doing just fine. Thankfully, he didn't ask the one question I was dreading: "When's Daddy coming home?"

Sheena was gazing out the window the whole time. I left her alone with her thoughts as we approached Wilder Hall.

The Town Car pulled up in front, where earlier in the day there had been a crowd of military, government, and law enforcement vehicles.

They were all gone now, replaced by two Dartmouth College Safety and Security cars. As we climbed out of the Town Car and into the frigid early evening, we were greeted by a man with a flattop.

"Ms. Aiyagari? Mrs. Bronik?" he said.

"Yes," I said.

"Steve Dahan. I'm with safety and security. I was told you two would be coming my way."

My eyes went to his belt, which had a pistol attached to it. In nine years hanging around Dartmouth College, I had never seen anyone carrying a firearm before.

"The only other person in the building right now is Beppe Valentino," Dahan said. "The state police should be here shortly. They want the Crime Scene Unit to be able to dust for prints while Ms. Aiyagari does her work. In the meantime, they've asked that anyone who goes inside wear these."

He held up a box of latex gloves. I took two, feeling the grit of the cornstarch as I slid them over my hands.

Then I walked inside with Sheena and started climbing the staircase. My plan was to hole up in Matt's office, so I wouldn't get in Sheena's way.

I was about to plunge through the **DO NOT ENTER** sign when I stopped and looked toward Sheena, who was already continuing toward the third floor.

"Sheena?"

She stopped and turned.

"Thank you for doing this. I really . . . I can't even explain how grateful I am."

Sheena bowed her head, almost like she was embarrassed, then brought it back up.

"You don't have to thank me," she said. "I'm just doing what I'd hope someone would do if it were my family."

I was desperate for more information. How long would this take? Entanglement was instant, wasn't it? Or would Sheena need to have another fit first?

But I stopped myself from asking any questions.

I already knew, from Sheena's testimony with the judge, there were no answers.

CHAPTER 45

Emmett tailed the Crime Scene Unit truck back to Hanover, then parked behind it, just outside Wilder Hall.

He briefly chatted with Steve Dahan, thanking the man for allowing the state police back inside—even though, technically, he didn't have a choice. With the Department of Defense out of the way, it was now a regular crime scene again. Which meant the state police could do as it pleased with it.

Haver Markham and her team quickly got to work. Sheena Aiyagari was already bent over some boxy metallic contraption whose purpose Emmett could not begin to discern. He still wanted to ask her about why she put Matt Bronik on her witness list, but that could wait until she wasn't quite so busy.

As the only person who didn't have a real purpose in the lab, Emmett excused himself and strolled down the hall.

He was, for lack of a better description, on standby. He had to stay ready to take Sheena wherever she wanted to go, as soon as she wanted to go there. There was just no telling when that would be. This precluded him from starting a trip down any of the avenues that might meaningfully move the investigation forward.

But it also meant he had time to kill.

Luckily, that was a game at which your typical detective excelled. He strolled down the hallway, looking at the folderol professors had tacked to their doors—the comic strips, the pictures, the funny quotes, most of which were physics references that sailed well over Emmett's head.

He was somewhere in the midst of reading a yellowed, brittle *The Far Side* cartoon when his cell phone rang.

The number came up as "Unavailable."

"Webster here."

"Detective, this is Gary Evans with army counterintelligence."

"Hello, Agent Evans."

"I've got some information about your victims in the forest."

Emmett permitted himself a brief smile.

The veteran's touch finally comes through.

"That was fast," Emmett said.

"Two fingerprints and a few phone calls. It's not that hard when you're dealing with nobodies."

"Come again?"

"The Chinese guys. They're not spies. They're not assassins. They're nobodies. Tourists."

"But they are Chinese?"

"Yes," Evans said. "They came here on tourist visas. One of them was Langqing Wu. He was thirty-two. The other was Yiren Jiang. He was twenty-eight."

Yiren Jiang. So he had used his real name on his fake license.

Evans continued: "We have an asset in China who checked them out. They're two ordinary guys who went to different technical universities in Fujian Province. Then they got jobs. They're with an outfit called Huangpu Enterprises Limited. They have no ties to the Chinese government that we know of. And we tend to know that kind of thing."

Fujian Province. Huangpu Enterprises. These were things beyond the reach of Detective Emmett Webster of the New Hampshire State Police.

"If they're nobodies . . . ," Emmett started but then couldn't decide how to end the sentence. "Why would two nobodies come to New Hampshire to kidnap someone?"

"No idea. To be honest, that's part of why I'm calling you. If they *were* government agents of some sort, that would actually give us something to go on. Civilians are more problematic. I was hoping we could work together. Maybe with what you know and what we know, we can put this together."

"In other words, we're all on the same team here."

"I seem to recall someone suggesting something to that effect earlier today," Evans said good-naturedly.

"Excellent. If you've got a Chinese asset"—Emmett felt ridiculous using the word—"could that asset maybe tell me a little more about Huangpu Enterprises? I can't exactly fly to China and start asking questions. Do they have any ties to American companies? Are they trying to develop some kind of technology that could benefit from this quantum-whatever thingamajig that Professor Bronik was doing? I'd love the lowdown on them."

"You mean a dossier?"

"Whatever you want to call it."

"Sure. I can have something put together. We're thirteen hours behind them, so it's already morning over there. Give me a little time and I'll send it to you. I assume the email on that card you gave me works?"

"Sure," Emmett said.

For once, he was fine with someone sending him an email.

CHAPTER 46

When I reached the second floor, I turned down the hallway toward Matt's office, a route I had walked many times.

Back before I had started working for Dartmouth—when Morgan was small and the boredom of stay-at-home parenting got particularly stifling—Morgan and I used to visit Matt regularly.

We called it going to Daddy's "office hours." Matt would let Morgan sit on his lap while he graded exams and would even talk through why a certain answer was worth full credit while another answer was only good for partial. Morgan would wear his most serious expression, absorbing every word, even while he couldn't possibly have understood any of it.

There was nothing all that exciting about it, and yet if I ever suggested we might go to office hours, Morgan would run through the house yelping, "Office hours! Office hours! Office hours!"

The boy just wanted to be with his father. He didn't care about the where or what.

How I yearned for office hours now.

It was mostly dark on the floor. There was only one light on. I slowed as I walked by it. Beppe Valentino was talking on the phone, with both his elbows propped on the desk and his head resting on one of his hands.

Rather than interrupt him, I continued on to Matt's office. The door was closed, but he never locked it. The lights, set on a motion sensor, switched on as soon as I entered.

I eased the door shut behind me, then looked around.

Earlier in the day, I had been convinced I would find something there that would help me make sense of what was happening.

I took a tentative step inside, touching my gloved fingers together, feeling the starch chafing against them. Army counterintelligence had surely been in here, snooping around, but any materials relating to Matt's research—the stuff the army would want—were upstairs, in the lab. Down here, it was mostly about teaching.

Nothing appeared to be out of place. The shelves that lined the right side of the room from floor to ceiling were their usual untidy chaos, books of all different sizes and colors, arranged arbitrarily.

A few years back, the anal librarian in me volunteered to organize Matt's collection into something that resembled sense—alphabetical, by subject, whatever. He declined, then astonished me by demonstrating that he knew where every single volume in his collection was.

I walked over and pulled out a book at random. It was called *How the Hippies Saved Physics*, by an MIT professor named David Kaiser. I opened it, scanned it idly, then replaced it on the shelf.

The next book I selected claimed to be able to explain string theory. I was lost after half a page.

Giving up on the bookshelf, I swiveled my gaze to the other side of the room, where a large whiteboard was affixed to the wall. It was covered in equations that were, both literally and figuratively, Greek to me.

A Nerf basketball hoop hung from the top of the board.

Behind the desk, under the window, were shelves with more books and a few knickknacks, mostly gifts—a lot of them pertaining to basketball, a few of them of the gag variety—given to him by students and fellow faculty members.

The desk was covered in sloppy paper piles of varying elevations, again with no apparent system.

I sat, feeling exhaustion wash over me. One of the piles was a stack of journal articles, printed out and stapled. I picked up the top one. It was beyond impenetrable.

My eyes then fell on the corner of the desk—the only part of it not overwhelmed by paper—where our once-simple, once-happy life was documented in a series of photos.

Morgan's school portrait, the one from two years back, when the photographer had somehow tricked him into smiling for real. A snapshot of Morgan and me on the Point Pleasant Boardwalk, taken during a trip to the Jersey Shore. A selfie of the whole family standing atop a bluff in Gile State Forest, with the fall colors spread out beneath us.

But there was one photo that really sent the memories flooding back.

It was of me. Just me. From our first fevered spring together.

We had gone canoeing on Lake Carnegie, one of those Ivy League absurdities—a man-made lake funded by Andrew Carnegie, who felt the Princeton crew team needed a better place to practice.

After paddling along for a while, we pulled the canoe up to a quiet spot along the lake, then walked inland a few hundred feet until we reached an abandoned canal. There, in a grassy spot under a tree, near a field of wildflowers, we had thrown down a blanket.

I kissed him first, which I usually did in those days, because he was still so shy. But his hesitancy never lasted long.

We ended up making love, right there under that tree, heedless that there was a popular biking path just on the other side of the canal.

Matt had taken the photo sometime after we had reassembled our clothes and started acting more respectably again. My face still had a flush to it. My hair was provocatively askew. I looked, above all, fabulously content.

I picked up the picture, studying my long-ago self. I was twenty-eight, unaware that the small bones in my ears were already starting to betray me. Matt was, what, twenty-three? I could barely remember us having been so young.

Ordinarily I might have regretted the passing of the years, just a little—perhaps felt a wistfulness in knowing I would never again be that beautiful and that Matt and I would never feel quite the same urgency toward each other. Then I would remind myself the passing of years had brought us many gifts. Morgan. Some form of wisdom. A love that was far more profound.

I allowed myself the fantasy that when springtime came, and we were somewhere near New York, we could leave Morgan with my parents for a day, and try to find that same tree again, and . . .

Wait.

There was something about the picture, about the photo paper itself—a slight warping near the edges of it. In a perfectly rectangular shape.

Like there was another piece of paper beneath it.

Had Matt hidden something behind this photo? Some kind of message, perhaps? This picture frame would be a perfect place for such a thing—out in the open, yet perfectly concealed.

I flipped the frame over. The clasps that held the back panel in place swung easily, having apparently been opened and closed many times before. Matt—or someone—had accessed this often.

Because the hidden message needed to be changed frequently?

I had thought my hunch about finding anything in Matt's office was baseless, but was there really something to it? Did I know all along I had been meant to find this? Were my and Matt's brains truly entangled as well?

My hands trembled as I removed the panel, then a piece of cardboard. And then, yes, wedged against the back side of the photo, there was a piece of white paper, folded in thirds.

I unfolded it and was soon looking at a printout of an email. From me.

2004 13 April 01:24 a.m.
From: BEzzell@West_Windsor.NJ.us
To: Matthew.Bronik@Princeton.edu
Subject: you
Matty,

I'm watching you sleep right now. Does that freak you out? Well, you're just going to have to deal with it, because I think you're so, so beautiful and I like watching you sleep.

You said earlier tonight that I had saved you from being a work-aholic physicist. But you're the one who saved me in so many other ways. I don't want to think about where I'd be right now if I hadn't met you all those months ago. You've made me feel happy, and beautiful, and loved like I've never felt before.

Yes, I daresay you have made me the happiest woman alive. I am very much in love with you. And if that freaks you out, you're just going to have to deal with that too. :)

All My Love,

B

I had no memory of sending the email, though I certainly remembered the sentiments behind it.

So this was Matt's big secret: He liked to revisit a romantic interlude with his wife. And he did it with reasonable frequency, if the way those clasps swung was any indication.

I slowly refolded the paper and, with pain squeezing my overwhelmed heart, returned it to the frame.

CHAPTER 47

For all the vastness of his fortune, five million dollars was still nettle-
some to Sean Plottner.

Not because of the actual amount. That was basically walking-
around money.

The issue was the form it came in. The majority of Plottner's wealth
was numbers in a computer somewhere. Want it as a wire transfer? No
problem. A check? Sure.

Want it as actual cash? Now there are issues. Five million dollars,
even meted out in hundred-dollar bills, is fifty thousand sheets of green
paper. And, little known fact, all US currency, regardless of denomina-
tion, weighs one gram per bill.

Therefore, five million dollars, in hundreds, weighs fifty thousand
grams, also known as fifty kilograms, also known as a hundred and ten
pounds.

Also known as a lot to lift for a guy who let his director of security
do most of his weight-bearing exercise for him.

The other issue was that your local branch of Ma & Pa National
did not maintain anywhere near that much hard currency on hand.
Depending on the size of the local population, a bank's vaults held
anywhere from fifty to two hundred grand.

Five million would have to come from the nearest Federal Reserve bank. Meaning Boston. And it would have to be delivered to Hanover. The bank would likely insist on an armored truck.

Once it arrived, Plottner wouldn't need an armored truck.

He had Lee.

Time to start the process. It was now after five. The banks were, technically, closed—except banks were never truly closed to a man of Plottner's net worth. He asked Theresa to get someone from the bank on the phone.

"Sir, why don't I make the first call," Theresa suggested. "That way if we need to increase the pressure later, we can have you intercede."

"That's a fine idea," Plottner said.

There was little doubt in his mind the money would be needed. He had a deal with this new person who had Matt Bronik, this Michael Dillman character. And now Plottner and Matt Bronik's wife had a deal too.

Plottner had few qualms about any of it.

Some might call it excessively opportunistic. But, really, what was life if not a series of opportunities?

You either seized them or you didn't.

CHAPTER 48

Having determined that Matt's office was not going to be a source of enlightenment, I decided to go up to the lab and check on Sheena's progress.

On the way, I passed Beppe's office, now dark, and Emmett Webster, who nodded at me and said . . . something.

I just smiled at him.

When I opened the door to Matt's lab, three state police crime scene investigators looked up at me.

But not Sheena.

She didn't appear to be there.

"Where's Sheena?" I asked.

A woman with strawberry-blonde hair turned toward me and said, "She left a little while ago."

I felt my face bunch into a frown.

"She left? Where is she?"

"I'm sorry, who are you?" the woman asked.

"Brigid Bronik. Matt's wife."

"Oh, sorry, Mrs. Bronik. I'm Haver Markham. I'm with the Crime Scene Unit."

"Nice to meet you," I said quickly. "Did Sheena say where she was going?"

"She seemed like she was upset about something. She said she was going down to the second floor for a second to talk to . . . someone."

"Beppe Valentino?"

"Yes, that's it."

"I just came from that way. She wasn't there."

Markham's brow furrowed, but she didn't speak.

Emmett Webster walked in. "What's going on?"

"Have you seen Sheena?" I asked.

"Yeah, she passed by and said she was going down to talk to Beppe."

"How long ago?"

"I don't know. Ten minutes? Fifteen? I didn't really pay attention. She said she'd be right back."

I immediately pulled out my phone and dialed Sheena's number.

It rang.

And rang.

Five interminable times.

Then it went to voice mail.

I hung up, then sent a quick text.

Where ru? Call me.

Then I redialed Sheena's number.

Same result.

"Maybe she just stopped in the ladies' room on her way back," Emmett suggested.

"Let me check," I said.

I exited the lab and turned left, toward the nearest bathroom.

It was dark. The light only turned on when I swung the door open.

"Hello? Sheena?"

But, of course, that was ridiculous. Sheena wouldn't just be sitting in blackness.

When I came back out, Emmett was in the hallway, looking at me expectantly.

I shook my head and said, "Let me check downstairs."

Emmett followed. I must have been confused about which office was Beppe's. Sheena was probably down there, right now, and I was getting myself worked up about nothing.

Except when I reached the office whose nameplate very clearly read VALENTINO, B, the door was closed. No light escaped from the crack underneath.

I tried the handle.

Locked.

"Let me check the bathroom down here," I said.

It was just a bit farther up the hall.

But also empty.

Since I was already down that way, I went to the postdoc office, a small room shared by three people. It, too, had no sign of life.

"Sheena?" I called out. "Sheena, are you down here?"

The ancient corridors of Wilder Hall offered no response. I felt at least twice as crazy as the look Emmett was now giving me.

"Maybe she's back upstairs by now," I said hopefully. "We just missed her somehow."

I resisted—barely—the urge to run back upstairs and only managed to do so because Emmett was still trailing me.

When I arrived at the lab, it was the same.

Three crime scene techs.

Still no Sheena.

"I'll call Beppe," I said. "Maybe she's with him and they just, I don't know, stepped outside for a breath of fresh air."

When the temperature was in the teens.

And the wind was gusting.

Whatever.

I dialed Beppe's number.

It went straight to voice mail. Like his phone had been shut off. I didn't know if Beppe texted or not, so I left a message to please call immediately.

Now fully frantic, I tried Sheena again.

Still no answer.

"What the hell is going on?" I asked.

"Just take a few deep breaths," Emmett said. "She's obviously somewhere. Let's go ask Steve Dahan. Maybe she and Beppe went to grab some coffee or something."

We trooped down the stairs and back out into the cold. Dahan climbed out of his car when he saw us descending the front steps.

I let Emmett take the lead.

"Did you see Sheena and Beppe?" he asked.

Dahan cocked his head. "You mean when they came in?"

"More recently. The last ten minutes or so."

"No. Why?"

"Something weird is going on," I said.

"They're not answering their phones," Emmett told Dahan. "And they don't seem to be anywhere inside."

"Well, they didn't come this way," Dahan said.

"Does this building have any other exits?"

"Yeah, in back. I locked it, so you can't get in that way. But you can get out."

"Think that's what they did?"

"We can find out," Dahan said. "There's a camera out there. It's mainly for the parking lot but I'm pretty sure it shows the back of Wilder. Hang on."

He went back to his car and retrieved a tablet. "Let's go inside. It's freezing out here."

I was barely feeling the cold, so I only noticed the warmth of Wilder so much. Dahan had stopped at the base of the stairs and was swiping at the tablet, talking as he went. I was missing a lot of it, but what I did manage to take in told me he was mostly just rambling.

Eventually, he produced an image showing a stretch of parking lot with just a few cars left in it, bathed in dim sodium halide light. On the left side of the screen, the back entrance to Wilder was visible.

"Let me roll the footage back and see what happens," Dahan said.

He slid a bar at the bottom of the image to the left. Time wound backward. For a short while, nothing happened.

Then a car entered the lot, then two figures exited the car, then they walked backward across the parking lot, then they entered Wilder. It was hard to make sense of it at high speed, going in the wrong direction.

"Stop there," I said.

"Let's go back a little further," Dahan said.

He slid the bar back, then set it going regular speed.

I concentrated on the screen.

The back door to Wilder opened. First Sheena poured through it, then Beppe.

They descended the steps. Beppe immediately glanced left, then right, in a manner that could only be described as suspicious.

Sheena was walking stiffly, strangely. When she reached the blacktop, she may have stumbled. Or not. She didn't go all the way down. It was more that she just slowed down.

Beppe, who had been tailing her closely—maybe too closely?—helped her along.

Or was he actually grabbing her?

Maybe even pushing her forward?

Or was I inventing that? Beppe's intentions were difficult to read. Helpful? Aggressive?

Beppe had one hand stuffed in his pocket. His other hand was on Sheena's elbow.

He led her to his Subaru, herding her into the passenger seat, then quickly walked around and hopped in the driver's side. His hand never left his pocket.

Because he was trying to keep it warm?

Or because there was a weapon in there?

I couldn't be sure what I was seeing. I reminded myself I had been under extraordinary stress. My mind's eye might be taking benign details and filling them with unintended menace.

Beppe Valentino was a theoretical physicist, not an armed kidnapper.

Right?

But Sheena wasn't answering her phone. Neither was he. And they had left in such a hurry. This, despite her saying she'd be right back.

It didn't require much imagination to think of how this might have played out in some horrible way. Sheena went down to Beppe's office, for whatever reason—maybe he even summoned her there—and he took the opportunity to complete the crime that the Chinese men he had hired had failed at.

But Beppe?

Really?

Why?

Beppe had been the one who called me to tell me about Matt's fits. All three times. Was that a department chair doing his duty or an attempt to establish an alibi?

I was surely being paranoid, yet there had always been aspects about Beppe that seemed a little too extravagant. Like that Maserati convertible, so impractical. Or the wife who spent her winters in an Italian villa.

How *did* he afford all that, anyhow? Or was that just it: he didn't. Had he gotten himself in a deep financial hole and, understanding the value of Matt's research—and betting on Plottner's desperation to acquire it—had he come up with this scheme to cover his debts and fund future profligacy?

The video ended with Beppe backing out of his parking spot, then speeding away.

The whole thing took maybe forty-five seconds.

"What did I just watch?" Emmett asked.

"I'm really not sure," Dahan said.

I couldn't summon any words.

"Could you go back to the beginning and zoom in on Sheena's face?" Emmett asked. "I feel like . . . I want to get a better look at her."

Dahan did as requested. The resolution on the camera was good enough that there was no mistaking it:

The pained expression. The wet cheeks. The puffy eyes.

Sheena was crying.

CHAPTER 49

Emmett watched the video four more times, asking Dahan to zoom in now and then.

It did little to clarify what may have transpired.

All that could be said for sure was that Sheena Aiyagari was distraught. And then she entered Beppe Valentino's car.

Whether it was voluntarily or under duress was still an open question in Emmett's mind.

But he was going to make every effort to figure it out. And quickly. He wouldn't have believed it twenty-four hours earlier—that a young woman's mysterious sixth sense would be his best chance to rescue the abducted professor—but this was now his reality.

They needed to find Sheena.

Emmett wanted to check Beppe's place first. Brigid insisted on joining him, and he didn't object. It would allow the Crime Scene Unit to continue working the lab undisturbed.

Before long, Emmett was rolling up outside Beppe's four-bedroom Cape.

There were no lights on, either inside or out.

"Doesn't look like they came here," Brigid said.

"Just sit tight a moment, please," he replied as he left the car.

He rang the doorbell.

No answer.

Was it possible, if you assumed the worst from that video, that Sheena was being held hostage inside? Unlikely. Beppe wouldn't bring her to his own house, would he?

Emmett returned to the car.

"We should try Sheena's place," Brigid said. "Maybe they went there."

With Brigid navigating, Emmett drove. He was still trying to think about Beppe Valentino as a suspect. Was there anything beyond the video—and his general proximity to Matt and Sheena—to implicate him? Did he have some motive Emmett didn't yet know about?

In between calling out the turns to take, Brigid was making phone calls—presumably to Sheena and Beppe. Every so often, he heard the tinny start of someone's voice mail. Brigid wasn't bothering to leave messages. She had already done so, and the dozens of missed calls would only reinforce the urgency.

When they arrived at Sachem Village, Brigid directed him to a multifamily home and pointed to the unit on the right.

"That's Sheena's," she said.

It looked every bit as dark as Beppe's place had been.

Emmett left his car running as he rang Sheena's doorbell. There seemed no point in turning it off when he already knew what was going to happen.

Sure enough: Ring, nothing; ring, nothing.

Except this time, Brigid was out of the car as he came back down the walkway.

"The neighbor was friendly," she said. "Her name is Lauryn Ward. I talked to her earlier today. She'd probably notice if Sheena showed up, even briefly."

Brigid was already walking toward the middle unit. Emmett joined her.

There were lights on. The door was answered by a woman with long light-brown hair swept into a haphazard bun atop her head.

"Oh, hi," she said. She eyed Emmett quickly before looking in Brigid's direction. "Brigid, right?"

"Yes. Hi, Lauryn. Sorry to bother you again. Can we come in for a moment?"

"Sure. The baby went down early and I didn't fight him, so it's only a little bit chaotic around here for a change. I'm sure I'll pay for it later."

"This is Emmett Webster. He's with the state police."

"Hello," Lauryn said.

Emmett dipped his head once.

"I was wondering if you had seen Sheena in the last hour or so?"

Lauryn was shaking her head before Brigid even finished the question. "I'm afraid not. I saw her briefly this afternoon, when she was with you guys. I was going to say hello but you were in and out so quickly."

"That was when we came back here to get her a change of clothes," Brigid said.

"Of course," Emmett said. "And before that . . . I believe you told Brigid that Sheena is usually back to her house by nine each night, but you were worried because you didn't see her last night?"

"That's right."

"If you don't mind my asking, what time did you go to bed last night?"

"Oh, gosh. I usually collapse around nine thirty. Maybe last night I made it to nine forty-five?"

"Did you see anyone out of the ordinary hanging around before you went to bed?"

"No, sorry."

Emmett had been hoping she might have seen the would-be kidnappers, lurking around. Then again, they didn't make their move on Sheena until after eleven.

Emmett pulled a business card out of his wallet.

"If Sheena comes home, or if you see anyone suspicious near her place, would you please give me a call immediately?"

"Yes, absolutely," she said, accepting the card.

She inquired about Sheena, and Emmett played it cautiously, walking the line between not getting the woman too alarmed while also impressing on her the gravity of the situation. Then he shut down further conversation by announcing they had to go.

When they returned to Emmett's car, Brigid asked, "What now?"

Emmett was still trying to decide. This might be an innocent misunderstanding. Maybe Beppe had decided Sheena, frazzled and overly emotional, simply needed a bite to eat. They could right now be in a restaurant, seated in back, in a spot with bad cell phone reception.

Or?

It wasn't so innocent.

Emmett had no way of knowing. But this was striking him as a time when it was better to apologize later for overreacting, rather than deal with the consequences of underreacting.

"I'm putting out a BOLO for Beppe's car and telling dispatch to call me as soon as someone finds it," he said.

Within a few minutes, every patrol officer in the area would be on the lookout for Beppe's Subaru Outback.

The lab appeared unchanged when Emmett and Brigid returned.

There was no Beppe, no Sheena.

And Haver Markham and her crew were still hard at work.

Or at least Haver was until she became aware Emmett had returned.

"Hey, I was looking for you," she said. "We got a hit on a print."

"Oh?"

"Yeah. It belongs to a Sean Plottner."

Whose prints were on file because of those long-ago arrests.

"Sean Plottner?" Brigid yelped. "What was he doing in here?"

"You know him?" Haver asked.

"I met him maybe two hours ago. He offered to pay the five-million-dollar ransom for Matt—but only if Matt would come work for him."

This was the first Emmett was hearing of the offer. It was straight-up strange. The kind of thing that made a seasoned investigator wonder what Plottner's motivations were.

"Did you say yes?" Emmett asked.

"I told him I'd think about it. I thought there was a chance Sheena was going to come through."

Emmett looked at Haver. "This print. Where did you find it?"

"Right . . . here," she said, crossing the room and pointing with the tip of a ballpoint pen to the door handle of a small white refrigerator that was resting on top of a counter.

"What's in that fridge?"

"Samples of some sort. Want a look inside?"

"Sure."

"That must be where Matt keeps the virus," Brigid said. "Be careful."

Haver capped the pen, then used the end of it to open the door so she didn't have to touch the handle, not even with her gloved fingers.

Emmett walked over and peered in. Even though he was close to it, he didn't feel much cool air. It reminded him of a hotel refrigerator in energy-saver mode, one whose temperature was set only a few degrees colder than the air conditioner.

Inside, there were rows of slender vials, all of them meticulously labeled with a letter and a four-digit number. The first, in the upper-left corner, was A0032. It went from there all the way down to M0102 in the lower right. Some of the numbers had more than one vial associated with them.

Emmett looked toward Brigid, who was gazing into the refrigerator with something like hunger. She walked closer to it, then stopped herself.

"Why was Sean Plottner opening Matt's refrigerator?" she asked acerbically.

"I don't know," Emmett said. "But I'd really like to ask him."

CHAPTER 50

The switchbacks—and they seemed to be endless—were making me nauseous.

Or, I should say, more nauseous than I was already.

As Emmett drove, I was thinking about the fingerprint on the refrigerator. How *had* it gotten there? Even if Plottner was involved in this somehow, it wasn't like he had done the kidnapping himself. He would have just been the guy who paid those three fake EMTs.

Had he come back to the lab later to steal a sample so that Matt could be forced to work on it? No. Gary Evans and the Department of Defense would have stopped him.

Besides, Plottner wouldn't want forced labor. He wanted the public recognition and lasting fame that would come from Matt's breakthrough, and he couldn't get that with Matt hidden away.

So what was the fingerprint about?

We made yet another hairpin turn up the mountain.

"I can't believe one person owns all this," I said.

Emmett mumbled something indistinct. By the time I caught up to what he was saying, he was midsentence: ". . . nice and casual about this. I'm sure Plottner's a smart fellow. I'd rather see if we can catch him off guard. So this is your visit. Not quite social, but not all business either. Ask him a few questions about himself, about the job he's offering your husband. I'll tack on my part at the end. Does that sound okay?"

"Sure," I said.

The terrain had finally leveled out. We were on top of the mountain now. We entered the large loop that fronted the house and drove around it counterclockwise before coming to a stop near the main entrance.

It was a beautiful home, though I couldn't begin to appreciate the details. I was too focused on Plottner, who invited us inside with breezy hospitality.

The very sight of him brought yet another wave of nausea. But I was determined to play this straight, so as not to tip off Plottner as to the real reason for our visit.

"Where's Lee?" I asked, looking around for Plottner's massive slab of a bodyguard.

"He's running an errand," Plottner said. "Come on in."

He led us into a grand living room that was too big for the amount of furniture in it. Plottner invited us to take a seat, and we did so.

"Can I offer you anything to eat or drink?" he asked. "I've got a chef who can whip up just about anything and the bar is fully stocked. I know the detective here is on duty, but I'm betting you could use something, Mrs. Bronik. A glass of wine, perhaps? Something stronger?"

At the moment, I would have rather drunk bleach, but I simply said, "No, thank you."

"Very well," Plottner said. "So, what can I do for you?"

I launched into a series of questions about the potential conditions of my husband's employment, as if I was seriously considering the possibility. It wasn't difficult to feign engagement in the answers—for all I knew, this would end up being our only option.

At every turn, Plottner had answers. Plottner Investments had an HR person who would tackle this concern, an IT person who could handle that one, a staff counsel who could set me at ease about another thing. Matt would sign a contract. Yes, it could be for multiple years, to give him some more stability. Yes, it was possible Matt could stay in Hanover, if that proved to be a sticking point, as long as he was willing to visit New York now and then. Yes, Plottner Investments had generous 401(k) matching and a no-deductible health care plan.

Once I had run through everything that came to mind, Plottner took one more chance to reassure me.

"I understand you have concerns, but I think Matt will find I'm a very reasonable man to work for," he said. "My management philosophy is pretty straightforward. It comes from my father, who got it from his father, so it's time tested: You get good people, then you treat them well. That's it. I'm sure if anything else comes up, we can work it out."

I offered a polite smile and said, "Thank you."

"We've got a deal, then?"

"I'm still thinking things through."

"Yes, yes, of course," he said. "Perhaps Sheena will come through. I take it she's at the lab, working hard?"

He said it innocently enough, like he expected nothing else. I looked toward Emmett, unsure of how to answer.

"Actually, we're not sure where she is," Emmett said cautiously.

Plottner's forehead wrinkled. "Oh?"

"She ran off a little while ago," Emmett said noncommittally.

"Well, I'm sure she'll be back," Plottner said, as if it were that simple. "You know these millennials. I have a few working for me and it's just drama, drama, drama, all the time. If it's not one thing, it's something else."

"Right, of course," Emmett said. Then he added, like it was an afterthought: "Oh, and as long as we're here, I was hoping you could clear up something pertaining to you that my Crime Scene Unit tripped across in Professor Bronik's lab."

Plottner's face immediately spread into a wide smile.

"Uh-oh. I don't need my lawyer, do I?"

Like this was all a joke.

Because wasn't that how the man who was gifted millions and turned it into billions thought of everything? Like the world was one big joke, and he might or might not let the little people in on it?

Whatever the punch line was in Plottner's mind, Emmett didn't bite. He just plowed ahead: "They found your fingerprint on the door handle to the refrigerator that holds the virus samples."

I watched Plottner's response intently. The smile dimmed perhaps a shade and a half.

"Well, isn't that something? I would have thought that'd be long gone by now," he said. "That must be from the day I visited Professor Bronik's lab."

"You haven't been back since?" Emmett asked.

"No. There was nothing there I really needed to see again."

"How did your fingerprint wind up on the door? I can't imagine that's something most visitors wind up touching."

"Professor Bronik was carrying a tray with both hands. He asked me to open the door for him so I—"

Plottner pantomimed opening a refrigerator.

"Weren't you wearing gloves?" Emmett asked. "Professor Bronik's lab is biosafety level two. I thought everyone had to wear gloves."

Plottner held up both hands and wiggled his fingers. "I'm allergic to latex. It's the strangest thing. Disposable lab gloves make me break out into a rash. I even have to use cloth bandages. Professor Bronik said the virus he was working with wasn't dangerous to people, and since I wasn't going to be touching anything vital it was no big deal to skip the gloves."

The fingerprint, smoothly explained.

Other than the way his smile had momentarily lost a small amount of luster, there hadn't been a hitch in his performance. I was sure it would have slithered through any lie detector without any deception indicated.

So why didn't I believe him?

Was it his smug, self-satisfied air?

Or that Sheena's disappearance benefited him, because it meant Matt's best chance of rescue was gone too?

Or because I didn't believe *anything* he had to say?

Emmett stood. "Thank you. Glad we cleared that up."

"My pleasure," Plottner said, also standing. "You're both welcome to stay here for the evening, if you like. It can get a little hairy going back down that mountain in the dark. We have everything you might need—toiletries, pajamas."

"No, thank you," I said, glancing at the time. "It's almost eight. I need to be getting home. I have a . . . a son."

I faltered, not wanting to give away what felt like personal information to this man I didn't trust. Which made no sense. Plottner surely knew we had a child. It was in Matt's bio.

"Absolutely," Plottner said. "Bedtime calls."

He escorted us back to the foyer.

"If you have any other questions—about the job offer, about the fingerprint, about anything—please don't hesitate to reach out," he said. "And to give you one less thing to worry about: Theresa has already been in touch with the bank. That five million dollars will be here first thing in the morning. Just in case."

Right. Just in case.

He had this enigmatic look on his face. It was not quite a grin—that would have been inappropriate. But maybe it wasn't as somber as it should have been.

After he bid us farewell, and once the front door had closed behind me, I started whispering furiously to Emmett. "He's lying about the fingerprint. It has to be more recent."

"What makes you say that?"

"There's no way that print would have lasted that long. A whole month? No way. Matt used that refrigerator almost every day. So did Sheena. One of them would have rubbed it off."

"Unless they always wore gloves," Emmett pointed out. "Fingerprints are made by the natural oils in the skin. If there were no other oils from anyone else's skin to disturb it, it might have stayed. Or he might have touched the handle in a different place than your husband and Sheena normally did."

"So you believe him?"

"I'm not saying I do or don't. I'm just pointing out the possibilities." We climbed back into Emmett's car.

"I just think this whole thing is so convenient for him," Brigid said. "The kidnappers have only been communicating with him all along. They're asking for an amount of money that we could never come up with. And then he looks like the good guy by coming up with the reward. In the end, he gets what he's wanted all along, which is Matt to come and work for him."

Emmett didn't answer. He just started driving.

CHAPTER 51

Emmett concentrated on the switchbacks as they wound back down the mountain.

Next to him, Brigid had settled into a quiet stew. She obviously suspected Plottner was more than just a nice rich guy who was being liberal with his checkbook, but was there really any evidence?

The fingerprint was inconclusive. It's not like the thing came with a time stamp.

Beyond that? It was interesting that the ransom demand had come to Plottner directly, but it was by no means incriminating. After all, Plottner was the one who had brought money into the picture when he first offered the reward.

They were at the bottom of the mountain, back on a state road headed toward Hanover, when Brigid's phone rang.

She looked at the screen and announced, "Sorry. It's home. I have to take this."

"No problem," Emmett said.

"Hello? . . . Hey, buddy!"

Thus began a conversation between Brigid and her son, then between Brigid and her sister, Aimee.

When the call was over, Brigid stuffed her phone back in her pocket. "Sorry about that."

"No problem," Emmett said. "Your sister seems like a handy woman to have around."

"Oh God, she's a lifesaver. She's beyond my best friend. We have this thing we say to each other. She tells me she'd take a bullet for me, and I tell her I'd walk through fire for her. But I seriously would. I don't know what I'd do without her."

"What does she do when she's not taking bullets for you?" Emmett asked.

"She's a forensic accountant and pretty much the best aunt in recorded history. Morgan adores her. She doesn't have any kids of her own, which is too bad. She would have been a terrific mom. But I guess it's for the best. The guy she married seemed great except that he was a lying sociopath. He traveled a lot for work, and it turned out he cheated on her constantly. But she didn't catch him at it until about two months *after* the wedding. Then he tried to claim he was a sex addict."

Emmett made a noise that was somewhere between a groan and a grunt. He never bought into the nonsense that men were somehow incapable of monogamy, that they had an imperative to spread their seed.

Whatever the biology was, it had nothing to do with that.

It was about your word.

If you made a promise to someone, you kept it.

Brigid continued: "Oh, my thoughts exactly. She actually caught the jerk because he—"

She was interrupted by Emmett's phone ringing. It was from 603 area, which was of course New Hampshire, and 643 exchange, which was Hanover; but, otherwise, he didn't recognize it.

He accepted the call and said, "Webster here."

"Yes, Detective, this is Professor David Dafashy."

His refined, almost-English accent poured through the car's speakers, which were connected to the phone via Bluetooth.

"What can I do for you, Dr. Dafashy?"

"Sheena Aiyagari is a fraud," he blurted.

"Come again?"

"She has a boyfriend," Dafashy said.

"What does that have to do with anything?"

"Are you really that thick? Don't you get it? She's lying. She tells everyone she has a fiancé in India and the whole time, she's polishing some other guy's knob. Some Tuck student named Scott Sugden."

"How do you know?"

"Leonie Descheun called me and told me. She was worried why the police were asking about me and so she checked in on me, because we have a *professionally. Cordial. Relationship.* She knows all about Sheena and her little games. They used to be quite close until Leonie learned what Sheena was really about. Then Leonie distanced herself. She said she didn't want to be friends with someone who could be so mendacious. I'm seriously thinking about flying Leonie back over so she can testify at the hearing. That ought to clear my name."

Emmett took a deep breath. "How so?"

"Because Sheena is lying! She's cheating on her fiancé."

"Even if that's true, cheating on your fiancé doesn't insulate you from being sexually harassed. That's like saying someone who shoplifted could never have her purse stolen. One has nothing to do with the other."

"Oh, right. Of course you would choose to see her side of it."

Emmett didn't have the brainpower to guess at what other game Dafashy might be playing here.

"There are no sides to this. A man has been kidnapped. The only side that matters is getting him back."

"And yet you waste your time investigating me when you really ought to be investigating her," Dafashy spat. "This is police malpractice. Your conduct is opprobrious. Opprobrious!"

"Sir, I'm merely—"

"Good *night*, sir!" Dafashy spat, then hung up.

Emmett looked over at Brigid, who seemed to have heard enough of the words that she was as mystified by the call as he was.

"That was strange," she said.

"I know," Emmett said. "I think I liked it better when he was invoking his right to counsel."

CHAPTER 52

After the weird phone call from David Dafashy—and the spurt of adrenaline it gave me—I could feel myself crashing as Emmett drove me home and dropped me off.

His final words were about getting some rest, because tomorrow would be a big day.

As I trudged up the front steps to the house, the weariness seemed to have invaded every part of my being.

My feet throbbed. My knees felt like someone had replaced the cartilage with glass shards. My back ached. My stomach was a pit of acid, my head a repository for mud.

Sleep deprivation. It was like being simultaneously drunk and hungover.

It was closing in on nine o'clock. I hadn't truly slept for nearly forty hours, since the previous morning. Before long, my body wasn't going to give me much choice. Every part of it was shutting down.

I barely even glanced at my CRV, which was sitting in the driveway, having been delivered just as Plottner promised. I just climbed the front steps. It took most of my concentration to get the house key in the lock, turn it, shove open the front door, which seemed to have doubled in weight since I last opened it.

The first thing I saw, resting on the small table by the door that served as a crash pad for mail and other objects entering the house, was the key to my Honda. I wondered how it had even gotten there.

Then my attention was diverted to Aimee, who came in from the kitchen.

"I put him down maybe fifteen minutes ago," she whispered. "I told him you'd kiss him good night when you got home."

"How's he doing?"

"He's fine. I think he's more worried about you than Matt. I told him Daddy would be back tomorrow and Mommy would be better once Daddy was home."

That was sure true.

I let out a long breath and said, "Thanks, Aim."

Aimee closed in, giving me the hug she knew I badly needed.

"We're going to be okay," she said. "Now go kiss your son and then let's call it a night. I'm beat."

I turned toward the stairs and trod up them, one deliberate step at a time. Morgan's door was the first on the left. I eased into the lightless room, picking my way across the minefield of LEGOs, cars, games, and stuffed animals—the detritus of prepubescence, which I had navigated in the dark many times before.

When I reached the bed, I didn't even see Morgan at first. It took a few seconds to pick out the small blond head, bobbing in the sea of covers.

I needed another moment to register the faint sound of his breathing, slow and tranquil. Morgan had been born a few weeks premature, just enough that his lungs weren't quite fully cooked. It required a brief stay in the neonatal intensive care unit, which was mostly terrifying for the front-row seat it gave me to all the things that *could* have gone wrong with my pregnancy—those babies born at twenty-seven or twenty-nine weeks gestation, hooked to ventilators, their grip on life as fragile as their tiny bodies.

After that, I promised myself I'd never, ever take Morgan's breathing for granted.

I sat on the bed. I should have just leaned over, given him a quick peck on the head, and gone off to my own room.

But I couldn't help myself. Sometimes the maternal drive felt less like a suggestion and more like a command. I stretched out beside Morgan, draped an arm over him, and snuggled as close as I could.

"Hey, my baby," I cooed, wondering if he would wake up and talk to me, hoping he would.

But his breathing was steady, somnolent.

I let myself melt into the bed, feeling its softness, sure that sleep would drag me down any moment. Truly, other than after childbirth, I had never been more exhausted.

And then . . .

My knees.

My back.

My stomach.

My head.

The very things that made being awake so unpleasant were now, cruelly, making sleep impossible. A dull pain radiated from my spinal cord down my arm. My hip barked at me.

Maybe if I readjusted my position, I'd be better. But I didn't want to disturb Morgan.

Once my brain realized the other parts weren't going to cooperate with its plan to sleep, it fired back to life and started throwing a succession of images at me. David Dafashy, sipping coffee. Sean Plottner, his enigmatic not-quite-smile. Sheena Aiyagari, crying.

I tried to ward them off, to think about the bed, or Morgan's breathing, or something not related to the forty hours since I last slept soundly, but the images kept coming.

Beppe Valentino, glancing around suspiciously.

The virus. Just sitting in those vials.

Matt. His bloodstained T-shirt.

His desperate, desperate countenance.

Sleep was hopeless. Really, I think I was gathering my resolve.

To do what I suddenly knew needed to be done.

Maybe it wouldn't work. Maybe it was reckless. By that point, I cared so little about my own well-being it didn't even matter.

Gingerly, so gingerly, I propped myself up, then slid my feet onto the floor and stood.

Morgan didn't move.

So far, so good.

I retraced my footsteps across the minefield to the door, then opened it into the landing at the top of the stairs. There was no light coming from Aimee's room.

Also good.

I slid into my bedroom, walked to Matt's nightstand, turned on his light, and pulled open the drawer.

In a small bowl, Matt kept a spare set of keys, which I pocketed.

There was also a pair of nail clippers. Thinking ahead, I took those too. Then I turned off the light.

I was soon creeping back down the stairs, into the living room. I grabbed the keys to the Honda off the crash pad table on my way out the door. Before long, I was on my way.

Back toward Wilder Hall.

When I arrived, Steve Dahan was still in his safety and security car. He got out to greet me as I pulled up.

I had been practicing this in my mind.

"I left something inside earlier by mistake," I said. "I'll be right back."

I had a full backstory prepared—about how my purse had spilled, about how it contained vital medicine for Morgan that must have rolled out. And now I needed to retrieve it, lest Morgan suffer consequences.

But Dahan just gave me a friendly grin and said "Okay" before hastily retreating to the warmth of his car.

Once I was inside, my next hurdle was the Crime Scene Unit. I had no idea how I was going to finesse them.

But it turned out I didn't need to. I got to the lab and used Matt's spare key to open the door. The lab was empty. The Crime Scene Unit was gone.

The lights came on automatically as I entered. Wasting no time, I crossed the room to the refrigerator. I pulled open the door, keeping my fingers in my sleeve so I wouldn't leave fingerprints, then selected one of the vials.

It was filled with a clear liquid. I set it down, still stoppered, on the table.

Then I pulled the nail clippers out of my pocket and snipped a piece of my inner forearm, emitting a quick high-pitched yelp as the blades sliced my skin.

A dapple of blood pooled on my arm. I cleaned it away, exposing the tiny half-moon gash I had created. Without hesitation, I pulled the stopper off the small vial and tilted its lip toward the open wound.

The liquid poured readily. Then I rubbed some into the cut, just to be sure.

Sheena's powers had started to show themselves after she had accidentally infected herself.

My infection wasn't going to be an accident. Was it reckless? Maybe. But Sheena had managed to have a fit and come out of it without any medical intervention whatsoever. So had Matt, assuming that the kidnappers didn't administer any medicine after they carried him out of Wilder.

I just hoped that by giving the virus direct access to my bloodstream, I would shorten the incubation period.

And then?

Two entangled brains had to be better than one.

CHAPTER 53

Emmett had managed to make it to the Tuck Inn and get his shoes off before collapsing on the bed.

That's where he still was a half hour later, watching the Celtics dismantle the Nets through closed eyelids, when he was startled out of sleep by a phone call.

It was the dispatcher.

"Hey, we got a hit on that Subaru Outback you were looking for," she told him.

"Where?"

"Parked in the driveway of the owner's house. Hanover Police were nearby on a domestic call. After they got that situation settled, one of them saw the Subaru and remembered the BOLO. Anyhow, I got him on the other line, waiting for further instructions. The BOLO said to call you first."

"Ask them to keep an eye on the Subaru and the house. If anyone comes out or tries to go anywhere, have them pulled aside for questioning. I'll be there in ten minutes."

The dispatch finished the call with, "You got it."

Emmett laced up his shoes, then fought frigid blasts of wind on his way to his car. Before long, he was rolling past two Hanover squad cars idling on the street.

He parked, then convened on the sidewalk just down from Beppe Valentino's place with two officers. One had a beard and an erect carriage. He introduced himself as Officer Harry Burnham. The other, Officer Danny Alvord, had a bald, perfectly round head.

Both seemed calm and capable and looked to be in their late twenties or early thirties.

"That's your BOLO vehicle," Burnham said, nodding toward Valentino's driveway. "We've been keeping an eye on the car and the house. There's been no movement."

Emmett quickly apprised them of the situation: That Beppe Valentino was anything from a harmless professor to an armed hostage taker. And they had to be prepared for either.

They agreed Emmett and Burnham would approach with caution from the front while Alvord would swing around back; and while no one would have weapons drawn, all would make sure the thumb releases on their holsters were open.

Once they had given Alvord time to get in place, Emmett and Burnham moved up the front walkway. As they approached the door, a floodlight clicked on.

Probably a motion sensor. But Emmett felt the unease of knowing anyone inside could now easily see him, and had him framed for an easy shot if they so desired.

He stepped up his pace, took the five front steps in three strides, and rang the doorbell.

A light turned on upstairs.

Burnham, just behind and to the left, had his hands resting on his belt in a way that was somewhat less than casual.

Finally, the door was opened by Beppe, wrapped in a bathrobe, his hair askew.

"Hello, Detective," he said. "What's going on?"

"Is Sheena here?"

"No. Why would she be?"

"She left Wilder with you, didn't she?"

"Well, yes. But I took her to Dick's House."

"Dick's House?" Emmett said.

"Sorry. The student infirmary. I'm sorry, what's this all about?"

"Sheena's not answering her phone. Neither were you."

"Oh, sorry. My battery was running low. It must have switched off. I—"

"Why did you take Sheena to the infirmary?" Emmett asked.

"She came into my office earlier, very upset. Hysterical, really. She was having . . . I guess you could call it a breakdown. She was concerned that these feelings of hers seemed to have gone away and that therefore anything that happened to Matt would be her fault. I tried to tell her that was ridiculous, but she was . . . beyond being reasoned with. She kept saying, 'I didn't ask for this. I didn't want this. Why is this happening to me?' We agreed it was best I take her to Dick's House."

"So you just dropped her off and left her?" Emmett asked, unable to keep the accusatory tone out of his voice.

"Well, I walked her in. She had calmed down some by then. She said she had texted a friend who would be meeting her there and that she would be fine. She was already getting checked in at the front desk and she insisted I didn't need to wait for her. And, I have to admit, I was hungry and tired by that point. I thought she was in good hands. So, yes, I left."

"Did she say who the friend was?"

"No. Just that it was a friend."

Emmett wondered if the friend was Scott Sugden, the Tuck student. Emmett was reasonably certain Dafashy really had gotten a phone call from Leonie. He wouldn't lie about that when he knew the police had already spoken with Leonie and might speak to her again. Therefore, it stood to reason Sheena probably did have a boyfriend—or at least a male friend.

"And you haven't seen or heard from Sheena since then?"

"No. But I'm sure she's just resting at Dick's House," Beppe said. "She's probably not answering her phone because they either made her turn it off or she's asleep. If you call over there, I bet they'll connect you to her."

Emmett bid good night to Beppe, then dismissed Officers Burnham and Alvord, thanking them for their time.

Fatigue was drawing Emmett back toward his bed at the Tuck Inn.

But hard experience had taught him there was no such thing as being too sure of something. And he knew he would sleep a lot better if he could confirm that Sheena was, in fact, in the care of Dick's House.

He looked up the number for the Dartmouth student infirmary and dialed it.

The woman who answered said she couldn't give out information over the phone. HIPAA regulations didn't apply to members of law enforcement who reasonably believed there may have been a threat to the health or safety of the patient involved. But the woman needed to confirm that Emmett was, in fact, a sworn officer and not just some random person claiming to be a state police detective.

That meant he needed to present himself—and, more importantly, his badge—if he wanted to know anything.

Emmett made the short trip across campus to Dick's House, where the front desk was empty. After a short wait, a nurse in brightly patterned scrubs appeared, looking substantially fresher than he felt. He introduced himself.

"Hello, Detective," she said. "We spoke on the phone. Can I just see some ID, please?"

Emmett pulled out his badge, which she inspected quickly.

"Thank you," she said, sitting down at the desk. "Now which patient were you inquiring about?"

"Sheena Aiyagari," Emmett said.

From under the desk, the woman slid out a keyboard, typed in the name, then pursed her lips.

"Can you spell the last name, please?" she asked.

Emmett did.

"That's what I typed. And the first name is Sheena, s-h-e-e-n-a?"

"That's right."

"I'm sorry, we have no record of Sheena Aiyagari receiving treatment here this evening."

"Are you sure?"

"Yes. According to this, Ms. Aiyagari was here a year ago February for treatment of . . . it looks like strep throat. She hasn't been back since."

"Is it possible she's back there somewhere but just hasn't been entered into the computer?" Emmett asked. "Sheena is South Asian, Indian, whatever you're supposed to call it. She's about five feet tall. She has a nasty bruise under her eye."

"I haven't seen anyone like that all night."

Emmett just stared at her, stumped. Had Beppe lied about walking Sheena in? Did he think Emmett wouldn't check his story?

Unless there was some kind of misunderstanding, and she really had been at Dick's House.

"Is it possible she was treated and released?" Emmett asked.

"No. That would be in the computer."

The nurse was clearly trying hard to be helpful. It was the computer that wasn't cooperating. One more reason Emmett preferred humans.

"When did you start working this evening?" he asked.

"My shift began at eight."

Which meant she wasn't there during the time when Beppe claimed to have dropped off Sheena.

"Who would have been here around seven or seven fifteen?"

"Donna Wolford."

"Anyone who came in here would have had to go through Donna?"

"That's right."

"Do you have a number for her?"

The woman hesitated, unsure whether she should hand over a colleague's number to a detective. And Emmett had no way of forcing her, other than pleading. So, in an earnest voice, he said, "Please. Ms. Aiyagari may be in serious danger."

The nurse pursed her lips again, then said, "I'll call her for you."

She pulled out her cell phone, tapped it a few times, then brought it to her ear. She held it there, waiting.

Then, after what seemed like roughly five rings, she left a message: "Hey, Donna, it's Sherry. I have a state police detective here who wants to talk to you. Would you mind giving him a call as soon as you get this? His name is Emmett Webster and his number is . . ."

She looked up at Emmett expectantly. He recited his number and added, "Please tell her to call me as soon as she gets this."

The nurse repeated both the digits and the request, then thanked Donna and hung up.

"I'm sorry," the nurse said. "You're just going to have to wait to hear from her."

Emmett glanced at his watch. It was now 10:03. It was entirely possible Donna Wolford, who got off her shift at eight, was now in bed, asleep.

And so were any answers she might have been able to provide.

CHAPTER 54

It was 4:31 a.m. when Sean Plottner's eyes opened for the first time. He had set no alarm. He hadn't needed one in years.

He might have lain there, tried to go back to sleep, but he knew there was no point. He could already feel his heart thumping in his chest, urging him awake.

If you had told twenty-one-year-old Sean Plottner that forty-six-year-old Sean Plottner couldn't sleep past five o'clock on a dare, the youngster probably would have gagged on the joint he was smoking.

Now? It was simply his routine. While most of the East Coast was still asleep, he typically read three newspapers—*Wall Street Journal, New York Times, Washington Post*—then dissected what had been happening with the markets in Asia and Europe.

So it wasn't unusual for him to immediately turn to the iPad on his nightstand before he even turned on a light.

What was unusual was that he didn't tap on any of the aforementioned publications or stock-checking apps.

He went to Facebook instead.

What he found was more exciting than any development in the Nikkei index.

Michael Dillman had finally answered:

"First, you will take a picture of the cash and send it to me. Then I will tell you how we proceed. The exchange will take place at nine o'clock. I'm moving up the deadline."

Plottner stared at the message. A muscle in his jaw flexed involuntarily. There were few things he liked less than people changing the parameters of a deal that had already been made.

He started typing:

"That's not possible. The money hasn't arrived yet. I told you I'd get it first thing in the morning. That's 9 a.m. I can't get it here any faster."

He hit send. Almost immediately, the dots started dancing.

Apparently, Michael Dillman was also an early riser.

"You are a rich man. Make it happen. Picture by 8 a.m. Exchange at 9."

Ordinarily, Plottner would never let someone dictate terms like this.

He would tolerate it this time.

What choice did he have?

"I'll do my best," he typed back.

If he didn't know any better, he'd think Michael Dillman was trying to scuttle the deal.

He took a screenshot of the exchange, sent it to his lawyer. Then he pulled on a bathrobe, walked down the hall to Theresa's door, and tapped on it.

She answered fully dressed but for her shoes, having already showered and dried her hair. She had made it a habit to wake even earlier than her boss. It was the only way she could guarantee at least a modicum of time to herself before the requests began.

"Yes?" she asked.

"Remember what you said about calling the bank first so that I could come in later and apply the pressure?"

"Yes."

"It's later."

CHAPTER 55

Emmett was making pancakes with Wanda.

It felt like a Sunday morning, but he wasn't totally sure about that. He just knew he wasn't in a hurry, and he smelled coffee, and that more than likely meant it was Sunday.

Emmett flicked water on the griddle, heard the sizzle that told him it was hot enough for the batter.

And wasn't it the damnedest thing. You'd think if his subconscious was doing him the favor of giving him a dream that involved Wanda, it also would have had them doing something a little more exciting. Making love, maybe.

But, no, they were making pancakes.

Still, it was such a vivid dream. She was chiding him about mixing the dry ingredients a little more thoroughly before he poured in the wet stuff.

And then the phone rang.

Not the dream phone. The real phone. It took another ring before Emmett realized it.

On the third ring, Emmett opened his eyes. He was at the Tuck Inn. He barely remembered driving back there the previous night. He looked down and discovered he had fallen asleep in his clothes again.

He hadn't even woken up in the middle of the night to pee. For a man in his midfifties, that was the sign of one hell of a hard night's sleep.

After the fourth ring, he glanced at the clock—6:06 a.m.—then located his phone on the nightstand and answered it.

"Webster here," he said groggily, propping himself up on an elbow.

"Detective Webster, this is Donna Wolford from Dartmouth. I got a message to call you as soon as possible?"

She spoke in a seen-it-all, done-it-all, matter-of-fact voice.

"Yes, Ms. Wolford. Thank you. I'm told you were working the front desk at Dick's House around seven last night?"

"That's right."

Emmett asked if she had seen a young woman who fit Sheena's description.

"Oh, yes. I was wondering if I might hear about her. She came in, probably about seven fifteen or so."

"Did she have anyone with her?"

"Yes. It was an older gentleman. I don't know his name, but I've seen his picture in *Dartmouth Life*."

"Could it be Beppe Valentino, the physics professor?"

"Yes, that sounds right. The young woman told him he could leave and he did."

So Beppe's story checked out.

"What happened next?" Emmett said.

"Well, I asked the young lady for her name and ID so I could get her checked in. And she said she just needed to sit down for a little while. I asked her if she needed anything, maybe a cold pack for the bruise under her eye. And she said no thank you, she was just going to sit for a little while."

"And you let her?"

"It wasn't a question of let her. That's what she was set on doing. She had obviously been crying. And she had that bruise. I thought maybe her boyfriend had hit her, or . . . well, I was just guessing, obviously. But a lot of times, with girls like that, you need to take it slow. You'll be able to do a lot more good for them later if you don't jump all over them at the start."

"Right, of course."

"I had some kids in back I needed to check on. I asked again if she needed anything and she said no. I told her I'd be right back and she said thank you. I was gone five minutes, maybe ten at most, but I really think it was more like five. And by the time I got back she was gone."

Emmett sat up a little straighter. "Gone?"

"Yes, sir."

"Did you . . . try to look for her, or—"

"No. We don't treat people unless they want to be treated. I have enough to do without chasing after students. They're too fast for me anyway."

"I understand. I'm just trying to figure out whether she was alone when she left."

"Couldn't tell you. I was in back."

"But would you have known if someone else came into Dick's House while you were in back? Is there some kind of bell that rings when the door opens?"

He was thinking back to his visit to Dick's House, when the woman in the patterned scrubs had appeared so quickly, like she had known someone had entered.

"Oh, well, yes. There's a chime that sounds. And now that you ask, I did hear that chime. Twice, actually. I thought I would come back in and find two more patients. But instead the waiting room was empty. So I guess it's possible she left with someone, yes."

Right. The first chime would have been someone coming in. The second chime was Sheena leaving with that person.

But again he found himself asking: Voluntarily? Or by force?

"Do you have any security cameras in the waiting room?" he asked.

"Oh, goodness no. Would you want a camera staring you in the face when you went somewhere for a treatment that's supposed to be confidential?"

"I understand. So you have no way of knowing who this young woman might have left with?"

"No, sir. Sorry."

Emmett asked the woman whether she had any other recollections about Sheena, but nothing seemed germane. He thanked her, then ended the call.

He was now imagining what might have happened: Someone was watching over Wilder, knowing that Sheena had gone in there, waiting for her to come out. That someone followed Beppe's car to Dick's House, then saw Beppe walk out. The person moved in, got lucky to find Sheena alone in the waiting room, and removed her by force.

The more benign possibility was that Scott Sugden, assuming that's who Sheena had been texting, had arrived and taken Sheena somewhere. Was Sheena not at Dick's House because she was holed up with Scott?

It was understandable, given the ordeal of the past two days, that she'd want some time with her perhaps-boyfriend. But then why hadn't she been answering her phone or texts? Had she simply fallen into a deep, exhausted sleep, like Emmett?

Time to find out. With effort, he swung his feet down to the floor and propelled himself toward the bathroom.

The address the DMV had on file for Scott Sugden was on West Street, just down the hill from the main Dartmouth campus, a short walk from the Tuck School.

Emmett pulled up to the curb in front of a ramshackle structure that looked like it could house seven or eight people, if they were young, single, and unpicky. It wasn't quite quarter of seven. There was no sign of movement inside.

There was also no doorbell. Emmett opened a rickety wooden screen door that didn't have a lot of Hanover winters left in it and knocked on another wooden door that wasn't much further behind on its journey to ruination.

Unsurprisingly, nothing much happened in response.

A second barrage on the door finally brought forth an unshaven, unhappy twentysomething white guy in a T-shirt, boxer shorts, and socks.

"Yeah?" he said, opening the door, which hadn't been locked.

"I'm with the state police. I'm looking for Scott Sugden. Have you seen him?"

"Umm, Scott? No. Not since yesterday morning."

"Do you know where he is?"

"Beats me, man. We don't exactly take attendance around here, you know?"

"Can I come in and have a look?"

The guy glanced over his shoulder, into the kitchen behind him.

"I'm not with narcotics," Emmett added. "I don't have time to make trouble over anyone leaving half a blunt on the table."

"No, we don't have anything like that," the guy said. "It's just a little messy."

"I'm not worried," Emmett assured him.

The guy led Emmett through the kitchen, where the only signs of intoxicating agents were a few empty cans of Milwaukee's Best.

"Is Scott in trouble or something?" the guy asked.

"No. Nothing like that."

They climbed the stairs to a hallway. The guy stopped at the second door on the right and tapped on it softly.

"Scott, you in there, man?"

There was no answer. He rapped his knuckles on the door a few more times.

"Scott," he said.

He waited another five seconds, then turned to Emmett.

"Sorry, man. No one home."

"Would you mind if I opened the door?" Emmett asked.

The guy's left cheek dimpled, pulling his face into a look of contemplation.

Then he tapped the door again and said, "Scott, we're coming in."

He turned the knob. The door opened with a creak into a small room whose main feature was a queen-size bed, which was empty but for a tangle of sheets.

"Is it unusual that he wouldn't sleep here?" Emmett asked.

"Couldn't tell you. It's pretty loose around here. People kind of come and go."

"Do you know if he has a girlfriend?"

"Oh, I have no clue."

"Have you ever seen him with a woman named Sheena Aiyagari?"

This seemed to spark recognition. "Uh, yeah, hot little Indian chick?"

Emmett wished he had a picture of Sheena so he could confirm it with a little more precision, but he supposed that description would have to do.

"Yes, that's her."

"Yeah, she hangs out here sometimes. But I don't know if they're dating or what."

Again, it only mattered so much. Whether or not Sheena was cheating on her fiancé didn't exempt her from being sexually harassed by an older professor.

"Do you mind?" Emmett asked, then stepped past the guy into the room.

There was a pile of clothes in one corner, but nothing else on the floor. The only furniture was a dresser and a bowl-shaped chair, both of which were serving as repositories for a disorganized collection of books.

Emmett walked to the closet. The space above and below the clothing was stuffed full—shoes, tennis rackets, golf clubs, boxes, bags, and so on. Nothing struck Emmett as being out of the ordinary for a Dartmouth grad student living in tight quarters.

He was in the midst of closing the closet door when, at the last moment, one word on one of the boxes jumped out and caught his attention.

A word he wasn't expecting to see in some country-club kid's closet.

WINCHESTER.

As in the firearms company.

Emmett reopened the door. Sure enough, in the upper-left-hand corner, sitting atop a milk carton filled with toiletry items, there was a box of nine-millimeter ammunition.

He blinked once, twice, puzzling over it. How many MBA students owned firearms?

"Is Scott ex-military?" Emmett asked.

"Scott? No. He's, like, ex-Yale."

"Do you know if he likes to target shoot?"

"Uhh . . . maybe? I don't know. I go to Thayer"—the engineering school—"so it's not like we hang out a ton, you know?"

Emmett brought down the box, which had a Walmart receipt stuffed in it. He studied the slip until he reached the time stamp. The bullets had been bought at 8:43 p.m. the previous evening.

This wasn't for target shooting. This was a guy trying to protect his terrified friend/girlfriend. She had texted him, he came to her rescue at Dick's House, and then one of them got the idea that they should get bullets for Scott's gun.

Emmett opened the box, which held fifty rounds, of which roughly a third were now missing.

He was now imagining this young man, loading a magazine, stuffing a few extras in his pockets, and saving the receipt, because he planned to put the unused ammo back in the box and return it when she—and this entire situation—calmed down.

But if that was the case, where were they now? Holed up at a hotel? With Sheena having either turned off her phone or unable to charge it for some reason?

Emmett put the box back, then turned to the guy.

"Do you have a number for Scott?" Emmett asked.

"You sure he's not in trouble?" the guy asked, having seen the box of ammo.

"He may be in trouble," Emmett said. "But not with me. I'm really just looking for Sheena, and I think she might be with him."

"Okay, hang on, I got a number for him in my phone."

The guy thumped down the stairs, to a room in the back of the first floor. Emmett followed and was soon plugging the number into his phone, thanking the guy for his help, and walking back outside.

There, he called Scott Sugden's number.

It didn't even ring once.

Just went straight to voice mail.

CHAPTER 56

My eyelids opened four minutes before my bed was set to start shaking.

Ordinarily, it was an act of will not to give in to the temptation of hitting the snooze button a few times.

I had no such issues now. That I slept at all was some combination of a miracle and a testament to the power of exhaustion. Already, the anxiety was coursing through me.

Sitting up, I turned on the light and studied the small cut on my forearm. I hadn't bandaged it, reasoning—with absolutely no scientific basis whatsoever—that this might allow any of the virus still living on my skin better access to my bloodstream.

I held still for a moment, trying to get in tune with whatever quantum forces might now be at work in my brain.

Had anything happened overnight? Would I recognize if it had?

How do you know? I remembered Detective Webster asking Sheena.

How do you know you're standing here? she had replied.

Was the feeling really that stark? I wished I could ask Sheena what, precisely, she had experienced. Was it a delicate fluttering in the brain or more like a headache? Would it develop slowly or come on suddenly?

I still wondered if I needed to have a full fit first. Wasn't it possible the virus was already having some effect? Once a virus got into your body, it began replicating immediately. Even if it needed time to reach critical mass, it was still in there.

That's what made the flu so pernicious. It was how one first grader could wipe out half his class, even though his parents kept him home: He had been spreading the germ before he was aware he had symptoms. By the time he sprouted a fever, the damage was already done.

I got to my feet, slipped in my hearing aids, walked into the bathroom, and began going through the motions of brushing my teeth when . . .

Yes. There was something there. I was sure of it. I pivoted out back into the hallway, back toward the bedroom and . . .

Again, there it was. I felt . . . *something*.

And didn't that make sense? Up until two nights ago, Matt spent at least eight hours a day in that bedroom. There had to be some trace of the virus left behind, which the virus in me was now reacting to. I hadn't felt it when I was just lying in bed, but once I separated from it just a little, I could feel the difference when I neared it again.

If I could detect something that slight, was it possible I could now locate Matt?

Maybe I just needed to give myself the chance.

And, really, no time like now.

I heard Aimee stirring. Morgan was still asleep, so I tiptoed over to my sister's room and softly tapped the door.

She opened it.

"Hey, I think I need to go out for a little bit," I said.

"Like you went out last night?" Aimee asked, raising an eyebrow.

"Something like that. You okay getting Morgan off to school? The bus comes at—"

"Just go," Aimee said.

I didn't wait for another word. I dressed hurriedly and was soon back in the CRV, even though I didn't know where to point it.

The morning was still, cloudy, like it might snow again. I relaxed, trying to get back in touch with the feeling of being entangled—on an atomic level—with Matt, the man I was entangled with in so many other ways already.

I thought about him, about our lives together. A memory came back. It was from just before our wedding, when we were taking a ballroom dance class so we wouldn't make complete fools of ourselves during our first dance.

With my tendency toward overanalysis, I had never been much of a dancer. Matt danced like a mathematical genius, which is to say poorly.

The teacher, a self-assured older woman with an air of wisdom about her, noticed us struggling. She sidled over to me and said, "Don't worry about the steps so much. Just think about how much that man right there adores you."

Then she closed in and whispered, "You're a lucky girl. There's not a woman in this room whose partner looks at her the way he looks at you."

And the woman was right. When the big moment came, I just focused on Matt, his loving gaze. Everyone later commented how radiant I looked during that dance.

All I did was reflect him.

That was the kind of entanglement I had experienced before. Now it was time to concentrate on this new kind.

As much by reflex as anything, I started driving toward downtown Hanover. Something about it felt right.

Until it didn't. As I neared the Dartmouth Green, there was a faint voice in my head—almost like the whisperings of that dance teacher— that told me I was no longer going the right direction.

Was this how the power evinced itself? Was it really just an instinct that you learned to pay attention to, a quiet conviction you allowed to take over?

I turned left on South Main Street, pointing myself away from downtown. I followed it down the hill as it became Route 10, not knowing why I was going that direction until suddenly . . .

Yes. Sachem Village. Where Sheena lived.

Without thinking too much, I made the turn and was soon parking in front of Sheena's place. This must have been the virus in her that I was feeling. Had she returned to her apartment overnight?

I got out of the car and rang the doorbell.

There was no response.

My eyes fell on the numeric keypad, whose code I had watched Sheena enter the previous day.

Having that knowledge and using it were, of course, two different things.

I paused, wrestling with the conundrum.

But not for long.

It was like the quantum forces were driving me. I typed 4-3-2-1 into the pad, then turned the handle and shuffled inside. I didn't fully shut the door behind me, just left it slightly ajar, as if this made my actions something short of breaking and entering.

Sheena's apartment was exactly as it had been the day before: tidy and neat, as if she was expecting company any moment. The walls were decorated with Rothko prints, whose lines and shapes must have appealed to the scientist in Sheena.

Behind the couch was an island with barstools that served as a transition into the kitchen area. I walked over to it. The only object on the island was a device I did not own but instantly recognized from its ubiquitous advertising: a Facebook Portal.

These things were essentially on all the time, weren't they? Always listening. Always following you. Creepy.

I studied the screen, then curious, pressed the power button.

The device informed me there had been a missed call. Bhabhu at 9:34 p.m.

And at 9:31. And 9:23. And 9:17. And 9:15. And 9:08. And 9:05. And 9:03. And 8:59.

The same thing happened the night before: missed calls, starting at 9:00 p.m. and lasting for the next half hour.

Then I checked the received calls and understood why. Bhabhu called every night—like, *every* night—around 9:00 p.m.

The calls typically lasted anywhere from fifteen to thirty minutes. One or two went longer. None were shorter.

They were all from Bhabhu. And only Bhabhu.

Suddenly, something Lauryn Ward had said was coming back. About how she tidied up the kitchen each night after putting her daughter to bed at 8:45 p.m., at which point she'd see Sheena's headlights swinging in.

She's usually home by nine o'clock at the latest, every night, without fail.

Obviously, Sheena was rushing back each night to video chat with Bhabhu.

I felt like I could already guess who Bhabhu was. But just to confirm, I googled the word and was soon looking at a Rajasthani phrase book.

Bhabhu was a colloquial word for "mother."

Who Sheena apparently talked to every night at nine o'clock.

Which wasn't that unusual in an Indian family. There was a large Indian community in the New Jersey library system I'd served, so it had been explained to me many times: according to cultural custom, the parents are considered to be responsible for their children—their daughters, especially—until marriage.

I immediately felt an ache for this mother, who was so far away from her daughter that her only means of connecting was through this cold, flat screen. I could scarcely imagine being so separated from my little boy, who gave me warm hugs every morning and night.

And what desperation Bhabhu must right now be feeling, not knowing where her daughter was, wondering why her calls hadn't been answered.

I had half a thought about calling Bhabhu and reassuring her, but how? At the moment, I had no more idea where Sheena was than Bhabhu did.

Or did I? I concentrated on Sheena, picturing her face, trying to feel her presence.

I closed my eyes, as if that might enable me to get in better touch with the elemental particles that were guiding me.

But my reverie was quickly interrupted by an authoritative male voice coming from near the front door.

I didn't know what it had said. Just that it was loud, demanding, and angry.

CHAPTER 57

Emmett was nearing the end of another rereading of Gary Evans's email.

The third time through was scarcely more illuminating than the first two.

Huangpu Enterprises was a subsidiary of MAI Holdings, whatever that was. It built cell phone towers across rural China.

Yiren Jiang, he of the sickle-shaped eyebrows, and Langqing Wu, with his dragon tattoo, were telecom engineers. Their job was to install and maintain the communications equipment systems in the towers.

Unanswered by the email: Why would two telecom engineers who worked for a private employer, Huangpu Enterprises—which had no known connection to the Chinese government—come to America to kidnap someone?

And then who killed them for doing it?

Emmett was no closer to coming up with answers when he got a call from Sheena's neighbor Lauryn Ward: Emmett had asked her to call if she saw anything unusual, and there was now a strange car parked in front of Sheena's place.

Lauryn said she heard the car door close but hadn't been able to see who had gone up the walk. But the person hadn't gone back down, and now Lauryn was pretty certain whoever it was had broken into Sheena's apartment.

Emmett closed the email and made quick time toward Sheena's place, remaining in emergency-response mode until he saw the CRV and recognized it as the one that had been parked outside Brigid's house.

After that, he was just curious. He walked up to Sheena's apartment and found the door had been left slightly ajar, which was auspicious for a police officer who had been called to investigate a break-in, because not even Captain Carpenter would later question whether he had the legal authority to enter the residence.

He walked in, saw Brigid near the kitchen, and asked:

"What are you doing here?"

He realized he should have knocked—or at least made some more noise—when Brigid leaped and clutched at her heart.

"Sorry," he said. "Didn't mean to scare you."

He wasn't sure she had heard him. So he walked closer, until she could see his face better, and repeated his apology.

"That's okay," she said. "I was just . . . drawn here and . . . I thought maybe I'd . . . find something or . . ."

"It's all right," Emmett said. "The neighbor called. She was worried it was a break-in. I need to let her know it's a false alarm."

"I should come with you," Brigid said. "I really ought to say sorry for scaring her."

He did not object. They left Sheena's door ajar, then walked over to Lauryn's, offering the appropriate apologies.

Then Emmett, who was still curious about David Dafashy's latest revelation, said, "This may seem like an odd question, but does Sheena have a boyfriend?"

"Boyfriend?" Lauryn asked, looking incredulous.

"Scott Sugden."

"Oh, he's not a boyfriend. Sheena's engaged to some doctor in India. I've never met him, but he's going through residency over there, just like my husband here. It's an arranged marriage, so she's known since she was, like, six that she was going to marry this guy. Scott is just a friend. Here . . ."

Lauryn had pulled out her phone and was shuffling through the photos.

"This is them at Halloween," she said, bringing up a snapshot of Sheena standing next to a tall broad-shouldered man with a movie-star square chin and collar-length blond hair. She was wearing a flowing red gown. He was dressed as a very dashing pirate.

"They were characters from *The Princess Bride*," Lauryn continued. "Buttercup and Westley. They'd make a totally cute couple. But they're not."

Finally, Emmett understood Dafashy's game. Create the illusion that Sheena and this beautiful young man were a couple, thus casting Sheena in a bad light. It was straight from the dirtiest page of the sexual harasser's playbook: when possible, make your accuser look like a hussy.

Which meant Dafashy was an awful human being.

But not, necessarily, a kidnapper. Because it meant he still believed he was going to have to go through this sexual harassment hearing.

Or at least he was smart enough to maintain that appearance.

Emmett studied the photo of the beaming youngsters, wondering once again where they were now. In hiding, perhaps. With bullets. And, he presumed, a gun—which they hopefully weren't having cause to use.

"I take it you still haven't heard from or seen Sheena?" Emmett asked.

"No. Nothing."

"Would you mind continuing to keep an eye on the place?"

She promised she would, and Emmett departed along with Brigid. When they returned to Sheena's place, Brigid showed him the missed nine o'clock phone calls.

Emmett just grimaced.

"On another subject, I wanted to ask you about something," he said. "Early this morning, I got an email from Gary Evans."

"The army counterintelligence guy?"

"Right. He was giving me information about Huangpu Enterprises. This is the company that employed those two Chinese men we found by the road out near Canaan."

"Okay."

"According to the dossier he gave me, Huangpu Enterprises builds cell phone towers across rural China."

"Okay," Brigid said. "And?"

"And . . . I don't know. I can't figure what it has to do with anything. I was hoping it might mean something to you. Have you ever heard of Huangpu Enterprises Limited? Did Matt ever talk about it?"

"No and no. Sorry."

"These guys who worked there, they were telecom engineers. Their area was the equipment that goes up in the towers. Is there anything in your husband's research that might have overlapped with what these guys were doing?"

"How so?"

"Oh, I'm just grabbing at straws here. This entanglement mumbo jumbo, if this is all about little bits of this and that being able to talk to each other instantly, could they be used to communicate somehow? Were these guys trying to steal something Matt was doing and put it in their cell towers?"

"I have no idea," Brigid said. "That's way beyond my understanding. David might be able to tell you."

"David, not Beppe?" Emmett asked, not relishing the thought of contacting Dafashy.

"He's the one who understands the technicalities. If anyone would know, it would be him."

"Okay, I'll deal with that later," Emmett said. "Now, to the issue at hand: What were you doing in here again?"

Brigid blushed. "I don't know. Maybe I'm just imagining it, but ever since I woke up this morning, I've been feeling something—the way Sheena was feeling something. The feeling led me here."

Emmett just nodded. Maybe without context he would have thought this was the stress of her husband's abduction, making Brigid have delusions. But after having been led to that remote cabin by Sheena's quantum instincts, he was beyond disbelieving anything.

"You were at the lab last night," he pointed out. "You think maybe you got some of this bug in you?"

"I don't know," Brigid said quickly.

"Well, did you find whatever it was you were looking for? Because otherwise we should probably be moving on."

"Right, right. Absolutely. And, no, there's . . . there's nothing here. I'm . . . I'm probably just imagining it."

Emmett bobbed his head again. "As long as we're here, I'm just going to have a quick look around, make sure nothing seems out of place. Then we'll lock up."

He strolled through the kitchen, then walked down the short hallway that led to the rear of the unit.

Brigid followed a few steps behind.

The first door was for the bathroom. He poked his head in. Mirror. Vanity. Toilet. Bathtub. Shampoos and bath gels and so on.

He opened the linen closet. The towels were folded and perfectly aligned. A shelf with extra soaps, deodorants, Q-tips, and whatnot had been arranged in neat rows.

The floor was dedicated to seasonal decorations neatly arranged by holiday, with Halloween being Sheena's apparent favorite. She even had an electronic atomizer, the kind that could be used with dry ice to create fog for trick-or-treaters.

Brigid nodded at it. "Looks like she did the haunted-house thing."

Emmett murmured agreement, though there was really nothing about this place that was even close to haunted. Everything seemed to be the product of an orderly mind. He moved on to the bedroom, where the bed was perfectly made and the pillows looked like they had been placed with the aid of a laser leveler.

His last stop was the bedroom closet. Unlike Scott Sugden's junk-filled hole, this one had been meticulously organized, from the shoe rack on the floor up to the stacks of sweaters above. A small stepladder leaned against the wall to help her reach them.

There were no bullets. Or guns. Or anything that suggested a person under siege. Whatever mayhem was circling around Sheena Aiyagari's life, it hadn't made its way into her apartment.

Emmett turned toward Brigid, who was lurking in the doorway.

"All right, I think we're—"

His phone rang.

"—done here," he said.

He fished the phone out of his pocket.

"Webster here."

Captain Angus Carpenter, with his usual zest for small talk, began: "Does the name Scott Sugden mean anything to you?"

"Yeah. He's a friend of Sheena Aiyagari's. Why?"

"Because Major Crime got called out early this morning to respond to another body dumped by the side of a damn road in the middle of nowhere," Carpenter said. "They just identified the victim as a Tuck student named Scott Sugden. What the hell is going on out there?"

CHAPTER 58

Sean Plottner did not bother apologizing that he had woken the bank's executive vice president from a deep slumber.

Once the man was done grumbling about it—or, more accurately, once he realized who he was talking to—he began a moving-heaven-and-earth effort to get five million dollars safely delivered to a mountaintop in western New Hampshire, an undertaking that ended with Plottner's helicopter touching gently down on his helipad.

Lee went out to retrieve the two metal cases that held the cash, then brought them inside to his boss's office, setting them on a table, then leaving without a word.

It was 7:15. Forty-five minutes ahead of schedule.

Plottner opened the cases, stopping briefly to soak in the sight: brick after brick of hundred-dollar bills, all of it neatly banded.

He ogled it for an overlong moment, then pulled out his phone, took a snapshot, and Facebook-messaged it to Michael Dillman.

The reply came two minutes later.

"Very good. You've passed the test. Now for the real thing. First, go to this website."

Real thing? What real thing? The five million dollars in front of him wasn't real?

Plottner typed the URL into his iPad so he could keep the Facebook conversation going uninterrupted on his laptop.

He was immediately looking at a small, apparently windowless room. Perhaps it was actually a large walk-in closet. The camera was affixed to the upper corner of the room, opposite the door. It was wide angle, so the edges of the image had some distortion.

In the middle of the room, two people had been securely bound to chairs—legs, arms, and torso—with a combination of rope and duct tape.

One was Matt Bronik.

The other was Sheena Aiyagari.

"Theresa!" Plottner called out.

Bronik was wearing the same blood-spattered T-shirt as before. He was staring straight ahead, though there didn't appear to be much to look at.

Aiyagari's clothing also hadn't changed from when Plottner had last seen it. Her chin was resting on her chest, and her eyes were closed, like she might have been sleeping. The only sign she was still alive came in the slight bobbing of her head with each breath she took.

On the wall behind them was a prominent digital clock that showed the current time to the hundredth of a second. It was now 7:17:47 and ticking.

Theresa appeared at Plottner's door.

"I don't want to be the only person seeing this," he said.

Whatever Theresa's reaction was to this sight—a video feed of two bound hostages—Plottner couldn't be bothered to notice.

He was already typing.

"Okay, you have them both. What now?"

Michael Dillman wrote back immediately.

"Do you require further proof of life? I want you to feel secure in knowing this feed is legitimate and happening in real time."

"It's fine."

"Are you sure? I can have one of them blink a certain number of times, or shake their head. Whatever you wish."

"No. I believe you."

So what now? Plottner was just starting to type when Dillman's next message came in:

"Are you familiar with Zcash?"

Plottner was, of course. It was a cryptocurrency, one of Bitcoin's lesser-known competitors. During an overlong dinner in Sonoma a year or two back, he had been subjected to a tech billionaire's excessive enthusiasms about Zcash's open-source protocol, the way its transactions were indelibly recorded in public blockchains, the proof-of-work mining that created the currency and sustained it, and so on.

The stuff that made techies swoon was only so interesting to Plottner. Really, Zcash wasn't fundamentally different from any other form of money humankind had ever created: it had value primarily because everyone agreed it had value.

Like Bitcoin, Zcash was a decentralized currency that did not rely on banks, governments, or other potentially unreliable third parties for its value. Unlike Bitcoin, Zcash had privacy features—through an ingenious bit of math known as a zero-knowledge proof—that allowed its users to remain completely anonymous.

Which meant Michael Dillman could disappear with his five million dollars and never be found.

So the cash had just been a diversion, a way of testing whether Plottner intended to go through with the exchange—all while keeping him off balance as to how it would actually happen.

Plottner had been outmaneuvered again. Truly, only a master negotiator could have come up with a scheme so well considered.

Both irate and impressed, he typed: "Yes, I know Zcash."

Dillman's reply came quickly, like he wasn't typing, but rather cutting and pasting from something he had already written.

"Very good. You will note that behind the hostages there are several improvised explosive devices with more than enough material inside to kill both doctors. The IEDs have been placed in a cage bolted next to the door. They have been attached to a timer. But I also have the ability to detonate these remotely, at any time I wish."

Plottner squinted at the feed on his tablet. Sure enough, next to the door there was a thick wire cage that might have originally been intended to protect an outdoor security camera. Inside were three lengths of PVC pipe, roughly four inches in diameter, that had been capped at both ends.

Pipe bombs. They had wires protruding from them. Some led to the timer. Others led to the door.

Another message had come in.

"At no later than 9 a.m., you will transfer five million dollars' worth of Zcash units into my wallet. If you fail to do so by that time, I will detonate the explosive."

Even before Plottner was done reading, the next message had arrived.

"Once this transaction occurs, the timer will begin. It is set for three hours. When the timer expires, I will provide you the location of the building, and you may safely enter the room. In the meantime, the door will be monitored by motion sensors, pressure sensors, and my own visual inspection. If any attempt is made to open the door before the timer expires, it will set off the explosive. If the power to the house is cut off, it will set off the explosive. Likewise, if there is any effort made to apprehend me, I will set off the explosive. Do you understand?"

Plottner understood perfectly. Dillman was giving himself three hours to run away. In that amount of time, he could travel anywhere from Connecticut to Canada. He would be impossible to find.

Which only concerned Plottner so much. Michael Dillman would either get away or not. Justice had seldom been of great interest to Sean Plottner.

He really only had one concern:

"How do I know you won't just kill them the moment you get the Zcash?"

"You will have the webcam. If at any time during the three hours you or anyone else wants to check on Drs. Bronik and Aiyagari, you may simply click the URL I've provided. It's all the proof of life you need."

No more than five seconds elapsed before Dillman wrote:

"Do we have a deal?"

Plottner leaned back.

The only thing to stop Dillman from killing his hostages the moment he received the money—or at any time during the three hours—was merely that it would complicate his escape. He wouldn't be able to use Bronik and Aiyagari as a kind of shield.

But that was hardly an ironclad guarantee. Once Dillman was in a place where he felt he was safe, he could set off the explosive.

Therefore, this was a terrible, terrible deal.

Probably the worst Plottner had ever struck.

And yet he had no leverage with which to improve it.

Michael Dillman held all the cards, the last of them being Sheena. By capturing her, Dillman had effectively cut off the only chance of finding Matt Bronik before the deadline.

The only way to get Bronik—and, now, Sheena Aiyagari—back safely was to act exactly as Michael Dillman ordered.

"Yes," Plottner wrote. "We have a deal."

CHAPTER 59

The last person to arrive at our house was, in so many ways, the last person I wanted to be there.

Sean Plottner. The devil himself.

But without him and his money, none of this was going to work. So I invited him inside and directed him toward our farm table, where he set up several laptops.

One was open to his Facebook account, so he could communicate with Michael Dillman.

The second one had the Zcash app up on its screen. It showed he owned 34,116 units. A plug-in on the lower part of the screen was converting that into US dollars. Its current market value was $5,010,833.

The final one was tuned to the webcam feed of Sheena and Matt.

When Plottner first brought it up, that image—and the shock it gave me—triggered a momentary disconnect between me and my senses. Had Aimee not been nearby to grab my arm, I probably wouldn't have remained upright.

It was like tuning in to a horror movie, except there was no maintaining any emotional distance from the screen, no ability to make it go away simply by hitting the power button, no comfort in knowing this was just some Hollywood illusion.

It was totally real. And the protagonist was the love of my life.

I could feel it like it was happening to me: the duct tape constraining my arms and chest, the ropes biting my skin, the ache of being pinned in place, the suffocating terror of knowing there was nothing I could do about it.

Once the sight absolutely overwhelmed me, I finally got the good sense to avert my eyes. From there, I could stomach no more than a few fleeting glimpses.

The only safe spot on the screen was the timer.

It was frozen at 3:00:00.

Three hours. Once the money changed hands, that timer would start counting down.

That's *if* this Michael Dillman guy lived up to his end of this wild deal.

And I didn't want to think about the alternative.

Plottner's arrival capped a hectic hour and a half, during which we had all gathered in our dining room, which now resembled a bizarre kind of war room.

I had returned there after my trip to Sheena's place, and after I finally admitted to myself that perhaps my own quantum compass had mostly been the product of an overly optimistic imagination.

Aimee had hurried back after delivering Morgan to school.

Emmett Webster arrived next, having gotten halfway to the Scott Sugden crime scene before his captain told him about the new demands from the kidnapper, then ordered the detective to turn around, head back to Hanover, and stay with me.

On the way back, Emmett had phoned David Dafashy and told him about Huangpu Enterprises, MAI Holdings, and the telecom engineers.

David had dismissed any possibility Matt's research could be used in current cellular communications. The quantum cell phone, while certainly imagined, was still a long way off.

Then Emmett told us what the state police had learned about Scott Sugden, which wasn't much. Sugden had been killed by a high-powered rifle. Otherwise, the scene was similar to the one where Yiren Jiang and Langqing Wu were found—a body, dragged off the side of a rural road, discovered by a neighbor. It was near Eastman, farther south of where the first two bodies were found, closer to where the abandoned house was.

Emmett also provided a full rundown on the lengths to which the authorities were going to make sure Michael Dillman couldn't get away with this crime.

They had Dillman's picture, courtesy of Dartmouth's security camera, and had distributed it broadly, along with Emmett's instructions that the best way to spot Dillman was the unusual slope to his forehead.

Between the state police and the considerable federal resources being mustered by Gary Evans, they were watching every nearby airport, train station, and bus station. Border Patrol agents had been notified, and every Canadian crossing would be on alert.

There were also observation posts in all directions on Interstates 89 and 91, staffed by officers with binoculars. Unmarked cars could be dispatched to follow any vehicles whose driver looked like Dillman—though they would do so at a distance, mindful of Dillman's threat to detonate the explosive.

Other, more noticeable efforts—helicopters, roadblocks, things Dillman might be able to see—were being held in reserve for that reason.

Half an hour before the deadline, there were more arrivals. One was Beppe Valentino, who was mostly there for moral support.

The other was the State Police Bomb Squad. The captain was an overexuberant man who was very excited to tell Emmett about the number of feet per second at which the shrapnel from the PVC pipe would be expelled if the bomb was set off.

I didn't ask to see his math.

Mostly, I was relieved when it became clear the Bomb Squad would be waiting *outside* the house.

Then, finally, came Sean Plottner, flanked by his constant companions, Theresa and Lee.

The billionaire had argued the war room ought to have been at his mansion—after all, it had more space. And it had the helipad, which would allow us to fly off somewhere quickly.

Emmett had vetoed that. A helicopter needed a place to land, and it was unlikely there was a helipad near Michael Dillman's hideout. And our cars would have to wind all the way down that mountain before we got anywhere.

So there we all were in our house.

Once Plottner had the computers working to his liking, he smoothly introduced himself to Aimee, then nodded grimly at Emmett and Beppe. He made all the right noises of concern. Still, there was nothing about Plottner's oily entrance that convinced me of his innocence.

The Zcash was only the latest log on that fire. How convenient that in the end the kidnapper asked not for real cash, but an untraceable cryptocurrency, with which he could do anything.

Including return it to the very account that had been used to fund it originally.

Then there was the room in which Matt and Sheena were being held. It didn't look like a rented warehouse or an abandoned cabin or any of the other kinds of places that might be available to a Chinese national who was improvising an abduction on foreign soil. There was something about it that seemed like it was in a rich person's house. The large closet for the fourth guest bedroom that no one used. Just remove the shelving and hanger bar and, voilà, instant hostage room.

Beyond that, why did Plottner keep documenting every interaction he had with Michael Dillman? It's like he was anticipating an accusation and wanted to have his defense well prepared.

Lastly, there was the final result: Matt Bronik working as a paid employee of Plottner Investments.

And, sure enough, once Plottner got his computers set up, his next move was to shove a contract in my face and ask me to sign it.

I did so without really reading it, then risked another glance at the webcam feed.

According to the large digital clock, the time was now 8:54:23. Less than six minutes to go until the deadline.

I hated that we were even cutting it this close, but Emmett's captain had insisted state and federal authorities needed more time to mobilize, to cover this port of call and that.

And whatever. Maybe they'd catch this Michael Dillman guy, and maybe they'd link him to Plottner, and maybe there would be punishments to fit the many crimes committed.

Revenge, retribution, and recriminations felt like secondary concerns.

First, get Matt back safely.

After tinkering with the three laptops a little more, Plottner announced, "Okay, I'm ready."

8:55:19.

Get on with it. Get on with it.

I was standing just to the side of Plottner, with a view of all three screens and his mouth. Emmett had stationed himself on the other side.

"Why don't you tell Dillman he's about to get the money," Emmett said.

Plottner began typing.

"Zcash soon to be inbound. You ready to receive?"

Eight seconds ticked away.

Then, from Dillman:

"Yes."

And:

"You are nearly out of time."

"All right," Plottner announced, turning his attention to the laptop with the Zcash app. "As soon as I hit this button, the transfer gets made."

"Hit it at 8:58," Emmett said. "My people are still getting in place. Right now, every minute matters."

I moaned. The detective shot me an apologetic look before returning his attention to the screens.

The room was silent, still. I barely dared to breathe.

The time ticked ominously onward.

8:57:09.

8:57:31.

Plottner's finger hovered over the button. Less than thirty seconds.

Then Emmett's arm shot out. He shouted something that overwhelmed my hearing aids, but he was pointing to the screen with the webcam feed, so that's where my gaze went.

And then I saw what had him so excited:

Matt's lips were moving.

His eyes were closed, but his face was lifted so it was square to the camera, giving me the best possible chance to hear his words, even though there was no volume on the web feed.

Then Emmett's frantic question finally reached me: "What's he saying? What's he saying?"

"Shh," I said sharply, and he quieted.

I poured all my concentration onto Matt's mouth—all my years of having been forced, by necessity, to know what people were saying by sight rather than by sound.

And suddenly it was like he was in the room with me, talking to me in such a normal tone of voice I could practically hear his twang.

I began repeating the words as they fell from his lips:

" . . . by a lake. It's a large lake. Sunapee. Newfound. Winnipesaukee. I'm on the west shore. The lake is at least a mile across, and several miles long. I love you, Brigid. I love you, Morgan. I'm in a house by a lake. It's a large lake. Start looking for us on the west shore of a large lake."

He stopped.

The atomic clock had not.

8:58:08.

8:58:23.

8:58:34.

Plottner still hadn't sent the money.

"What do I do?" Plottner asked, apparently frozen. "Do I hit the button?"

"Yes," Emmett said. "Hit the button."

Plottner brought his finger down on the laptop's touch pad. The app made a noise, then popped up with a dialogue box saying the units had been sent.

The Zcash app was now showing Plottner's wallet was empty. The plug-in lagged for a moment, then flipped to $0.00.

No one spoke.

I looked back at the webcam screen, in particular that 3:00:00. It hadn't moved. Dillman now had the money. When would the countdown begin?

I took a deep breath, feeling like I wouldn't be able to release it until that number started ticking down.

"Well," Plottner said, "I guess that's—"

He didn't finish the sentence.

The webcam feed had gone black.

CHAPTER 60

Sean Plottner frantically swiped at the touch pad of the laptop.

As if this was merely some kind of technical issue. A screen saver switching on or something.

Except no. The cursor was there, floating across the dark screen like a small triangular ghost in the night.

A light-gray *X* had appeared at the top of the screen. At the bottom was a light-gray bar. Just above that were the words Hit Esc to exit full-screen mode.

But where there had once been a brightly lit room, two captives, three pipe bombs, a clock, and a timer, there was now just an inky gloom.

"What's happening?" Plottner demanded. "Why did it cut off?"

He punched the Esc button. All that accomplished was to make the black square smaller and put more graphics around it.

The important part, the middle, was still a void.

Brigid Bronik, who had let out a small shriek when the feed cut out, was just behind Plottner. She had covered her mouth with her two clenched fists.

From in front of her laptop at the head of the table, Aimee said, "I don't have anything either."

"The feed is just . . . gone," Plottner announced.

Brigid groaned.

She staggered toward the table and flopped in a chair. She had a hand across her heart.

"I can't," she mumbled, but couldn't seem to get anything else out. She just kept repeating, "I can't, I can't, I can't . . ."

Aimee came around behind her, shushed her, and rubbed her back.

Plottner crossed his arms. He was attempting to shift into that sixth gear of his, to find the brilliant solution, to think this problem through to some heretofore unseen logical solution.

No fortune had ever been made by panicking when a plan seemed to be falling apart. But a lot sure had been lost that way.

"He's just toying with us," Plottner said. "We can't allow ourselves to get rattled. This doesn't change anything. We need to start focusing on lakes. Which lake? Can we at least start narrowing down lakes within, say, a two-hour drive that loosely fit the parameters Matt has given us? We need to stop thinking about the webcam. It wasn't really telling us anything anyway."

"It was telling us they were still alive," Emmett said, his voice a low growl. "How do you know he didn't just set off the explosives?"

"Because he'd be giving himself away," Plottner said. "An explosion like that would get called in, maybe even start a fire. We'd be able to zero in on his location almost instantly. Plus, he'd no longer have Drs. Bronik and Aiyagari as a shield. Nothing would stop the authorities from going full-court press with helicopters and everything else they could put in the air and on the ground. He's got to keep us believing they're alive."

"Then why not keep the feed going?" Emmett asked. "It would give us that much more reason to think he was going to be a man of his word and reveal the location in the end. Does this mean he doesn't plan to do that?"

"It's unclear," Plottner said. "Maybe yes. Maybe no. I'd just be guessing."

"I hate to say this, but even if he didn't set off the explosive, he could have shot them. It's quieter," Emmett said.

"True," Plottner conceded. "But I don't think so. His main focus is getting away, not leaving two more bodies. When he first directed me to the feed, he was insistent on demonstrating that the feed was real, and happening in real time. He didn't want anyone to make an issue out of it later, because he wanted to be able to take off the moment I agreed to the deal, to give himself a head start. He knew the hostages were secure, so it's not like he needed to stick around for anything else. He was giving himself an extra hour and a half to run, and he was doing it before the authorities could put up roadblocks or anything like that. He could be a long way from here already."

"Even if that's true, why make the screen go black?" Emmett asked.

"Maybe because he saw Professor Bronik's lips moving?" Plottner said. "Or maybe it's just to distract us, to make us waste time and energy by having this very conversation. At this point, it doesn't matter. Is there some kind of database of lakes? An environmental nonprofit that catalogues them by square mileage so we can home in on the larger ones? Something like that?"

No one answered. Brigid was still barely holding herself together. Aimee was mostly soothing her sister. Detective Webster was quiet too.

It was Beppe Valentino, who had been sitting quietly in the corner, who broke the silence.

"It's Schrödinger's cat," he said.

Plottner turned toward him. "What do you mean?"

"The kidnapper. He's recreating Schrödinger's cat," Valentino said. "We have a closed box. We have a death mechanism. We have a certain chance that mechanism has been triggered and a certain chance it hasn't. I don't mean to sound so clinical about it. But right now, according to the logic of quantum physics, Matt and Sheena are both alive *and* dead."

CHAPTER 61

Emmett hadn't liked anything about this setup.

The Facebook messaging.

The webcam.

The Zcash. (What, exactly, was a cryptocurrency again? And how was it people were willing to pay real money for it?)

Then that screen went black, and it was almost like it jolted him out of a bad dream—one where the machines had taken over—and back into a simpler world, the one he was comfortable in all along.

He needed to stop trying to rely on Facebook messaging, Zcash, and Schrödinger's cat to tell him who his perpetrator was.

How did they *really* know that Michael Dillman was the man with the Neanderthal forehead?

Be honest: they didn't.

The third Chinese man could have been killed, just like the other two Chinese men. Except the body was tossed down a well or stuffed under a log or stashed someplace where no one would find the body until spring—or ever.

The person pretending to be Michael Dillman might have even planned it that way, making sure two bodies would be easily found and the other wouldn't be. Just to make everyone think it had been the third guy doing the killing.

What could Emmett say for sure about Michael Dillman?

He was someone who had it in for Matt Bronik and Sheena Aiyagari.

He used fancy words.

And he was damn, damn smart.

All of which neatly described David Dafashy. Who else, besides a physicist, would turn a hostage exchange into a real-life Schrödinger's cat?

Eliminating Bronik and Aiyagari was the only way Dafashy could salvage his career. And he had subsequently discovered a way to compensate himself handsomely for doing it.

What's more, he had created, in Michael Dillman, the ultimate fall guy:

One who didn't really exist.

The state police and the federal government were right now pouring a thousand human hours into finding an apparition.

All the while, the real perpetrator was hiding in plain sight, in that shed tacked onto the side of that falling-down house.

Just waiting for everything to blow over.

Such a cunning, cool customer.

He must have somehow found Sheena, holed up with Scott Sugden. Maybe Dafashy made a lucky guess? Maybe he lured them into a meeting? Sheena thought she was safe with her armed friend. But she obviously wasn't. And Sugden had died trying to defend her.

Soon Aiyagari and Bronik would pay the same price. Because there was no chance Dafashy would leave them alive. He was just waiting three hours to hit the button on his remote detonator, because that's what a fleeing suspect would do.

Eventually, the authorities would call off their search for Michael Dillman. They would conclude the bad guy, whose real name they never knew—and who obscured his electronic tracks every step of the way—had slipped their noose.

Then Dafashy would go on with his life, free from sexual harassment charges and independently wealthy on top of it. He would spend the money slowly, carefully, in a way that didn't attract too much attention.

Yes, Dafashy had thought of everything. And he would trust in his sterling intellect, and the perfection of his scheming, to protect him.

So how did you capture the perfect criminal?

Easy. Use his perfection against him.

Dafashy's one vulnerability was that he had to continue acting innocent. Which meant Emmett wouldn't need an army of cops or a massive manhunt to find the man.

One phone call, and Dafashy would be forced to come running.

If only to keep up his masquerade.

Beppe was going on about Schrödinger's cat—the context for it, the debates it had spawned, how it had been misunderstood—when Emmett interrupted him.

"Actually, Beppe, would you mind making a phone call for me?" Emmett asked.

Beppe looked startled to have been interrupted in the middle of his lecture.

"Yes, of course. What is it?"

"Could you call David Dafashy and ask him to come over here immediately?" Emmett asked. "Tell him you're meeting at Brigid's house, and you need him to join you as soon as possible.

"And don't tell him I'm here."

Dafashy's hands.

This was all about his hands. If they were visible, and not clutching a cell phone or some other device that might be used to set off an explosive remotely, then Emmett could apprehend him, cuff him, and end this thing.

Beppe had made the call. Dafashy eagerly accepted the invitation. He said he would be there right away, even said he had something he wanted to share with Beppe.

Of course he did.

No doubt it was something that would further obfuscate matters. Dafashy seemed to be an expert at that.

Emmett gave Brigid her instructions while Dafashy was en route. She was to open the door, then clear out of the way so Emmett could get the drop on Dafashy.

It was a simple plan. No webcams or cryptocurrencies.

Old school.

Just how Emmett liked things.

The only thing that could thwart him was if Dafashy's hands were in his pockets. Emmett would have to use a move he had learned long ago. If you kicked the backs of a man's knees while you landed on his back, he went down every time.

He also instinctively took his hands out of his pockets to brace his fall.

Emmett waited until he saw Dafashy pull up, then hid on the hinge side of the door. Dafashy's boots were heavy on the front steps. He rang the bell.

Brigid made eye contact with Emmett, pausing as she approached the door.

He nodded at her.

His pistol was drawn, with the safety off. He was as ready as he'd ever be.

Brigid opened the door, and said, "Hello, David, thank you for coming."

Her voice was high pitched. Wooden. Would Dafashy notice?

"I came as soon as I could," he said gravely.

Emmett still couldn't see the man yet. Where were his hands? Sides or pockets?

Then Dafashy closed the door behind himself.

Sides.

Emmett stepped forward and said, "Put your hands up. You are under arrest."

Dafashy startled, but soon recovered himself and his natural arrogance.

"What is this about?" he demanded, turning toward Emmett.

"Keep your hands where I can see them," Emmett said, leveling the pistol at Dafashy, staying just out of arm's length. "If you fail to comply, I will consider it an act of aggression and I *will* use deadly force."

"What are you talking about? This is—"

"Put your hands on your head."

"I'm not—"

"Put your hands on your head now."

Dafashy's face signaled his annoyance. But he complied.

"Turn around," Emmett said.

"This is absolutely ludicrous," Dafashy said, even as he turned his back to Emmett.

Ludicrous. The fancy words, right to the end.

"Very slowly," Emmett said, "I want you to put your hands behind your back."

"Haven't you gotten tired of harassing me yet?" Dafashy asked, tossing his hands back with dramatized exasperation.

Emmett's answer was to snap a pair of handcuffs on him.

"Lie down on the floor," he ordered. "Facedown. Now."

"Is that really necessary?"

"Lie. Down."

With a roll of his eyes, Dafashy got to his knees, then paused. "Honestly, how am I even supposed to do this with my arms behind my back?"

Emmett grabbed the back of his jacket and lowered him until he was facedown on the hardwood floor of the Broniks' foyer. From the dining room, everyone else—Beppe, Brigid, Aimee, Plottner and his entourage—looked on anxiously.

Quickly, Emmett rifled through Dafashy's pockets—jacket and pants. This produced a wallet, keys, a cell phone, and a wadded handkerchief.

But nothing that looked like a detonator.

Which meant he must have been using the cell phone.

"Okay, where are they?" Emmett said when he was through.

"Where are who?"

"Matt Bronik and Sheena Aiyagari."

"You honestly think I know?"

"Yes."

"Well, you're wrong. As a matter of fact, I was just getting ready to call you and tell you about MAI Holdings."

"What about it?"

"As soon as you said the name it rang some bells. I had to look it up to be sure. And it turns out I was right. Sheena's father is a wealthy businessman. His company is called Marwari Aiyagari International—*M. A. I.* It's a multinational corporation that builds cell phone towers all across the globe. India and China. Russia. Parts of Africa. Even America. MAI Holdings is the shell company he created to possess its assets, including Huangpu Enterprises. If these telecom engineers worked for a company owned by MAI Holdings, it means they worked for Sheena's father."

"Why would Sheena's father kidnap his own daughter?" Emmett said. "That's ridiculous."

"No, not Sheena's father. Stop being so thick. It's Sheena herself."

"Why would she do that?"

Dafashy twisted his neck in an attempt to shoot Emmett a withering glance. He didn't get very far, so he had to impart most of his scorn with his dismissive tone.

"Are you really that daft? She had a front-row seat for what Matt was doing with the quantum virus. She saw enough to be able to steal his methodology. If Matt publishes that paper, she's not even a footnote in history. But if Matt disappears and *she* publishes it? She makes Matt second author—posthumously of course—but she could claim to be the one who made the final breakthrough. And then she reaps the professional spoils. A Nobel Prize. Tenure anywhere she wants. Lasting fame.

"That's why she kidnapped him instead of just killing him outright. She wasn't sure if she could bring it home herself. She might need him for additional help or information."

It was a theory, for sure. Emmett was still a long way from accepting it.

Chief among his doubts: "If all that's true," he said, "why did she also kidnap herself? And kill her own friend. And what's with the five-million-dollar ransom demand?"

"How should I know? The woman is certifiable. Look, obviously something went wrong on her way to the Nobel. I know you think there's no way cute, adorable little Sheena could be involved in something so awful. But open your eyes, man. She's in it up to her neck and beyond."

Emmett glanced into the other room. Were any of them buying this? It was difficult to tell.

He thought about when he first met Sheena at Baker Library, with her battered face and her apparent terror. Michael Dillman hadn't even surfaced at that point.

Was that all an act? Had she inflicted those injuries on herself in order to deflect any suspicion? To make herself look like one of the victims?

"And other than the Huangpu–MAI Holdings connection," Emmett asked, "what proof do you have that Sheena is involved?"

Dafashy sighed dramatically. "Well, I obviously haven't connected *all* the dots for you. So here's an idea. How about you let me up off the floor so I can help you investigate?"

Emmett was sure Dafashy would like that. Really, how was this new so-called revelation different from the version of truth Dafashy had been pushing all along?

Sheena was the evil harpy, the wanton harlot, the monster in every single one of Dafashy's fairy tales.

For that reason alone, he might have dismissed anything Dafashy had to say out of hand.

But how to explain the fact, confirmed by Gary Evans's best spies, that at least two of the men who carried Matt Bronik out of that building worked for Sheena's father?

Emmett thrust his hands on his hips, then glanced at his watch. It was 9:23. Assuming that Michael Dillman—whoever he was—had started that three-hour timer when he received the Zcash, it was set to expire at 11:58.

At which point he might reveal the hostages' location.

Or blow them into very tiny pieces.

So what did Emmett do about Dafashy?

Then, from the other room, Aimee called out, "Emmett, could you come in here, please?"

Emmett took a few steps toward the dining room and said, "Yes?"

Aimee was sitting in front of her laptop, which she tilted so he could see it.

It showed, of all things, a Google Maps satellite image, zoomed in close on a house.

"I've just been doing a few searches," she said.

Searches? Emmett thought. *What kind of—*

Then he remembered: Aimee was a forensic accountant.

She continued: "MAI Holdings owns a house on the west shore of Lake Sunapee."

CHAPTER 62

We tore down Interstate 89, lights flashing in front and behind, whipping past traffic that had pulled to the side for us.

I was toward the end of the caravan, just after the Bomb Squad, pushing the CRV's engine to rpms it had never seen on my many trips to swim practice and the grocery store.

Aimee was in the passenger seat. Her twin jacket was crumpled at her feet. She was balancing her laptop on her knees, pumping her hot spot for more information on MAI Holdings.

So far, nothing seemed all that relevant. It was privately held, so there were no SEC filings to mine. Most of its work in America seemed to be in Appalachia or the rural West. The Lake Sunapee house was the only asset MAI owned anywhere nearby.

It made sense that Sheena's father, who was apparently quite wealthy, wanted a place to stay when he visited his daughter. And a house on Lake Sunapee would double as a fine corporate retreat.

But I was still having a difficult time absorbing the rest of this. The kidnappers worked for Sheena's father? And Matt was being held at his house?

Which meant . . . Sheena had started all this?

The same woman who politely chatted with me at all those physics department functions? And unfailingly asked me about how my son was doing in school? And talked to her mother every night at nine o'clock?

I wasn't ready to believe she could be so duplicitous. Weren't there some things a person wouldn't do for a Nobel Prize?

Or was the pressure to achieve greatness really that strong?

We departed the highway at Exit 12A, having picked up an additional police escort, and ripped through the small town of Sunapee, which was mostly empty this time of year. After a few more turns on ever-smaller roads, we were suddenly slowing.

On our left was a driveway with two stone pillars. It was long, paved, and plowed—all signs of a wealthy owner.

I followed the caravan down, toward the lake. The house was a sprawling, multiwinged, two-story colonial that couldn't have been any less than ten thousand square feet.

My clock read 10:06. An hour and fifty-two minutes remaining.

Aimee and I got out of the car. Dafashy remained in the back seat of Emmett's vehicle—probably on the detective's orders—and Beppe had stayed with him.

Emmett and the other state troopers quickly huddled near the Bomb Squad truck, paying little attention to the civilians.

Meanwhile, Plottner's limousine, which had followed the caravan down the driveway, was suddenly on the move again. As I stared at it dumbly, it completed a five-point turnaround—made complicated by the presence of the other vehicles, the snowbanks, and the limo's own unwieldiness—and was now rolling back up the driveway.

"Where's he going?" I asked.

"I have no idea," Aimee said.

The limousine disappeared from view.

Then my phone rang.

Plottner.

"Hello?" I said.

Then I read: "Lee informs me that there's a significant chance the house may be booby-trapped. There's also a chance Michael Dillman is still monitoring the premises and will detonate the explosive when he becomes aware of our presence. As my director of security, Lee has advised me to wait at a greater distance. So that's what I'm doing. I'd suggest you do the same."

Right.

Except.

Wasn't it possible Plottner had done his research and discovered that Sheena's father owned Huangpu Enterprises/MAI Holdings? Then Plottner had hired men from that company, knowing it would cast suspicion toward Sheena?

He could have also found the house that belonged to MAI Holdings and decided to use it, knowing it was unlikely anyone else would be going to a New Hampshire lake house in March. It was just like Plottner to think of every detail in his efforts to create more misdirection.

In which case, he was right now just continuing playing his part—to be cautious, and to encourage others to do the same.

But, truly, nothing here was going to explode. Plottner wouldn't want Matt to be harmed.

"Thanks," I said. "I'll take my chances."

Then I hung up.

The state police, having finished their deliberations, had apparently also decided the front door might have some kind of trap or trip wire, because they had entered the house through a window. Two men in bomb suits had shattered it with a battering ram.

Nothing exploded except the security alarm, whose shrieks were soon bouncing off the frozen water nearby, alerting the other empty lake houses that one of their own was being assaulted.

After thirty seconds, the alarm abruptly silenced. The central monitoring company must have been informed that this was a police matter. Then one of the bomb-suit guys came around and opened the front door for the rest of the team.

Over the next twenty minutes, we lurked outside the house as members of the Bomb Squad crept room by room through the first floor. Every now and then, I could hear them yell something that sounded like "Clear."

As soon as I saw them through one of the windows, tromping upstairs, I started toward the front door.

Aimee said something, which I ignored. She then hurried around to where she was blocking my path.

"What are you doing?" Aimee asked.

"Looking for my husband," I said, then repeated my theory about Plottner not blowing up anything, least of all Matt.

"Okay," she said. "I'm coming with you."

Because of course she was.

We crept in the house through the still-open front door. I had decided to start my search on the north side of the house and then work my way south, just to be systematic about it.

It was 10:36. One hour and twenty-two minutes to go.

The house was, unsurprisingly, expensively furnished. I began in the mudroom, where there was no sign of mud. Just a top-of-the-line washer and dryer that probably cost more than any piece of furniture we owned.

Across the hallway was a guest bedroom that felt little used, despite a magnificent view of the water. It didn't take long to search. Both it, and its en suite bathroom, were mostly empty.

The kitchen came next. But here, what caught my eye wasn't the pricey brands—Viking, Sub-Zero, Bosch—it was the food, both perishable and, more tellingly, nonperishable.

Eggs. Milk. Sandwich meat. Cheese. It was all fresh. None of the sell-by dates had been met yet.

Someone had been using this kitchen. And had perhaps planned to continue using it for a while.

In a kind of trance, I pulled out the trash, finding it full of spent take-out containers, frozen meal boxes, and fast-food wrappers—not exactly the kind of fare consistent with an MAI Holdings corporate event.

"What are you doing?" Aimee snapped from the other side of the room. "Don't touch that. It's been handled by the kidnappers. It's potential evidence."

"Right, sorry," I said, lifting my hands in the air, leaving the trash can where it was.

I moved on to the cabinets and drawers, moving quickly but leaving nothing uninspected. They were so neatly organized it didn't take long to see there was nothing out of the ordinary.

The same could not be said for the living room, which had an empty spot where it looked like a couch may have been. And a large rust-brown stain on the carpet behind it that looked like dried blood.

Like someone had been killed there. Perhaps one of the Chinese men? Or Scott Sugden?

I pointed it out to Aimee.

"That's not Matt's, you know," she said.

"I know," I said, then moved quickly away from it.

A sitting room came next, but again, there wasn't much to see. Because this was not anyone's full-time residence, all the rooms had an impersonal sparseness to them.

Then I arrived at the other guest bedroom on the lower floor.

Immediately, things felt different.

There were more pillows on the bed. More knickknacks on the dresser. There was a sitting area by the window, which had another terrific view; but there was also a desk shoved up against a wall, like someone wanted to be able to do work here.

This was no longer the product of an interior decorator on a nearly unlimited budget, looking to show off. This was a more functional space. Someone used this room.

And I could already guess who. There was a Rothko print on the wall.

I slowed down. Enough so that Aimee, still trailing, nearly ran into me.

"What's up?" she asked.

"I think this is Sheena's room when she stays here."

"Okay," Aimee said, and left it at that.

I inspected the dresser, which was perhaps quarter-filled with Sheena-size clothing. Most of it was summer appropriate.

Then I moved on to the nightstand and opened the drawer. It was again filled with assorted stuff—scrunchies, moisturizer, tissues, a small teddy bear.

And a framed photo.

It had been placed facedown.

I was less concerned about disturbing evidence in here—this was just Sheena's stuff, after all—so I turned it over.

It was a selfie of Sheena with Scott Sugden, who looked like Westley from *The Princess Bride* even when he wasn't in costume. It had been taken at sunset on the shore of the lake. She was wearing a bikini. He was topless. She had her arms snaked around his torso and her cheek pressed against his bare chest.

I immediately recognized the flush to Sheena's face, the way her hair was just a little askew, the look of extravagant contentment.

It was the same look I wore just after Matt and I made love that day at Lake Carnegie.

These were not merely friends. These were two young people, very much in love.

Sheena really was having an affair. Just like Dafashy said. And apparently it had been going on for a while—since at least last summer.

I showed the picture to Aimee, whose raised eyebrows told me she immediately understood the implications.

Even the location of the photo—tucked away in a drawer, rather than out in the open—was suggestive of a hidden relationship. She must have shared stories about Scott with Leonie Descheun, who had apparently been a close confidante for Sheena; but she had kept it from everyone else, including the neighbor she only sort of knew.

I continued into the bathroom that was attached, recognizing the same products that had been in Sheena's bathroom at Sachem Village.

This had to be some life for Sheena. Especially in the summertime. Sneaking away to a multimillion-dollar vacation home on Lake Sunapee with her boyfriend. I was somewhere in the middle of that fantasy when I opened the bathroom closet and saw the towels.

They weren't quite as perfectly square and flat as they had been in Sheena's other bathroom closet.

There was something wedged behind them.

Something hidden.

I moved the top towel and uncovered a small box.

It was white with a blue band across the top. I reached for it, extracting it from the closet.

My close vision was rapidly failing with age, so I couldn't make out all the small type. But I could easily read the larger lines.

ROMPUN.

SEDATIVE AND ANALGESIC.

FOR USE IN HORSE AND CERVIDAE ONLY.

"Check this out," I said, holding up the box for Aimee to see. "What is Rompun?"

Aimee pulled out her phone. As she jabbed at it, she shuffled around in front of me so I could hear her, then started reading.

"'Rompun,'" she said, "'is a sedative reserved for veterinary use, primarily horses and cattle. Absorbs and metabolizes rapidly. It's banned for human consumption because it causes a dangerous combination of hypotension'—that's low blood pressure—'and bradycardia,' which I'm pretty sure is a slowed heart rate."

Low blood pressure. Slowed heart rate.

That was the one-two punch that nearly killed Matt both times he went to the hospital.

I could feel myself losing my bearings again. I had to lean against the sink for support.

"Rompun is the brand name," she continued. "The generic name is xylazine. It's described as 'an opioid, many times more powerful than heroin. In recent years, humans have started abusing it as a recreational drug. It—'"

Aimee abruptly stopped reading and took in a sharp breath.

"'It induces a coma-like state that, at low, nonfatal doses, causes the user to walk around hunched forward, in a state of semiconsciousness. For this reason, it is known as . . .'"

Aimee was having a hard time continuing.

"'As *the zombie drug*,'" she eventually said. "'Because it causes the user to resemble a zombie in appearance. The effects usually last'—oh God, Brigid—'approximately six hours. The drug can be difficult to detect by conventional toxin screens because it voids rapidly from the body. The primary aftereffect is a thunderous headache.'"

"A thunderous headache," I repeated.

"The zombie drug," she said.

We just stared at each other, neither of us needing to say more.

The effects of xylazine were a perfect match for Matt's symptoms.

His inexplicable fits, suddenly explained.

And the drug was in Sheena's bathroom. Sheena's private, personal bathroom.

"Sheena," I said, still a little stunned. "Did she really do this to Matt?"

"She must have," Aimee said.

"But how did she get the drug into him?" I asked. "Did she pour it into his coffee or something? Wouldn't Matt have noticed the taste?"

Aimee looked down at her phone. "It says here it can either be injected or administered as an aerosol."

"An *aerosol*? Oh my God."

"What?"

And then I told her about what Emmett and I had found in Sheena's other bathroom.

The electronic atomizer.

A device that expels a liquid in aerosolized form.

If you used dry ice, the atomizer would create a fog, perfect for a haunted house. But with a room-temperature liquid? It would be invisible. And the hum of the laser would easily cover whatever noise the atomizer made.

Matt wouldn't have heard or seen a thing. Just been stricken as the cloud floated down on him.

As for me, it was like a cloud had been lifted. Beppe said the visible spectrum of light was like one inch on the journey from New York to Los Angeles.

I was seeing everything now.

All twenty-five hundred miles.

Because I even knew where Sheena had hidden when she delivered this poison. Those old retrofitted air-handling ducts that ran through Matt's lab and the rest of the third floor of Wilder.

They were big enough for a large child to crawl through.

Or a small adult.

Sheena could have hoisted herself up into the ducts from a closet somewhere—anyplace the air-handling system had an intake port. She would have worn a mask, so she didn't sicken herself. Then she let the atomizer and the xylazine do the rest.

She had started weeks ago, dousing him twice to establish the pattern that something was wrong with Matt, even if medical science was powerless to explain it.

Such that when the third time came around, and three EMTs showed up to carry Matt away, the people watching would think this was normal.

Just Matt Bronik, having another fit.

Matt wouldn't have been able to fight those EMTs off. He was incapacitated, not even aware of what was happening.

Aimee had said this was an inside-Dartmouth job. She had been absolutely right.

It wasn't just inside Dartmouth. It was inside Matt's own lab.

I thought back to the judge's chambers, and Sheena's hysteria when she thought the Department of Defense was going to kill the virus. That would have been a serious setback, having to recreate Matt's work. Perhaps she wouldn't have been able to. In which case all her efforts would have been for naught.

Dafashy, unlikely prophet, had been right. She was going to publish Matt's work as her own, then ride it to academic stardom.

"It was Sheena," I said. "It all started with Sheena. And now Matt is—"

Aimee reached out, took my hands.

"He's going to be okay," she said. "I don't know how, but he's going to be okay. You have to keep believing that. You have to."

She squeezed hard.

"Okay," I said, shaking off her hands. "We should tell Emmett about this."

It was exactly eleven o'clock.

Fifty-eight minutes to go.

CHAPTER 63

Emmett had never heard of Rompun or xylazine. But he had seen the atomizer. Even before Brigid talked him through it, he already grasped the key details.

He went to his car to retrieve some gloves and an evidence bag, then carefully placed the Rompun box inside. It would surely have Sheena's fingerprints all over it. He took the item back to his car, and was just returning to the house when he met the Bomb Squad captain, who was rushing down the steps, wild eyed.

"There you are," he said breathlessly. Then he took a big gulp of air and said: "We found them. They're up here. Come on."

The Bomb Squad captain led Emmett upstairs, through a bedroom, to a door of what appeared to be a closet. Then the captain treated Emmett to an overexuberant explanation of just how perfectly Michael Dillman had engineered everything.

The wiring that had been connected to the explosive appeared to be powered by the house's electricity *and* by a backup battery—the work of a man who knew what he was doing, and had done it well.

The door was monitored by both a pressure sensor and a motion detector, a difficult combination. On their own, either could have been defeated.

But both together?

That, the Bomb Squad captain said, was impossible. And while he might have been able to go through the ceiling to lift the hostages out—there appeared to be a good-size attic above them—they couldn't, because Dillman might be watching remotely.

There were redundancies on top of redundancies. The perp had thought of everything.

And now he had disappeared to who knows where.

But, Emmett realized, there was at least one person who knew who he was.

And, at the moment, that person was tied up and trapped behind a heavily wired door. Emmett walked up to it and stared at it for a long moment, letting out a long breath before he started talking.

"Sheena? It's Emmett Webster."

"Oh my God, do you have a way of getting me out of here?" Sheena chirped, her voice high and panicky. "Because these Bomb Squad people are worthless."

"We'll get you out," he said. "I want to talk about what happens after that. We found the Rompun in your bathroom downstairs. And we found the atomizer in your bathroom at Sachem Village. We know you were the one behind the kidnapping."

"I don't know what you're talking about," Sheena said petulantly.

"Look, I'm just trying to help you here. Once we get you out, you're going to prison. There's no question about that. The only issue now is for how long. And that's going to depend on how much you cooperate. That cooperation starts *right now*. Do you understand me?"

There was no reply.

Emmett continued: "See, here's the problem. We keep finding all these bodies. Langqing Wu. Yiren Jiang. Scott Sugden. Now, kidnapping is one thing. And it's bad, don't get me wrong. But if you cooperate, and the prosecutor decides you didn't mean to hurt Matt, and we're able to determine you weren't involved with those murders, you'd probably be looking at a class B felony. Three and a half to seven years in prison. Given that you don't have a record—and, again, if you cooperate with us—you'd do the three and a half.

"Now, personally, I think you got double-crossed by the people working for you. So I don't think you had anything to do with these bodies. But if you stonewall us, it'll look like you *were* involved. Even if you didn't pull the trigger, you would be convicted as a coconspirator. Murder for hire is a capital offense in New Hampshire. Kidnapping and murder together is also a capital offense. We don't have the death penalty anymore, but a capital offense conviction is punished by a mandatory life sentence with no parole. So, really, it's up to you. Do you want to be in prison for three and a half years? Or do you want to be there for the rest of your life? Like I said, cooperation starts now. And it had better start fast, or I'm out of here."

At first, there was silence from the other side of the door.

Then came the low murmuring of a man's voice. Matt Bronik. Talking to Sheena in the gentle tones of a professor, correcting an errant student.

Emmett couldn't hear exactly what was being said. He held his breath, put his ear close to the door. It was still too soft.

Then:

"Okay," Sheena said. "I'll cooperate."

"Are you sure?"

"Yes, I'm sure. I'll cooperate."

"I can't have you holding back on me. I need you to be a hundred percent straight with me about everything. If you lie to me now about even the littlest thing, I can't help you later. You understand that?"

"I get it, I get it. I'll help you."

"Very good," Emmett said. "Now tell me about the men you've been working with. We know Langqing Wu and Yiren Jiang worked for a subsidiary of your father's company in China. Who's the third man, the one who used the alias Michael Dillman?"

"His real name is Johnny Chang. He worked for my father, too, but in America. He's total scum. He's the one who has been killing everyone."

Emmett glanced behind himself. Brigid and Aimee had wandered into the room, though they were being kept at a distance by the Bomb Squad. Emmett turned back to the door.

"So you hired Johnny Chang, Langqing Wu, and Yiren Jiang to come here and kidnap Matt?" Emmett asked.

There was a short pause. "Not exactly. I didn't hire Johnny. He had been stealing from my father's company and he got caught. Our deal was that I was going to destroy some evidence my father had so he couldn't press charges. In return for that, Johnny was going to help me. He was the one who brought Wu and Jiang over. Johnny's deal with them was that they would get the money he had stolen from my father—it was something like a hundred thousand dollars. But they weren't supposed to hurt Matt. I swear. They were just going to do the kidnapping. Then Wu and Jiang were going to go back to China with my father's money, and Johnny was going to hold Matt while I . . ."

Her voice trailed away. Emmett thought he could hear her crying.

"While you what?" he prompted.

"My own research was hot garbage, okay? It was this big dead end. My postdoc was ending in a few months. I didn't have any job offers. I wasn't even getting interviews. My father had given me this deadline: Once my postdoc was up, I was going to have to return to India and marry this . . . this asshole that I had been promised to when I was, like, six. This stupid, arrogant doctor. And there was no getting out of it. I had tried to explain to my father that I was in love with someone else, but it didn't matter. All my father could think about was the shame the family would suffer if I broke off the marriage. He told me if I didn't come back home to India, he was going to cut me off. I literally wouldn't have a dime to my name. All my bank accounts, all my credit cards, it's all my father's money. And Scott . . . Scott was just a student. He didn't have anything. I couldn't . . . I couldn't ask him to support me, it . . . it was just a mess.

"But then I had this amazing idea about how to get Matt's project across the finish line. And I was going to just tell him, but you know how that goes. The professor publishes the big paper. The postdoc gets thanked in the acknowledgments. Then I thought, wait, if *I* was the one to publish Matt's research, I would have all the job offers I needed. I could tell my father to go to hell. And Scott and I . . ."

Again, she couldn't finish. Emmett did it for her: "You could be together. You could be with the person you loved most. You'd do anything for that."

Emmett certainly understood that. All too well.

"Yes," Sheena said in a small voice.

"So those three guys kidnapped Matt. Then what?"

"Those idiot feds came in and closed down the lab," Sheena said. "Without access to the lab and the virus, I wasn't going to be able to do anything. So I . . . I came up with the whole idea of my brain being entangled with Matt's. I thought once I dangled out the hope that I could find Matt, the Department of Defense would let me back into the lab."

"That was all made up?"

"Yes. There's no quantum compass. That cottage I led you to, I had found that earlier in the day. I made it look like someone had slept there. Then I told Johnny to go out there and plant that potato chip bag with Matt's fingerprints on it. I thought that would convince the government that I needed to get back into the lab."

Emmett shook his head. Of course the quantum compass was a fraud. He should have known. But he wasn't the only one who had been fooled. People much smarter than him had fallen for it too. That was the power of the quantum physics. It felt like magic, enough that everyone had started to believe in the impossible.

"But then everything got crazy," Sheena continued. "There was that million-dollar reward and . . . Jiang went rogue on us, trying to get the million. Wu was in on it too. Then Johnny figured out they were up to something and he . . . he must have killed them. All I know is, Johnny suddenly told me he wasn't taking orders from me anymore and that our deal was off. I guess he figured that if he got five million dollars from Plottner, he could disappear to an island somewhere and live like a king. He was just going to kill Matt and so Scott and I, we . . ."

Sheena was again struggling to get the words out. But Emmett could finish the story by himself.

In short, Sheena had an experience with a very different kind of interference.

"Scott told you about the gun he had in his closet," Emmett said. "You thought you could come out here, get the drop on Johnny, and set everything right."

"Yes," Sheena whimpered.

"But Johnny Chang was waiting for you guys. He killed Scott Sugden with a high-powered rifle, then took you hostage."

"Yes," Sheena said again.

"And do you have any idea where Johnny is now?"

"No. I just . . . no."

"He didn't say anything about where he might hole up?"

"No. Originally he was just going to fly back to Colorado when it was over. But I doubt he did that. I have no clue what his plan is."

"Matt," Emmett asked, "did you overhear anything that might help us?"

"I wish I had. But no. He didn't exactly talk to me much."

Emmett looked down at the ground, then up at the others in the room. Brigid seemed to take this as her permission to walk closer to the door. The Bomb Squad captain let her go, though he remained close enough that he could grab her if she got too close.

She stopped about five feet short.

"Matty," she said in a shaky voice. "Matty, it's me, baby."

From inside, Matt yelled, "Brigid! Get out of here! Get out of here *right now!*"

Brigid continued: "Matty, I love you. I love you so much. You are the most amazing man in the world and I love you and we're going to get you out of this, don't you worry."

Matt screamed, "You have to go! I don't want you anywhere near here! I love you too. But go. Go!"

"I love you," Brigid said, tears streaming. "I love you. All I want you to think about is how much I love you."

This brought a new and even more urgent plea from Matt, though it didn't seem to move Brigid any more than the last one had.

Finally, Emmett got it: Brigid might have been able to hear him, but she couldn't make out the words.

He walked up and seized Brigid gently by the arm, making sure she could see his mouth.

"He wants you out of here," he said softly. "It's really not safe. You have to think of your son right now. If something goes wrong here . . . the boy shouldn't have to lose his father *and* his mother."

Her tears were coming harder now.

"I know. I just—"

Wanted to say all the words to her husband that Emmett wished he could have said to Wanda one last time.

"Please," Emmett said firmly. "We have to go."

His grip on her arm tightened.

"Okay, Matt," Emmett called. "I'm taking her out now."

"Thank you!" Matt called. "Thank you! Go! Go!"

"I love you, Matty," Brigid kept calling as he guided her down the hallway. "I love you so much."

CHAPTER 64

Emmett kept his hold of Brigid's arm until they were out of the house by a good fifty feet.

"I need you to promise me—to promise *Matt*—you won't try and go back in," he said.

He could tell by the look on her face he wasn't necessarily going to get that promise, so he turned to Aimee.

"I'm serious. You have to keep her out of there."

"I understand," Aimee said. "She does too. It's about Morgan. We're going to think about Morgan, right?"

Brigid was still trying to contain her sobs, not doing a very good job at it. Emmett left them and returned to the Bomb Squad, which now had men up in the attic. They were cutting away the insulation to expose the drywall of the attic floor.

That was as close as they dared get. The fear of Johnny Chang seeing them coming through the ceiling stopped them from going any farther.

Once they got the word it was safe, they would cut a hole in the drywall and hop down. The captain said that thanks to still photos sent from headquarters, and with what Matt Bronik had told them from the other side of the door, they had figured out how to disarm the pipe bombs safely.

The whole operation would take about three minutes.

It would also take about three minutes to vacate the house from the attic while wearing bulky bomb suits if they determined all was hopeless.

They would be awaiting word either way.

Emmett thanked him, then went back down to the lower level of the house to begin his own search for clues that might lead him to Johnny Chang.

Sheena's culpability really only changed things so much. At least immediately. His greatest concern was still getting everyone out of this alive.

And, by his count, there were really only two ways that could happen.

One, Chang would be a man of his word and allow the hostages to leave the room when the three-hour timer was up. Since that seemed unlikely, that left:

Two, they find Chang and either capture, kill, or disable him before he could set off the bombs.

There was little Emmett could do to control the first option. He focused on the second.

Where was Chang?

Emmett attempted to think like a fleeing suspect. Plottner thought Chang had taken off around 7:20, right after agreeing to the deal. Emmett didn't believe that. Chang would have needed to stay close. What if Plottner, or someone else, had insisted on one last proof-of-life demonstration before handing over the Zcash? What if there had been some other unforeseen wrinkle?

No, Chang had at least stayed nearby—close enough to be able to return to the house, if necessary—until a few seconds after 8:58, when he finally received the money.

At that point, his options were more limited. He would have guessed there was a massive search for him. Bus stations, train stations, and airports would be dangerous, even off limits.

He obviously had some kind of vehicle. He and the other two men had transferred Matt Bronik into something—a van? a truck?—when they vacated the ambulance.

Whatever he was driving, the real question was where he had gone. He'd know there was a good chance the highways and other major thoroughfares were being watched, but New Hampshire had thousands of miles of quiet back roads. Even with the combined efforts of the state police and the federal government, there wouldn't be enough officers to monitor all of them.

Emmett was in the living room now. His search was not systematic. He was just keeping his eyes open.

Even if Chang had been smart enough to stick to back roads, he still had other issues. Sleeping in a van or truck in New Hampshire in March wasn't just unpleasant. It was dangerous. You either risked freezing to death, or you kept the engine on and risked carbon monoxide poisoning.

He needed somewhere to stay. If he used a credit card, the authorities would find him quickly. Even if he stayed at some off-brand place that accepted cash deposits, like the Tuck Inn, a hotel clerk would be able to identify the subject of a manhunt as well as anyone.

Then there was the even more difficult problem of how to escape the country. Having five million dollars in untraceable money was only so good if you couldn't eventually go somewhere to spend it.

Emmett was in the kitchen, lost in his thoughts, not even looking at anything in particular.

Then his gaze fell on a garbage can that was in the middle of the floor. Which was odd. It hadn't been there the first time he had been through the kitchen.

Brigid or Aimee must have taken it out. But why would they?

He walked over and looked down at it. His eyes fell on a Walmart receipt that was sitting atop some of the other trash. He didn't want to touch it, lest he spoil any fingerprints on it, so he cocked his head to the side to read it.

The item that jumped out at him was third down.

Thetford Qk Dslv Tiss 4pk2.44

Thetford. He knew the company. And he knew the product: quick-dissolve toilet tissue. It was specially made for the septic systems of boats and RVs. He had bought some himself for his own RV.

And didn't that make sense? Whether you wanted a place to stay while you visited your grandchildren or a place to hide out while there was a massive police manhunt for you, a recreational vehicle was a solid choice.

It would be comfortable. And warm enough. Many models had electric heat that you could keep on all night without having to run the engine.

Wherever Johnny Chang was hiding, he was doing it in an RV.

Emmett covered the ground leading back outside with long, urgent strides.

It was 11:14. Forty-four minutes to go.

Brigid, Aimee, Beppe, and David Dafashy had gathered near Emmett's car. They turned toward him as Emmett approached.

"I think he's in an RV," Emmett said. "Johnny Chang. He bought the kind of toilet paper that's made for RVs."

Aimee asked, "So what do we—"

"We call every RV-sales-and-rental place in the area, starting in the Lake Sunapee region and moving outward. Tell them it's an urgent police matter and ask if an Asian man with a sloped forehead has been in their store anytime in the last twenty-four hours."

"And if they have?" Beppe asked.

"Hand the phone to me."

Aimee, who had a laptop under her arm, brought it up and set it on the hood of Emmett's car. A few keystrokes later, she had a list of potential places.

They split it up, started calling.

Emmett's first try was with the Granite State RV Emporium in nearby New London.

He struck out there.

His next call was Upper Valley RV Sales & Rental in West Lebanon.

There, a woman answered the phone. After Emmett explained who he was and what he was looking for, she electrified him by saying, "We had a man like that in here this morning. He came in a little after nine."

"Tell me more, please," Emmett said.

"Well, he wasn't picky, that's for sure. We've got plenty of stock this time of year. He could have taken pretty much any RV on the lot. He said he didn't care, just that he'd need it for about a month or so. I told him our midsize option was ninety dollars a day, plus thirty-five cents a mile, and he could have it as long as he liked. He said that sounded great. I asked him if he wanted to see it and he said no, he just wanted to get on the road. We filled out the paperwork and he left."

"How long ago was that?"

"I probably had him out the door by nine forty-five or so?"

Meaning he could still be anywhere within a fairly wide swath of New Hampshire or Vermont.

But at least they now knew what he was driving.

"What's the license plate on that vehicle?" Emmett asked.

She gave it to him, along with the make and model.

"What name did he use?"

"Jonathan Manchu Chang. He was real polite. He said people called him Johnny."

"What kind of ID did you get from him?"

"License and credit card," she said. "Same as everyone else."

"And they were both in the name Jonathan Chang?"

"Yeah. The license was Colorado. Don't see a lot of those around here."

"Did you photocopy it?"

"Scanned it, actually. Front and back. Want me to email it to you?"

"That'd be great," Emmett said, providing his address. "And the credit card went through no problem?"

"Yes, sir," she said. "It was a Visa. Want the number?"

Emmett took it. The credit card companies required a subpoena before they gave out most information. Emmett didn't have that kind of time. But maybe it would be useful later.

"Thank you. Now if you could do me a favor, please assemble and save any evidence you have on Johnny Chang. I'm going to send someone by for it in a bit."

She said she would; then he rushed her off the phone, eager to call this in to Angus Carpenter. Before long, they would have hundreds of eyeballs looking for Johnny Chang.

And that was a good start.

But he worried it wouldn't be good enough.

Johnny Chang was one man in one RV in an area of the country that was primarily sparsely populated wilderness.

Impossible to find.

Except.

Emmett was getting an idea.

He called Gary Evans.

Emmett gave the agent a brief rundown of the situation, finishing with, "And now he's in an RV. He pulled out of Upper Valley RV Sales & Rental on Miracle Mile in West Lebanon at approximately nine forty-five. Would you have any satellites that could tell us where he is now?"

"Officially," Evans said, "the army doesn't use its satellites to monitor the activities of American citizens."

"Unofficially?"

"I'll call you back in ten minutes."

CHAPTER 65

My lipreading allowed me to eavesdrop on Emmett from a distance. I missed a word here and there, but I got the broad strokes: he had called Gary Evans and asked for the army's help.

He was then immediately back on the phone, pacing around the driveway, asking his captain to have a SWAT team at the ready.

I related all of this in real time to Beppe and David, who had huddled with me in front of my car. Aimee was sitting in the passenger seat, only half listening through the open window. She was mostly pounding her computer in an attempt to learn more about Jonathan Manchu Chang.

After a few minutes, she called us over.

"Okay, according to what I've learned so far, Johnny Chang went to Rice as an undergrad, then Berkeley for grad school."

"Sheena went to Berkeley," Beppe said. "They must have met there."

"Well, then that explains Johnny signing on with Marwari Aiyagari International after he left Berkeley," Aimee said. "He was the chief technology officer for MAI USA. That's all according to his LinkedIn profile. And if you only looked at LinkedIn, you'd think he was still there.

"But then I found an article about him in the *Denver Post* that tells a much different story. Johnny Chang was fired by MAI, and he's facing a criminal charge for embezzlement in Colorado state courts. It looks like he had set up fake companies that were invoicing MAI for fake services and equipment. He had been arrested, arraigned, and was out on a personal recognizance bond. He was facing at least five years in prison."

Which corroborated part of Sheena's story. The rest was easy enough to believe. Sheena preyed on her friend Johnny's desperation. That it was one more way to stick it to her controlling father only sweetened the deal for her.

David was about to offer some kind of observation, but I immediately shushed him. Emmett had received a phone call.

I didn't bother with the long-distance lipreading this time. I walked up to him so I wouldn't miss a word.

Except he was mostly just listening with a look of stony concentration on his face.

As soon as he ended the call, I asked, "What's happening?"

"The army tracked Johnny Chang for a good while after he left the RV rental place," Emmett said, talking fast. "But then they lost him. Apparently the satellite they had immediate access to couldn't see through the trees. Last they saw, he was headed into a place called Gile State Forest. It's a few thousand acres. We're starting to search it now."

I felt an electric charge surge through me. "I know every road and every trail in Gile State Forest. I've hiked there hundreds of times."

He studied me for half a beat, then jerked his thumb toward his unmarked car.

"Why don't you get in?" he said. "I think the Bomb Squad wants you out of here anyway."

Without another thought, I climbed into his passenger seat.

"I'm coming too," Aimee said, moving toward the back seat.

Emmett offered no objection. Within twenty seconds, we were on the move.

It was 11:32. We still had twenty-six minutes. Gile State Forest was a big place, but there were only a few roads in and out. It might not be impossible to find Chang there.

And then?

And then we'd figure it out.

At the top of the driveway, we passed Plottner's limousine, idling by the side of the road. I thought about calling him, then dismissed it.

His money wasn't going to help us now.

As Emmett drove, he got his radio connected to the same frequency as the SWAT team, which had been hanging out near the highway. They would make it to Gile ahead of us.

"Evans said Chang went into Gile on Route 4A. Not long after Sugar House Road, he made a turn and that's where they lost him."

Another charge went through me. "I know exactly where that is," I said. "It's an old logging road that runs through the heart of the forest. It goes up a way and then splits. The left fork heads to an abandoned mine. The right fork dead-ends at some trails."

Emmett relayed that information to the SWAT team. As he drove, I watched the minutes tick away.

11:38. Then 11:39.

We crossed under the highway, then turned on Route 114. Johnny Chang would have traveled this direction on his trip to Riddle Hill Road and the abandoned house. It made sense that he had scouted out the area and remembered it when he was looking for a place to hide in his RV. Gile State Forest could get crowded during the warmer months, but not this time of year. I was often the only person there when I visited. It was a good place to lie low.

11:43. We pressed on. We had reached Route 4 and made the turn toward Gile.

Then Emmett's radio crackled.

It was the SWAT team. They had found the RV. Chang had taken the right fork and pulled off to the side of the road in a clearing. The SWAT team was now assessing its options.

Driving at terrifying speeds, we were just a few minutes behind. Emmett turned on the logging road. 11:45. Then 11:46. The road surface was snow covered, with some combination of gravel and mud underneath it. His tires kept spinning, slowing us down.

"We're running out of time," Aimee said.

"I know," I said.

Emmett didn't reply. It was taking all his concentration just to keep us on the road. The trees leaned in close on both sides, forming a kind of tunnel over us. No wonder the satellite had lost track of Chang.

We reached the fork and turned right. Emmett kept gunning the engine until we arrived at a spot where the road had been blocked by a half dozen state police vehicles.

One of them was a green truck that had SPECIAL WEAPONS AND TACTICS emblazoned on the side.

11:48 now.

Ten minutes to go.

"What's the plan?" Aimee asked.

"Just stay here," he said, coming to a stop and opening his door.

Then he jogged briskly away.

From behind me, Aimee was putting on her twin jacket. She said something I didn't hear over the rustling of the fabric.

"What?" I asked.

"I said: 'That's a really crappy plan.'"

CHAPTER 66

Emmett's boots kept slipping on the slushy mud as he covered the ground between himself and where the rest of the officers had convened in a rough clump.

Captain Angus Carpenter was in the middle of the gathering. He had binoculars slung around his neck and a radio in his hand.

Toward the front of the group were four officers from the SWAT unit, dressed in body armor, carrying long rifles with scopes, ready for action.

"Okay, what's the situation?" Emmett asked.

"There's an RV with a license plate that matches the one you gave us," Carpenter said. "It's up ahead in that clear-cut area. The road runs through it, and he just came to a stop in the middle of the road. He's got at least fifty yards of open space on all sides. Whether he knows it or not, that was a really smart move. There's no sneaking up on him."

Emmett nodded toward the SWAT guys.

"That's what those scopes are for, aren't they?" Emmett said. "Just wait until he walks past a window and take him out."

"Can't. Curtains are drawn."

Emmett looked toward the distance, where he could just see the clearing.

"The only advantage we have right now is that Chang doesn't know we're here," Carpenter said. "Or at least I think he doesn't. Other than that, it's all advantage Chang."

And Emmett already knew the road dead-ended somewhere beyond where Chang was. So there was no sweeping in around from the other side.

He toed the ground, trying desperately to think of something.

"Are there any blind spots we could use to approach the vehicle?" he asked.

"There are no windows in the rear of the RV. Problem is, he's got a pretty good view out the side. Plus, if he was in the driver's seat, he could see us coming in the mirrors. We wouldn't truly be in a blind spot until we were maybe ten, fifteen feet away. It's too risky. Then there's the problem of what to do once we got there. He'd still be inside somewhere, and we'd still be outside."

"I could pretend to be a lost hunter," Emmett suggested. "Use that as a way to at least get closer. Maybe draw him out so we could take a shot."

"The way you're dressed?" Carpenter asked, looking skeptically at Emmett's khakis. "He'd see through that in three seconds."

"Well, we have to establish contact soon. We have"—Emmett checked his watch—"eight minutes until that explosive goes off. And the Bomb Squad needs three minutes to extract the hostages. We have to move *now*. I'll walk toward him with my hands up. At least that way he'll know he's been caught. Maybe he'll be reasonable and—"

He stopped because Brigid was running up from behind him.

As he turned to face her, out of the corner of his eye, he saw a shape moving quickly through the wilderness, nearly at the tree line.

It was Aimee.

Emmett sputtered, "What is she . . ."

Heads turned.

"Oh God," Carpenter said, seeing it now too.

"The last thing she said before she got out of the car was that one of us had to do something, and it couldn't be me because I was a mother," Brigid said, panting.

Aimee was almost to the clearing. Without pause, and without a single glance behind her, she plunged through the last of the brush.

She was now out in the open, on the snow-covered field, a black-jacketed dot set against a white background, marching toward the RV.

"Aimee," Emmett called, as loud as he dared. "Aimee, no!"

But she either couldn't hear him or wasn't going to pay attention to his warning. She was walking without hesitation toward a man who had killed three people in the last twenty-four hours and wouldn't hesitate to kill another. He obviously had the means—that powerful rifle he had used to blow away the back side of Scott Sugden's head.

She might as well have been striding into a tornado.

He had to stop her.

Or protect her.

Or something.

The other cops were just standing there, flat footed, unable to act. They had many hours of training in how to respond when an enemy did something erratic but were a lot less certain when that unexpected action came from an ally.

Emmett dashed toward the clearing, snatching a rifle from a very surprised SWAT team member on his way.

"Hey, what are—"

Emmett ran to where the road met the clearing, then partially hid behind a tree that was too small to conceal him completely. He could see the RV, which meant anyone inside could see him.

He had no body armor. Or shield. This was madness.

There was an impulse, a fleeting one, that told him to keep going. If Wanda was waiting for him on the other side, wouldn't it be worth it?

Then the impulse left him. There were too many other people who wanted him to stick around for a while longer. His kids. His grandkids. His friends.

"Aimee," he said in a fierce whisper. "Aimee, for the love of—"

There was no point. He was only increasing the chance he'd get noticed.

He raised the rifle, tucked the stock against his shoulder, and looked at the RV through the scope. The vehicle instantly ballooned in size. It was older, boxier than the newer models. Still, a twenty-four-footer. Just like the one he owned. The one he and Wanda were going to travel the country in.

The way it was angled, Emmett could see both the rear bumper and the entire right side, including the door that served as the only exit.

The door was closed. And the windows were curtained, just as the SWAT guy said.

Emmett kept the rifle up, but took his eye out of the scope. Aimee was walking up the middle of the road now.

Completely fearless.

Completely foolhardy.

Completely vulnerable.

He could sense Carpenter coming up behind him.

"Stay back," Emmett said. "No sense in you being in the line of fire too."

"What's she doing?" Carpenter demanded.

"I don't know. She's—"

And then, when she was about fifty feet away, Aimee sat down on the snowy ground and started scooching forward, using her hands and her bent right leg to propel herself.

She trailed her left leg behind her, like it was useless.

"Help," she called out. "Hello? Is anyone there? Help me, please!"

And then Emmett got it.

He had been thinking about the lost-hunter gambit.

She had decided to go for injured hiker.

"Hello? Please?" she called. "I think I broke my ankle. I can't walk. Help!"

"Does she have a death wish?" Carpenter asked, awed.

"I don't know. Maybe this will actually work."

Emmett's eye was back in the scope. It wasn't giving him the kind of wide view he might have liked, so he kept sliding it between the door and the curtained window. His finger was resting lightly on the trigger.

"Just tell everyone to stay back," Emmett said. "If Chang is looking out, I don't want him seeing anything but her. That's the only way this works."

"Can you see him? Do you have a shot?"

"No."

Aimee's protests were growing louder and more inventive—about the rock she hadn't been able to see, about how she knew she shouldn't have gone out alone, about how she was worried about hypothermia. All the while, she continued scooching closer to the RV, gaining maybe two feet with each lunge.

"What time is it?" Emmett demanded, not daring to take his eye out of the scope.

"Fifty-three," Carpenter said.

Five minutes. But really two. They needed to give the Bomb Squad three minutes to get through the ceiling and disarm the explosive.

Or three minutes to get the hell out.

Aimee unleashed another "Please! Help!"

She had roughly halved the distance from where she had started, and was getting closer with each lunge. There was no chance Johnny Chang hadn't heard her yet.

He was probably just deciding what to do about her.

Stay in the RV with the door locked and let her bellow until she went hoarse?

Pretend to be a Good Samaritan—just a nice guy in an RV—and take her in?

Or shoot her without a word?

"Fifty-four," Carpenter said. Then, like he was reading Emmett's mind, he added, "Sixty seconds until I have to tell the Bomb Squad what to do."

Emmett was trying to keep himself steady. Nothing ruined a shot faster than if you let your breathing get out of control.

He swiveled his scope from the door, to the window, back to the door.

Then the door swung outward.

Emmett increased the pressure on the trigger, looking for a target, finding none. The door didn't seem to have anyone behind it, at least no one Emmett could see.

Realistically, he would have exactly one attempt at this. If he missed, Chang would realize this was a trap, close the door, and retreat back into the RV.

"Thirty seconds," Carpenter snarled softly.

What happened next took maybe three of those thirty.

But it didn't feel like real time. Not to Emmett, anyway. And it wasn't that he had changed.

Time itself had changed.

Emmett finally understood what Beppe Valentino had been talking about when he described being pulled into a black hole. The galaxy was pinwheeling around, faster and faster. But to Emmett's frame of reference, from somewhere inside that churning blur, everything was happening much more slowly.

The first thing he saw was a figure emerging in the doorway, standing on the lowest step of the RV.

It was a man with his own rifle, raised in a firing position, its barrel pointed at Aimee. She was perhaps forty feet away. Practically can't-miss range.

Emmett took in a breath and centered the crosshairs of his scope on the man's forehead.

It had a slope to it.

Like a Neanderthal.

Unmistakably, this was Johnny Chang. Michael Dillman.

Whatever his name, it didn't matter. He was about to be a dead man.

Emmett didn't wait another beat.

He just squeezed the trigger.

A bullet travels faster than sound. And you certainly can't see one in flight. So Chang had no way of knowing, as he took careful aim, that a projectile was hurtling toward him at supersonic speed.

He was focused on his own ministrations, and his own trigger, which was also in the midst of squeezing.

And that, in turn, sent his own bullet flying.

Toward Aimee.

In what order those bullets landed, not even Emmett and his pinwheeling galaxies knew for sure.

CHAPTER 67

Silence is not truly a thing.

It is the absence of a thing.

In the same way that white is a lack of color, silence is a lack of sound, which can make it a very hard quality to describe, even for someone whose life is largely shrouded in it.

So what I heard was the thunderclap of simultaneous gunshots, followed by a silence that was, in all its absence, the most deafening thing I had ever not heard.

It seemed to stretch out, creating a void in every direction, filling the world with the totality of its nothingness.

The man with the rifle had fallen out of the RV and landed on the ground face-first. His arms were splayed. His weapon had hurtled out of his hands, almost like he had thrown it, and had speared itself in the snow, stock down, muzzle up, several feet away.

Aimee was lying on her back. From the distance that separated us, I couldn't tell if it was because a bullet had knocked her down, or if she had simply gone horizontal to make herself a smaller target.

The first thing that ruptured the silence—at least to my damaged ears—was me.

Shouting, "Aimee!"

Then I started running toward her.

There was a roar from the men behind me. I'm sure it was "Stop" or "No" or "Don't." But I couldn't hear it.

Or, more accurately, I wasn't listening.

I just ran up that slope, alternately crunching and slipping on the snow, powering toward my sister.

As I got closer, I became hopeful. There was no massive wound, no great mess of blood, nothing apparently wrong with her.

The bullet must have missed.

Somehow, someway, through some miracle of fortune or aerodynamics—or just bad aim—the projectile had gone high, or wide, or low, or who knows.

As I reached her, Aimee's eyes were open and she was staring up at the sky in a way that was somehow peaceful, like a child searching for pictures in the clouds. Her legs were still akimbo underneath her, bent like the injured hiker she had pretended to be. Her arms were resting at her side.

I knelt beside her.

"Aimee, Aimee," I said, trying not to shriek.

She studied me but didn't seem to comprehend what she was seeing.

Her mouth opened. No words came out.

Then I looked down at her black jacket, the one that was identical to mine—except hers now had a small hole high on the right side of her chest, out of which a few down feathers protruded at odd angles.

And the feathers weren't white.

They were dark red.

"Aimee, honey, what happened?" I asked. "What have you done?"

They were stupid questions.

And she wasn't answering.

I stared down into that hole, and all I could see was wetness. But then, around the edges of her back, there was a new color creeping into the snow.

Crimson.

"Oh God," I said. "Oh God, oh God."

It was a prayer, a plea, and an expletive all at once.

I grabbed her one hand in both of mine and squeezed. She did not squeeze back, just let me mash her hand.

Then, rattling out of her, there came a sound.

"Brig," she said.

There was a wheezy quality to her voice. Almost like she was inhaling water as she spoke.

I brought myself close to her face so she knew I was there. She didn't seem to be capable of saying more.

"Stay with me. You have to. Come on, Aim. You and me together now. Like always. Just stay with me."

She was back to looking up at the sky, which was a monolith of gray.

"So cold," she groaned.

"I love you, Aimee," I said. "I love you so much. Now stay with me."

There were suddenly hands on my shoulders, moving me from Aimee with gentle but insistent force. Someone was saying something.

"No," I moaned, trying to fight it.

But the hands were large, strong, and attached to a member of the state police SWAT team. They were suddenly under my armpits, and I was brought unwillingly to my feet.

They needed me out of the way so they could get to Aimee. I turned and staggered into the arms of Emmett Webster.

There were two SWAT team members now on either side of her. One of them was digging quickly through a medical bag. The other had torn open the buttons of Aimee's jacket, exposing a gruesome mess of red. He barked out an order to another SWAT team member just behind him.

Emmett started speaking.

"What?" I asked, now looking at his mouth.

"We got the bomb in time. It was disarmed safely," he said. "We got Matt out. He's going to be okay."

I nodded, then sagged against him for a moment before I turned back toward Aimee. She was still supine. Her eyes had closed. The SWAT team guys were working on her furiously.

She let out a weak moan. One of the men was pressing hard against the wound.

Emmett had to restrain me from running back to her. "Just let them work," he said. "They're trained for this."

There were tears falling off my face in large drops.

"Aimee," I bawled. "Aimee."

I sank to the ground, my knees planted into the snow, my eyes aimed toward the sky, where a medical helicopter was now angling aggressively toward us, closing in fast.

CHAPTER 68

A feeling was coming over Sean Plottner.

He was sitting in the lobby of Dartmouth-Hitchcock Medical Center, with Theresa on one side and Lee on the other, when it began.

At first, it was just a mild tingling.

He thought perhaps it was a reaction to the hospital. Plottner hated hospitals—the smell of disinfectant and death; the haughtiness of the doctors; the irrational worry that even noncommunicable diseases, like appendicitis or diabetes, might somehow be contagious if you hung around them long enough.

But, no, it was more than that. Because the tingling quickly progressed to an itch.

They were waiting to see Matt Bronik, who had been admitted a few hours earlier in what Plottner thought was an overabundance of caution. Bronik had apparently walked out of that MAI Holdings house under his own power: bruised, scratched, and stiff, but otherwise fine.

He was certainly faring better than his sister-in-law, who had been shot and was now in surgery.

But Plottner was having his own issues. Because now the itch was more like a burn. All he wanted to do was talk to his newest employee—and prove what a compassionate boss he was—before jetting off to somewhere that wasn't New Hampshire in March. Yet this odd, uncomfortable sensation wouldn't leave him alone.

He was being called upon by a strange visitor, one that normally kept its distance, never bothering him when he was trying to get something important accomplished. And as much as he tried to ignore it, it didn't seem to want to leave him alone this time, until finally Plottner had to acknowledge the presence of this infrequent and unwanted companion:

His conscience.

It was telling him this deal he had struck with Brigid Bronik wasn't right. She didn't really want her husband working for Plottner Investments. And Matt Bronik had already made it clear he didn't want it either. Yet Plottner, blinded by his typical single-mindedness, had used circumstances to his advantage anyway, because that's what he always did.

And it simply wasn't right.

Oh, Plottner tried to argue with his conscience. He had given Brigid what amounted to a five-million-dollar signing bonus. And he would be paying Matt a million dollars a year. It wasn't exactly indentured servitude.

Nevertheless, his conscience was insistent. This was coercion. There were some things money shouldn't be able to buy, and a human being was one of them. Even if it meant a return to the stultifying boredom of his billions, he couldn't force himself on Matt Bronik.

"I've been thinking," Plottner said slowly, "that maybe I won't hold Brigid Bronik to our contract. She signed it under duress. I'll leave it up to them. If her husband wants to come work for me, great. If not, so be it."

Theresa, brightening, shoved her round glasses farther up on her face.

"Sir, I've been thinking too," she said. "What if you just funded Dr. Bronik's research another way? The right way?"

"What do you mean?"

"You could do it through Dartmouth. Endow an institute and have Bronik installed as director. That way, Dr. Bronik would get to be an academic, freely sharing his research with the world, and you'd still get to be associated with whatever contributions he and his colleagues were able to make to the advancement of knowledge. It would be a win-win. We could call it the Plottner Institute."

"The *Plottner* Institute," he repeated. "That's a fine idea."

"Thank you, sir," Theresa said.

And then Lee cleared his throat.

And spoke in a fathomless voice.

"I like it," he said.

Plottner's eyes widened for a moment before he recovered from his shock.

"Well, okay," Plottner said. "It's settled then."

Plottner turned to Lee.

"Nice speech, by the way. Really won the day."

Lee just nodded back.

CHAPTER 69

Two millimeters.

Matt did the math on the back of a napkin, using a formula he had probably mastered in the second grade—and the magnificent calculator in his head—and told me that, assuming Johnny Chang's aim had originally been true, the impact of Emmett's bullet, which must have struck some incalculable number of nanoseconds before Chang had finished squeezing his trigger, had lifted the barrel of Chang's rifle by two millimeters.

Well, 2.176, to be Matt-exact.

That had the corresponding effect of sending the bullet fifteen centimeters—sorry, 15.24 centimeters, or about six inches—high and to the right of the middle of Amy's sternum.

Which, in turn, meant the difference between Amy sustaining a mortal, center-mass wound and what she was dealing with instead. According to the doctors, it was a "through-and-through" wound. The bullet had entered just beneath her collarbone on the right side and exited out her back.

Even if Chang had missed high left instead, she probably would have bled out: the left side of the chest has many more major veins and arteries, and if the bullet had nicked any of them, she never would have survived.

The right side is less complicated. So while she had lost a lot of blood, she would live.

Still, she was facing a long, painful rehabilitation. The knowledge of that—and our awe over the sacrifice she had made for our family—had muted my reunion with Matt. For as much as it was a relief and a joy to be back in each other's arms, our emotions were tempered by what it had cost my sister.

And also what it had nearly cost her, but for the gift of those two millimeters.

We were in Matt's room, awaiting word that she was out of surgery. His medical issues amounted to some superficial wounds and a bit of dehydration. He was expecting to be discharged soon.

In the meantime, he filled the time by reading *Harry Potter* to Morgan, who had crawled up into bed with him.

It was one of the parts with Grawp. Matt did do a good Grawp.

Eventually, Morgan had to depart. He would be spending the night at a friend's house.

Shortly after he left, we were informed Aimee had made it through surgery "beautifully." After some time to make sure there were no further complications, she was ready to be brought into her recovery room.

I wanted to be there when she woke up. Matt insisted on coming along and simply unhooked himself from his IV, leaving behind what would undoubtedly be a mystified medical staff.

When we entered Aimee's room, she wasn't there yet.

But Emmett Webster was.

"What are you doing here?" I said. "Shouldn't you be, I don't know—"

"Standing guard over Sheena?" he asked, amused. "We don't have to worry about her anymore. She was taken into custody right after the Bomb Squad got her out."

"What's going to happen to her?"

"That remains to be seen. It certainly helps that she's confessed to everything. And at least so far her story is lining up. We found the burner phone she had been using to communicate with Johnny Chang. We found his phone in the RV. The history of calls between them starts two months ago. There were also a number of texts that make it clear she knew everything that was happening and was calling the shots—right up until Chang turned on her. From there, it seems like it really was Chang, acting on his own. It'll be up to the prosecutor how to charge her exactly. The three-and-a-half-years scenario I floated for her may have been a little optimistic. It might end up being closer to ten. But that will ultimately be up to the courts."

I bowed my head. Now that Matt was safe, I was mostly just saddened by Sheena.

Such a waste.

"So I'm worried about your sister instead," Emmett continued. "Any word?"

"The surgery went well, I'm told. Should be anytime now."

"Do you mind if I stay for a little bit?"

"Not at all," I said.

He nodded. "I talked to David Dafashy a short time ago. I owed him an apology, and then we got talking. He and Mariangela are going to try and patch things up. He told me he came clean to her about Leonie Descheun and begged Mariangela for forgiveness."

"That's a start," I said.

"I may give Mariangela a call myself a little later, because I also spoke with Sheena. Among the other things she confessed, she confirmed that she invented her allegations against David. She had gotten the details about David's advances—the conference in Montreal, the trip to Les Jardins—from Leonie. Sheena then added her own embellishments about the compliments and whatnot. They took on the air of truth because of all the specifics supplied by Leonie."

"Why did Sheena feel the need to frame David in the first place?" I asked.

"You know, I didn't ask," Emmett said. "But David and I talked about that. He thought perhaps it was because if the department lost *two* tenured professors, it would create more opportunity for Sheena to get hired at Dartmouth, which is what she wanted. To me, it was just another false trail. If we didn't bite on the Chinese guys as suspects, we were supposed to bite on David Dafashy. It was more diversion."

"Well, I hope David and Mariangela will give it another try. He's not perfect but—"

I was interrupted by an orderly calling out, "Knock, knock. Patient coming."

The orderly wheeled Aimee in, then parked her in the middle of the room. Her right side was heavily bandaged. An IV bag hung on her bed.

"Aim?" I said. "Aim, can you hear me?"

Her eyes were closed.

But it didn't matter. Her ears were open, right?

"I love you, Aimee," I said. "Thank you for saving Matt's life. That was incredibly brave, even if it was incredibly stupid. Thank you. Thank you. I love you so much."

I wasn't sure if there was more to say. Aimee didn't appear to have heard any of it. I just stood there, clutching her left hand, overcome by the gift of her life.

Then she weakly croaked, "Brig?"

"Yes?" I said, leaning close.

A dreamy, narcotized smile spread across her face as she said, "Always told you I'd take a bullet for you."

ACKNOWLEDGMENTS

This is my tenth published novel, a number that astonishes me even as I type it.

If I had been told, when I was a struggling young newspaper reporter, that someday I would have ten books with my name on them, I would have said I could die happily.

Since I'm now only forty-five—and still have kids to put through college—I'm going to backtrack on the dying thing. But even ten books in, I can assure you: authoring doesn't get old. I'm thrilled to be able to share this story with you and for you to make the characters a part of your life, just as they have become part of mine. And I'm deeply grateful to the real-life people who helped make this work possible.

That starts with the physicists whose research on quantum mechanics I borrowed and twisted for my storytelling purposes, in particular David Kaiser, the Germeshausen Professor of the History of Science and Physics at Massachusetts Institute of Technology. Dave was endlessly patient explaining the heady concepts that appear in these pages to this social science guy. If there are any technical mistakes, it's only because I decided to ignore his brilliant counsel.

I'd also like to thank:

Audiologist Leah Ball and my delightful neighbor Melissa Schutt for their insights about hearing loss.

Dr. Randy Ferrance (whose caller ID inexplicably shows up as "Reiner," hence that character name) for help with the medical stuff.

Kara Williams, who made a generous donation to the Virginia Institute of Autism so that I might give Scott Sugden a glorious death.

My fellow author Daniel Palmer, who spitballed ideas with me (and helped inspire a certain scene in the book when he said, "The only thing I know about physics is Schrödinger's cat").

The outstanding team at Thomas & Mercer, including the wonderful Jessica Tribble Wells, who is such a joy to work with it has me rethinking certain long-held writerly prejudices against editors; developmental editor Charlotte Herscher, who stepped in with a critical eye and helped sharpen the final manuscript; author relations manager Sarah Shaw, who ensures the author never lacks for swag; cover designer Anna Laytham, who may be the only reason you picked up this book (cool cover!); production editor Laura Barrett; copyeditor Susan Stokes; marketing wiz Lindsey Bragg; and the boss, Gracie Doyle, who has assembled a fantastic group of professionals and made me feel so welcome at Amazon Publishing.

On a personal level, I also need to acknowledge the people who keep me sane on a daily basis—no easy task with any writer.

That begins with my beloved agent, Alice Martell, even though she told me I needed to blow up the first draft of this manuscript (alas, she was right—as she always is). I am lucky to have her as an advocate, sounding board, and friend.

I'm also grateful to the breakfast crew at Hardee's, where I continue to write my novels during the morning; and Chili's, for when the work spills into the afternoon. Both establishments keep me supplied with inspiration and Coke Zero.

Then there are my writer buddies, who I should know better than to list—because I will surely kick myself for leaving people out. But just to name-drop a few who have been through the wars with me for a long time now, a big shout-out to Lou Berney, Carla Buckley, Hilary Davidson, Peggy Finck, Chris and Katrina Holm, Jamie Mason, Erica Ruth Neubauer, Daniel Palmer, and Chris Pavone.

My parents, Marilyn and Bob Parks, are still my backbone in this world (and, not for nothing, they're also the most aggressive members of my book sales force). I feel blessed that they remain a vibrant part of my life.

Lastly, there's my reason for being: my wife, Melissa, and our two children. With every laugh, every hug, every kiss blown at me from the other side of a car window, I am reminded that my extraordinary good fortune in this world goes far beyond merely having authored ten books.

Thanks, family. I love every day with you.

ABOUT THE AUTHOR

Photo © 2016 Sarah Harris

International bestselling author Brad Parks is the only writer to have won the Shamus, Nero, and Lefty Awards, three of American crime fiction's most prestigious prizes. His novels have been published in fifteen languages and have won critical acclaim across the globe, including stars from every major prepublication review outlet. A graduate of Dartmouth College, Parks is a former journalist with the *Washington Post* and the *Star-Ledger* (Newark, New Jersey). He is now a full-time novelist living in Virginia with his wife and two school-age children. A former college a cappella singer and community-theater enthusiast, Brad has been known to burst into song whenever no one was thoughtful enough to muzzle him. His favored writing haunt is a Hardee's restaurant, where good-natured staff members suffer his presence for many hours a day, and where he can often be found working on his next novel.